Kierlyn,
Thank-you for
such an te
to our fam,
part of Gracie
as a young

Cynthia's Dance

A Christian fantasy novel by

TERRY HARRIS

Enjoy the read!

Tmy H

Ps. 34:4-5

 FriesenPress

Suite 300 - 990 Fort St
Victoria, BC, V8V 3K2
Canada

www.friesenpress.com

ISBN
978-1-5255-6072-9 (Hardcover)
978-1-5255-6073-6 (Paperback)
978-1-5255-6074-3 (eBook)

1. FICTION, CHRISTIAN, FANTASY

Distributed to the trade by The Ingram Book Company

This story is dedicated first and foremost to the
glorious King who planted the idea in the soil of
my heart some thirty-five years ago and nurtured
it until the time came for it to be written.

To my sweet Laura Marie, who gracefully endured the pain
of losing our three babies. Thank you for listening to the
Holy Spirit and holding on to the hope of a "third child."

And to our dear children:

Nathan – Our incredible firstborn whom
I wish to be like everyday

Gracie – Our most precious and beloved
daughter who inspires me daily

Jordan- Our third child – a true gift from God

Baby Harris – Our first baby in Heaven

Joseph – Our second baby in Heaven

Angela – Our third baby in Heaven

Join our community at Cynthiasdance.com

1

ON A SUMMER NIGHT OF LOUD ROLLER COASTERS AND sticky, pink cotton candy, Madeline Brewer Richards stood on a grassy green hill in the center of a popular theme park called Ziggy's Island.

She was waiting for Danny Richards, the love of her life and the owner-operator of Ziggy's. They had met just twelve months earlier when Madeline began working there. He had told her she was the most beautiful creature he had ever seen and he couldn't live without her. She found that her God-given looks had opened many a door in her young life but seeing one of the most distinguished men in all of the county propose to her on one knee confirmed the fact she was a "catch."

They quickly fell in love and married. But Danny made it clear that between his lousy childhood and living on his own since he was a teenager, he had no interest in having kids. He was convinced he would be the world's worst dad, and he wasn't about to spend the rest of his life swimming in guilt and regret.

A week before their wedding, his rude behavior at dinner caught her off guard. "Let me put it this way," he said while chewing his asparagus, "you let yourself get pregnant and you'll be raising that kid on your own."

With a hard gulp of her wine, she responded the only way she knew to keep them on the same page. "Don't worry, I'll never let myself get pregnant."

Despite taking precautions, four months and two days into their marriage, Madeline discovered that she was carrying their child.

She was scared to death.

They had just launched enormous plans to expand Ziggy's Island and make it the largest theme park in North America. With its time-travel experience, it was already different from its competitors (Ziggy would take you back to the 1950s and let you indulge in all things from the decade). Madeline intended to grow the park to include the 1960s, 70s, 80s, and even the 90s. For the price of one ticket, you could travel back in time, as it were, and relive the memories of your youth.

But now she was pregnant, about eight weeks along, and the zest for building an empire with Danny was secretly replaced by dreams and desires to raise a child.

She had created an excuse to meet privately with a doctor earlier that week. What took place was unforgettable: hearing the heartbeat of the child inside her. The repetitive, fast swishing sound was not what she expected. The noise was odd at first, but the sonographer assured her that the baby's heartbeat was strong and healthy. It was the most glorious thing she had ever heard. That extraordinary day changed her feelings about life and the future.

Though the ultrasound could not yet confirm the baby's sex, Madeline strongly suspected the child inside her was a girl. In their home perched atop a cliff, overlooking the blue ocean, she secretly began planning a girl's nursery. Theirs was no ordinary home; it was more of a castle, with eleven bedrooms, two kitchens, and its own personal, private stretch of beach. Madeline smiled at the thought of a mermaid-themed room for her daughter.

Her joy turned to anxiety, however, when she thought about how Danny would take the news. She had been smart and careful. *How in the world could this have happened?* she asked herself over and over. The whole situation had come as a complete shock, but she couldn't shake the feeling of absolute joy of carrying Danny's child.

Perhaps Danny wouldn't be so offended after all. Perhaps he would forget about their discussion some months earlier and, hearing the news of being a father, have a change of heart.

Or perhaps he would leave her to raise the child on her own, just as he had said he would. She had already decided that if he did, she would choose the life of her baby over his fantasy of a marriage without children.

Or would she?

She had chosen their favorite rendezvous spot, a grassy area overlooking the lights at Ziggy's, to break the news, hoping it would play in her favor. But now she wondered. The more she wondered, the more anxious and nervous she became.

This night, the park was filled with distinguished and influential visitors for Ziggy's black-tie inaugural summer ball, which was Madeline's brainchild. CEOs, politicians, and even celebrities were dancing, mingling, and probably making deals. These were the people who could help Ziggy's grow through investments and influence. In the distance, she heard laughter and music, and she knew the event was a huge success. But the evening's victory took a back seat to her feelings about having a baby girl.

Madeline reflected on the doctor's visit and her daughter's heartbeat. It was all so real to her now. With her hand on her belly, Madeline spoke her first words to the child. "Hey, Baby. I'm your mommy, and this is Ziggy's Island. I want you to know that I love you so much and …"

"There you are!"

Madeline jumped, wondering if she'd been overheard. It wasn't Danny, it was Ziggy's newly appointed chief financial officer, Radcliffe Finklemeyer. A short and stubby man who dressed to impress others, tonight he wore a fine custom-made Italian tuxedo that assisted in covering his bulging belly. Madeline didn't like Radcliffe. Ever since she challenged him at a board meeting on a financial decision months earlier, she always felt a strange awkwardness between them. There was a coldness about him. He never seemed happy. But, overall, he was very good at numbers and keeping Danny in check with financial matters, so Madeline tolerated him.

"Oh, hello, Radcliffe. Why aren't you enjoying the party and schmoozing the bankers?"

"I could ask you the same question. I was told Danny was coming up here. I need to talk to him about some financial issues I discovered today. Were you aware of the amount of money that this event is …"

Madeline cut him off. "Yes, Radcliffe, I'm aware of how much we spent on this ball, but tonight is not the night for this. We will be in the office on Monday morning, and we can address your concerns first thing."

"Concerns? What concerns? Tonight is a party!" Danny bounded up the slope, sporting a smile. "Hello, sweetheart." He kissed Madeline and gave Radcliffe a dismissing grin, which prompted a small sneer on his CFO's plump face which rein-forced Radcliffe's look of disdain towards Madeline.

"Walter," rebuked Radcliffe.

"Radcliffe, I prefer to be called Danny."

"I was just reviewing our expenditures for this extravagant debacle and I crunched some numbers. Are you aware that the dance floor alone cost us-"

"Radcliffe, I do appreciate your due diligence, but let's talk about this some other time. There are a lot of important people down there that I need to entertain, and I just can't handle any more tonight, all right?"

"Of course ... Danny." Radcliffe smirked as he walked away, but only Madeline noticed.

Danny finally turned his attention to Madeline. "So, I got your page. What's up?" He looked down at the pager strapped to his belt as it lit up with another green message.

She avoided eye contact, which was unusual for her. "Just thought it would be nice to be alone for a little bit tonight."

"Alone? We have over six hundred VIPs and their dates dancing under the stars at our park, which means more open doors for me to get on the boards of a few more Fortune 500 companies."

Madeline paused. She knew Danny loved having his name splashed on whatever plaque, marquee, advisory board, or building front would let him. If his name could be in lights, he was there, regardless of the inconvenience or cost. Typically, she would encourage him in his quest to be among the elite. Tonight, she wanted him focusing on her.

"Did you see the governor was here?" he flirted.

"Yes," she said quietly. "I accepted his RSVP last night."

"So why are we standing here and not over there hanging with the most important people in our time zone?"

She took a deep breath. "I got some news the other day and I wanted to share it with you."

A strange ring sounded, breaking the awkwardness. Danny reached down and, like a revolver, drew his pet toy—his cellular phone. It was almost the size of a blow dryer and came with a carrying holster. It rang again, the sound chirp-like, and Danny answered it.

"Hello. Oh hi, Susan. Yes, yes, I understand. Please tell the governor I had some business to take care of and I'll be there in ten minutes to give him a personal tour. Thank you, Susan."

Madeline's eyes were filled with tears. She snapped her hand up to wipe them away.

"Are you crying?" he asked as he replaced the oversized phone in its waist holder.

"No. I think I got some mascara in my eye," she lied.

Danny heard a new song kick in. He started to dance in place. "I really gotta get back down there, hon. Is this something that can wait till later?"

Madeline hesitated, her mind racing. How should she break the news to him? A thought struck her that she believed would get his attention. "Danny, have you given much thought to retirement?"

"Retirement?"

"Yeah, you know. You. Me. Sailing off into the sunset on our hundred-foot yacht?"

"Sounds good to me, in about thirty years."

Madeline smiled. She had him hooked. "So, who's going to inherit Ziggy's when we're ready to do that?"

"I don't know. I guess we'll sell it to the highest bidder."

"We could do that." She took a step away from him and leaned close to a small willow tree. "I was thinking it would be a lot better for us and everyone else to, you know... keep it in the family."

"Well, since I don't have family, that would mean your mom, and I don't see her outliving either one of us."

She sighed to herself. *Why does he have to make this so hard on me?* She took a deep breath and nervously turned and looked him in the eye. "I was thinking more of our family. You, me, and our..."

"Look, Madeline, I told you before we got married that I'm not interested in having kids, and that means adopting, foster kids, none of it. Just the idea of..." His pager chimed, interrupting him. He snatched it up and stared at the green light.

"Okay. The governor just paged me. Now we really have to get down there. We can't keep this guy waiting. He means too much to our future."

Madeline was discouraged and wondered for a moment about *their* future, regardless of who was governor.

"Come on," Danny flirted. "Let's adjourn this meeting for now and reschedule for some other time years down the road, when my hair starts to fall out. Okay? We've got a whole lot of stuffy shirt VIPs I want to show my wife off to." Danny held out his arm and waited for her to join him.

Madeline was stuck. She forced a smile, placed her arm in his, and strolled down the grassy green hill toward a long red carpet, the pathway to the grand ball.

Since Madeline was a young girl, she had dreamed of a starry night like this where she and her true love would spend the night dancing and romancing like a prince and princess. She had pulled it off. The place. The night. The man. Even the stars were cooperating.

But the only thing she could think of now was how to break the news that she was pregnant.

Life didn't seem fair. She was filled with mixed feelings of regret, anger, hurt, and confusion. After all the hard work she had put into a night she had dreamed of for years, now she only wished she could go home, lock the bedroom door, and curl up with no one to interrupt her crying. *What is wrong with me?* Not wanting to appear weak, Madeline took a deep breath. *Must be hormones.*

The two walked arm-in-arm across the red carpet that guided them to the top of a sunken amphitheater, where they could see all the guests dancing and partying below. Ziggy's normally used this space for dances and high school reunions associated with the 50s, but tonight's occasion was their biggest and most expensive event yet. With all eyes on them, the striking couple descended the steps and stopped at the edge of the dance floor.

The evening was so beautiful. The small lights hanging over their heads, beautiful white and red flower arrangements, and hundreds of votive candles strategically placed throughout. The expensive Italian hardwood dance floor provided the perfect setting for couples to fall in love, whether for the first time or the hundredth time. Couples swayed and twirled as they danced to the romantic ballad the ten-piece orchestra played.

By appearances, everything was perfect, including Madeline. So why didn't she feel like dancing?

"Care to dance, my lady?" Danny waited and then, not getting an immediate response, pulled her close. They foxtrotted their way across the dance floor toward the governor. Danny was handsome in his tuxedo. His hair was combed back, not one out of place.

Nearby women looked on her with envy. He was the obvious catch of the crowd. She stared at him, torn. Her love for the man she had admired since the moment she met him had been arrested and was held in contempt of his behavior just moments ago. She wanted him to want their child.

She awkwardly and abruptly stopped the dance. "I'm sorry, honey. I'm just not feeling well. My head's pounding. You go ahead and chat with the governor, and I'll just sit here and rest."

Danny snapped, "What is with you tonight?" He spun on his heels and left her standing alone on the dance floor.

Madeline stared at his back as he walked away. She was ticked and squelched a desire to throw something at him. She groused to herself and looked her husband up and down, noticing a spot where his hair had begun to thin. Suddenly, he didn't look so hot. She stepped off the dance floor and stood uncomfortably near the edge.

Danny joined the governor and his guests. To Madeline's dismay, they laughed and patted each other on the shoulder. True to form, Danny was the life of the party. Madeline pouted;

it didn't seem as though he missed having her by his side. She even suspected she was on the brunt end of their crude jokes.

Angry, and now paranoid, Madeline sat back in her chair and crossed her legs. The mother-to-be was in for a long, miserable night, though she acted like she didn't care. Her heart sank, as she truly did care—a lot.

During the ride home that night, Danny was like a little kid on Christmas morning. It was obvious that, in his mind, everything had gone off without a hitch, and he couldn't contain his excitement. The night's success was a turning point for Ziggy's Island and the company's growth. He complimented Madeline up and down for her phenomenal work and attention to detail, but his words meant nothing to her. He didn't even seem to notice that she hardly spoke a word the whole ride home.

After arriving home, Madeline immediately went to bed, with no further explanation of her behavior other than saying she didn't feel well. She laid there consumed with how she was going to tell Danny that she was pregnant. The more she obsessed about it, the more restless she became. Finally, frustrated and wide awake, she turned over to see if she could talk with him, but of course, he was sound asleep and in fact, slept like a log that whole night.

Over the next several days, Madeline struggled with how to find a way to tell Danny about the baby. She would sometimes distract herself by thinking about names. She celebrated the moment she decided to name the baby Cynthia. She would not allow the name to be reduced to Cindy; Cynthia was a name of distinction and class. It boasted in part of some mythological Greek goddess, and that was inspiring to Madeline. Her daughter—*their* daughter—would be groomed into the finest young lady she had ever known; a young lady Danny would be proud to call his own.

But even those thoughts were often short-circuited by a bolt of fear that Danny would never stomach the interruption to their busy lives. He had already stated that he was not interested in a discussion about having children, and she was scared to death he would continue resisting it. Even worse, what if when she finally did tell him, he gave her an ultimatum—him or the baby? Her skin grew cold. Fear and terror invaded her fantasies of being a mom and robbed her of the joy she deserved.

In the depths of her soul, losing Danny was not an option she entertained. But neither was giving up the baby. Somehow, she would have to convince him that nothing would change. She would be there for him in building Ziggy's and everything would be better.

As the war inside her soul raged, Madeline continued working long, hard hours. She devoted herself to making sure Danny saw a stronger work ethic than ever before. Once he learned of the pregnancy, she imagined, he would see no threat to building Ziggy's Island into the largest park of its kind. She often rehearsed that thought when she felt powerless; it was her defense in the courtroom of her mind, providing a sense of control that she needed desperately.

As a reward to herself, she spent her brief lunch breaks window shopping for baby outfits and little dresses. The small children's clothing store in the center of 1955 Boulevard proved a fun place to peruse. It also happened to be one of Danny's favorite streets in the park.

On one such day, she ran into Cecilia, an old friend from her college days, and they had lunch at a local malt shop. Cecilia surprised Madeline with her response to the baby dilemma.

"You cannot afford to lose that man of yours, Mattie." She panned the park with her left hand, showing off her perfectly polished nails.

"Of course I'm not going to lose him." Fear stormed Madeline's brain, causing her spine to stiffen. "Danny will completely understand and support me in this." She looked down at her salad and took a bite, feeling Cecilia's stare.

"Hey. I'm not here to scare you or anything. I'm just telling you as your friend who has a quasi-functioning husband that you have got yourself a million-dollar man there, and *nothing* is worth losing him over. Nothing! But you gotta figure it out quick. He's gonna notice sooner or later." She smacked her lips and sucked the last few drops of her malt from the bottom of her glass. Madeline cringed at the annoying sound.

"Let's talk about something else. I'm not worried about losing my Danny. We're deeply in love." She threw a hinting wink at her friend, hoping to steer the conversation another direction. Cecilia shook her head as she stabbed her salad with her fork.

The lunch meeting with Cecilia heightened Madeline's fear. Feelings of anger and distance took root in her heart along with bitterness and resentment. But was her resentment toward Danny or baby Cynthia?

None of these feelings had been a part of Madeline's thought life before because nothing ever meant so much to her. If something became too contentious, she would either win the battle through her smile or let the matter go, indifferent to the possible consequences. Feeling happy and getting what she wanted was always the priority for her. But now there was something— someone—to fight for. She knew that a smile and a wink would not win this battle, and it scared her to death.

Days passed and she was still unable to sit down and talk with Danny. Her conversation with Cecilia played over and over in her mind, creating waves of anxiety, tons of questions, and truckloads of anger – anger at herself for not telling him, anger at Danny for not knowing what she was going through, and even anger that she had to deal with this immense struggle.

On a couple of occasions, she and Danny clashed over their vision for Ziggy's future, which caused fierce arguments. He often inflamed the situation by saying under his breath, "I can't believe I married my chief communications officer." His plans for the expansion were on the line, and he showed no patience or flexibility.

On the heels of one such tumultuous day, Madeline woke up in the middle of the night, sensing that something was wrong. She quietly went to the bathroom and closed the door. Anxiety and deep fear filled her as she stared at red liquid in the toilet. She had no idea what the blood meant, but her instincts told her it was not good. She put on a feminine pad and went back to bed. Not being able to go back to sleep, she tossed and turned and dreaded the worst. Time dragged like a two-ton anchor being pulled through the mud.

The clock seemed to stand still. When the sun finally started to come up, she rose from the bed and made her way to the kitchen, fumbled through her address book, and called her doctor's office. The message on the other end asked her to call another number in case of an emergency. She hesitated. *Was this an emergency, or was it just her wild imagination? After all, she felt fine.*

She scribbled the number down and called it. It was a voice-mail message center that routed emergency messages to the doctor's beeper. She dialed the digits and cleared her throat. "Uh, hi. This is Madeline Richards. I saw you a couple of weeks ago and, um ..." She started to cry. "Um, I saw blood in the toilet tonight after I went to the bathroom, and I'm not sure what it means. Can I get in tomorrow, I mean, this morning?" Not knowing what else to say, she left her home number and hung up the phone.

A few hours later, she received a call back while Danny was in the shower. She was told to go for another ultrasound. She was thankful for the chance to find out what was going on, but at the same time, scared out of her wits at what the news would be. She felt so out of control.

She dressed and drove to the medical building, anxiety rushing through every cell in her body. Her first visit here had been a great day. Deep inside she prayed today would be the same. She slipped her sunglasses up on top of her head and stepped up to the window, softly announcing her name. The front desk attendant, who was on the computer, smiled at Madeline and directed her to sign in.

Her hand trembling, Madeline scribbled her name onto the appointment sheet. She was the fourth person that morning. She briefly looked at the clock to indicate the time of her arrival. It was nine minutes before nine a.m. Though it was early in the day, she wondered, was it too late to help her baby?

She glanced at the names on the list again and wondered if the other women were also there because they were afraid for the life of their baby. She couldn't help but turn and scan the room. Two young moms, both very pregnant, sat in the front lobby. Sitting opposite each other, they were each engrossed in a gossip magazine. It was apparent neither one of them was too concerned about any immediate danger. Feelings of envy and jealousy, uncommon to her personality, sprung up inside her heart. She felt so desperately alone and scared.

She bit her nails as she waited for the nurse to call her name. She had not done that since she was in college. Those days of exams and crazy long hours with no sleep reminded her of recent nights. Her mind wandered back to the days when she was single and carefree. She had the world by the horns, and she was going to steer it in the direction she wanted it to go. Oh, how she longed to be that girl again.

Minutes dragged by as she did her best to keep distracted by thinking about Ziggy's Island expansion plans. Work made her feel good about herself. She knew she was, in many ways, irreplaceable, and it provided her much-needed feelings of power and control. She looked up to realize she was the only one left in the room. Just then the nurse called, "Cynthia Richards."

Madeline jerked with a shock. "Excuse me? Don't you mean Madeline Richards!?"

The round, short woman of Philippine descent glanced down at her chart. "That's what I said, Madeline Richards." She smiled, opened the door, and gestured for Madeline to enter.

Madeline was unnerved and unsettled by hearing her daughter's name called instead of her own. She clung tightly to her purse and walked down a narrow hall that led to the same tiny, dark ultrasound room. It seemed different than the last time she visited—smaller, claustrophobic, and lifeless. Madeline outwardly remained calm, but her mind raced uncontrollably as she contemplated various possible outcomes of this visit. None of them felt safe.

"Please undress and put this on. The sonographer will be in shortly." The nurse handed Madeline a baby-blue gown with Velcro adhesive on the back and left the room.

Madeline undressed and cautiously laid down on the cold leather exam table. Her eyes stared at the white-tiled ceiling. Again she waited, trying to reason why she was going through this alone and why her husband wasn't with her. Anger rose up in her soul. *Why didn't he see me? Couldn't he tell that something was going on inside me? Why didn't he pay as much attention to me as he does his precious amusement park?*

She eyed a plain white calendar hanging on the wall that displayed the date in big black letters: September 1. She stared at it and pondered if it would be a day of celebration or grief.

A young Persian woman entered the room and introduced herself as Sonia. She rolled a table alongside Madeline and asked her to lie still.

Sonia took the handle off the equipment and apologized for the cold goo she had to squirt on Madeline's belly. As Sonia stroked the device around Madeline's stomach, she boasted about the new 3-D Volusion ultrasound equipment they were using. Madeline didn't hear a word, fixated on hearing the swishing heartbeat. Each second of silence confirmed Madeline's deepest fears.

"Is it on?" Madeline desperately asked.

"Yes," Sonia replied. Then she said words Madeline dreaded to hear: "I can't seem to find the heartbeat."

Adrenaline surged through Madeline's body. She held her breath and anxiously asked, "What does that mean, you can't hear a heartbeat? Is my baby okay?"

"Let me get the doctor," Sonia calmly stated as she removed her gloves and left the room.

Madeline asked her again if everything was okay.

The sonographer smiled with compassion and said, "The doctor will be in shortly."

The moment Sonia stepped out of the room Madeline sat up. She couldn't stand the vulnerability of lying down any longer. She longed for some sense of control. She gazed at her belly, tears welling up in her eyes. "Baby? Are you okay?"

Just then, the doctor appeared in light-blue medical attire. Madeline looked for signs of hope in her facial expressions.

The doctor grabbed the ultrasound wand and went over Madeline's belly once more. "Madeline, was there any sign of spotting before last night?"

"None that I know of," Madeline stated insecurely. The quiet in the room was deafening as she waited to hear any sound of life from the machine.

With a slight smile of sympathy, the doctor put down the wand and delivered the news Madeline did not want to hear. "I'm sorry but there is no heartbeat."

Anxiety gushed through Madeline's body. She went numb. "No. No. We just heard the heartbeat nine days ago, and you said it was strong. Check again!"

"It's fetal demise," the doctor said with compassion. "There is no heartbeat."

"You mean, my baby is …" Madeline dropped the last word, unable to say it audibly.

"I'm so sorry." The doctor touched Madeline on her right shoulder. "I would like you to stop by my office and schedule a D&C so we can get you cleaned up inside. Okay? Is there anyone we can call for you?"

Madeline shook her head and mustered the strength to squeak out, "I'll be fine."

The doctor left the room. Never before had Madeline's life so completely fallen down around her. She felt devastation and loss to her bones. Her hopes, dreams, and future died in her womb along with her child. She wanted to burst out in hysterics and scream and cry.

Instead, she got up and dressed. She was a shell of a woman walking down the hall, using all her strength to suppress her emotions. Very calmly, she made her D&C appointment and slowly walked to the parking lot.

Finally, she made it to her car and the solace of her driver's seat. Once she closed the door, she couldn't restrain herself any longer. She had never cried so hard in her life. So much of the emotion she had buried for weeks flooded her body in uncontrollable convulsions. Her baby was gone. *She failed. She failed her baby. What did she do to cause this? What didn't she do to cause this? This was her child she was supposed to protect.*

I'm so sorry, Cynthia. I'm so sorry! I didn't protect you! The last thought played over and over in Madeline's head until she couldn't take it anymore. She cried and cried. *Why, God? Why?*

After an exhausting hour of sitting in her car, questioning and pleading for answers from God, Madeline got angry at God, at Danny, even angry at the doctor. "Fetal demise, are you kidding me? This was my *baby!*"

With each tear she cried, Madeline subconsciously placed another brick in the wall she was building around her heart. When she wiped away her last tear, she decided that no one would ever hurt her like this again. Internally, she posted a "No Trespassing" sign over the door to her heart, and instead of going home, she drove straight to the office.

On her drive to the park, Madeline traced her thoughts of the night before, to when she sensed with all her being that *something* happened with baby Cynthia.

Questions flooded her mind, driving splinters of pain into her soul. *What happened to my baby? Where did she go? Is she ok? Will I ever see her?* Madeline knew she didn't have the answers to these questions, nor did she know of anyone who did, so she turned up the volume on her radio, hoping to tune out the voices that blamed her for the loss of her baby.

The years slowly passed. Madeline never told Danny about baby Cynthia. Madeline's secret festered inside of her, and she carried a deep hurt and anger toward Danny that he couldn't understand. Danny's heart eventually softened to the idea of parenthood, but when they finally did attempt to have children, they were unable to get pregnant. Danny shrugged parenthood off as it "wasn't meant to be." It was obvious that he had no idea of the hole his attitude left in Madeline's heart.

She never released the guilt of Cynthia's loss years before and was certain that God was punishing her. Her secret battle ate her up inside. She had to endure alone the pain of being unable to conceive. Their multiple attempts to get pregnant failed again and again.

Every month for years, Madeline would see her doctor, use her ovulation kits, be with Danny, take a pregnancy test ten days later, and be disappointed. Every negative test made her more jaded, and Danny began to feel more like a sperm donor than a husband. Their intimacy was now restricted to dates on a calendar. Spontaneity or true affection were gone. They both agreed that they wouldn't try IVF, and as the years went on, they eventually stopped trying.

The agony of infertility added to the distance between them, especially as Madeline's friends, including her friend Cecilia, had no problem having children. Madeline would put on a happy mask at baby showers and hospital visits. Every time she would see a pregnant woman or a mom with a baby, she physically felt a jab in her gut. Danny was completely disconnected from her during this time and focused his energy on Ziggy's. Madeline suffered alone.

Eventually, the pain grew too great, and Madeline and Danny ended their marriage in divorce court.

The day Madeline signed the divorce papers, Danny proposed a strictly business relationship and named her chief operating officer and marketing manager of Ziggy's Island. He had learned in those years just how important Madeline was to the park's future and, more poignantly, his success. Ziggy's catapult into a new level of success was his estranged wife's brainchild. And perhaps, if she worked for him, he might win her back.

Madeline, on the other hand, went back to her maiden name, Brewer, and convinced herself her new position at Ziggy's was exactly what she needed to move beyond her pain and make a life for herself. She liked seeing Danny squirm in his admission of needing her help to expand Ziggy's the way they had envisioned. Madeline was keenly aware that Ziggy's Island was Danny's baby, as it were, and it would require her vision and marketing savvy to make it everything he wanted: one of the greatest amusement park experiences in North America.

She buried the deep ache in her soul for a child. But no matter how hard she tried, her thoughts often returned to the haunting question of what life would be like if Cynthia were alive.

She made up a myriad of rules to protect herself from emptiness. One of the first rules was that no one would be allowed close enough to crush her like the miscarriage and her infertility had. A second rule: there would never be another ball at Ziggy's Island.

It was in these pain filled years that Madeline and Danny's business relationship grew as Ziggy's expanded. Madeline stayed true to her promise, keeping walls around her heart and focusing on work, on the other hand, Danny was twice divorced and on occasion had some young, attractive gold digger after him.

2

DURING THIS TIME, ON THE OTHER SIDE OF HEAVEN, Cynthia matured from the baby Madeline lost into a young woman and a beautiful daughter of the King.

A unique part of that growth was a deep yearning and desire to meet her mother and father; this became part of her conversations with her heavenly family. Her childlike desire to leave Heaven and go see them on Earth seemed reasonable to Cynthia, even though, to this moment, that type of journey had never been allowed by the King.

But neither Cynthia, nor anyone else, for that matter, knew that her unusual desire was actually initiated and nurtured by the King Himself. For His own reasons and glorious purposes, He had ordained in the secret places of His throne a plan that could never be conceived by the human mind: to change the world through the life of a young woman who had never been born.

As with each of His children who arrived as an unborn child, Cynthia was cared for and loved by the citizens of Heaven, for everyone was like family. As Cynthia grew, she had a deep love for children and took it upon herself to care for a newly arrived orphan girl named Angela. Angela matured under Cynthia's care and the two became like sisters, doing everything together.

Cynthia and Angela served together in the King's court, teaching and leading small children in dance and worship. They demonstrated an extraordinary passion for their service and taught each of the children how to express their own voice and skills in the act of worship.

"Angela, I am so excited about the festival! The children have been working so diligently on their routines," Cynthia bubbled as the two of them walked along a bright, golden street. The road was transparent and brilliant in its colors. The surface was soft to the touch and always warm. It led to anyplace you might want to go in the Celestial City.

Both were dressed in dazzling white, pure-silk gowns that were far brighter than any mortal eyes have seen. They danced, as it were, along the road in their crystal shoes. The shoes were flat-soled with a soft-colored tint to them. Each daughter of the King wore her own pair of crystal shoes as unique to that soul as their fingerprint. Each son of the King owned a pair of soft leather sandals customized according to his particular identity.

The two of them suddenly darted off the main road and rushed down onto a pure, silver-white sandy seashore. The shore surrounded a magnificent body of water; its end had yet to be seen. Cynthia removed her smooth crystal shoes, dropped them, and then ran across the silky soft sand and onto the glassy sea. She did not sink but stood atop the water just as firm and sure-footed as the golden road on which she had just walked. Angela, just a step behind, slipped out of her glass footwear and joined Cynthia in a splashing contest.

After a bit of splashing and laughing, Angela removed a beautiful white-stone necklace engraved with her name, Angela Marie, and tossed it high into the air. She and Cynthia watched it sink into the depth. The water was as clear as day, all the way down to a level that could not be measured but could be seen by their perfect vision. As the necklace freely dropped, Angela waited, as though testing it. Finally, she bent over and without so much as a strain, snatched it up.

"Ha-ha!" she exclaimed. "That's the farthest I've seen it sink."

This was a game that the "sisters" loved to play. Cynthia removed her own necklace, which bore the name Cynthia Hope, from around her slender neck and tossed it up in the air. Again, the girls watched it plunge into the deep. Cynthia watched and waited.

Angela seemed confident that her friend would not be breaking her new achievement. Cynthia felt differently and waited some more.

Angela peered down at the necklace dropping further than she had ever seen. She glanced at Cynthia, who knew Angela thought she was done, but did not move to stop the necklace from its seemingly never-ending descent. Angela was being tested. This had never happened before.

The necklace continued to drop farther and farther. Cynthia watched her friend's expressions and could tell she was thrilled at the anticipation of what would happen next.

Finally, Cynthia reached down and yanked up her priceless treasure by its chain. The depth was unimaginable but certainly not unattainable. She revealed the pure solid-gold chain in her hand and then dangled it playfully in her friend's face.

Angela let out a gasp and a loud, "Ahhhh!"

"Nothing is beyond your grasp when you know to Whom you belong," Cynthia informed her friend.

They shared a hug and a laugh. Angela loved learning from Cynthia. This girl knew how to live out every moment as though it was an original moment, never to be duplicated again.

Just beyond them, great blue-and-white-colored whales glided through the waters and engaged playfully with schools of dolphins. The stunning lights of the city glistened off the water and created rainbows around the girls. In the distance, beautiful snowcapped mountains gave a feeling of majestic provision.

Water flowed into enormous waterfalls and eventually made its way into the sea of Heaven.

From the heart of the city's center, a loud trumpet blast was followed by a roar of excitement from the citizens. It was time to eat.

Cynthia and Angela waltzed across the glassy sea and onto the silky soft sand, where they replaced their shoes and made their way to the Great Hall, the gathering place for meals and festivities.

The King's Throne Room, situated behind the Great Hall, was the focal point of the entire kingdom. It overlooked the city, which held at its heart the King's chamber. Placed all around the city were the dwelling places of the citizens, which rested on the hillsides in a step-like fashion. Each dwelling place had door-ways but no doors and open windows but no glass or locks of any kind. The dwelling places were the private settings in which saints old and new could gather and enjoy fellowship.

The golden streets that led to the Great Hall were lined with breathtaking gardens. Profound mixtures of blues and yellows, greens and purples, pearl whites and sharp pinks tantalized the eyes, evoking a deep gush of praise and worship. The King's children encountered nature's magnificent beauty and a plethora of colors as common to them as black and white are to the souls of those on Earth. Paradise cannot be imagined—only experienced.

On their way to the Great Hall, a small boy with curly brown hair and big blue eyes asked Cynthia about her now-famous request to meet her parents. Josh had arrived in glory as a nine-month-old and found a special place in Cynthia's heart as he developed into the young boy he was now.

"I'm waiting to hear," she said. "Hopefully, I will know soon. Real soon…" She hugged him and then watched him skip ahead, singing as he went.

She turned her attention back to Angela. "It seems that nearly all the city is aware of my request to visit my parents on the other side."

"There is a ton of excitement about your request," Angela reassured her.

"But how do you enter time if you have only known timelessness?"

"Yours is not the first wish for such a miracle, only the first to voice it." Angela wrapped her arm around Cynthia.

In Cynthia's development and growth, the desire to meet her father and mother in person grew perpetually. This desire is common among babies who never had the opportunity to be born. There is an unspoken but known longing to meet and love the biological parents who have been part of their soul since arriving in Paradise.

Sadly, some children wait patiently to meet their parents but will never have the chance because their parents ignored the King's calling to trust Him as Savior. They choose to reject His love; therefore, they will never be united with their child in Heaven.

But, one day, in grace and compassion, the King will put each child's disappointment to rest. Memories, desires, and tears of separation will be wiped away forever.

Others meet their parents and are allowed to be the first ones at the portals of glory to greet them on their arrival. As one can imagine, those moments of joy and completion are fulfilling for both the child and the parent.

Cynthia's desire was unique; she wanted to go to them on Earth. The King had never permitted this before. Over time, she had also developed a deep desire to dance with her father, perhaps learned from her duties as a worship leader, or perhaps just the innocent desire of a young lady.

The sisters entered the city's courtyard, joining thousands of others who were gathering for the great feast. The sounds of talking and laughter were considerably loud and celebratory, but Cynthia clearly heard a soft, deep voice call her name.

Her perfectly shaped legs came to a peaceful halt. She turned to see Sebastian standing in the distance among some prominent men of the city. Sebastian was a dominion commissioned to care for the girls as they matured. He was in the second sphere of angelic beings and served the King as a governor of heavenly matters.

Around Sebastian were beasts of every kind: lions, lambs, dogs, rabbits, bears, squirrels, cheetahs, and so many more perfectly formed animals who all lived in unity with no fear of demise.

"Sebastian!" Cynthia ran to him and graced him with a hug, with Angela following close behind.

Cynthia was as close to being a daughter to Sebastian as a human can be to an angel. He admired so much about her— her beauty, character, and exuberant smile that conveyed much love. He often teased her that the crown of her head had been rounded as though made to wear a diadem.

"I have something to discuss with you," Sebastian informed her as they walked in step. "I believe you will find it exhilarating."

"I'm all ears," she said as a gesture of interest and respect. Indeed, she had slightly oversized ears, like her mother, but on Cynthia, they were charming.

"You have been granted the privilege of sitting with the King at this festival."

Her face beamed with light and her heart was raptured. She began to thank Sebastian incessantly.

"My child, please. I am only the messenger of this good news, not its initiator. The King gave the order, and I am simply here to announce it to you."

"I'm so glad it was you who told me. Thank you. I cannot wait to sit with Him!" She turned to Angela, who was beaming with joy for her friend.

The two friends locked arms and sang songs of rejoicing as they drew closer to the palace. With no pole or wire for support, exquisite banners that proclaimed the many names of the King hung above them on either side of the golden street. Their gentle wave served as reminders of His many victories.

The fine silk flags represented every language and tongue. *Jesucristo* (Spanish for Jesus Christ), *Yeshua* (Hebrew name for Jesus), *Princeps Pacis* (Latin for Prince of Peace), *Re Dei Re* (Italian for King of Kings), and *De Zielzorger* (Dutch for the Shepherd) were just a few of the titles that flapped in the windless air. The King's favorite of them all, Son of Man, was proclaimed prominently in various languages such as Swahili (*Mwana wa mtu*). The declaration of His mighty name provided an ambience of majestic splendor and royalty.

The stairs to the Great Hall were a flawless blend of pearl and sapphire. The crowd of every tribe, tongue, and nationality moved harmoniously into the banquet room. Their entrance into the massive gathering place left them in awe, regardless of how many times they had entered it.

Its walls were covered with untarnished gold. Pillars of translucent marble adorned the corners and were used to hold red silk curtains draped across the top of the room from corner to corner. Laid within the gold walls were thin strips of purified silver that accentuated the streams of silver light that shone around the room.

The hall was massive but intimate in its settings. Its length appeared to be greater than one hundred football fields, and its width broader than fifty, yet it was immeasurable. Innumerable tables filled the vast space, positioned around the main walkway, which led to the platform that hosted the King's table. Three translucent golden steps encircled the King's dining table, providing full access to Him at any time.

The people celebrated being in His and each other's presence. Each person knew his or her place and took it at one of the many large, three-sided tables, which resembled the ancient triclinium. These allowed a reclining posture for dining instead of sitting upright in a chair. The three sides also promoted an intimate setting and a space where the servants could serve the guests.

Cynthia took her place at a table and reclined next to a gentleman of stature. He had large hands that bore the scars of a great fisherman who had spent the better part of his life toiling with fishing nets. But the hands were also gentle, as was his Galilean face. Peter had a strong jaw, a bright smile, and a large nose. His hair was dark and curly.

Cynthia smiled. "Hello, Peter."

"Cynthia, my child," he responded. "I heard a wonderful story about your father today from Sebastian."

"Oh, please tell me," she pleaded. "I want to hear everything you can tell me." Oftentimes, a person in Paradise will be told stories, as it were, about the life of a loved one on the other side. The stories are told as though they have already happened, even though in many cases, such as with Cynthia's father, they have yet to take place. This is because the person's life is not viewed from what he or she is at the moment, but what that person will become and accomplish once their heart is united with the plans and desires of the King. All lives are seen from the perspective of eternity, whether for good or for evil. In Cynthia's case, she had heard story after story of a brave father and a loving mother who together lived in a mansion that served the needs of many children who otherwise would have no home, no life to celebrate, and no one to love them.

As Peter was about to share his story, Naomi, a young girl with a very big grin that accentuated her tiny nose and long, flowing blonde hair, nearly tackled Cynthia with an oversized hug.

"Ahhhh!" Cynthia cried out.

Naomi stepped back, soaking wet, and laughed with Cynthia. "You should have seen the dolphins. They were so hilariously fun. We traveled across the sea at outrageous speeds."

Cynthia understood every word perfectly, even though Naomi spoke her native Russian.

Peter bellowed. "Naomi, you are such a girl of the water," he said in Aramaic.

"Says he who swims with the whales," Naomi jabbed back.

"But I am a fisherman." They roared with laughter.

Applause suddenly filled the vast room. Conversations ceased and songs of celebratory expressions rang out. As an outsider, you would hear thousands of native languages. But as a citizen of Paradise, they sounded like one perfect language.

Shouts of the King's name resounded. "Melchizedek, Melchizedek. The one great King."

The King appeared. Everyone rose to their feet, then bowed in complete humility and honor to the One they adored and loved. They shouted out His name in every dialect ever created: "Jesus!" It was a sound beyond description. The heavens shook to their core, yet not one soul trembled in fear.

Bright light emanated from His being. Angels and cherubim circled high above and honored Him with a chorus of thundering shouts. "The Highest! Glory to the Highest, who reigns now and forevermore."

All citizens bowed low, filled to the brim and overflowing with joy and celebration that erupted in shouts of personal gratitude and thanksgiving. Smiles of jubilance covered the faces of all citizens. Creatures of every kind—lions, lambs, cattle, and others—took their rightful place as invited beasts of the King's court and paid homage to their maker.

The King was elegant and strong. His eyes were clearer than transparent gold but looked as soft as a baby's brown tone. He stood a tall six feet, and His posture was that of a general who had seen battle and walked away victorious.

As He drew near, they lifted their heads to receive His smile. No one could take their eyes away from His deeply compassionate face. Beams of joy exuded from His glance. Love was not an emotion that came from Him; it was His very essence. His royal garments were a brilliant white with gold trim accentuated by a golden belt. The sash held small stones of amber and amethyst that hung with just the right tension.

His feet were housed comfortably in soft sandals that exposed marks of victory. His hands were partially hidden by His low-hanging gown, but as He gestured toward those He called His own, you could see perfectly healed scars on his wrists just above his palms.

The sight of the scars brought tears of incredible joy and gratefulness to the eyes of many—but not all. There is a sweet, intimate understanding about the meaning of those scars between the King and those who once lived life on Earth. It was similar to the look of understanding that two people share when they have been through a battle together and come out victorious. The battle's price was known only by those intimately familiar with it.

There were also many in the crowd who had never seen the light of day outside the womb. They were not fully aware of life's battles or the price that the marks in His hands and feet represented.

Cynthia was one of those. Oftentimes, she found herself staring at those who shed tears at the sight of the King's scars. It always made her curious. Sebastian, her dear angelic friend, had tried to explain it to her, but he too was limited in his understanding of the deep intimacy between the Eternal Prince of Peace and His children who wore His forgiveness like a crown.

Angels do not have a savior. Those that chose rebellion would forever remain banished from glory. Forgiveness of any sort had not been provided to them by the King. Human beings were the only creatures to be offered such a remarkable gift and only those who had lived on Earth and received His forgiveness understood the depth of the meaning of the scarred hands and feet.

The King made his way down the middle of the aisle and touched those around Him with a hand of blessing. He approached Cynthia and stopped. Cynthia bowed her head in reverence, her insides vibrating with life and energy. He lifted her chin and gazed into her eyes. She had no reason to look away. There was not even a partial hint of shame or embarrassment that intruded the moment. He paused.

"Will you dine with Me?" His eyes sparkled.

Thrilled and humbled, Cynthia nodded with a beaming smile. She rose to her feet and followed the King to His rightful seat of authority atop the platform. Together they ascended the wide steps of pearl and sapphire. The incline was steep, yet it seemed short in its distance.

The King's table looked much like the others, but it had a designated place for authority. He motioned for her to recline at His right hand.

She had not noticed that the music and celebration had paused. The city was enjoying a slice of perfect life, and no one dared to interrupt.

A great bright smile crossed His lips. "Let the celebration begin!" He announced.

Instantly, the music resumed to a perfect level and joy-filled laughter filled the hall once again. Trumpets, harps, violins, horns, and even percussion instruments played beautifully in the background.

Magnificently prepared food was placed before the King and Cynthia. Fruit, luscious and large, dripped with beads of clear water and was laid open on a pure-gold serving plate. Figs, berries, nuts of every kind, and other delicious delicacies were spread on the table within arm's reach.

All eyes were on the King as He rose from His seat and served Cynthia. She had seen this holy moment many times before, but she had never personally experienced the magnitude of what was taking place. She was like a newborn baby who lacks the capacity to fully understand the great depths of love bestowed on her by her loving parents.

Dancers and singers began to offer their gifts of celebration in front of the King's table. Men and women ascended and descended the stairs as they honored their beloved King.

"May I join them?" Cynthia asked the King.

"By all means, My child."

Cynthia launched out of her seat and joined the dance. Her feet and legs moved gracefully amid the other dancers. A choir of children rushed to the front and joined in a choral. Cynthia moved toward them and choreographed their moves to the rhythm of the music and the other dancers. Angela joined Cynthia in the jubilation. A lovely maiden named Jeannette, who was of Lithuanian descent, ignited a great round of clapping in time with the music from the vast crowd of worshippers. Wakeyia, a shorter African woman, joined Jeannette and they both beamed while shouting out words of adoration.

The music rose to a new level. The clapping morphed into applause and filled the city. Not even the walls of the Great Hall could contain the praise. The rejoicing and celebration swept over the Celestial City like a tsunami, bringing all living things to once again fall down on their face in gratitude and humble devotion.

Magnificent brilliant streams of translucent and multicolored light radiated from the King's face. Its weight penetrated the skin of each person and creature present. Unbridled ecstasy flowed from His presence into His creation, leaving them speechless.

After this culminated and the applause settled down, Cynthia took her place next to the King.

He sang a soft and personal melody of love over her. Words of blessing clothed her and without her knowing it, draped providential protection and provision over her. When He had finished, He smiled and then playfully ruffled her dark hair. They shared a laugh.

"What is it you wish, Cynthia?"

"Only to be here, with you, my King. I need nothing more."

"Hold out your hand, my child."

She lifted her right hand and mysteriously the necklace she had been wearing now laid flat across her palm. She touched her neck where the precious stone once hung.

"What name does it bear?"

"Cynthia Hope," she answered.

"And such a beautiful name, at that. But there is more to it, and the time has come for you to discover it."

"My Lord?"

"Tell me the yearning of your heart."

She pondered the request. Not because she had forgotten that yearning, but because she searched her mind for any desire outside of this very moment. "That I might meet my mother and father. If only but for a moment, that I might tell them how much I love them and how grateful I am to them for all they have done to help so many."

She paused. There was more. The King waited for her to finish.

"And if I may, Your Majesty, I pray that I might dance with my father, if but just one time."

He touched her cheek and replaced the necklace around her neck. "Your petition has been granted." His words roared through her soul and lifted it to a new height. Her King, the Creator of all, had just granted her permission to do something no other person had ever done.

As the words of the King moved throughout the city, a sudden loud applause erupted from the citizens and a new celebration rang out. Cynthia blushed with warmth and awe as those around her congratulated her.

The King turned and drew Cynthia into an embrace. "Daughter, remember who you are." As He let her go, He made His way through the hall, touching His people.

Angela ran to her friend and held her tightly. "This will be a moment to be celebrated by all who have ever longed to meet their family."

Cynthia scanned the throng of well-wishers surrounding her as she pondered what Angela had just said. Then it occurred to her that Angela too would love the opportunity to meet her own mother or father.

With compassion, Cynthia turned to her friend. "I wish it was you taking the journey to meet your parents."

"This is the perfect will of Him who made us both," Angela said. "It is right. I celebrate this incredible moment with you and will intercede as you do what you have been called to do. My joy is complete. I am content with the King's plan."

"I must go at once and thank Sebastian. Surely he had a hand in seeing this come true," Cynthia declared.

Sebastian chimed in with a chuckle, "We have a long journey ahead. You will have plenty of opportunity to thank me then."

Cynthia spun on her heels and saw her guardian standing behind her with open arms. She gave Sebastian a strong hug of gratefulness. Tears of joy rolled down her lovely face.

As the enormos crowd made its way out of the room, taking their laughter and conversations with them, a holy silence filled the space, which allowed Cynthia a moment alone to ponder all that had just happened.

She scanned the Great Hall. "What did the King mean … 'Daughter, remember who you are'?"

"It will make perfect sense when the time comes," Sebastian answered.

She considered the thought more deeply. "Yes, I suppose there will be many surprises in my time there. What's it like down there, Sebastian? Surely you've been there many times."

"Not as many as some of my fellow angels. Let me just tell you this—expect the unexpected and remain true to who you are. Never forget that. Never deny it."

"Why would I ever do such a thing?"

"You will be on the other side of the veil. What often seems to be true is not, even though it feels true. Your feelings will deceive you. Remember who you belong to, and let faith take the place of feeling."

"Faith? What is that?"

"It is how you will live your life while absent from our city. Are you ready to begin your journey?"

"Now, Sebastian?"

"It is the appointed time."

Cynthia unconsciously rubbed her necklace between her fingers. She took a long pause to process it all. She looked up and locked eyes with Angela. Angela reached for her hands and held them tight.

"The silence of this Great Hall pays homage to the remarkable event that is about to take place. Now we, as citizens of the kingdom, will watch in awe as you begin your new journey to a world you have never known."

Cynthia's eyes sparkled with excitement. She squeezed Angela's hands in anticipation and turned to Sebastian. "Let's go!"

Together, they disappeared.

⤲ 3 ⤳

SEBASTIAN AND CYNTHIA SET OUT ON A SLOW WALK across a tranquil, glassy sea. The sky was electric with bright rainbow colors that changed in hue and tint. It was sheer ecstasy, unimaginable to a person who did not live in Paradise, as was the simple act of walking on water, which Cynthia loved to do. She had enjoyed so many moments with her friends playing, running, even dancing atop the sea of Heaven.

But now it served as the transitional path to a place she had only dreamed of that would not offer her the privileges she had known.

"Sebastian?" she asked curiously. "Why don't we just travel to Earth by thought, as we do oftentimes in the Great City?"

"Your journey to Earth requires both development and preparation, and those critical elements require time. Each step will lead you closer to your destination."

She pondered his words for a moment. "I promise to learn all I need to know."

As they walked and talked, Sebastian shared what he knew about life on Earth and the boundaries she was called to live by. So intent in her listening, Cynthia was slow to notice that the shades of color surrounding them had morphed into pale streams of light.

The backdrop of colors that surrounded them were simple earth tones. Blues and grays and some pink now dominated the horizon. The beautiful banners that had displayed the many names of the King and waved so effortlessly were gone. Above and around them was an empty horizon with an occasional flash of lightning that left dark clouds in its wake. She pondered the changes in atmosphere.

Cynthia truly appreciated Sebastian's tutoring and occasionally asked questions like, "What is sleep?" or, "What do you mean by suffering?"

Total and unquestionable dependence on the King had been as natural to her as breathing would soon be. She had never needed a breath of air in her existence. But where she was going, it was different. From the physical to the emotional and all areas of life in between, her conscious need for the King would be on a whole new level. Sebastian knew what she would face in her journey and understood that much of her dependence on the King would have to be learned the hard way.

"You must remember that while you are here, your time with the King, the time to learn from His book and listen to His voice, is of the utmost importance. While you walk the unstable shores of your new city, you must not forget who you are and to Whom you belong. Is this understood, Cynthia?"

"It is, Sebastian. I will not forget." Streams of anxiety and nervousness flowed through her body, but she did not understand what they meant or if they needed her attention, much like a child who feels growing pains but doesn't necessarily stop and acknowledge them.

Sebastian stopped and revealed a small brown book. It was bound by old, authentic leather, and its pages contained handwritten text on an ancient plant skin. "For those times." He handed it to her.

She received it with gratitude and opened it. Small writing in Latin filled each yellowed page. It was an early copy of the

Canon of Scripture. Cynthia had never seen one before. To her, the Word was a living Person, and knowledge was shared through personal stories among the saints.

"It is the written Word of the King," Sebastian informed her.

"Thank you, Sebastian. I will cherish every moment I spend with it."

"This book will keep you from sin, or sin will keep you from this book."

"What is sin?"

"It is that which separates you from your Father." He motioned with his hand to resume walking.

Cynthia presumed Sebastian was referring to her earthly father but said nothing to clarify the statement. Her ability to fully understand his thoughts had begun to dissipate. Consequently, she was unable to grasp that she had surrendered that gift of communication. She was about to ask Sebastian about the change but was startled out of her thoughts.

At that moment there was a crack of thunder and peals of lightning flashed. From behind Sebastian's right and left shoulders, large gray wings of muscle and thick tissue emerged. These were used strictly for battle and were protected by a layer of tight collagen scales, much like that of a rhinoceros.

Sebastian swept Cynthia behind his body and covered her with his right wing. With one quick motion he withdrew a flaming sword from his left side. He stood his ground as three ugly creatures possessed by demon spirits growled and stalked the travelers.

The demons let Sebastian know by their roar that he and Cynthia were trespassing. It was not the roar of a mighty lion but more of a hyena fighting for the last morsel of a carcass.

One of the ugly creatures spoke with a snarl and hiss. "Where is she, this daughter of the *King*?" He spoke his reference to the King in tones of disgust and vile temper.

Cynthia poked her head out from behind Sebastian's protective wing and the beast caught a glimpse of her and hissed loudly like a barbarian. She gasped and tried to hide again.

The beast snarled at Cynthia. "What is it, my child? Do you seek your mother and father? Look no more, for I am your mother."

The beast transformed into a tall woman with silver blonde hair, dressed in a long silk gown.

The woman took a step toward her. "Come, girl, I will take care of you."

Sebastian furled his brow and set his chin for battle. The sweet, kind, and gentle angel who walked the streets of glory and shared jokes with young children was now in full battle mode, ready to take out the threat to Cynthia's arrival at her earthly destination.

Cynthia closed her eyes and held onto Sebastian tightly. She had never encountered such hostility and was being baptized in the realities of angelic warfare, of which she had only heard stories.

Sebastian raised his sword to strike the beast closest to him. All at once, out of nowhere, an immense force struck the three beasts from the side, knocking each one hundreds of feet into the darkness.

Six strong, angelic beings dressed for battle spun around and replaced their swords in their sheaths. The leader, a mighty warrior with dark skin, flashed a smile toward Sebastian.

"We were in a realm close by and heard you drawing your sword. Figured you might appreciate a little backup." He grinned a handsome smile. The other five beings relaxed their stance.

"You assumed correctly, my good friend. I was about to have some demons for lunch, but to be honest, I wasn't really that hungry." As Sebastian was chiding with them, he lowered his ominous wings, which revealed Cynthia. She stepped out from behind him and breathed a sigh of relief.

The leader of the holy group spoke with humility. "We have heard of this great calling you are about to engage in, my child, and we wish you Godspeed in your journey." The angels bowed their heads in honor to Cynthia, who graciously accepted the gesture and returned it with a bow of her head.

"See you, my friend," he said to Sebastian and flew away just as fast as he had arrived. The others followed.

Cynthia looked to Sebastian. Her eyes spoke in volumes of her fright.

"Are you well?"

"Yes. I think so. You were my shield, and I felt your strength."

"That is the strength of your King, my child. Remember it well as you go about His business."

"I will. I promise." She drew close to him and held his arm for security.

With that they resumed their travel and the tutorial on the wisdom she would need on her journey. A curious concern that the evil beings would return, and that she would have no one to defend her, burrowed its way into Cynthia's soul and created a cavity of doubt that she had never known before.

After a long time, they came to a stop at the shoreline of a beach community. The trek had taken them the equivalent of many weeks in human time. Together, they stood atop the water a short distance from the shore of the quiet beach. The sky was dark, with dawn about to break. Cynthia had never experienced darkness before and she found it alarming, yet compelling. She squinted until her eyes adjusted to her surroundings, finding comfort in the white glow from the unfamiliar moon in the sky.

"Cynthia," Sebastian said hesitantly, "before you cross over onto this temporary terrain, I want you to know you can change your mind; you do not have to go. This journey is not mandated in any way."

She pondered his words and turned toward the highway that separated the sandy ground from the row of houses on the other side of the blacktop road. Cars drove by. Like much of what she saw, the automobile was new to her. It all seemed so unreal. It didn't feel anything like she had been used to. As she and Sebastian stood upon the water, a frigid wave licked up the back of her legs and the shock from the cold startled her.

Cynthia latched onto Sebastian's strong arm in order to keep her footing. The gentle waves that lapped the beach had moved her closer to the shore. She peered down through the early morning light into the murky water. It was unsettling.

"What happens when I step onto the land, Sebastian?" Cynthia asked curiously.

"You surrender your immortality and resume being mortal, as you once were."

Cynthia had learned of how she, and other babies like her, had arrived in Paradise. Their journey from the womb to the King's presence was as blessed and meaningful as one who lived a full life on Earth. In her unique case, Cynthia would be doing something that no one except the King had done before, though so much of what He did in that display of humility and love was unfathomable to her finite mind: He had set aside His royalty and eternality to become mortal—and so much more.

She felt prompted in her heart to take the step and learn what her Master had in store for her. Her heart worshiped Him, and she realized she could trust Him and move forward.

"I wish to go ashore."

She handed her copy of the Scriptures to Sebastian to hold and then bent down to scoop up a handful of ocean water. He watched her as she pondered the texture and color of the salted sea.

"As you desire. First, we must change your appearance." He pointed at her shining white silk gown. When she looked down, it was transformed into a plain blue cotton dress with a cream-white belt.

"Your footwear, please?"

"Will I get them back?" Cynthia loved her glass shoes, which had been designed uniquely for her and given to her by the King.

"Most assuredly. When your journey here is complete and you are ready to return home, they will be waiting for you."

She stared down at her shoes and then obediently removed the right one. Then Sebastian held her hand to balance her as she slipped out of the left one.

She handed them over to him and instantly sank about three feet to the bottom of the shallow shoreline.

"HELP!" she shrieked, reaching out to her friend for help. The water was cold and unnerving. She felt out of control. Her feet searched for sure footing. She was terribly uncomfortable and had a hard time maintaining her balance. About the time she settled on a secure spot, a strong wave crashed against her and pushed her forward, face down on the beach.

Fear struck her soul, different than anything she had felt before, even the surprise attack of the demons in the heavens. She was now fully mortal and completely vulnerable in her thoughts and feelings. Before she could grasp her new reality, another wave hit her from behind. Cold for the first time and feeling out of control, Cynthia began to cry.

Sebastian flashed a hint of a grin. "Not quite what you're used to, hmm? Don't worry. You'll adjust." He stretched out his strong hand and helped her up.

She peered down at her blue dress. It was soaked and covered with green muck that she did not recognize. She started to shiver. She didn't like being cold. It felt threatening in a strange way.

Cynthia took a step forward. Her sadness quickly turned to shock as she stepped on something sharp and jerked her foot up. "Ouch! This is horrible!"

She sneaked a glance at Sebastian, hoping for some sympathy.

"We will provide a new pair of shoes that will suit your needs."

Fighting back the tears, she took another step and winced as relentless waves pummeled her to shore.

Taking her by the hand, Sebastian led her forward, away from the cold water.

Finally reaching dry sand, Cynthia sighed and surveyed her new surroundings. *This is what she wanted for so long?* Cold and wet, she glanced towards Sebastian and forced a smile. Triumphantly she tossed a fistful of sand into the wind; it blew hard against their faces. They both spit profusely, trying to remove the sand from their mouths. Cynthia giggled and wiped sand from her face.

"There are some final instructions that you must embrace to carry out your task," Sebastian announced in a tone of impatience.

"Yes, sir. But… may I ask you a question first?"

"By all means."

She hesitated, shivering from the cold. A myriad of questions filled her head, but she didn't know where to begin. She looked back—at the water, the sand, and the shoes she once wore. "Will everything be different for me here?"

"Not all has changed. There are many attributes that you will carry into your experience to help you as you go."

She smiled, feeling a bit better. "Okay. I think I know what you mean. Who I am hasn't changed. Just some of what I can do."

"Exactly." He grinned. "Now may I continue?"

She grinned too and nodded.

"Though you may not realize it, what you have chosen to perform is a heroic endeavor for the kingdom. Therefore, your identity is of great interest to those who do not share the same goals as those of the King, nor you, for that matter, as you have already encountered with the beasts. Therefore, it is of immense consequence that no one, until the appointed time, know from where you came."

"But isn't that the purpose of my journey? Meeting my father and mother?" she asked.

"Only at the appropriate time. Until then, you are to steer clear of any discussions about your parents. However, and I caution you gravely, you are never to deny that you are the King's child. Such an act will have dire consequences. Is that understood?"

"How will I know when to reveal my identity?"

"The time will present itself as clearly as I am standing by your side. Until then, when talk about your identity comes up, simply tell them your name is Cindy Hope and you are visiting family."

She smiled, then frowned. "Sebastian, why would I deny the King? I cannot imagine hurting Him so."

"The secret is to remember." He handed her the leather book of Scripture.

She changed the subject. "What is my mother like? I've heard many wonderful things about my father but so little about her."

"She is as lovely as the sunrise and as wounded as a sparrow with a broken wing. Bitterness robbed her of her destiny."

Another frown appeared on her lips.

He continued. "But it is her ache that got the King's attention."

"Ache for what?" she asked.

"Not what. But rather, for Whom!"

Cynthia didn't follow what he was saying. She could no longer perceive his thoughts. But she could read his expressions. "Me?"

Sebastian nodded. Cynthia pondered the thought of her mother hurting so badly. He then turned back to the water, walked out a few feet, reached into the water, and pulled up a large-mouthed fish squirming for its life.

Gently, he removed a coin from its mouth, tossed the fish safely into the water, and handed Cynthia the coin.

She took it and examined its beauty but said nothing.

"Your first order of business is to find shelter, food, and appropriate clothing."

Cynthia glanced at her wet clothes. The bitter cold pierced her innocent body, especially her feet. She started to shiver again.

"I miss my shoes and gown already."

"As promised, your royal attire will return when you complete your task."

They trekked up the sandy beach and stopped near the road. The sun was beginning to rise in the east.

He concluded his tutorial of the journey. "Go to the town over there and find Ninth Street." She followed his point toward a serene street with a row of offices and stores. "There you will find a coin shop called Finklemeyer's. They will exchange the gold coin you hold for the funds necessary until you find employment. Once that is accomplished, find suitable clothing and go to 721 Marigold Lane. There you will find Miss Eunice Casselberry. Let her know you are in need of her attic and a pair of shoes. She will help you."

"Attic?"

"Yes. That is where she keeps her shoes. It will serve as your living quarters for the time being."

Cynthia tucked the instructions into the back of her mind and moved to the next question demanding an answer. "Where will I be of service to my employer?"

"A theme park called Ziggy's Island."

"Theme park?" she asked.

"That's a term used to describe an amusement park, where people pay money, myriads of it, to have fun."

She contemplated his comment for a moment. "Is that where I will find my father and mother?"

"It will lead you to them in due time, my child."

Sebastian held her by the arms and looked into her eyes. "I admire your courage, young lady of the King. What you are about to experience is so magnificent that we angels hold our breath, as it were, and would leave our posts immediately to take your stead, if only we were qualified."

He smiled. "You, among women, are most to be admired."

She gave him a strong and lengthy hug.

"You are not alone. Remember." He disappeared.

She scanned the beach, then the water, then the community across the highway. Sebastian was gone.

"Goodbye," she whispered, though she did not understand why. She had never said goodbye to anyone before, yet here she was saying it as though she knew what it meant. She was becoming in touch with her instincts.

She breathed a prayer and took inventory of her feelings. She stood in an unfamiliar place but felt at peace. A feeling of adventure surged through her body. Adrenaline gave her a sense of purpose and focus. Then her body gave her its first hunger pains. The odd gnawing sensation was unsettling but then she remembered Sebastian telling her about hunger and pain and their part in the proverbial human existence. She breathed another quick prayer of thanks for the privilege of her unique experience and felt encouraged.

I need to find food. She looked around and her lovely brown eyes landed on an elderly woman rummaging through bright blue-and-yellow trash cans. *I wonder if she's hungry too.*

She winced with each step as she approached the vagrant. "Excuse me, please."

The lady was annoyingly surprised and dropped the piece of hamburger she had just hoisted to her lips. She eyed Cynthia. "What can I do for you, Your Highness?"

Cynthia did not react to the reference to royalty; she understood that, as a child of the King, she was royalty.

Cynthia drew close to the woman but leaned back when a stench filled her unsuspecting nostrils. The sweet lady's body odors were unfamiliar to Cynthia. Then, for the first time, she saw the effects of age and neglect. She unintentionally stared at the elderly woman, who had deep, dark wrinkles and reddish sores on her face; her skin sagged; her nose looked bent and unusual. The citizens of Heaven were all in perfect health. There were no such blemishes on one's body or creases in one's skin.

There was no sign of aging or dying in the King's presence. All of this was new to Cynthia and she couldn't help but peer at the imperfections in the woman's face.

Cynthia pondered what she was looking at. Then she realized she was gazing at a woman made in the image of the Creator. Compassion filled her soul; she leaned back in and drew close to her.

"Where might I find Ninth Street?"

Cynthia's inviting smile disarmed the woman. "Not typical for folks 'round here to…" She grumbled to herself but didn't finish. "What do ya give me if I tell ya?" the woman barked.

"What would you like?"

"Could use some food. A little drink would be proper." The old lady adjusted her rugged and dirty blouse in an effort to look formal, as if something about Cynthia made her want to be better.

"Food it is! Where might we find the Great Hall?" Cynthia locked arms with the woman's dirty arm, which caused the woman to shrink back. "What's the matter?" Cynthia inquired of her new friend.

Cynthia moved the woman's mucky, matted hair back from her face and placed it behind her ears. Then she smiled and looked into the woman's eyes.

The lonely lady chomped her toothless gums. "Alrighty then. Let's go ta' town."

"Alrighty then," Cynthia agreed and spun them both around to face their destination.

Together, they stepped from the sandy beach onto a small crop of grass and then onto the sidewalk. Cynthia winced again once she hit pavement.

Cynthia spied the old lady's ragtag shoes, if that's what you could call them. She had a painful hobble to her walk. Her feet were swollen and red.

"Are all the roads here so hard?"

"Need shoes," she muttered.

"Then that's what we shall get… along with the food." Cynthia's stomach growled. "What was that?" she asked with a shriek in her voice.

"You're hungry!" exclaimed the old woman.

Cynthia cringed as her hunger pains grew.

"Don't worry. You'll get used to it!"

"This has happened to you too?" Cynthia groaned.

"You betcha! Every day."

Cynthia couldn't imagine. "What is your name, please? I do not know it."

"Violet," the woman matter-of-factly stated.

"Violet. I'm Cynthia, uh… Cindy. It's a pleasure to know you." They shook hands.

A small, toothless smile emerged from Violet, which gave Cynthia a sad feeling. *This woman needs more than food or shoes. She needs love.* Cynthia decided she would be the one to give it to her.

As the sun peeked its head over the trees the two new friends waddled and winced their way across the slow highway, feeling the hope and light of a new day.

∽ 4 ∾

THE QUAINT BEACH COMMUNITY OF PARADISE BAY WAS perfectly poised as the link between two larger beach cities along a paved California coast. Just a stone's throw from the cold blue ocean was the stretch of highway that provided an easy excuse to pass through, and the town's approximately three thousand residents loved that so many passersby did not notice the tiny sign boasting the town's name.

The town's hand-painted signs communicated a salute to a simpler time. Center Street was the predominate access point to the various picturesque shops, restaurants, markets, hardware stores, and even the post office. It did not intersect with the coastal highway, which was why most travelers didn't notice it.

At Ninth Street, Cynthia and Violet found the coin shop. They quietly entered the front door, looking for help.

While Finklemeyer's Coins and Collectibles was what you might expect of a coin shop, the opening of the door rang an angry buzz that made them feel more like intruders. Cynthia was sensitive to the sudden jerk of Violet's body at the sound of the door closing behind them. She put her arm around Violet's left shoulder, then smiled and gave a squeeze of comfort.

An older Middle Eastern man stepped out from behind the door of the back room and greeted them in a strong Egyptian accent. His face was ashen from too many years of smoking. His eyes were almost covered with black eyebrows that had not been trimmed since the mid-1970s. He was quick to cough and slow to apologize for it. The harsh odor of his breath left Cynthia gulping ever so slightly for fresher air.

"How may I help you?" he muttered with an unwelcoming tone, looking at the ladies with a furled brow.

Cynthia forced a smile and offered her hand to him as she spoke in perfect Egyptian. "Hello, my friend. We are looking for help in trading this coin for money." She made a mental note that she had retained her knowledge of languages and breathed a short prayer of gratitude.

The man appeared annoyed and regretfully obliged the handshake.

She handed the coin to him.

He glanced down at the coin and then examined it carefully. "How did a girl such as yourself come to own a rare coin like this …?"

Cynthia began to reply, but he continued in an accusatory tone. "… of which there are only two, maybe three, known coins like it in the entire world?"

Cynthia remained optimistic. "A dear friend gave it to me for my expenses until I acquire employment at Ziggy's Park."

"I will make phone call," he said in broken English.

The private phone in Radcliffe's office rang loudly, interfering with scouring the budget on his computer. Without even looking up, he knew who it was on the other end. "Yes, Jacob. What is it?" He listened as Jacob told the short tale of this Caucasian woman, who wore wet clothes, and her homeless friend, walking into the store with such a rarity as a flawless, first-century gold coin with the face of Caesar Augustus on it.

Radcliffe spun his chair around and stared at multiple monitors stationed ever so carefully behind his desk. They showed the store from six different angles. He moved close to the screen for a better look at the two women.

His eyes glanced at Violet and dismissed her as a potential threat immediately. But there was something about Cynthia that made him paranoid. The screen did not do her justice, but he could tell she was not from around the area. Her clothes did not match her beauty. It was as though she had disguised herself to look like a pauper, much like a royal person would do if he or she wanted to visit a town unnoticed.

Radcliffe rose to his small feet, encased in tight, custom-made black leather shoes. He leaned down and with a hanky swiped a speck of dust off the front tip of the left shoe. It annoyed him to have a spot or anything else uninvited on his handmade Lodings. His looks had not changed much in recent years, except for the thinning, gray hair that now crowded out the sides of his once-coveted brown strands.

His suit was casual at a glance but impeccable in its fit. It concealed his portly figure. The ensemble was one of more than a dozen that he owned. His ideas on how the world should operate were even less in variety than his suits. If you think of Ebenezer Scrooge, you understand who Radcliffe was and the condition of his soul. But based on his clothing, one might not guess that this was so.

"Describe the coin to me in detail," he instructed Jacob.

Jacob described a small, thick gold coin with the figurehead of Caesar Augustus on the front with the words *Divus Augustus* inscribed around the head. The coin was not perfectly round, as it was formed in the fire with a hammer. "On the back…"

Radcliffe interrupted him. "What year do you estimate the coin to be?"

"No later than twenty-seven to thirty-two AD," Jacob said as he blew his nose three times.

"What do you estimate the value to be?" Radcliffe demanded, annoyed at the obtrusive sound. He hated it when Jacob did that, especially while on the phone.

"Maybe fifty thousand."

"Offer them twenty-five thousand, not a penny more."

"Yes. Yes, yes. I will do this," Jacob assured his employer.

"One more thing. Close the store and bring the coin to me when they leave." Radcliffe slapped the phone in its cradle and turned back to the monitors to watch the store. He spied Cynthia, with her back turned to the camera, and then saw Violet leaning over the counter as if to reach behind the glass case and remove an item. The glass door was ajar. "Foolish Jacob," he muttered as he picked up the phone to call Jacob. *How many times had he warned him not to leave the glass cases open when unattended?* He returned the phone to the cradle when he saw Violet abort her reach just as Jacob reappeared from the back room.

Jacob scowled as he mumbled to Cynthia. "Not worth much to us. We give you twenty thousand dollars and not a penny more. Take it or leave it. I do not care."

Cynthia looked at Violet, who shrugged her shoulders, then back at Jacob. Her spirit warned her that something was wrong. She sensed the presence of sin and felt a darkness in the man. It scared her, but she confidently reminded herself, *I am a child of the King.* Looking in Jacob's eyes, Cynthia questioned his intentions. "Is that the best price you can offer us? And remember... lying is a sin."

"I'm a very fair businessman; you ask anyone. All right, twenty-five thousand US dollars. Not a penny more."

Cynthia pondered the offer. Her spirit still said something was wrong, but she was unsure of why. She felt nervous, as though she was about to make a mistake. It was uncomfortable and caused her to squirm in her partially wet dress. "That sounds fair, but I'm sure you …"

Jacob cut her off. "Twenty-five thousand is my final offer. Take it or leave it. I do not care."

Violet grew restless. Cynthia agreed just to finish with the ordeal and leave. She gave Jacob a simple nod.

Jacob opened the safe sitting in the corner behind his register and quickly entered the code to open it. He pulled out a stack of bills and counted out twenty-five thousand dollars in one hundred-dollar bills in front of Cynthia. "You wish for a receipt?"

"Receipt?" she asked.

"Yes. A receipt," he impatiently repeated.

"Sure," Cynthia said with a smile. She didn't know what it was but figured it could be important.

Jacob wrote it up and handed it to her. She stared at the stack of cash in her and and looked back at him. "Do you have something I can put this in please?"

Annoyed, he grabbed a brown paper bag from under the counter and handed it to her.

"Thank-you," she said politely and put the money into the bag.

Before she reached the door, he yelled out, "Hey, you tell your friends about Jacob. I am an honest man! I treat them fair if they come to me."

She slid back toward him and gracefully offered her hand. "Okay. I will do that."

He obliged the gesture and shook her hand. She held his hand for a sustained moment, which seemed to make him very uncomfortable. "I'm grateful that we were able to meet such a fine man as yourself who could help us," she said just above a whisper. "You were very kind," she continued in perfect Egyptian.

His eyes betrayed his own greediness for a moment and reflected a smidgen of sorrow and regret. He slipped his hand away from hers and turned around, ducking back into his dark room without saying a word.

Violet grew weary of waiting and left the shop. Cynthia paused, then followed.

Outside the coin store, Cynthia stopped and breathed a big sigh of relief.

Violet rocked back and forth. "Got money. Can we get me my food?"

"Is this enough money for us for food and clothes?"

"Oh yeah. That's plenty!"

"Then let's eat!" Cynthia calmed her friend with a touch on the shoulder and walked her across the street.

They spotted a quaint Italian deli and meandered to a table alongside the big window. It smelled of breakfast and teased the ladies with promises of delight and satisfaction. The older woman who served them was a family member of the proprietor's, so she offered them a quick rundown of food options, which amounted to ten varieties of eggs and five choices of meat.

Cynthia was a novice at this, and Violet was distracted by the condiments placed atop the small wobbly table.

"What would you suggest?" Cynthia asked quietly. Hunger pangs were unsettling to her, and she just wanted to satisfy them.

"Our number one is what most folks order. I think you'll find it appetizing." The woman's voice had a hint of tenderness that was difficult to muster, as she had her own personal troubles to deal with in life.

"Okay. We'll have two number ones, please." Cynthia laid her elbows on the menu, which seemed to annoy the woman. She held out her hand and nodded toward the menus. "Oh, I'm sorry." Cynthia quickly handed them back to her.

Conversation with Violet was not easy, so Cynthia was grateful when the food arrived a few moments later. She stared at the food, curious. The meal that stared back at her from the diner's cracked plate looked so different than what she was used to. For Cynthia, it was the antithesis of food in the King's Great Hall: fresh fruits, nuts, berries, olives, and other perfect delicacies.

Cynthia gave thanks for the breakfast and started to eat with her hands. Violet chose to do the same. Both women struggled with placing the scrambled eggs in their mouths. It was not until Cynthia noticed other patrons using their forks that she realized what the utensils next to her plate were for. In Heaven, they always ate with their hands. But the food was quite different than what was in front of her.

She observed the way others used their silverware and followed suit. It proved to be a much easier way to eat. Violet stuck with eating by hand.

Cynthia forced down the eggs and the rubbery toast. Even the water had a strange, unappealing taste to it. She did, however, enjoy the sweet, small packages of jelly.

When the meal was finished, Cynthia didn't feel well. Her nauseated stomach now growled for different reasons. She rose from the table and began to walk out, forgetting that she had to pay for the food, another oversight on her part. The waitress intercepted their path out the door and handed Cynthia the bill.

"Oh, another receipt!" Cynthia exclaimed.

"Not exactly," replied the waitress. Cynthia looked at the piece of paper and realized her mistake. Her face turned red as she apologized and handed the waitress some money to cover the cost.

"Is that all?" the waitress asked, wanting a tip.

"Oh and thank you!" Cynthia grabbed her hand and shook it.

The woman accepted the shake but reflected an odd smile back. As Cynthia and Violet left the deli, the woman grumbled under her breath and cleared away the dishes.

Once outside, Cynthia and Violet made their way to a brightly colored woman's shoe boutique sandwiched between a candy store and an antique shop. When they entered the front door, a bell rang announcing their arrival.

Violet swatted at the noise and grumbled. Cynthia, on the other hand, smiled at the sound of the bells. Her spirit suspected something uncomfortable, but she tucked the feeling away and started to venture down the aisles.

This was all new to Cynthia. Shoes of every kind were hoisted atop petite shelving spaced oddly about the walls. Items were marked with signs telling Cynthia what was being sold. Sandals, handbags, scarves, and stockings were piled high into an open bin with a "half-off" sign stuck precariously in the middle of it all. She wondered what "half-off" meant.

A line of simple-looking clothing hung on racks placed here and there. A "sale" sign hung above them.

Two plain-looking young women with heavy makeup and clothes that matched what Cynthia saw in the store appeared out of the back room. "May we help you?" they questioned in unison without seeing to whom they were speaking. Their name badges identified them as Portia and Deidre.

Suddenly their eyes popped open wide with disgust. They stared at Violet's appearance and then grabbed their noses "Ewww." They then looked Cynthia up and down and stepped back with a sneer of jealousy.

"Who might … you be?" mocked Portia, the short and rotund one. "A princess looking for Prince Charming?" They giggled to each other.

Cynthia's spirit was insulted by their demeanor and she felt her heart beat faster as a desire to fight back roared up inside her mind. She chose to remain amiable.

"My friend and I are in need of some shoes and clothing, please," Cynthia said.

"We don't have anything that will fit you, I'm afraid," snarled Deidre, the slightly taller sister, with red streaks in her black hair.

Portia stalked Cynthia and Violet like a lion pursuing its prey. She ran her fingers across the shoulders of Cynthia's blue dress and sniffed the air around Cynthia. "You smell fishy."

Cynthia moved forward a step to get away from the woman.

Violet had wandered off a few feet and started to touch various shoes, looking to replace her old worn-out loafers.

"Eewww!" screamed Deidre. She grabbed a pair of nice-looking sandals from Violet's hands. "What ARE you doing? Please *do not* touch our merchandise unless you are planning on paying for it."

"How much are they?" Cynthia inquired, hoping to disarm the awkward rigidity.

"It doesn't matter because they're not for sale," Portia said.

Violet turned around and wobbled out the front door, grumbling to herself of how stupid she was to let Cynthia's kindness convince her otherwise.

"Well?" the sisters asked in unison as they attempted to stare Cynthia down. After a moment one tapped her feet and the other folded her arms.

Deidre raised an eyebrow. "Don't you have someplace to go… Your Highness?" They turned to each other and laughed hysterically.

Cynthia looked about the shop and saw items that she needed but would have to acquire elsewhere. She felt confused about what she did wrong. Why would they treat her and Violet so badly? She searched for the right words to say to the women, but none came to her. Hurt and dismayed, she slowly left the store.

This time, the bells ringing as she exited the store brought a frown to her lovely face.

Cynthia looked up and down the street. Violet was gone. Cynthia felt sad that she didn't say goodbye or get the shoes Cynthia had promised her. She prayed quietly, "Please show me some love and beauty in this place." She set out alone to find her new home.

She spotted an outdoor kiosk selling sunglasses, sunscreen, and sandals. She bought a pair of white sandals and put them on her aching feet. They brought relief and renewed a bounce back into her step. She thanked the clerk and made her way down the street. Seeing the beautiful blue sky, a surge of excitement welled up inside her once again. She knew she was loved, and she knew she was here for a purpose.

A few brief encounters with some nice people passing by and Cynthia was directed successfully to Marigold Lane and the address Sebastian had given her: 721. As Cynthia walked down the street, two stray cats, a small dog, and a squirrel happily walked behind her, reminding her of the furry friends she left in Paradise. Even the birds flew around her, singing a happy melody. She smiled and hummed a tune of worship.

Seven twenty-one Marigold Lane was a white, two-story house overdue for some paint and roof work, but its structure was solid, and the steps were new. Much like its inhabitant, Miss Casselberry, the house had occupied the same space for many decades.

Cynthia approached the dwelling with a simple sense of surrender and trust. She didn't know where she was or where she might be going, but she was invigorated by her journey on this planet. She stopped at the foot of the steps and whispered a word of gratitude heavenward for helping her find the place she would call home.

She opened a loose gray metal gate that defended the house from predators and ascended the stairs. The worn-out welcome mat on the porch looked to be of another era. Cynthia straightened it and brushed off the dirt and dust. It read, "Angels welcome. All others must sing."

Cynthia grinned ear to ear, enjoying the providential care that the King had provided. Instead of knocking, she began to sing a song about butterflies and kisses that welled up inside her eager soul.

Her song was melodious and perfect in pitch.

Cynthia sang another verse, finally getting the attention of the resident inside.

The door creaked and the woman poked her large head through, spying to see who might be singing outside her front door. Her narrow brown eyes scanned the porch, looking at Cynthia, and then for others who might be with her.

She brushed her uncombed graying hair back behind her ears. She moved towards Cynthia. Cynthia sensed the singing was effective in drawing the woman out of her suspicious state. The door opened farther.

Cynthia muted her song. There was a long moment of silence. Tears streamed down the woman's tanned, wrinkled cheeks, glistening like drops of pure gold oil. She didn't reach to wipe or stop them in the hallowed moment.

"Who are you?" Eunice asked, breaking the silence.

"My name is Cindy. I was told you had a place for me to stay, Miss Casselberry."

"Eunice. You can call me Eunice. That song you were singing, it's so … I haven't heard anyone sing that since my daddy left."

"It just came to me as I stood here reading your note," Cynthia said.

"My note?"

Cynthia stepped off the welcome mat, exposing the faded writing.

Eunice broke out in laughter. "I forgot that was there. It's been so long since I even noticed it. My father gave that to me as a present because he loved singing so much. I can't sing a lick, but boy could he sing." She hesitated and thought for a moment, turning sad in her tone.

"He left several years ago after he and mom divorced, and that song was one of his favorites. He'd sing it to me over the phone when I was in a bad place. I'd always call him when things got crazy and he would tell me everything was going to be okay because God was in His Heaven and all was right with the world."

The tears began to flow again. "I thought…" She changed her volume to a whisper. "I thought you were like my… you know… my angel or something, and maybe you were going to… Let's just say it's been a little lonely. Mom died a few years back and Dad has never bothered to call me since."

Cynthia stepped toward her and held her. They hugged each other for a long minute or two.

"How did you know my name?"

"A dear friend told me," Cynthia said, stepping back.

"Are you an angel?" Eunice whispered.

She grinned. "No, I'm just Cindy."

Eunice looked around curiously, wiping her nose with a hanky she kept close by.

"I'm here to see about lodging…" Cynthia resumed the conversation.

"I'm sorry, but you're mistaken. I don't have a room to rent, and I certainly don't take in pets!" Eunice motioned to the animals gathering around Cynthia's feet.

Cynthia laughed. "Oh. They are not with me. Time to go now!" She waved her hand and the animals scurried off.

Eunice slowly opened the door. "Please come in."

The house was pleasant, with blues and whites and sand-colored walls. Pictures depicting isolated sunsets and contemplative mornings hung crooked around the living room.

"You have a lovely home, Miss Casselberry."

"Please call me Eunice. Did you say someone told you I have a room to rent?

"My friend that I mentioned told me about it. I hope you don't mind."

Eunice frowned a peculiar disapproval look. "I don't mind the idea. I actually like you very much, even though we just met. It's just that, well, I don't have a room for rent. I'm sorry. There are only two bedrooms here; my nieces share a bedroom and I have the other."

"Oh, I'm sorry," Cynthia offered quickly as she moved toward Eunice, hoping to dispel the awkwardness. "Perhaps I misread the number on the house. I'm looking for seven-twenty-one Marigold Lane."

"That's my address. May I ask who told you this?"

"A dear friend who always tells the truth," Cynthia answered, a little confused. "He directed me to this address and instructed me to ask to use your attic."

"My attic?"

"Yes, where you keep your shoes."

Eunice's face dropped. "How in the world ...?"

She motioned for Cynthia to follow her up a narrow wooden staircase that ended at a tall, dark-blue door.

The door opened with a groan, revealing a spacious room filled to the slanted ceilings with shoe boxes of every imaginable color, size, and design. Cynthia stared at hundreds of brightly decorated shoe boxes. Each box seemed to be crammed against another begging for room to breathe.

"So many," Cynthia pondered aloud.

"I just *love* shoes," Eunice blurted out. "You don't think it's an addiction, do you?" She looked away, avoiding eye contact.

"I don't think so," Cynthia assured her.

Eunice glanced down at Cynthia's flimsy sandals. "What size do you wear, dear? Your feet look rather small."

"I don't know. I've always just worn the pair the King gave to me."

"The King?" Eunice asked as she searched through box after box as though she were on a wild hunt.

"Um, yes. Where I come from."

"Oh, so you are a princess, just as I thought." Eunice dropped a couple boxes on the floor and scooted a small chair over so Cynthia could sit down.

Cynthia changed the subject, as she wasn't prepared to explain the purpose of her journey just yet. "How long have you been collecting shoes?" Her eyes scanned the room.

"When I was a young girl, my daddy took me to see Cinderella. Ah, when she put on those magical glass slippers... I fell in love with shoes." Eunice paused, her eyes shifting back and forth. "I'm sorry. I got lost in a memory..." She removed Cynthia's sandals and slipped a pair of light-colored flats on her feet.

"Cinderella?" Cynthia asked in all sincerity.

Eunice raised an eyebrow. "You know, the fairy tale. Cinderella, the ball, Prince Charming, all that stuff?" The soft, flat-soled leather shoes she slipped onto Cynthia fit perfectly and their light-blue color matched her dress.

"Perfect!" she said as more of a congratulatory to herself.

Cynthia stood and beamed a grateful smile. "Thank you, Eunice. They are divine."

They hugged, Eunice obviously enjoying the moment. "You said something earlier about knowing I had shoes in my attic. How did you know that? No one but me and my nieces knew they were here, as we just moved them up yesterday from the warehouse."

Before Cynthia could respond, Eunice said, "Oh, and of course Radcliffe. He seems to know everything that goes on around here. I'd swear sometimes this place is bugged."

"Radcliffe?"

"My cousin," she whispered, her cheeks blushing slightly. "Radcliffe Finklemeyer. Sometimes I'm a little embarrassed to admit we're related."

"The coin-shop owner, I presume?" Cynthia asked.

"Oh, he owns a lot more than that. In fact, it seems he owns nearly everything in Paradise Bay. This house is his. I get to stay here rent free as long as I look after his daughters. It's a long, odd story, but I'm their godmother. Their mother ran off with the banker and I was left in charge of the girls when their dad complained he had no time for them. They prefer to call me Aunt Eunice, so that's why I call them my, uh, nieces . . . Anyway, if he knew I had so many shoes from the store, he would have a fit."

"Your love for shoes will be our secret. I promise."

That seemed to put Eunice at ease for the time being. She began to pick up the unopened boxes.

Cynthia glided toward an open space near a window that overlooked the small community and beyond that the vast blue ocean. She wondered how she had been able to cross such a mighty expanse. She recalled her moments of skipping across the pure, still waters of Paradise with Angela. *Oh Angela*, she thought, *I wish you could be with me on this journey*. She knew Angela would find humor in it all and let out a hearty laugh at the craziness of walking the hard, dusty roads of a planet she was not born to.

Cynthia took a step back and then sort of waltzed about the room, squeezing her thin frame between the rows of shoe containers. The wooden floor creaked under the thin carpet strips as she crossed it. She could see the stained strips of cloth were more of a bandage than an actual floor covering. The shreds of cloth reminded her of how the King was once cared for as a baby wrapped in strips of cloth, lying in a manger.

And though she had never been born, Cynthia now walked among the living because He had been born those many centuries ago. She paused and smiled a thought of thankfulness.

A beautiful stream of sunlight bursting through the dirty windows highlighted dust that hung in the air. It reminded her of the streams of silver that embellished the Great Hall in Paradise. She knew she was home.

Cynthia's eyes twinkled. "It's lovely."

Eunice made an uncomfortable decision. "It might not please the girls too much, but I'm going to move the shoes to our garage and make a livable place for you till you find a place of your own."

Cynthia interrupted Eunice's introspection. "I have no desire to impose on your family."

"I think the girls could use a little time with someone like you," Eunice assured her. "You're probably the sweetest thing I've come across in some time, and I'm certainly not going to let you sleep on the streets."

Cynthia gave her a hug of gratitude. "You're so kind. Thank you. I have money to pay rent." Cynthia pulled out the wad of cash she received from Jacob.

"Will five hundred a month be okay?" Eunice asked hesitantly looking at the stack of cash in the brown bag. "I think it will keep my miserly cousin off my back if there's some sort of income generated from it."

"That is more than gracious. Five hundred it is." Cynthia beamed, feeling as though she had a family already. She handed Eunice the first month's rent.

Eunice reached down and handed Cynthia an empty shoe box. "Here, you can store your money in this. Hide it where you wish."

Cynthia accepted the box and put the bag of cash into it and closed the lid.

Eunice took a breath, then gazed into Cynthia's doe-like eyes. "You don't look like you're from around here. Is your family anywhere nearby?"

"I believe so, but I am uncertain at this point as to where."

"Do you have a job lined up?"

"I've been instructed to go to Ziggy's Island and seek employment there."

"Wow! You are in the right place." Eunice hesitated. "My cousin Radcliffe just happens to work there. He's the CFO. Perhaps we could take a drive over there when we're done here. I can't promise anything, but at least it's a start."

"I'd be eternally grateful for any assistance you could provide."

"I believe you would." Eunice grabbed an armful of boxes and walked down the stairs, headed for the garage.

Cynthia surveyed her new dwelling. It was light years from what had been her home in Heaven, but her spirit rejoiced in the room's simplistic beauty, its view of the sea, and the heart of the woman to whom she would pay her rent. Excited to help clear the space, she breathed a prayer of thanks, set her book and the box holding her money down under the window sill, and loaded her arms with shoe boxes.

∽ 5 ∽

HOURS LATER, CYNTHIA AND EUNICE STACKED THE LAST shoe box in its place. They had filled one complete stall of a two-stall garage. Eunice stared at the sea of shoes that now robbed her nieces of their parking space. "The girls are not going to like this so much," she mumbled under her breath.

"Pardon me?" Cynthia asked.

"Oh, nothing. I'll handle it. Let's go clean up and change our clothes before we head over to the park." Eunice took a step toward the house.

"What I'm wearing is all I have," Cynthia said.

Eunice flashed a curious look. "Oh. Well, you can borrow one of my niece's dresses until we can go shopping…"

Cynthia waited patiently for her to finish her thought.

"A lovely thing like you has only one dress?"

"I guess." Cynthia shrugged with a smile.

Inside the house, Cynthia stared wide-eyed at a large bedroom closet that was crammed full of dresses of every color, design, and style imaginable.

Cynthia gasped. She had never seen such excess. Clothing had never been a concern of hers before now.

"I know," Eunice quipped. "This is for just one of my nieces. The other one has a closet twice this size with three times the dresses."

"Where did they get them all?" Cynthia had to know.

"They buy up for themselves all the good inventory that's supposed to go in the store," Eunice said as she feathered through the enormous selection of dresses. "If you can call it 'good.' Not a place I would shop. Here." She handed Cynthia an almost child-like white dress, which accentuated her flawless, supple skin. "She won't even know it's gone."

Cynthia wanted to mention her experience earlier that morning with the girls in town, but she hadn't the heart to embarrass Eunice with stories of their rudeness, in case they were the nieces that Eunice was talking about.

"Not bad," Eunice declared as she held it up to Cynthia's delicate frame. "And never been worn before." She ripped the tags off the back of the garment.

Cynthia examined herself in one of the four full-length mirrors in the room. She liked it. "Is it all right that I wear it?"

"If you don't tell, I won't tell."

"I would want to know, wouldn't you?" Cynthia looked at her reflection, then into Eunice's eyes through the mirror.

"I'll be sure to let her know that we borrowed the dress," Eunice stated softly.

Cynthia smiled and returned her gaze to the mirror. It seemed dim in its reflective light compared to the perfect translucent light she was used to.

"I'll get the car. See you downstairs in a few." Eunice stepped out of the room and closed the door.

Cynthia breathed a prayer of gratitude and changed clothes.

Moments later, Cynthia waited in the driveway wearing her borrowed white dress. Eunice backed out a bright-yellow VW convertible, the car that had filled the other stall of the garage. She stopped directly in front of Cynthia.

Cynthia eyed the car in curiosity.

"Never been in a convertible before?" Eunice inquired.

Cynthia just nodded.

Eunice reached over and opened the passenger door. "Your chariot, my lady."

Cynthia stepped into the car and sat down in the soft leather seat. "This looks nothing like the chariots I've been in."

Eunice shook her head, backed into the street, and stepped on the gas, thrusting Cynthia back in her seat and eliciting a laugh.

The freeway to the park was clear, and Eunice took full advantage of it, averaging more than seventy miles per hour all the way there. Cynthia raised her arms as if riding a roller coaster and sang at the top of her lungs. Onlookers from neighboring cars didn't know what to think of Eunice or Cynthia, and that was fine by them. Both were euphoric and showed no signs of leaving that state.

At least not until Eunice pulled into a long line of cars waiting to enter Ziggy's parking lot. The lot was massive; the park employed hundreds of part-time and full-time staff. Eunice crawled her way to a reserved spot and shut off the car.

Cynthia was beaming ear to ear. Her hair was windblown, and her nose was pink from the sun. "That was absolutely hilarious. Can we do that again?"

"Anytime you wish. Where did you learn to sing so beautifully?" Eunice asked as she closed the car's convertible top.

Cynthia stepped out of the car and gazed at the massive lot full of cars. "Sebastian says I was created to sing."

"Sebastian?"

"A dear friend." To change the subject, she pointed to a thirty-foot statue in the far distance and asked, "Is that Ziggy?"

"It sure is. Come on, let's grab a ride on this tram; it's a long walk to the gate."

A crowded tram of a couple dozen Ziggy patrons pulled around and stopped. The front and back of the tram each displayed a slightly sun-faded banner depicting a flourishing green tree with the name "Palmer Labs," along with their marketing slogan, "DNA Testing – Made Just for You."

"Palmer Labs has been a sponsor of Ziggy's Island for nearly six years," Eunice informed Cynthia. "They even offer discounted DNA testing to employees and its customers." Eunice pointed to a couple open seats.

Cynthia followed Eunice and squeezed between a bench full of men and women dressed in various retro fashions. All eyes seemed to be on Cynthia. She smiled back, feeling as though she owed them a "thank you."

A young, red-haired daughter of a woman clad in 1980s garb ran her fingers along Cynthia's dress. The little girl had a patch over her left eye. Cynthia smiled at the little girl and offered her an open door for conversation.

"Are you a princess?" the girl asked softly.

Her mom reached up and moved the girl's hand away from the dress. "That's the other park, Daphne."

The young girl studied Cynthia up and down and then looked away.

Cynthia looked at Eunice, confused. "Other park?"

Eunice smiled. She was about to respond when the tram arrived at the front gate.

Cynthia gazed at the enormous statue that begs each visitor to stop and get a photo. Ziggy was more than thirty feet tall and twelve feet round, an all-American boy riding a rocket ship. He held banners displaying the various decades, from the 1950s to the 1990s.

The crowd scurried to the entry turnstiles and pushed past Cynthia, who was gazing up at the unusual décor welcoming patrons to Ziggy's. She studied the different colored flags waving in the wind, looking for the various names of the King, of which she was used to seeing in Paradise, but saw none. Each flag had its own colors, stripes, animal, or symbol. She spotted a black-and-gold placard that stood in the middle of the tall flag poles. It read: *A Salute to Our Fifty States.*

She turned her attention to a crop of bright-colored flowers several feet in front of her. She smiled and reached down to touch one. Cynthia frowned. "They're plastic," Eunice said matter-of-factly as she walked past her. Cynthia rubbed the flower with her fingers and shrugged.

Eunice flashed a special card to the attendant that allowed both of them to walk on through. As soon as they entered the park, they were greeted by trains made to look like rocket ships, a different train for each decade.

"The admin office is off 1957 Street in the fifties lot. We'll take this one," Eunice said as she led Cynthia to a 1950s train. A time stamp was placed on the right hand of each of the ladies. Cynthia was all smiles, much like a child in a candy store for the first time, as she drank in the sounds of the park. The noise of the roller coasters and the sudden, high-pitched screams of the people riding them were all new to her, yet the sweetness of the laughter reminded her of the Great Banquet Hall. It was a small taste of Heaven.

The journey back in time immersed the train's passengers in all things 1950s. Unlike the other passengers, Cynthia's awe wasn't based on memories, but was rather a result of her virgin experience. Things were so simple down here, yet her King was in the details and she knew it.

As the rocket ship turned the corner and slowly made its way down 1955 Street, the passengers' "oohs" and "aahs" filled the air along with the song "Wake Up Little Susie" by the Everly Brothers. Many of the die-hard patrons were dressed in full '50s attire, such as poodle skirts, pedal pushers, leather jackets, and other popular clothing from the era. Each lot had its loyal annual pass holders who dressed from their favorite decade.

Perfectly restored Chevrolets and Studebakers sat in front of malt shops and full-service filling stations. The storefronts depicting that wonderful postwar era were as real as if one had traveled back in time. On each street corner sat a small, middle-class home with a green lawn and picket fence, reminding park visitors of a simpler lifestyle.

Each year of the 1950s had its own unique street and bragged of details so minute it took visitors' breath away. That was also the case for the other decade lots. Each era was an exquisite re-creation of life at that time.

The ladies exited the tram along with the crowd of ambitious visitors.

"My cousin's office is in this building over here. Why don't you wait while I go talk to him? He doesn't care much for surprises; especially when it interrupts his money counting. I may be a while. Make yourself comfortable."

Cynthia nodded and accommodated herself on a bench in front of a small malt shop, the kind of establishment you would have seen on the corner in any small town in America back in the 1950s and early 1960s.

She gazed through the window and observed couples dancing on the malt shop floor, wondering for a moment if one of those couples was her mother and father. An unfamiliar tune vibrated the glass in front of her.

Cynthia giggled and turned to watch the crowd of people flowing past. Perhaps, just perhaps, one of them would be her mother or father. A thought shouted at her: *How would I know who they are?*

She reminded herself of what Sebastian had said: "When the time comes, you'll know." Knowing Sebastian only spoke the truth, she sat back with wide-eyed wonder and watched the throng of people milling about.

Many of those passing by slowed down, stared a little, and walked away, seemingly talking about her.

She smiled at the strangers with a compassionate gaze and giggled when she noticed two sparrows perched atop the bench she was sitting on. She hummed a tune for them and watched them fly away.

A young mom walked by holding her young daughter by the hand.

A sudden melancholy came over her when she thought about Paradise and the children she had known and served with in the King's court. She experienced feelings of missing them, which was a first for her. She felt as though there was a hole in her heart. Surveying the crowd, she hoped to find children to play with. It was one of her favorite duties in Paradise.

She spotted a toddler a few feet away. The little boy danced happily to the tunes of the early rock music blaring through hidden speakers. His recently soiled diaper did nothing to slow him down.

Cynthia approached the little guy and pretended to dance with him. He stopped, sucked on his bottle, then rocked back and forth some more. Cynthia kneeled down to mirror his dance steps and then reached out to pat him on the head.

A mid-sized woman with sandy blonde hair pulled back in a ponytail snatched her son away from Cynthia and told her son, "No—we don't play with strangers."

Cynthia stood up, wounded and surprised by her comment. Before she could explain or apologize, the woman slid her sunglasses down onto the bridge of her nose and walked away. The little boy stared back at Cynthia over his mother's shoulder, which left Cynthia dejected.

She looked around for a sympathetic person to talk to, but there were none. She felt alone. *Everyone is so different here.*

A few moments later Cynthia found herself in a conversation with a friendly older woman who was visiting the park for the one hundredth time. Her story was anecdotal and chatty. Their time together ended when her husband showed up with some buddies who wanted to check out the muscle cars on the 1970s lot. It was a pleasant experience and recharged Cynthia's emotional batteries.

She found her way to a nearby bench and sat down, gazing at the people who passed by. They seemed to be rushed and frantic. It was obvious to her they lacked a peace and joy with which she was intimately familiar. She pondered how she might help them discover that serenity.

The loud sound of a balloon popping over her left shoulder caused her to squeak, which quickly turned to a giggle. Turning toward the sound, she saw a man in his late twenties crouched down with a Canon camera in one hand and a small sharp pen in the other. The remains of the deflated balloon rested at his feet.

"That was perfect," he said, looking at the image on his camera. He was tall, thin, and had a boyish grin. "Just the reaction I was hoping for."

She sat quietly, unsure of what to say.

The handsome stranger looked up from his camera. "You're, uh, not from around here, huh?"

"I must confess it is my first time here. Can you tell?" Cynthia replied.

"Just a little, but that's what makes you so unique. I mean, your dress is pretty snazzy, but the 'Hey, I'm pretty but don't know it' look does something for you. In fact, if I was a bettin' man, I'd say you're exactly what I'm looking for."

"Exactly what are you looking for?"

"Viral material. Social media. I'm lookin' for someone not from around here." He moved closer to her and gestured as he spoke. "I've been hired by the park to find that one person who says, 'I'm a fan of Ziggy's and you should be too.' They want me to capture what you've got."

"And what is that, mister…?"

"Bobby Eckert." He stuck out his hand to shake hers. As they shook, Cynthia was drawn to the fun-loving awkwardness about him. She liked how his long brown hair laid across his shoulders and yet hung partially in his eyes.

"If I had to define it, I'd say 'stickiness.' Care for some?" He whipped a box of Cracker Jacks out of his right back pocket and offered her a handful.

"Does this make me sticky?'

He laughed. "It can. Really, though, we're looking for someone who sticks with you after you see them, you know what I mean? Someone who can help attract new ticket buyers to the park."

She munched on a few kernels of popcorn as she eyed the camera coddled in his hands like a baby. "Here, take a look." He pulled up several shots of her that he just captured.

Cynthia stared at the images. "Is that me?"

"Yeah! Doesn't that lighting make you look great?"

"I don't know. I've never seen myself like this before." She examined her image a little closer. "Does this grab my image?"

"Yes. This is a camera," Bobby joked in a condescending tone. "Like on your iPhone."

"iPhone?"

"Oh! Are you a Galaxy girl?"

"Why, yes!"

"Cool. What's your name?"

"Cindy."

"Just Cindy?"

"Cindy Hope."

"Where you from, Cindy Hope?"

She smiled. "Let's just say I'm visiting family for a while."

"Oh. I get it. You're a princess in disguise from one of them small countries I read about?"

"Not exactly."

"What are ya doing right now? You waitin' for somebody?" It was obvious he was hoping she would say no.

"Yes, as a matter of fact, I am. Eunice is setting me up for an employment interview with her cousin."

"A job here?"

She nodded. "Perfect. Then they won't mind if I steal you away for some shots." Cynthia glanced around for signs of Eunice, uncertain.

"Come on. They're for Ziggy's. It'll be fun!" Bobby put out his hand.

She thought for a long moment. A part of her surged with excitement, but it was quickly replaced with a pause of hesitancy that served as a caution to her. In her innocence, she was still learning to cope with unfamiliar feelings of fear and doubt. She weighed it out in her mind. She had just met him and had no idea who he was. "I told my friend Eunice I would wait here."

He pulled out a Ziggy's employee badge displaying his photo. "No worries. I work for Madeline Brewer, head honcho of Ziggy's, and I promise we'll stay right here in the park. I just want to get some shots of you for an idea I have in mind. As soon as we're finished, we'll come right back so you can meet up with your friend. Deal?" He stuck out his hand to take hers.

She felt secure in his explanation. "I'd love to, Bobby."

Bobby kept a hold of her hand and pulled her into the crowd. His touch sent tingles through her skin, a sensation she hadn't known before but which she definitely enjoyed. It made Cynthia giggle.

For the next couple hours, Bobby gave Cynthia a personal tour of Ziggy's Island, showing her his personal favorite spots of each decade. He led her out of the 1950s attractions and over to the 1960s, where there was a blend of people dressed as hippies and beatniks.

As they were walking, Cynthia noticed an older woman struggle to sit down on a bench. Without saying a word, Cynthia stepped over and slowly helped her find a comfortable spot. The lady smiled and thanked her. Bobby caught the moment on camera but thought nothing of it.

He led her to an underground beatnik joint and explained to Cynthia the superficial aspects of the Beat Generation. While there, he captured shots of her posing as an intellectualist. Curiosity drew her to a Woodstock field where loud rock music blared at maximum volume. She plugged her ears, hoping to spare them from damage. It made a great shot for Bobby, who then sympathetically moved her to a crowded '60s street where her picturesque face was perfect for a pose in a pristine 1964 Mustang. At each stop, Cynthia was drawn to a person in need.

A man on crutches who was being pushed along in a crowd needed someone to act as a barrier for him. Cynthia helped the man to the side. She helped a pregnant woman trying to pick up a sippy cup that the small toddler she was carrying had dropped. She provided a kind word to an angry teenager who yelled at his cell phone and then hung up.

Upon finishing a conversation with a man on crutches she noticed Bobby waving his camera at her. He seemed anxious, running his fingers through his hair while looking at his watch. She said goodbye to the man and acknowledged Bobby with a smile. "I'm sorry, Bobby. I just love hearing the stories of these incredible people. There are so many who seem to be hurting. Where to next?"

"No worries," he said with a shrug.

He resumed the guided tour and led her to a roller coaster. Her eyes furled when she saw the long line of people waiting. He flashed his VIP pass to the attendant and moved them to the front of the line, so she just tightened her lip and stepped up to the cart as it stopped in front of them. She had never been on a roller coaster; her eyes widened to the size of saucers as the speeding rocket ship zipped along at breakneck speed. She screamed, she laughed, she giggled. She allowed herself to feel whatever the moment provided, and Bobby captured it all on a shaky camera.

Next, he quarterbacked her down 1976 Street, where muscle cars stacked up along the curb and bicentennial memorabilia hung from the lampposts like a Fourth of July parade. They eventually landed in a '70s discotheque jammed full of patrons adorned in bell-bottom pants and polyester shirts. Disco and funk pumped through speakers above the lighted dance floor. Cynthia, captivated by the smoke and disco-ball effects, suddenly found herself in the center of a line dance. As soon as the dance finished, Bobby ushered her off the dance floor and to the 1980s lot.

The '80s crowd congregated at bars and restaurants. This gave Cynthia an unusual and unforgettable experience with hair band music and videos. Bobby found some vintage '80s clothing hanging along the walls for visitors to try on and convinced her to model some of the bright and trendy fashions of the time. She finally agreed and stepped into a dressing room with hot-pink work-out pants and a top.

When she reappeared, Bobby choked back a laugh. The spandex looked goofy even on her lovely figure. Bobby captured several shots of her comical reactions to the clothing, as she pulled on her spandex pants and tripped on her high-heeled shoes. She finally gave up and changed back into her borrowed white dress.

"I must say, white does serve you well."

"Thank you, but I miss my robe."

He smiled, not fully understanding what she meant, and offered his hand to her. She accepted it and together they continued their tour.

They came to the center of the park, where a large rocket ship with Ziggy on board went through the stages of lift off and rumbled the ground around them. It was loud, and smoke filled the area. Cynthia held her hands over her ears. She laughed as she felt the rocket shake and vibrate the ground, just as if Ziggy were actually lifting off.

Fire from a pit below spewed flames. More smoke bellowed out from under the ship.

"What is that?" she hollered over the noise.

"Ziggy's journey through time. It goes off twice a day. You ought to see it at night. It's so cool. That thing uses a ton of fire that lights the whole place up." Cynthia didn't hear everything he said but nodded as though she did. The noise finally died down, leaving the smoke to hang in the air.

Cynthia's mind drifted back to her memories of entering the King's Throne Room, the rumbling, the smoke, the peals of fire. She looked for the eternal rainbow that encircled the King's sovereign chair but found only blue sky. An amused expression emerged on her face as she was glad to remember that she belonged to Him and was here under His direction.

Bobby watched her with interest. "How's the princess holding up? You look a little worn."

For the first time, she felt tired. She had been up since the rising of the sun and so much had happened to her on her first day.

"Let's go chill for a while." Bobby ushered her out of the crammed '80s park into a mellow '90's coffee shop.

On their way, Eunice spotted Cynthia in the crowd and approached her. Eunice gave Bobby a once over, then stared at Cynthia, who carried a melting ice cream cone that dripped strawberry ice cream on her niece's dress.

"Hello, Cindy." A parental protectiveness came out in her tone.

"Eunice!" Cynthia sensed awkwardness by the way Eunice shifted her eyes. "I'm terribly sorry I left my place. Bobby has been showing me around and we've had an absolute ball. Ziggy's is a wonderful place!"

Bobby extended his hand to Eunice. "How ya' doing? Bobby Eckert."

Eunice spied his camera. "You're a professional, I take it, Bobby?"

"I am. Mattie hired me."

"Oh, Madeline hired you. My cousin works for Madeline and Danny. He's the CFO. Guess he's the one who will write your check."

"Guess so." Bobby let the comment slide. He turned to Cynthia. "Cindy, it's been a pleasure. You care to do this again?"

"As much as you would care to," she said with a tired smile.

"What's your cell? I'll text you a time and place later this week."

"Cell?"

He shook his mobile device in the air. "Cell phone…"

"I don't have one."

"You're kidding me, right?"

"Here's mine." Eunice handed her phone to Bobby. He entered the digits into her cell and left the two ladies with a flirtatious grin.

He turned back. "See you soon, Cindy." He winked at Eunice.

Eunice turned to Cynthia. "What was that all about?"

"He wanted to show me Ziggy's Island and take pictures of me," Cynthia answered.

"I bet he did," Eunice sarcastically replied. "Look, I have great news. Radcliffe agreed to help you get a job in the park. He wants to meet you first, of course, but don't worry about that. I'll be right by your side the whole time. Are you available a week from Tuesday at nine a.m.?"

Cynthia threw her arms around Eunice in gratefulness and weariness. "You are so kind. Thank you, Eunice. I am available anytime you need me."

"Let's grab a burger and get you home," she suggested emphatically.

The drive home was a slow one. Traffic was bumper to bumper, and Cynthia had her first experience in rush-hour traffic. "It feels as if all of Heaven is on the same road we are, but no one's moving," she admitted with a dose of perplexity.

Eunice smiled painfully and referred to it as a road to hell.

When they arrived back at the house, Eunice pulled a cot and mattress out from the garage and the two of them carried it up to the attic, finding a place for it near the window. After some sweeping, straightening of tables and chairs, and dressing the bed in sheets and blankets, Cynthia finally had a place to rest her head.

She had never been tired before. It was one of many surprises in her new journey. She was curious why her eyes wanted to shut and her body felt so heavy, but her mind was too tired to figure it out.

Eunice said good night and then closed the door. The sound of her heavy steps was the last thing Cynthia heard before falling fast asleep for the first time in her new world.

6

LOUD NOISES, GIGGLING, AND ARGUING FROM FAMILIAR-sounding voices woke Cynthia several times in the night, startling her. The room's darkness and the odd sounds from raucous voices were unnerving and frightening. *Remember who you are.* She prayed and fell back to sleep, knowing that she was not alone.

With the morning sun came light that filled her room through a bare window. She smiled at a bird singing outside it. She cracked the window open. The bird started to fly away but oddly changed its direction and flew into the attic, where it perched itself on the back of her chair. It was a rare black thrush with a bright-orange neck and dramatic yellow-and-black streaks above its eyes. It chirped and she laughed.

A moment later it flew out and searched for food.

Cynthia browsed the room. To her surprise, several soft-colored dresses sat atop a small dresser in the corner, waiting for her to choose one. She took a deep breath, feeling the nearness of her King, and surrendered to a growing desire to worship Him. As she danced about the room and hummed a familiar worship song, the adventure of a new day sprung up inside her like a bubbling stream. She wanted to soak up every moment of her life on Earth.

Her time in the attic became a time of singing and praise. She opened the Scriptures and feasted awhile on the Psalms; she knew them well. Being on the same planet the writers had once tread upon gave her a whole new perspective.

When she finished her study and prayer, she capered down the stairs and found Eunice at the dining-room table eating breakfast.

Cynthia instantly felt hungry—a new sensation that was less than desirable.

"The dresses are beautiful. Thank you, Eunice. But I do think I should buy my own."

"I'll make you a deal. You pay for the dresses and I'll provide the shoes. I have all kinds of ideas for your shoes."

"If you insist." Cynthia played along, enjoying Eunice's obvious desire of wanting to help her.

"We have that boutique I mentioned over on Center Street. We can go later this morning and see if there's anything you'd like to wear. I have to open the store today. My nieces were out late last night. I certainly hope they didn't wake you. They were much too loud... as usual."

"I'm just grateful for a place to stay," Cynthia said softly.

No sooner did those words leave her lips when Deidre stumbled into the dining room, her hair hanging in her face and her PJs disheveled and stained. She grabbed a glass and filled it with orange juice before turning toward them. She groaned. "God, I feel awful."

Deidre blew her hair from her eyes and saw Cynthia. Deidre shrieked and dropped the glass of juice she was holding. It shattered, making her scream again. She jumped back only to land hard on her rump.

Immediately, Cynthia stepped forward and started to assist in helping her to her feet.

"Don't touch me," Deidre growled.

Cynthia grieved at Deidre's hostility, but she respectfully stepped back. Her eyes offered compassion, but Deidre jumped to her feet and turned away, rejecting the gesture of kindness, "I don't need your help, *Princess*."

Portia entered the room looking better, though not by much. "What is *she* doing here?" Portia demanded with even more contempt than Deidre as she pointed at Cynthia.

"Enough!" Eunice stepped between the unhappy pair after Deidre rose to her feet. "Both of you are behaving rudely and I will not tolerate it in our home. Cindy is our guest and will be treated as family ... or should I say *better* than family. Cindy, these are my nieces Deidre and Portia."

Cynthia smiled politely but only received harsh stares back from the pair.

"A transient? Does Father know about this?" Portia jabbed.

"Your father has an appointment with Cindy a week from Tuesday to help her find a job in the park."

"You didn't answer her question, dear Aunty," Deidre said. "Does he know this ... this ... homeless princess has invaded his house at your request?"

Portia stepped into Cynthia's space. "Where's the bag lady? She living here too?"

Eunice furled her brow. "Your father may own the property, but this is *my* house as long as I live in it. I will judge who stays and who doesn't. There is room for her in the attic and if you push me one step further, I will see to it your bags are packed and the both of you land on your father's porch this very night."

The room went quiet.

Eunice took a breath. "We all know how he feels about his own daughters living in his home, don't we?"

Deidre and Portia were abruptly quiet, which made Cynthia wonder what their relationship with their father was like.

"I expect you both to be at the store by noon," Eunice said calmly as the sisters sat down and started eating. "Cindy, why don't we go do some shopping for you?"

Cynthia wanted to fix the awkwardness in the room, but the moment did not permit it. Instead, she prayed silently for an opportunity to address it later.

Deidre and Portia squirmed in their seats as they scarfed down a breakfast prepared for Cynthia.

The next several days flew by without much drama. To avoid another encounter, Eunice told Cynthia that she would keep the girls busy with separate schedules.

Cynthia adapted quickly to her earthly self and began each day sitting at the open window of her room, singing songs from a grateful heart to her King, and meditating on His holy writings. The veil between them was not an issue; she felt His presence. She heeded Sebastian's advice and always stayed close to Him in her heart.

It was a habit of hers, as it was in Paradise, to speak His name with each moment that presented itself to her. She enjoyed sensing His smile of complete approval and acceptance. Now she had to hear His voice in her spirit, without the joy of seeing Him.

Her time of adoration was often followed by a stroll around the small town's center and along the beach, oftentimes with Eunice by her side. The water was a keen reminder that she was just a visitor. She knew whatever she faced was not forever and she would return to her place in Paradise and to a seashore that was familiar.

Everywhere Cynthia went, she would look at passing faces wondering if they might be her parents. She also hoped to find her lost friend, Violet, who was nowhere to be found. It was important to Cynthia that she do whatever she could to help this lonely, deprived woman. Violet held a special place in her heart and there was no giving up on her.

Meanwhile, she continued to pray for Deidre and Portia. They had told her that no matter what occupied their time, getting her out of the house for good was their top priority. Although she was confused as to why they held such disdain for her, Cynthia remained optimistic about a future relationship with the girls. She believed somehow her prayers would be answered.

To demonstrate this hopeful outlook, after decorating the attic, she gave a fresh coat of paint to the hallway that led to the girls' room, making it bright and attractive. The girls said nothing.

On the morning of Cynthia's interview with Radcliffe, Eunice got a text from Bobby.

"Hi Eunice, this is Bobby. Can you ask Cindy if she's available to meet up today?"

Eunice texted back. "I'm sorry, Bobby. She has an interview at the park today."

"OK. Let her know that her pix are done and I'm taking them over to Madeline. Have her call me if she would like to see them. Thx."

Eunice decided not to respond to his request. She felt a protective spirit rising up in her and wasn't sure she wanted this guy near her girl. She sat on the couch and tried to comprehend what she was doing and why. This was unlike her to fight for control over someone. She had always enjoyed an easy-come-easy-go mindset. Why was she so protective of this young woman?

At that moment Cynthia descended the stairs and greeted her with a huge smile. Eunice's heart leaped, and she realized that Cynthia was more than just a friendly houseguest. Eunice viewed her as the daughter she had so desperately wanted but never had. Was this stranger an answer to her unspoken prayers of so many years?

Tears slowly ran down her cheek. She was slow to wipe them away.

Cynthia noticed the glistening drops of emotion and rushed to Eunice's side. "Are you all right?"

"Couldn't be better, sweetheart."

"Are they happy tears?"

"The happiest I've ever cried." She kissed Cynthia on the cheek and rose to her feet. "You are a lovely young lady, Cindy. If I had a daughter, I would want her to be just like you. I appreciate you so much."

Cynthia sensed that Eunice was not her mother, but left room in her heart that she might be. "It is I who am grateful for you. You have been such a kind and charming friend."

"We must go." Eunice wiped her tears away and grabbed her keys off the hall tree. "Don't want to be late for your interview."

She checked Cynthia's shoes. "These are right for the occasion, a perfect fit for the day." Eunice smiled big and gave her a thumbs up.

Cynthia hugged her shoulder and they made their way to the car.

When they opened the garage door their jaws dropped. Eunice's VW was completely buried in shoes. Sometime in the night, the girls had dumped all the shoes on top of the car and put the empty shoe boxes inside it.

"I was wondering when they would finally say something about their parking spot," Eunice commented.

"I'm so sorry if they did this because of me." Cynthia turned and looked deep in Eunice's eyes.

Terry Harris

"My dear, you are not responsible for the foolishness of someone else."

"What are you going to do?" Cynthia asked, befuddled.

"Nothing. Absolutely nothing. And it will drive them batty."

Cynthia gazed at her and tried to understand.

"I won't say a word about it and that will make them absolutely crazy. They'll be dying for me to say something, but I won't." Eunice gave Cynthia a grin and a wink. "Come on, we'll move them out of the car now, and when we get back, we'll stack them up just the way they were."

Cynthia didn't really know what to think, so she started removing shoes from the car and put them to the side. Eunice joined her.

Bobby had only been to Madeline's office one time. That was about three weeks earlier when she discussed launching a social-media campaign for Ziggy's, based on the idea of a fan club. Bobby further suggested she build the tribe off a single person who would be the face of Ziggy's fan club; someone who appealed to all ages and could possibly create a viral response.

Madeline hadn't been too sure such a person existed; she'd explained to Bobby that today's theme park guest was much different than yesterday's. When she had first launched her ideas to expand twenty-five years ago, things were a lot simpler. Even a few years ago, they only used billboards, TV, and radio ad campaigns to draw the crowds in.

This generation's use of social media demanded more of diverse strategy, but Bobby believed those concerns would be put to rest by his pics from his afternoon with the stunning girl in white.

He found the wait outside Madeline's office was a long one. Looking about the walls, his eyes were drawn to two large black-and-white photos perfectly aligned and hanging side by side. Their frames were identical, white with large white mats.

Bobby leaned in to inspect the quality of the photos. The shots were of Ziggy's Island on a foggy day. The first photo showed the vacant stores of the '50s lot. There were no visitors, and there was no movement, just the stillness of hanging fog on Ziggy's empty streets. The second photo showed the top tracks of a popular rollercoaster from the '80s lot, peeking above the layer of fog. The photos conveyed that Ziggy's Island could not only be a place of joy and fun but one of cold and loneliness. Bobby was jolted out of his thoughts with the abrupt sound of a door opening.

"Bobby." Madeline leaned out the door. She possessed a stark beauty in her eyes and cheekbones. Her neck was slightly long, but her flowing dark hair that draped her shoulders covered it well.

Bobby stepped into her office and noted some new furniture. "Redecorating?"

"Not exactly," she stated. "So, what do you have for me?"

"Okay," he sighed, wishing they had a little bit more warm-up time.

He pulled out several shots on stock paper and placed them into a picture-frame book that was a mock-up of Instagram and Facebook. He had done his research and knew that Madeline was one who demanded and appreciated a good presentation, and clicking through digital shots on his camera was not a professional way to present his ideas.

He stepped back, waiting for her to ooh and aah over his work.

Madeline was silent as she drank in the details of each shot.

Bobby waited. She said nothing.

As he waited, he couldn't help but get caught up in his own work. He reacted to various shots with smiles, grins, and self-congratulatory smirks. Then, unexpectedly, Bobby saw something familiar with Madeline. Bobby's eyes subtly shifted between Madeline and the pictures of Cynthia. To his surprise, a strange similarity between them began to emerge. He saw a striking resemblance in the face and the curve of the neck. After a while he forgot to be subtle.

Sensing his stare, Madeline slapped the book closed, startling him. "Is there something you'd like to say?"

"No. No, not at all. I was just wondering ..." he stopped, pondering if he should ask.

A gesture with her eyes and a furled brow indicated she didn't appreciate his behavior. She resumed her review of the shots. He went back to staring at her.

He couldn't resist. "You don't have a daughter, do you?"

This time, she kept examining the photos and answered him coldly. "I do not. Do you?" He let that one sink to the bottom without retrieval.

Madeline didn't react to many of the images until she flipped to the last few pictures. Her pause gave him a hint of hope. He stared over her shoulder at the pictures she was studying. They were simple shots of Cynthia helping people, the man on crutches, the distressed mom, even the elderly woman.

"Was this staged?" she asked, flashing the shots in Bobby's direction.

"No. Why would I stage that? That's not what you asked for. These," he said as he flipped through shots of Cynthia's first-time experience with speeding roller coasters, high drops, and terrifying twists, "are what I see as the money shots."

"I disagree. I believe this is your starter," she said as she held up a shot of Cynthia giving a high five to a group of middle-aged women in matching T-shirts. "I want a full campaign on Facebook, Twitter, Instagram, Snapchat, and any other sites that can communicate this message. This girl could be worth a million bucks. What's her name?"

"Cindy."

"Is she a model?" Madeline asked quickly.

"I don't think so."

Madeline glanced at him, but Bobby just shrugged. "That's all I know."

"I have a gut feeling that this girl, whoever she is, really cares about people and that's the draw, especially for social media. Find out what you can on this Cindy and make sure there's no background baggage that's going to come back to haunt me."

"Absolutely," he said, congratulating himself for landing the job. He looked at the photos of Cynthia and the women again and was surprised that it was these Madeline liked so much. Ultimately, he didn't care. His work had pleased her and now he just landed the biggest job of his career. Hopefully, these photos could be the beginning of more jobs to come.

"If everything checks out with her, I want to meet her in my office early next week to secure a contract. I'll show these to Danny. Knowing him, he'll have her at every one of his building dedications till the end of eternity."

She started to leave then turned back. "You can get in touch with her, right?"

"Not a problem," he said shaking his phone. Madeline walked out of the office with Bobby in tow. He sneaked a peek at his cell, hoping to see a text from Eunice. There was none. He texted her again.

Around the corner and down the hall to the right, Cynthia waited with patience beside an obviously agitated Eunice.

Cynthia gathered information about her potential employer by studying the way he swanked the lobby with all his accomplishments. She noted framed certificates of recognition and honors that were old and outdated. The once-clean paper was now yellowed on several of the business and CPA awards. The odd way they were all displayed shouted insecurity. A large picture of Radcliffe standing next to a pile of money gave her an odd feeling of pity for the man. The awards focused on those whom he had crushed in his business dealings.

She prayed. Her spirit was moved to be on the alert.

The office door jerked opened. Radcliffe grunted. "Eunice."

Cynthia followed Eunice and then smiled as she walked past him into his office. "Good morning, Mr. Radcliffe." She could've sworn he raised to his toes to make himself look taller. Odd.

"Radcliffe, this is Cindy. She's the girl I told you about. She's looking for a job and I think she'd be an excellent employee for..."

"Have a seat, Cindy," he barked as he clomped behind his desk and landed in his seat. He looked intently at Cynthia over his reading glasses. "You look familiar. Have we met before?"

Cynthia remained calm. "I do not believe we have." She knew he was fishing. She wasn't going to be easy bait. He was going to have to work for his knowledge.

Her gaze was drawn to the collection of TV monitors behind him. She looked across his desk and recognized the interior of the coin shop she had visited the first day. She spied Jacob on the monitor, standing behind the counter and conversing with a customer.

Radcliffe's gaze followed Cynthia's as he turned around to see what she was watching. Cynthia sat down next to Eunice. Eunice smiled at her reassuringly.

"Radcliffe, Cindy brings a lot of experience in music. She would be an excellent addition to the talent that performs in Ziggy's musical shows."

"So why did you bring her to me?" he snapped. "I have nothing to do with that side of the business. I thought you wanted her to work in the accounting department." His tone was indignant.

Eunice was visibly aghast at her cousin's rudeness.

"I'm more than honored to work wherever you have need. I will serve you as though I were serving the King himself," Cynthia said.

"What king? We have no king in this country. Where are you from? England?"

"A great deal farther, Mr. Finklemeyer."

"This is nonsense. I don't have time for this conversation. This meeting is over. Good day."

"Then, I'll just have to go around your short behind," Eunice snapped back. "Come on, Cindy."

"I'll see to it she never earns a day's wage on this lot," he said as he shot out of his chair. He moved towards the door, heading them off.

Eunice glared down on him. "You're a pitiful little man."

Cynthia looked at him with sadness. Sebastian had warned her of human beings who were not of the family and opposed to it. She was getting another taste of that. It was a bitter pill. Nonetheless, she accepted Radcliffe's position toward her.

"Good day, Mr. Finklemeyer." Cynthia had barely cleared the room when the door slammed shut, leaving both her and Eunice to shudder with a chill.

"I'm so, so sorry, Cindy. I … I don't know what to say. I never expected him to …"

"Oh Eunice, please don't apologize. You have absolutely nothing to be sorry for. You have been nothing but kind and considerate."

"But I thought I could help you get the job you said you were supposed to have. Now I've ruined everything."

She gave her friend a hug, which caused Eunice to let out a sigh. "You've ruined absolutely nothing. All is well. If I am to work at Ziggy's, nothing can stop it."

"Where do you get such courage?"

"From my Father."

"I wish I had a father like that. I thought I did, but when he left me…"

"There is someone who would like very much to be your Father. Would you like to meet Him sometime?"

"Umm. Yeah, I think so."

Cynthia made a mental note to look for the right opportunity to introduce Eunice to her Father God.

On their way out of the office Eunice noticed two new texts on her phone from Bobby but chose not to say anything to Cynthia. More than ever Eunice felt responsible for protecting Cynthia from untrustworthy people; unfortunately, Bobby fell into that category.

Down the hall from Radcliffe's gloomy, pencil-pushing office was Danny's oversized two-room bungalow, which served as both an office and part-time sleeping quarters. He had spent many nights sleeping on a single cot after working endless hours on the maintaining and growth of his one and only baby, Ziggy's.

Ziggy's was everything to this now-graying, dark-haired man. He hated aging, but he refused to paint his hair or tighten his skin with some false coloring or injection to make himself look like an out-of-work actor trying desperately to maintain his earlier glory days. Danny, always looking to stay ahead of his world, did not look back.

Madeline walked into his office unannounced, as she often did, and plopped down in the brown leather chair near his desk. "We need to talk." She suddenly sank below his eye level. The chair she sat on was made to sit lower so his guests would feel "below" him. He grinned to himself.

She grimaced, pounced to her feet and pulled a thick book off the shelf of his floor-to-ceiling bookshelf. It was his favorite place to showcase pictures and awards showing him as a leader in the community and a first-class philanthropist. She plopped the book onto the chair and sat down, now at eye level with him. It was a game they had been playing for twenty-five years now. Danny felt he had won more times than not.

"I think we found our 'Ziggy's Biggest Fan,'" she stated. "Only it's a different direction than we first discussed. Take a good look at these."

Madeline rose to her feet and handed Danny a couple of pictures of a pretty girl helping people. She sat back down and waited for him to respond.

Danny glanced at them and tossed them back her way. "What am I supposed to be looking for? I don't see anything worth my time."

"Her name is Cindy. Look at her eyes, her face, her concern for these people." She stood again and moved around his desk and stuck a photo in front of him. "Our numbers have plateaued and even dropped the last two years because of our inability to attract the younger ticket buyer. The baby boomers are dying and we're not replacing them."

"So, what does a picture of a pretty little do-gooder have to do with any of that?"

"Every one of our competitors on the West Coast has a social-media campaign about all the great things they're doing in the community. 'Buy a ticket, have fun, and while you're at it, help save the whales, or help the illiterate, or buy a hamburger and send a kid to camp.'"

Danny rose and went to his trophy case of pictures and awards and picked one up in each hand. "What do you think I've been doing for the last thirty years? I'm probably the most decorated and recognized philanthropist known to mankind. I've got my name plastered all over hospitals and schools and recycling centers as far as the Mexican border."

"Have you ever bothered to sit at the bedside of one of the patients of those hospitals? Do you even know who it is you're helping? When's the last time you stepped foot inside the halls of a school that bears your name?"

Danny lowered the framed awards and then returned them to the bookshelf. He took an extra moment to ensure they sat exactly perfect. He liked them in their place.

Madeline moved closer to him and posed the second picture in front of his nose, a close-up of the girl, helping an aged woman.

"She cares about people. If she represents Ziggy's, that means Ziggy's cares for people, young and old. That's our campaign."

Danny looked closely at the picture. His eyes focused on the girl's face. He acknowledged to himself she was unusually pretty. She might very well be a good image for Ziggy's. In fact, she looked a bit familiar, as though she reminded him of someone else. Suddenly, he noticed a strong similarity in her nose, eyes, and the curve of her neck. The dark hair… he glanced up at Madeline, then back down at the photo.

She glared at him, perturbed. Danny studied it closer. Madeline lost patience with him and snatched the photo out of his hands.

"I'll arrange a meeting. You can meet her yourself and we can make the decision then."

She walked out the door, leaving him to ponder.

Why was he fighting Madeline on this? He didn't really understand his resistance. And what did she mean about the hospital and knowing people's names? He thought he'd made a difference in people's lives.

He looked out the window of his plush office and contemplated the uneasy feeling rising in his gut.

Radcliffe removed his earphones, disappointed in what he had heard. He had the offices of every executive in the building bugged, except Madeline's, which she kept locked when she was not in it. It was Radcliffe's dubious pleasure to listen in on conversations that were worth his time. The information he compiled ensured him of retirement on his grounds and no one else's.

The meeting between Madeline and Danny seemed, as often times it was, to be a waste of his time. He made a note of the conversation in a private log he kept hidden under his desk, just in case he might need it one day.

Terry Harris

∞ 7 ∞

AFTER BREAKFAST AT THE LOCAL CAFÉ THAT SUNDAY, Cynthia and Eunice strolled down Center Street, arm-in-arm, enjoying each other's company. A stray black-and-white cat followed close behind them. Suddenly, Cynthia stopped in her tracks. In the distance, she heard a children's choir singing "Great is thy faithfulness. Great is thy faithfulness." Cynthia shrieked with excitement at remembering where she had come from. She began to run toward the sweet music as she unashamedly and loudly joined in the singing. Clutching her purse, Eunice awkwardly chased Cynthia, trying to keep up.

The small church sat on Center Street between a mom-and-pop bakery and a bank, just two short blocks from the shores of Paradise Bay. It was a lovely white chapel, straight out of a Thomas Kincaid painting, with its tall steeple perched on top and a broken church bell.

Cynthia got to the church far ahead of Eunice and eagerly darted through the foyer, singing loudly. The marble floor down the center aisle was covered with red carpet. On the ten rows of pews on each side sat matching red cushions. At the front, high above the platform, hung a crucifix. Cynthia was taken back a bit; she was not used to an image of someone she knew hanging dead on a golden cross. She stopped singing, just for a moment, as the congregants all seemed to turn in unison to look at her.

Cynthia continued to belt out the last of the song and then stood quietly in the aisle, reverent. She glanced over her shoulder. Eunice had stayed at the back of the church and looked uncomfortable, so Cynthia went back to retrieve her friend.

"This is as much your home as anyone's," Cynthia whispered to her. "You are welcome here, and I am so delighted to be by your side."

"I've never been in a place like this before. What should I do?"

Cynthia hugged her friend. "Absolutely nothing. It's who you are that the Father loves ... not what you do." Grabbing her hand, Cynthia led Eunice to their seats.

The children began to sing a second hymn, and Cynthia couldn't hold back her emotion. She worshiped with a glad song, remembering her friends, her home, and her loving King. Tears filled her eyes as her perfectly pitched notes and her authentic praise reached the Heavens, leaving no soul around her untouched. With her hands held high, she sang along with the choir, their eyes fixated on her.

Visitors touring the church sat near her and listened. She smiled at them and encouraged them with a gesture to join her in the sacred moment. Some began to sing, others just cried. When the children had finished, Cynthia excitedly cheered and clapped for the young worshippers. This was contagious. Everyone in the church joined her and applauded the choir. The children grinned from ear to ear.

The cheering subsided and slowly everyone started to leave the church. Cynthia closed her eyes to quietly thank her King. She could see Him before her so clearly. When she finally opened her eyes, she saw the pastor making his way toward her. She figured he was coming to speak with her, but she was more concerned about getting back to Eunice. He introduced himself as Pastor Timothy and proceeded to jump headlong into a string of compliments to Cynthia about her singing. An invitation to sit and chat quickly followed. She thanked him for his kind words but deflected all credit to her King in a way the pastor was not used to. "I cannot take credit for that which has been given to me. If it pleases Him, I am blessed and grateful."

Cynthia proposed a get-together on another day and time. He politely invited her to call and set up the appointment. She thanked him and made her way back to Eunice. When their eyes met, Cynthia saw she was trying to process what she had just experienced, but all Eunice communicated was her desire to leave. Cynthia obliged the unspoken request and remained silent as they left the church.

The walk home was a quiet one.

Eunice didn't speak during dinner that night, or afterward, for that matter, and gave Cynthia a good-night kiss on the cheek before going to bed. Cynthia graced her friend with all the space and time she needed and kept the conversation light.

That night Cynthia prayed for Eunice, Deidre, and Portia before falling asleep.

The next morning a freezing bucket of cold water was mercilessly splashed across Cynthia's face and body, startling her from a deep sleep. The two ladies she had just prayed for a few hours earlier apparently thought it would be funny to awaken her with the melted ice water from their champagne bucket.

Cynthia chose not to say anything to Eunice of the incident. She cleaned and dried their ice bucket and returned it to its rightful place in the kitchen cupboard. The girls said nothing to her about it.

For the next few days, Cynthia did chores around the house, but always made time to take her morning walks on the beach and stop by the chapel for a quiet time of music and reflection. Because of the impact her singing had on the church and its attendees, she was asked to share a song or two each time she stopped by. It became a distraction to her own personal time, but she didn't mind giving her time and talents to those in need.

When the day arrived for Cynthia to meet with Pastor Timothy, she was greeted by the organist instead. "Pastor Timothy took a sudden leave of absence," she told Cynthia. "For what it's worth, something is going on with him, but I don't know what it is. This is very out of character for him."

Cynthia wasn't sure how to respond, as the news of his departure came as a bit of a surprise. "When you hear from him, let him know I was here. I would love to reschedule our appointment. Please also tell him that I will be praying for him." Cynthia left the church with a promise she would be back soon.

One morning later that week, Eunice and Cynthia sat at the breakfast table. Eunice quietly sipped her coffee, letting her food go cold while Cynthia enjoyed a hot bowl of oats and fresh fruit. Cynthia offered small talk and remained patiently optimistic as she waited for Eunice to open up with whatever was on her mind. She suspected it had something to do with the chapel and Eunice's concerns of her own spiritual state of affairs. But she would remain quiet and let Eunice broach the subject when she was ready.

The phone next to Eunice vibrated on the small antique dining table.

"Everything okay?" Cynthia asked.

"It's Bobby. He's been texting you, says it's urgent."

"I hope everything's all right."

"He's been trying for several days to reach you. I haven't been honest in letting you know about it. I'm sorry. I've been acting stupid and selfish."

Cynthia processed what she was hearing. Right now, Eunice was her priority, but she would love to see Bobby again. "Stupidity is certainly not one of your characteristics. Now, overprotective … ehhh," she said, moving her hand in a so-so manner.

Eunice laughed, almost choking on a mouth full of coffee. "Is it that obvious?"

"Deliriously so, I'm afraid."

"I'm sorry, Cindy."

Eunice handed her phone to Cynthia so she could read the messages. Cynthia gave her hand a love squeeze and smiled. She scanned the texts. There were no specific mentions that she had the job as spokesperson for Ziggy's, but he did say that he had something important to discuss with her.

Eunice showed her how to text back. Cynthia simply replied, "I'm available to meet today. Where and when would you like to connect?"

"Noon today. Danny's office. Do you know where that is?" Bobby responded.

Cynthia showed Eunice the text. "Tell him yes."

"Perfect," Cynthia said as she texted Bobby back.

Cynthia handed the phone back to Eunice and sang a worship song as she removed dirty dishes from the table. Once the task was completed, she ascended the stairs, giving thanks in her heart and asking for wisdom. She sensed something paramount was about to transpire.

At the stroke of noon, the elevator chimed as it arrived on the fifth floor, which was the very same floor where they had their less-than-stellar meeting with Radcliffe. Eunice scurried past his ominous door and down the hall, pulling Cynthia by the hand as she went. Cynthia chuckled inside. She understood why Eunice was acting so odd, yet she felt sympathy for her. Slavery of the soul to another's opinion was a hard taskmaster from which one is rarely freed.

Cynthia admired the courage that Eunice displayed on a few different occasions on her behalf and was appreciative for her loyalty, even at the price of Radcliffe's wrath.

A door on the far end of the hall opened and chatter filled the corridor. Eunice nearly jumped out of her skin. They turned around to see Bobby and Madeline emerge from Madeline's office and advance toward them in step.

Cynthia rubbed Eunice's shoulder a bit to help calm her anxiety.

"Cindy! So glad you could make it." Bobby practically leapt to her side. "This is Madeline Brewer, chief marketing officer and COO of Ziggy's and newest fan of your work."

Madeline shot Bobby a look of irritation. "Good to meet you, Cindy."

Cynthia shook her hand firmly. "I'm honored to meet you, Mrs. Brewer."

"It's Ms. Brewer, but you can call me Madeline."

Madeline turned to Eunice and shook her hand. "Good to see you again, Eunice. Does Radcliffe know you're here? Perhaps you'd like to visit with him while we spend some time with this young lady."

Eunice froze for a second then blurted back, "Uh, no. I'm sure he's very busy. I know he hates to be bothered when he's scouring the books." She smiled awkwardly.

"If it's all right with the two of you, I'd prefer she remain with me. I'm indebted to her for her wisdom and guidance and could use it as we discuss certain matters, I'm sure," Cynthia stated with an unusual authority and humility.

Bobby piped up. "Maybe she can hang out in the park while we talk?" Cynthia gave him a hard look and smiled a firm opposition to that thought. "Or, maybe she can join us," he said with resignation.

Eunice squeezed Cynthia's hand a big thank you.

"Right this way," Madeline said as she grinned at Cynthia's moxie and opened the door to Danny's office lobby. Cynthia was the first to enter and gave Madeline a warm thank you with her eyes.

Madeline entered his inner office alone, leaving Cynthia, Eunice, and Bobby waiting in the lobby.

Much like his inner office, the lobby was decorated with photos and plaques displaying his name on various community awards. Hospitals, schools, low-income housing, and even educational institutions all paid tribute to the generosity of Danny and Ziggy's Island. Many of them were inscribed with *Walter Daniel Richards*. Some were less formal, like the still of an orphanage that simply read, *Danny Richards, our hero*.

Cynthia admired the man's work but felt it lacked something. People. In reality, each photo praised the giver but said nothing about the people receiving the gift. It all smacked of pompous grandeur to someone like Cynthia.

The inner office door opened and Madeline called them in.

Cynthia again gave Madeline a clear-eyed message of gratitude as she entered first. "Thank you, Madeline." Her voice was soft and yet firm. Madeline shook her head a tad as the others entered.

Danny ended a call as they all took their seats. Eunice sat on the couch in the far corner, behind the chairs in front of Danny's desk.

Cynthia sat upright in the chair facing Danny's desk, positioning herself as though she were in the company of royalty, something she had been accustomed to in Paradise. For in that place all citizens were royalty and addressed their King as such.

Bobby slouched down in his seat as Danny put his cell phone down and looked everyone over.

"Hi, Cindy, I'm Danny Richards. Nice of you to come today."

"So pleased to meet you, Mr. Richards. I deeply admire your support of the community."

Danny tossed Madeline a look that could've been either impressed or skeptical. "Just call me Danny, please. Thank you for your admiration. We try to support those in need when we can."

She stood up. "May I?" She pointed to the pictures on the bookshelf.

"Sure," Danny said with a grin.

She scanned the framed pictures of self-promoting poses with local VIPs in front of educational institutions, benevolent societies, and medical buildings. She wanted to understand his heart. The closer she looked, the more distant she felt from him. She spotted a couple of pictures from many years earlier. A woman holding a small, dark-haired boy with a six-year-old Danny squeezed in next to them. They were family shots. Danny's face spoke of loneliness. Cynthia gently touched the frame with her right forefinger.

"Is this your family, Mr. Richards?"

"Yes. That was taken when I was about six or seven."

"Cindy, why don't you take a seat and tell me about yourself?"

Cynthia ignored the invitation and continued to gaze at the photos.

"It seems you have had such an impact on so many people. Thank you." She turned and looked over her shoulder at Danny.

Danny tossed a look Madeline's way. She shrugged.

"Have you met any of the people you've helped, Mr. Richards?"

He retorted back quickly, "Yeah, on their way back from the bank after they cashed my check."

Madeline closed her eyes and winced slightly.

Cynthia furled her left brow. Such arrogance was not appreciated.

Danny responded to her stare. "I do my best to meet people I need to meet."

"Children especially know when they are liked…" Cynthia returned a photo of a large-framed check made out to an orphanage to its original spot on the shelf and exposed dust, indicating it had not been moved for some time. "… and when they're not."

Bobby jumped in. "Cindy remembers the name of every person she met at the park that day, after hearing their names just once."

Danny glared at Bobby. "I know the names of nearly every one of the presidents and founders of every organization I've ever given to."

Madeline, looking uneasy, said, "Cindy, why don't you take a seat and we'll …"

Danny interrupted Madeline. "What she's trying to say is, if you want to continue this interview to work for 'me,' I suggest you take a seat and let 'me' ask the questions."

Cynthia remained calm and moved back to her seat. "I apologize, Mr. Richards, if my concern for the welfare of the children seems bold. They are my passion and I see the world through their eyes. I'd certainly love to answer any questions you may have for me. I would very much like to help you in any way I can."

"I'm not so sure we need help, as you say, Cindy, but I'm willing to consider using you as the face for our next marketing campaign as Ziggy's ambassador, if that's what Madeline and I determine to be in the best interest of our company."

"I must tell you up front I'm not here to be used by anyone, Mr. Richards. If you so deem, I'd be more than pleased to represent you to the larger groups of people who are not currently attending your theme park."

Eunice raised an eyebrow.

Cynthia continued. "I am willing to consider acting as your ambassador, if that's what's best, as you say, for the company that you have so magnificently built. It is a lovely theme park and can be of immense enjoyment to so many and, better yet, of huge benefit to children everywhere who are in great need of love and care."

Danny rolled his eyes and shot a glare at Madeline.

Madeline stepped behind Danny's desk and put her hand on his shoulder. "Cindy, do you have any current employment that would conflict with a trial contract?"

"I currently do not."

"How about a manager or agent?"

"No."

"Even better. Do you have the capability to be available to us on a moment's notice?"

Eunice spoke up, her voice jubilant. "I can have her here in less than an hour's time—or any other place you may need her to be." She glanced at Cynthia, as if asking if what she'd said was okay.

"I'd be delighted to serve you whenever you need me."

"All right then." Madeline smiled. "Bobby knows how to find you, so let us discuss this and we'll get back to you."

Cynthia rose and offered her hand to Danny. "Mr. Richards, thank you for your time, and on behalf of so many children, thank you again for your kind generosity. I hope to see you again."

Danny shook her hand but wouldn't look her in the eye. They all left the room, leaving Madeline and Danny alone.

Cynthia, Bobby, and Eunice exited the building and were greeted with sunshine and blue skies, a perfect day to visit Ziggy's. The sounds of the park were a delight to Cynthia's ears. As the laughter, chattering, and of course the music, gave her a sense that all was well with the world. She was enjoying her life on Earth and she wanted to see more.

"Bobby, I'd like to take you up on your offer to sip on an orange…" She paused.

"Orange Julius. Don't tell me you've never had one!"

"Eunice, would you mind if Bobby brought me back to the house later?"

"Not at all, my dear. You enjoy yourself and I'll catch up on some errands. I have some ideas for drapes for the attic."

Terry Harris

"Sounds like a plan to me," Bobby said.

He gave Cynthia a thorough tour of the '80s lot. They shopped, sipped on their drinks and enjoyed the performances of break-dancing on the streets of 1985 and 1986. Cynthia laughed as she tried her best to keep up with the dancers, but the cardboard head-dance spins proved to be too much.

Bobby captured some true-to-life shots of her mixing it up with the street performers and tourists. She was sensitive to the time she promised him, so her interactions remained brief but impactful. It was so natural for her to strike up a conversation with a stranger.

Cynthia spoke with a strikingly handsome Swedish young man in his native tongue, and invited Bobby to share in the conversation as she interpreted for the happy foreigner, but Bobby used the camera as an excuse not to participate and was suddenly distant with an obvious change in his demeanor.

When she was finished, she said her goodbyes and then turned to Bobby. "Okay, where to next?" she asked.

He fumbled with his lens. "You know what, there's a couple things I need to get done that I suddenly remembered. Do you mind if I drop you off a little early? Maybe we can go to the beach later this week and get some shots there."

She was keenly aware that his attitude towards her had suddenly turned a bit cold and she felt a rift between them. But now was not the time to ask him about it. "Whatever works best for you, Bobby."

"I'll take you home now," he said in a muffled tone.

There was an awkward silence between them as they made their way to his truck and down the road. Cynthia set her mind on giving him space. She was learning that human relationships on Earth were quite complex and oftentimes frustratingly difficult. She longed to know his thoughts and feelings as she was accustomed to doing in her previous home.

"You know what?" he said as they drove down the freeway in his overpriced Jeep Cherokee. "Ten to one I get a call from Madeline within forty-eight, asking when I can get you back to the park to ink a deal."

"I would like that."

"Yeah, it'll be a game changer for us both. Know what I mean?"

"We would have something in common to work on."

They finally reached the house. Bobby smiled and nodded. "I'll be in touch."

"Goodbye, Bobby. Thank you."

She stepped down out of the vehicle and closed the door. He backed out of the driveway and left her standing there alone and confused.

Eunice was not home when Cynthia walked through the door. But the girls were. They had three friends over, and evidence of a food fight and other raucous behavior was scattered about the living room.

Cynthia smiled at the girls and started toward the stairs, but Portia stepped in front of her and blocked her from going any farther. Her breath smelled of strong liquor and her eyes were glazed.

Cynthia stopped and looked around. Everyone was staring at her. The silence was intimidating to Cynthia's sense of well-being.

Deidre joined her sister, leaving the boy she had been sitting with on the couch. "Where ya' headed, Princess?" Deidre teetered against Portia, splashing the drink in her hand all over Cynthia's light-yellow skirt. "Oops. I'm sorry." Some of it hit Cynthia's face, putting a strain on her sweet spirit.

Portia laughed. "Maybe we could use her dress as drapes for her room. I heard she was looking for some." They all laughed at her. Cynthia suddenly missed the silence

Adrenaline rushed through her body, giving Cynthia an odd burst of energy. This was a new sensation with which she wasn't comfortable. She quickly prayed, looking for wisdom. Nothing came to her.

Portia lunged towards Cynthia and pushed her back into Deidre. Cynthia felt Deidre lose her balance but then was shoved back into Portia. Cynthia's body hit Portia hard, causing the rotund girl to fall backward. Thrown off balance, Cynthia reached out to grab something to keep from falling. Finding only Deidre's arm, the two of them landed awkwardly on top of Portia.

Cynthia jumped to her feet and stood back. The sisters' friends laughed. Infuriated, the girls tried to get up, only to stumble over each other.

Cynthia moved past them, quickly made her way up the stairs, and locked the attic door. On her side of safety, she listened as they swore at her and each other.

She backed away from the door and plopped down on the bed. The late afternoon sun was now blocked by clouds. Gloom hovered over the room. She felt totally and utterly alone and unsafe. She fidgeted with her necklace, rubbing it again and again between her fingers. "Cynthia Hope," she said to herself.

Tears flowed, and after a while she used her bedding to wipe them away. She couldn't grasp why she was being rejected and despised by people she had not offended, at least not that she could remember. Her expectations of what this journey would be like were being shattered. Disillusion and disheartened groans erupted inside her soul. Her heart ached as she tried to understand what she was feeling.

She thought about Bobby, then Radcliffe, then Danny, but finally felt a glimmer of hope when she thought of Eunice. However, with Eunice came the pain of the girls.

Her mind drifted to Madeline. She replayed their interactions in her mind and looked for a thread of commonality. She sensed that there was more to Madeline than the bottom line, but was convinced that Madeline would drop her immediately once Ziggy's no longer had any use for her. She concluded it was Madeline's way of conducting business and nothing more.

She searched her mind's eye for any evidence of her parents. She trusted her King. She trusted Sebastian. She knew she was here because of a plan that was preeminent to anything she might dream of, yet there was no sign of anyone she perceived could be her mother or father.

The father that was often described to her and for whom she was looking was a great man, a king, as it were. He was a kind and gracious man, putting others before himself. The mother she had heard so much about was humble and gentle, one who cared for her children and served them, putting their needs before her own. She thought of Eunice again, but then remembered that she had never had children, so she was not a candidate.

Not thinking of anyone to match those profiles made her sadder. She prayed for relief from her growing burden. She did not find it in prayer this time, so she scanned the pages of her Bible, thirsty for something true to lift her spirits. The words seemed flat, with little life to them. Frustrated and deeply hurt, she fell asleep in her alcohol-stained clothes.

The angels in Heaven, especially Sebastian, watched over her that night, feeling her pain. They wanted to go down and tell Cynthia that the parents she was looking for would one day be revealed to her. Yet they understood that young Cynthia must now walk by something of which they knew nothing of, a thing called faith.

Neither angels or anyone else in Paradise needed this mysterious inner strength, which demanded setting aside one's feelings and insights. Faith was a relationship that could only develop in people on Earth. Once her time on Earth was complete, the rewards of the faith she developed would forever remain as her testimony to the King's promises.

What Cynthia had to learn was the importance that faith played in the relationship between the King and His children. There was nothing more sacred to God than pure trust and total faith in Him as their heavenly King and Creator.

Sebastian sighed. If only he could lend a hand to ease her burden. He knew darker days and difficult nights were in store for this young girl who gave him so much delight.

8

A FEW DAYS LATER, CYNTHIA WAS MEDITATING ON PSALM 34 when she heard a soft knock on the attic door. After a moment, she opened the narrow portal. Eunice stood before her with a timid smile on her face.

"Sorry to disturb you, Cindy. Bobby called. He asked if you would meet him and Madeline at the children's wing of the hospital near the park."

Cynthia raised a brow. She had begun to doubt her employment with the park when the two-day window in which Bobby had been so confident had passed. But she was excited to hear that she would be seeing children. She missed them greatly. "Give me fifteen minutes and I'll be ready to go."

While dressing, she wondered if she would run into the girls; they had not seen each other since their encounter the other afternoon. No word had been spoken about their behavior, as Cynthia knew she was in their home and Eunice was probably not up for another argument with them, especially regarding Cynthia's presence in the house.

United Memorial Hospital was an older institution with a fairly new children's wing, named the Walter Daniel Richards Children's Hospital. It had broken ground ten years before and was now growing. At the time, it had cost Danny and Madeline nearly three million dollars. Madeline disagreed with the substantial investment back then but as Danny saw it, it was a chance to be known for their goodwill in the community.

Ten years later, the hospital had outgrown its space and was expanding by adding another dual-floor unit dedicated to critical care. The hospital board made Danny an offer he couldn't refuse by allowing him to have full public credit for only partial funding. They had offered to use Danny's additional gift as a matching grant and leverage that money to raise the complete amount they needed. Madeline had let Danny convince her that the move was perfect for their marketing needs, but she saw right through him. She knew what he really enjoyed was the idea of having his name dropped in every conversation with the local investor types. It gave him great satisfaction to be the lead guy in this type of fundraising. But the question in Madeline's mind was whether it really benefited their new marketing plans.

This day was another ceremony celebrating breaking ground. Madeline knew this was a perfect opportunity to introduce Cynthia as their goodwill ambassador, but she wanted to ease the idea into Danny's mind prior to saying it publicly. She surprised him when she suggested that they drive together to the ceremony, giving her the opportunity for a one-on-one talk with Danny about the new marketing strategies involving Cynthia.

It was one of the few times they had ridden in a car together since their breakup, about twenty-five years ago. Things seemed to be fine between them until Madeline brought up Cynthia.

"I'm in the dark here, Mattie, as far as what she has to offer us," he said as they sat at a long red light. "We're already doing so much in the community."

"To be honest, Danny, today's generation doesn't give a hoot about a name on a building. What they want to see is how you change the world by what you do. I think this girl can give us that."

"Sorry, I don't see it." He floored the gas, letting her know of his frustration.

She waited for him to finish making his point and then lightly put her hand on his right knee. "Have you ever actually entered the doors of the hospital that bears your name?" It was the first time she had touched him like that since the divorce.

"Yes," he said dogmatically. "I used the bathroom once. All right, I'll go along with this little game for now. But know this, I'm not putting her name on my building or anything else, for that matter."

"I can live with that," she said as she smiled to herself.

Bobby was waiting at the ground site, milling around with senior hospital staff, when Madeline and Danny approached him.

"Where's wonder girl?" Danny chided Bobby.

Just then a man with a dark-gray suit and very expensive glasses called out, "Mattie! Walter!" It was Tom Diaz, president of the hospital's board of directors. He was a successful local businessman who had been friends with Madeline and Danny for several years.

Madeline walked over to meet him, turning on the charm and giving him a glistening smile. "Tom, how are you? So good to see you." They exchanged hugs. Danny approached and offered his hand to Tom. For whatever reason, Madeline liked the fact that Danny was a good two inches taller than him. It gave her a sense of superiority.

"Hey, listen," Tom said, sort of under his breath. "I've got a little surprise for you guys. You're gonna love this."

"Why don't you guys go talk and I'll catch up with you a little later," Madeline said, turning to look for Bobby. She noticed him several feet away and walked towards the stage where he stood. "Where's Cindy?"

"She should be here any time. Got a text a little while ago saying they'd be here," he said, looking at his phone.

She took him aside to be updated on Cynthia's background check. "Can't find a thing," he said, shuffling his feet and staring at the ground. "There must be a hundred Cindy Hopes, just in the US, and she doesn't match the profile of any of them."

Madeline's mind paused at hearing the "Cindy Hope," but she dismissed it as she was too distracted to give it any further thought. "Keep looking. Last thing I need is to be surprised by this girl's past." Then she walked away toward the crowd.

A small stage covered by a canopy stood erect at the front part of the grounds, next to the current children's wing. A couple of ribbons and shiny new shovels waited to be used as props in the photo shoot. Several local photographers approached the set. Eunice trailed behind them, followed by Cynthia.

She was dressed in a soft, off-white dress with light-blue shoes. Her hair was back in a ponytail. Madeline immediately decided she didn't like the ponytail. She was the opposite of Danny and preferred formality over casual.

Madeline waited as the ladies approached her. Eunice stepped back behind Cynthia when they arrived.

"Hello, Cindy. You look lovely today."

Cynthia shook Madeline's hand warmly. "I'm excited to be here."

"We've decided to hire you as our goodwill ambassador, and I thought today's event would be the perfect time to introduce you," she said as she stood behind Cynthia, undoing her ponytail. She fluffed Cynthia's hair out and then draped it across her shoulders. "Better," she said, mostly to herself. She then straightened Cynthia's necklace and studied it. "Pretty," she noted of the smooth, white stone, not knowing Cynthia's name was engraved on the back.

"Thank you. I will do my best to represent you with the highest integrity."

"We'll discuss the details of your pay later today."

"Oh, I don't wish to be paid. But thank you."

"Of course you want to be paid. Why else would you take on the job?"

"To help the children."

"How will you eat, pay your bills…?" Madeline asked with a motherly tone.

"I am well cared for. I have all that I need for the moment."

Cynthia smiled and turned to Bobby, who seemed to be struggling not to stare at her.

"I have you to thank for this, Bobby. If it wasn't for you, I would not be here today," she said with a warm smile that made him gulp and erased any awkward feelings between them from their last encounter. She leaned in close and gave him a kiss on the cheek. *He smells good.*

The doors opened to the hospital and several children came out to be part of the event. Some children were in wheelchairs, one on crutches, and others walked but were dressed in hospital gowns. Each of these children had one thing in common: they were orphans cared for by the state.

Tom leaned into Danny. "You asked for kids, you got kids."

Danny smiled. "Perfect."

Everyone turned to see the children. Cynthia's heart leapt. She left the adults and made her way to the young boys and girls. Her spirit grieved at seeing them in pain. She was not accustomed to seeing children in this way. In Paradise, they were all in a perfect state, free to be whole and happy.

She knelt down to a nine-year-old boy dressed in a red shirt, who was sitting in a wheelchair. She smiled big. He wouldn't make eye contact with her. His demeanor bordered on despondency. His legs were thin but didn't show signs of disease or ailment. "Hello. What's your name?" she asked. He said nothing.

Cynthia looked around the small crowd and resumed her attempts to connect. "Are your mom and dad here?"

A nurse spoke up. "Uh, Logan is an orphan. He doesn't have any guardians."

Cynthia frowned inside but smiled on the outside. She wanted to speak to the nurse about putting labels on children, but she held her tongue and said nothing. After all, one could officially call her an orphan.

"How long has he been in the wheelchair?" Cynthia asked the nurse amiably.

"Since the day after he arrived here. He was walking when he showed up, but since he learned he wasn't going back home, he's needed the chair."

She touched Logan's arm gently. He moved it away ever so slightly. Cynthia smiled, understanding his reluctance. Rejection was a cancer to one's heart and could do great damage to a person, including a will to walk.

Cynthia moved to a little girl who had a large bandage over her left eye. She stood next to her and put her arm around her. The girl received the love and hugged her back. A boy leaning on crutches and dressed in a hospital gown that was starting to fall off piped up and asked Cynthia a question.

"Hey, lady. Do you sing?"

"Actually, I do sing. Do you?"

"No. But I play the harmonica." He whipped out the shiny silver instrument concealed in his right hand and began to blow. Some notes were on key and his tune was catchy, so Cynthia sang a few made-up lyrics as she went.

The other kids slowly smiled. Some started to clap. Others sang along. Logan remained still.

Eunice drew near to Cynthia and joined in with the singing. Bobby snapped a few pictures and gave her the thumbs up.

Madeline had shuffled her way inconspicuously over to Danny's side, expecting a blowup any moment. She was just about to tap him on the shoulder when Tom leaned into Danny and grinned.

"Who's the girl?"

"Thinking about hiring her as an ambassador for the park," he said. Madeline raised an eyebrow.

Tom scanned the crowd, which was growing. It was like a wall of smiles.

"Brilliant, Danny. Great idea. Is this why you called and asked to have some kids at the event?"

Danny stalled a half-second. "You bet. Perfect opportunity to launch the campaign." He turned and smiled at Madeline who grinned and stepped back, not saying a word.

Once the music stopped and the singing ended, Tom walked up to the platform and called Danny to join him. Danny did so, and with his usual self deprecating monologue, thanked the good people of the community for supporting Ziggy's Island, the best park in the United States. Then, he thanked the hospital for providing him the opportunity to give back.

After the ribbons were cut and the ceremony concluded, it was time for photos. The children who weren't in wheelchairs were invited on stage next to Danny, who put on the charm and shook hands with each one. Cynthia beamed a pleasing smile seeing that he had taken the time to meet some of the children and get their names, though he appeared to have forgot most of them as soon as he heard them.

The children in wheelchairs took their pose in front of the platform on ground level.

After several moments of picture taking, the children called for Cynthia to join them. She had been standing next to Madeline during the ceremony.

Danny and Madeline exchanged stares. Madeline nodded, led Cynthia by the hand up to the platform and stepped onto the stage. The children all cheered. Their kindness warmed Cynthia. She noticed Logan sitting alone in the back, behind the rest of the kids.

Madeline took her place next to Danny but took command of the microphone. "Ziggy's Island is very pleased to introduce our new goodwill ambassador, who is here with us today. Cindy, would you like to say a word or two?"

Cynthia prayed. She knew this platform was not hers to use for her own purposes. "A child who is loved, accepted, and understood has much to contribute to their world and little to demand from it. A child without love is at great risk and vulnerable to that which their Father did not intend."

Madeline looked at Danny with concern. Danny glanced away as if to say, "Told you so."

Terry Harris

"I come from a place where, as a community, we work together in nurturing and restoring what is missing from a child's life, and that is what I see here today at United Memorial Hospital. So much gratitude is due to Walter Richards and Madeline Brewer of Ziggy's Island for their outstanding generosity in adding a critical-care unit to the children's hospital. With the help of kind and caring medical staff and the gift of modern medicine, untold thousands of children will have their bodies restored to health within these walls. It is our duty, then, to pick up where they leave off and help bring restoration and healing to their broken souls. That is what I pledge myself to do, and I hope you will join me."

The children began to erupt in cheers as the adults applauded. The praise lasted a little longer than normal, which created a frenzy of photo-taking. Bobby greeted Cynthia as she descended the stairs of the platform and made her way to the children. "That was pretty amazing what you said up there."

"Thank you, Bobby. I meant every word."

Moments later, the crowd had thinned. Cynthia heard more times than she cared to about how great she was. Some people had missed the point of her remarks.

The children each gave her a hug and then the staff corralled them back into the hospital. Cynthia noticed Logan lagging behind the others as he pushed his wheelchair listlessly toward the door, where a nurse stood waiting.

His chair stopped. He paused a long moment. Then he spun it around and rolled toward Cynthia, who was standing a short distance away, watching him try to navigate his wheelchair through the thick grass with his weak arms. He stopped and tried again, going at it from another angle. When that didn't work, he tried again. And again. Finally, out of sheer frustration, he flung his hands off the wheels and stared at Cynthia, defeated.

She felt a voice inside her whisper, "Stay where you are." So she did.

He tried again, only to tip the chair ever so slightly. On the verge of tears, the boy rocked back and forth. Upset that he couldn't get to her, his hands began to shake.

"I'll wait for you, Logan. You can do it," she encouraged him.

Logan paused a long while, as if he were battling within himself.

All of a sudden, he did it. With both arms, he forced himself up and stepped off the pedals of the wheelchair. He caught his breath and regained some strength. Then he moved his right foot. It worked. So, he moved his left foot, then his right again. Eventually, he had put four or five steps together, which formed a walk.

Cynthia could bear it no more and ran to him and embraced him. The little boy hugged her, his tears leaving wet splotches on her dress. "Please come back," he said. "Please come back."

"Every moment that I can," she promised. She loved this little boy with a love that was bigger than her own heart could contain, and he seemed to know it.

He smiled as Cynthia helped him back into the chair. His thin legs shook from exhaustion. Cynthia stepped around the back of the wheelchair and pushed Logan to the sidewalk where the nurses stood waiting. The two ladies looked at her with doubt and oddity, but she said nothing.

Cynthia hugged Logan one last time and carefully observed him as one of the nurses rolled him back into the hospital. He turned around and gave Cynthia a huge grin and a big wave goodbye.

Cynthia turned to Madeline and Danny just as they exchanged glances. Danny, for some reason, looked disappointed.

Tom was the last to leave the premises. He sat in his new BM and hit a speed-dial number on his phone. A quick glance in the mirror and a toss of his thinning blonde hair was long enough for the person to answer. "Hey, it's Tom. Thought you might like to know you're going to be seeing a hailstorm of posts on an event that just took place here at the hospital with your new goodwill ambassador."

"What ambassador are you talking about? We have no such person here," the voice on the other end of the phone grumbled with irritation.

"You do now, and she seems to be able to make the lame walk! I'd be careful if I were you." Tom stated emphatically. He enjoyed being the bearer of "new information." There was oftentimes a reward for it.

"I can't discuss this now. Send me the details."

"Sure thing. I assume this is worth something to you."

"If it is, you will receive recompense. Now just do it." A loud click at the other end followed.

Tom laughed to himself as he set his phone down and started the car. "Jerk."

In his darkly lit office, Radcliffe sat back in his chair. He mulled over in his crusty mind what he had just learned from Tom. He hated surprises, especially of this nature, and it sounded like Madeline and Danny had just pulled another fast one on him. But he would find out before they told him and thus be a step ahead.

Tom's irritating words rang loud in the back of Radcliffe's grave mind. He hated things that reeked of "miracles" and such nonsense. He believed, as he had been taught by his miserly father, that goodness was a thing found only in fairy tales. None of us were more than a vapor in time brought about by a succession of evolving events, and we certainly had no place beyond the grave, so life was about one thing only: getting all you can get while you can get it. "Goodness" was a sign of weakness and self-pity, and those who chose to live in its blinding light deserved to be squished like a meaningless cockroach.

He spun his chair around and two men from the catering department sat, nervously quiet. One man was balding and in his late forties. He wore an inexpensive wedding ring that Radcliffe, being a jeweler, hated. The other man was much older, with gray hair. He was divorced with an older son living at home. This reminded Radcliffe of his failed marriage and what the divorce cost him, which he hated even more.

They waited for the grueling scrutiny they were under to continue. "If you care for your jobs, your numbers on this report better improve—significantly!" Radcliffe groused just above a whisper. They both swallowed hard. It was more than obvious they were in trouble.

Eunice was quiet as she drove home. Cynthia listened to music on the radio and sang along to tunes she liked. Eunice felt free to let an occasional tear flow down her cheek, only to feel Cynthia gently wipe it away for her.

There was one parking space open on the highway along the coastline where they lived. Eunice grabbed it and uttered "thank you" under her breath.

They parked and Eunice asked if they could take a walk.

"Yes," Cynthia replied, "I'd love a beach stroll and know of the perfect place to clear one's mind and connect with whatever is important."

Terry Harris

But Eunice was already out of the car and didn't hear it. Instead of going to the beach, she trotted across the street to a little old-fashioned café that she knew had been owned and operated by locals for nearly four decades.

Eunice walked in and plopped down in a corner booth. It had seats made of church benches and tables covered by plastic, with old newspaper clippings underneath for you to read.

Cynthia followed suit and plopped down across from her, looking a little perplexed.

A rangy redhead food server greeted them and took their orders. "Mind if I order for us?" Eunice asked.

Cynthia nodded in submission.

"We would like your hot bread pudding with caramel sauce and extra, extra whip, please. Oh, and two ice-cold waters and two coffees."

The server smiled and trotted off.

"They have *the* best bread pudding," Eunice said. "No one can beat it."

"I can't wait. I've never had bread pudding before."

Eunice looked around at the décor and started talking about her younger years of growing up with a simple mom and dad. She had been close to her dad, more so than her mom. She and her father had a special relationship and he was the sunshine of Eunice's life.

When Eunice began talking about what it was like when her mom had passed, she spoke of her mom's death as though it just happened, but it had been nearly twenty years.

She admitted to being left "hanging" by her dad's sudden disappearance from her life, with no idea as to what she had done wrong. She looked for a reason all this happened, and it was clear to Eunice that she was stuck in a place of confusion and hurt. She was convinced that she had done something wrong but was too scared to find out what it was.

The dessert and coffee were served, but never really touched, as Cynthia listened intently. Eunice knew that her story was a jumbled mess of hurt feelings.

She abruptly stopped talking and sipped her coffee. She had nowhere else to go with her tangled thoughts and feelings, so she decided to eat her dessert.

Cynthia spoke up. "Do you blame your mom?"

"My mother!?" Eunice piped back.

"Not because she did something wrong against you, but simply because she left?"

"I'm afraid you're confusing me, Cindy. My mother did not choose to die, she just died. That's not her fault."

"You are right, Eunice, but when she was alive, your father was part of your life. Perhaps there is a part of your heart that blames her for your father not being here now, with you."

Eunice looked away but stayed in tune with what Cynthia was trying to tell her.

"I come from a place where healing and reconciliation flow as natural as water from a faucet in our family. It must hurt deeply never hearing back from your father when you needed him to be there for you."

"Everything was so much better when she was alive," Eunice said pensively as she looked out to the ocean. "I just wonder sometimes if I did something wrong, you know?"

"I'm so sorry you lost your mother," Cynthia offered. "But I'm even more sorry you lost your father too, even though he's still alive. He was supposed to be there for you. It's not your fault that he wasn't. And it's not your mother's fault either." Cynthia lovingly grabbed Eunice's hand. "You needed someone to be there for you, but he wasn't. So in reality, both of your parents died at nearly the same time."

The tears began to flow as Eunice wept quietly. Cynthia didn't let go of her hand and waited. Finally, Eunice wiped her face with her one free hand and pushed her hair back from her reddened face.

She smiled a little genuine smile. She took a bite of her bread pudding and invited Cynthia to do the same.

"May I ask a silly question?" Cynthia nudged as she released Eunice's hand and turned to her plate.

Eunice nodded.

"Why did you bring me here, to this café?"

"This is where I got the news of my mom dying. I got a call on my cell and was sitting here in this booth when I spoke to my dad. It was the last time we talked. Or at least really talked. He didn't say a word to me at the funeral."

"Maybe you should just call him."

Eunice was surprised and giggled uncomfortably. "What? He left *me*. I think the ball's in his court!" She nervously took a sip of her coffee.

After a long pause, Cynthia looked Eunice in the eyes. "You know what?" Cynthia said just above a whisper, "You have another Father who loves you and will never leave you or reject you."

Cynthia smiled long enough for Eunice to process her words.

"I never really believed that before," Eunice said, "but I know you believe it. I don't get it. But I want to know what you know. I want to feel like you feel. I do want a loving father!" Eunice squeezed Cynthia's hand again.

"I would love to help you."

They both took a deep breath and quietly sipped their coffee.

When they were done and had paid the tab, the two ladies rose from the booth and laid a tip down on the table. Cynthia hugged her friend. Eunice sensed a deep closeness that had not been there before. She loved this girl dearly and was so glad to be part of her life.

"What did you think of the bread pudding?" Eunice asked with a grin.

"Heavenly. Best I've ever had." They shared a laugh.

That night as the ladies sat on the patio of their backyard, Eunice prayed and was introduced to the King. Her heart leapt with an inexpressible joy when she invited Him to be part of her life. She felt a great weight of despair and guilt lift from her shoulders, causing her to giggle as though she were a child. She and Cynthia laughed and hugged and hugged and laughed. It was a truly remarkable transformation for a woman who had felt the weight of the world just hours earlier.

"By the way, Eunice, you should see the party that's going on in The King's court right now," Cynthia said.

Eunice shrugged, not knowing what she meant.

"I'll tell you about it sometime." Cynthia smiled and made a gesture. "Great big party—for you!"

As they stepped into the living room, Eunice stopped Cynthia. "A couple times today you have referred to the place where you come from and now you mention The King's Court. Where are you from? If you don't mind me asking."

Cynthia paused. "It's on the other side of the ocean. A wonderful city with so much to see and do."

"Is that where you grew up?"

"Yes, it is."

"And you said your family was here. Why would they ever come here without you?"

"There was a death in the family… and it separated us, so I grew up without my father and mother. Recently, I was told I would find them here."

Eunice gasped. "Oh Cindy, I'm so sorry. I didn't know you were an orphan."

"I'm not an orphan. I was raised with the purest love and complete acceptance, and I know who I am and to Whom I belong. I feel my Father's love even though I can't see Him. He is always with me."

"For the first time I can tell you I feel much the same. I can't explain it. I feel like a child being born into a family I never knew I had. Everything feels so new. Does that make sense?" Eunice asked with a heart overflowing with gratitude.

"It certainly does," Cynthia encouraged her.

Eunice looked at her. "Can I ask one more favor? Will you pray for me? I really feel the need to call my dad."

Without skipping a beat, Cynthia held Eunice by the hand and interceded for her. When she was done, Eunice let out a deep breath and gave Cynthia a hug. Cynthia said goodnight and turned toward the stairs. She stopped. "Eunice, why aren't you a mom?"

Eunice sighed. "I always wanted to be a mother. I had some health issues in my early twenties that would have made pregnancy difficult, if not impossible. And then there's always that little detail of not finding the right man! I thought about adoption for a short time, but with practically raising Portia and Deidre for most of their lives, it just wasn't meant to be, I guess."

Cynthia gave her friend an understanding smile and nodded. "So, you've never been pregnant?" Cynthia bit her lip nervously, indicating she was not sure she should pry any further but really wanted an answer.

"No," Eunice gently replied with a slight shake of her head.

"Call your dad before it gets too late," Cynthia replied with a smirk. "Good night."

Disappointment filled Cynthia's soul as she began to climb the stairs. In her heart of hearts, she knew that Eunice was not her mom, though she carried a flicker of hope that her feelings were wrong. With all the events of the day, Cynthia felt no closer to finding her parents. She began to wonder if she was missing something, if there was something she should be doing.

Had she walked right by them on the street? Was the waitress from the café actually her mom? Was the mailman her dad? How would she know?

She had been taught about this thing called faith, but she didn't realize how difficult it could be to live it. It was an emotional day, and Cynthia felt an exhaustion she had never known before. *I trust You,* she said to herself as she crawled into bed. Her mind then quickly turned to the amazing blessings of the day, and her spirit lifted. She was transformed by all that had transpired that day in Eunice's life as well as Logan's. She sang herself to sleep with a song of praise with the window open and the stars shining down on her. Moonlight bathed her as she rested.

Her last thought before she plunged into a deep slumber was, *I wonder how Eunice's new birth will affect Portia and Deidre.*

❦ 9 ❧

SOCIAL-MEDIA POSTINGS ABOUT THE LITTLE BOY IN THE wheelchair walking to Cynthia spread like wildfire, oftentimes exaggerating what really happened and sensationalizing the events to make Cynthia look like a saint and miracle worker. It marked an escalation of events in Cynthia's life.

Ziggy's Park received an avalanche of press stemming from the viral videos. Homemade videos of Cynthia helping people at Ziggy's created a social-media frenzy.

Madeline became Cynthia's contact for speaking engagements and appearances. She handled the requests with a keen eye and watched over Cynthia as though she were family. She said no to several inappropriate television and radio invitations that were geared toward embarrassing a person instead of interviewing them.

Instead of relying on Eunice, Madeline began sending a limousine to pick up Cynthia for work, or she would drive Cynthia herself when they attended an event together. On this particular day, Madeline had a packed day of appearances scheduled for Cynthia that would include a visit to a daycare committed to children with special needs and a visit to United Memorial Children's Hospital. She knew that Cynthia was excited about her ministry opportunities, especially the hospital visit, as she was looking forward to seeing Logan again.

Eunice was hurt at the start of Madeline's and Cynthia's growing relationship, but in her infant steps of praying, she found release from anxious and jealous thoughts. She was growing in her faith as she obeyed the convictions she felt in her spirit toward those she loved. First, she made small strides in the relationship with her father. In their phone conversation, he was reluctant in the beginning but accepted Eunice's invitation to reconnect. It would prove to be a long process but a healthy one for each of them.

Eunice's attitude toward Portia and Deidre also began to change. She thought of them from a whole new perspective. Anger and distrust were replaced with compassion and sorrow over the condition of their souls. She became burdened to the point that she invited them to have tea with her in the village. It was something they did when the girls were young, and they used to love it. As they grew older and more stubborn in their ways, Eunice stopped doing things with them and treated them, more or less, as unwanted but tolerated roommates. The girls begrudgingly accepted the invitation but insisted on meeting Eunice there rather than walking together.

While the sisters had stood her up the first time, after a few weeks of relentless invitations and refusals, both reluctantly promised Eunice they would join her.

Eunice thanked Cynthia for her prayers and then gathered her courage to go meet the girls for tea. The prayer encouraged Eunice to remain hopeful that Deidre and Portia would actually show up this time.

Terry Harris

When the girls showed up just a few minutes late, Eunice sat scared in her chair, unsure of what to say or do. She felt, however, impressed to be boldly honest and compassionate. After fifteen minutes of useless small talk, Eunice abruptly spoke up. "Girls, I owe you both a sincere apology. For years now, I know that I have been distant and unaccepting of you. I have been angry and critical of you when I should have been compassionate and loving. You've needed a mother, or at least some guidance, and I failed to give that to you. You've had to rely on each other to get by, and that's not right. I am sorry for failing you in so many ways."

The girls fidgeted with their teacups. Deidre tapped hers with a silver spoon, which caused Portia to get irritated and grab the spoon. Finally, she released it and returned her attention to Eunice.

Eunice bravely continued. "Your mom is gone, your relationship with your dad is strained, and I've pushed you out. You deserve better, and I promise to do just that. You are like my very own daughters, and I do love you. I am sorry. Please forgive me."

Portia's sniffles interrupted the silence. Tears filled her eyes and emotion choked her up. Deidre clanked her spoon against the teacup over and over. She stood up and pushed the chair away loudly. "I don't believe you, and I certainly won't forgive you." She walked out.

Eunice turned to Portia and touched her hand. "Do you believe me, Portia?"

Portia looked away. Eunice squeezed her hand. "Will you forgive me?"

She couldn't look at Eunice but cried and nodded yes. They ended their time together with a hug. It communicated that there was still work to do but they had initiated something new.

The days became weeks and the weeks became months as Cynthia and Madeline worked together to shape and mold Ziggy's new image. In Cynthia's mind, the park was no longer looking to sell tickets and apply Band-Aids to problems that plagued their community; they were now actively involved in finding solutions and helping others. Cynthia believed herself to be blessed beyond words as such an opportunity unfolded before her. She knew that Madeline, however, was still about promoting the park and building the bottom-line sales revenue.

One day, Cynthia and Madeline were walking into Ziggy's offices when Cynthia noticed a homeless man digging through the trash in the parking lot, looking for bottles and cans. Madeline became irritated at Cynthia when she walked over to him and not only talked to the man but gave him a hug.

"Don't you realize how dangerous that is?" she chastised Cynthia as she returned to Madeline's side. "He could've had a knife or something."

Madeline barked at a security guard nearby. "What are we paying you for?" She cocked her head over her shoulder toward the direction of the man. "He's scaring the guests."

Cynthia gave the homeless man a slightly sad smile and waved goodbye as the security guard took steps toward him. Just then, Cynthia gasped with delight. "Madeline! I have an idea," she exclaimed.

Madeline rolled her eyes as she unlocked her office door. "It's your job to be pretty and sweet, not to think."

"Hear me out," Cynthia boldly commanded. "Why don't we have a promotion that every person who brings a canned good, jacket, or blanket to the park saves fifty percent off admission? We can use them to help the homeless in the local soup kitchens and shelters!"

"Fifty percent? No. Maybe ten." Madeline paused. It wasn't a bad idea. "I'll think about it," she said with a wink.

"I'll take that as a yes," Cynthia replied back with her own winking smile. By day's end she had sketched out the plans on paper and got the formal green light from Madeline. Neither one bothered to ask Danny what he thought of the idea.

Within a week, they had launched the marketing and social-media campaigns, inviting the world at large to help Ziggy stomp out poverty one person at a time. They offered tickets to the park at a ten-percent discount for anyone who brought a bag of food or blankets for the needy.

From the start, the idea was so brilliant that it drew in an additional thousand guests to the park in one month. However, the logistics of where to store the items became a nightmare. Cynthia received notice that the city regulations regarding food items was causing unexpected stress for the legal department, which they did not have time for. Canned food, blankets, and jackets were stacked in corners of the park in odd, obscure places, causing many of the annual pass holders to mumble and complain on social media and in phone calls to the office. Cynthia feared what might happen to her plan.

Eventually, the complaints of Ziggy's new "poverty reduction" incentive made their way to Radcliffe's office, and he vowed to use them to shuffle the hierarchy and get himself promoted to a higher position on the staff and ultimately the board. This type of nonsense and goodwill seemed outdated and of considerable cost to the park, and he would personally see to it that their goodwill ambassador would pay for her righteous acts of foolish benevolence. He would wait for the right moment and then strike.

One rainy and cold day, Radcliffe took it upon himself to once again eavesdrop on Danny's phone conversations in his office. After several minutes of hearing one-sided conversations, Radcliffe heard Danny say his goodbyes. Now was the time to strike. Radcliffe marched his stout figure down the hall and right into Danny's office without announcement.

"Walter, have you misplaced your mind?"

Radcliffe slammed the door shut and stood directly behind the chair that faced Danny's desk. "It seems to me, Walter, that you have lost sight of who we are as a company and have egregiously turned a blind eye to the antics of your ex-wife, who continues to appease the wild and financially careless promptings of that hireling referred to as our goodwill ambassador!"

"Hireling?" Madeline asked as she stepped out of the shadows and placed her slender figure directly in front of Radcliffe.

Radcliffe startled, as he had not seen Madeline in the room and was caught off guard, a feeling he despised.

He craned his neck and spotted Cynthia watching the action from the corner. He looked back up at Madeline.

She towered over him. The two-inch difference seemed greater, as she was able to look down on him. Beads of sweat slowly appeared and rolled down his bony nose, finding their resting place on his freshly shined shoes.

"Madeline. I... I thought you were off site."

"I'm sure you wish I were," Madeline said, not moving an inch.

Radcliffe stepped back and pushed his glasses up. "I'm only saying this because of the risk we run in losing..." He stopped mid-sentence, knowing it was falling on deaf ears.

He moved around Madeline's stance to direct his comments to Danny, whom he hoped would be the rational mind in the room. "If you had heard the number of complaints I've received in just the last two weeks..."

Madeline took a step closer to him, which forced him to go around her and right up to Danny's desk. "Complaints from staff, from board members, from the very ones who pay our salaries—the ticket buyers themselves."

Danny stood up and moved to the front of the desk and leaned against it. "Have you looked at the numbers lately, Radcliffe?"

That was an insult to Radcliffe and his position as chief financial officer. He knew those books better than God himself, or so he thought. "Of course! What do you think I do all day, Walter?"

"Then you would know our sales are up nearly twelve percent over last year at this same time. That's a double-digit increase that we haven't seen in over five years."

"I'm well aware of the increase, but are you considering the risk factor long term? We have food stacked in the corner of our seventies lot. We've become a Goodwill, for Pete's sake, storing jackets and blankets inside the gate of the fifties lot. Why, we have enough blankets to give away to the entire county!" He said the last few words with increasing volume.

"That's wonderful!" Cynthia exclaimed. Radcliffe gave her a dirty look and turned his attention back to Danny.

"What do you propose we do?" Radcliffe inquired.

"We're working on a solution for those problems and will have the items stored in the proper facility within the week," Danny said matter-of-factly. "Anything else?"

Radcliffe felt smaller than he cared to, so he exited the room, but not before throwing his opinion out as if something to be seriously considered. "She's trouble, Walter," he said, pointing at Cynthia. "Mark my words, she's wrong for this company." He vacated the room with a slam of the door.

"I want that stuff out of this park, now!" Danny barked at the ladies as he moved back to his chair behind the desk.

Cynthia wanted to defend the state of affairs and assure him all would be well, but Madeline responded first. "I'll take care of it personally. Come on, Cindy."

Cynthia hesitated and then stepped directly in front of Danny's desk. She was bubbling over with passion for the children but held her tongue. "Thank you, Danny. I promise you won't regret your generosity."

He shivered when he heard her speak his name. She had no idea how much she sounded like Madeline in that moment.

The ladies left the room to head back to Madeline's office as Danny went back to his paperwork.

Passing Radcliffe's office on their way, Cynthia stopped. She wanted to go in and correct the misunderstanding that he had toward her.

Madeline looked backed to Cynthia. "He's not worth the trouble, Cindy."

"But he misjudged my intentions. I only desire to help the children, nothing more."

"News flash for you, girl. You can't be a hero to everyone. Sometimes you have to go it alone. Come on."

They entered Madeline's office and Madeline motioned for her to have a seat. Madeline rolled up her sleeves and hit speed dial.

"Like Chinese?" Madeline asked while waiting for someone to answer her call.

Cynthia shrugged and smiled.

A young female voice politely answered and Madeline ordered a couple of chicken dishes with brown rice for the two of them.

Cynthia watched Madeline. Her hands moved succinctly from the phone to the computer keypad to the paper notebook in front of her as her eyes darted back and forth from her two large monitors. She admired how there was purpose in what she did. She knew Madeline well enough by now to know that, in

Madeline's mind, there was a list of things to do, and they were being attended to and marked off as she accomplished each task.

The task at hand now, as they waited for dinner, was to locate and secure proper containers for the donated items. "We need to find the highest rated and most efficient repository for our budget," Madeline stated. Cynthia scooted her chair around the desk and sat close to Madeline so she could look on as they scoured the computer screens.

Madeline paused a moment. She seemed bothered by something. Madeline squirmed in her chair and stared at one of the computer screens as Cynthia leaned in closer. Madeline pushed herself back from the desk and rose to her feet.

"Are you all right, Madeline?"

"I'm fine. I just remembered something. I'll be right back," she mumbled as she climbed out from behind the desk and abruptly left the office.

Madeline stepped into the hall and leaned against the wall. Her heart was beating fast and she felt flushed. *What is wrong with me?* she grumbled to herself. She couldn't figure out why she suddenly felt so anxious and disturbed. She took a deep breath and closed her eyes. Memories from years before flooded her mind. She remembered sitting at her desk, six weeks pregnant, and dreaming of working alongside her daughter. *Where are these thoughts coming from?* she wondered aloud.

As Cynthia awaited Madeline's return, she walked the room and scanned the pictures hanging up and set atop the bookshelves.

Many of them were of Madeline alone. A couple shots included Danny, but those were work-related and conveyed no sense of connection or family. Cynthia looked for pictures of Madeline's family but only found a picture of Madeline's mom from thirty years before. It was a headshot and portrayed nothing out of the ordinary.

Who is Madeline? Why has the King brought us together? Cynthia looked closely at the photos of Madeline and her mother. They were both strikingly beautiful and very winsome, but there was an absence of connection with others. Cynthia picked up a shot of Madeline by herself in a stylish ski outfit, skis in hand, smiling on a snow-covered mountain.

"Park City, Utah. Great weekend. Lots of snow and tons of skiing," A newly composed Madeline said as she resumed her place behind the desk.

"Did you go alone?"

"Actually, I did. A boyfriend canceled at the last minute and left me hanging. But I thought, what the heck. Why not go and make a good memory of it? As I remember, it was the coldest winter in decades that year. Brrr," she said with a smile.

"Where I come from, mountains are covered with pure white snow that's not cold at all." Cynthia said, doing her best to bring the walls between them down. She gently returned the photo to its proper place and took her seat next to Madeline.

"That would be heavenly," Madeline muttered as she began typing on her keyboard.

Cynthia smiled. "I'd love to see you join me there when the time is right."

Madeline continued typing. "You know… let's just focus on getting these donated items out of here, ok? Oh, would you mind giving me a little elbow room? I'm feeling kinda cramped right now."

Cynthia smiled small and submissive and moved her chair around to the front of the desk, opposite of Madeline.

Terry Harris

The computer screens filled up with various nonprofits to contact as Madeline typed. "Looks like we have a few options. Let's get to work." Madeline turned one of the monitors around so Cynthia could follow along from her side of the desk.

Cynthia glanced at Madeline over the computer screen with a large grin. It was obvious an idea erupted inside her, and she couldn't resist announcing it. "Have you ever considered having a grand ball for all the children who have no parents?"

"*No!*" came a bark from the other side of the monitor.

"We could host it here at the park and ..."

"Cynthia, I said *no!*" There was a shocked pause before Madeline said, "I mean, Cindy ..."

Cynthia was taken back. She didn't know what to think or feel. The silence in the room was thick.

The phone rang, breaking the silence.

"Hello," Madeline muttered coldly into the receiver. "Send him up." She hung the phone up. "Food's here," she said toward Cynthia. She finished typing, then went to the door to retrieve dinner. She stopped at the door and turned around to say something to Cynthia.

Cynthia sat quietly in her chair with her back to Madeline.

Madeline chose to say nothing and exited the office to get the food.

A few days later, Cynthia arose early and walked to the beach. Then she made a brief stop at the chapel for a time of peaceful adoration of her beloved King.

When she sat down in a pew, she was tapped on the shoulder by Pastor Timothy. He grinned a peculiar smirk. "Hello, there. Remember me? We were going to get together."

"Of course, Pastor Timothy. I sincerely apologize. I did stop by to see you but was told you had left town."

"Oh yes, this is true. I, how do I say ..." He mumbled to himself in his native German. "... found myself rather perplexed after watching you sing."

"Oh?" Cynthia stood to her feet to hear more.

"I've never met anyone quite like you before. You seem so genuine in your faith. It appears so real to me, not like others I have known. Or myself, for that matter."

He hesitated, then peered into her eyes over his wire-rim glasses, which hung low on his nose. "You make me wonder about my own beliefs. That's why I had to take some time off. I needed time to …" He paused then emphasized the word dramatically. "*Think* about such matters."

Cynthia genuinely cared about the struggle he was bringing to light. "And?"

He held out both hands in exasperation. "You know something about this King that I do not know." He lowered his hands and sighed.

Cynthia's eyes moved from his face to the large crucifix at the front of the chapel. She whispered near his left ear. "He's alive!"

"Huh?" Timothy grunted.

She pointed to the crucifix and shook her head with a warm, convincing smile. "That's not Him. He's not on the cross anymore. Alive! I've seen Him."

The pastor turned and gazed at the figure hanging on the metal cross. She continued to smile on Him as she waited expectantly for an outburst of joyous validation. "It's true," she encouraged him.

The moment of stillness morphed into an awkward silence. Cynthia turned to the pastor and took inventory of his face.

He patted her on the arm and smiled. "You have given me much to consider. Thank you for coming in today." With that, he left her and meandered toward his tiny office.

Cynthia returned to the pew and poured out her heart to her King. He met her in her quest and encouraged her mightily.

Terry Harris

Later that afternoon, the phone in Radcliffe's office rang. It was his cell. He scowled as he recognized the number. "What is it?" he demanded as he put it on speaker phone.

"Daddy... I mean, Dad?"

Radcliffe paused. He did not care to hear the voice, and he certainly did not like the term. "What can I do for you, Deidre?"

"We need to talk. It's about Eunice and this girl Cindy."

His nose twitched. He was now indignant. "What about her?"

"Can we meet someplace? I think you should know what's going on."

"I'm sure we can discuss it now, over the phone. Just tell me what's on your mind."

"Did you know she's living with us?" He didn't, but he refused to admit it.

"I had my suspicions."

"Well, anyway, Aunt Eunice... she's different now. She's praying and talking to us about weird stuff. I'm really worried about Portia. She's not herself. She doesn't text the way she used to, she doesn't talk the way she used to ... I'm afraid this Cindy is brainwashing everybody."

Radcliffe conceived an idea as she was bantering on. "On second thought, yes, let's meet. I'll see you at Dickeys' Café on the fifties lot tomorrow morning at nine. Don't be late." He hung up the phone.

His eyes twinkled. The plan that he had just conceived was now birthing itself into a full-blown strategy to not only disgrace the pesky brunette they called Cindy, thereby removing her from her throne, but perhaps even take down Madeline at the same time. He was so excited he worried he might not sleep that night.

That next morning, Radcliffe gathered himself and made his way to the lot. He had slept well and so he was full of an unusual amount of energy. He loved removing obstacles that stood in the way of his complete and total control. This descendant of a

Neanderthal was going to lose her place as ambassador quicker than she had ascended to it.

Deidre found him sitting at a table in the corner of the café, looking mean and inattentive.

"Hello, Daddy."

"Sit down and stop calling me that."

She took her seat.

He refused to look at her and said nothing for a long moment.

She pulled out Cynthia's leather-bound Scriptures and slid it over to him. "I found this in her room. It looked kind of different to me, so I thought you might like to see it."

His eyes enlarged a bit then his eyebrows furled when he saw what it was. He detested Scripture and was opposed to its existence. Something about this book made him curious, though. He scanned it briefly and noted the ancient plant-type pages. He also noted the receipt from his coin store, which had served as a bookmark.

He groused. "Probably nothing, but I'll look into it." He shoved the book into his satchel and slid the coffee he had been sipping to the side. He leaned in so he could whisper, "I have a job for you."

His whisper was soft, so she leaned closer. He could tell she was trying to avoid his offensive breath, but he didn't care and chose to breathe even harder as he unveiled his plan.

10

CYNTHIA ROSE EARLY THAT MORNING AND ENJOYED A melodious time of singing and communicating with her King. She sat in the windowsill and gazed out across the majestic blue ocean. She drew a deep breath and smiled. Chills ran up her spine as commanding waves of seawater crashed on the shoreline and roared like a proud lion. Farther out, the sea appeared to be calm. She marveled at how the sun rays danced across the water and caused it to sparkle like a diamond ring under a brilliant light. It reminded her of how the light in Paradise glistened off the pure blue sea. She felt homesick.

The beauty of her Lord's creation implored her to draw near, so she slipped into her sandals and went to grab her Bible. It wasn't there. She looked high and low but did not find the book. After several moments, she sat down and wondered what could have happened to it.

Her spirit was bothered. It was such an essential part of her life on Earth. Where could it be? *Had someone taken it?* That thought scared her. She was not familiar with the feeling of being violated. Then, darker thoughts penetrated her mind. She was vulnerable. If someone did take it, what could she do about it? What *should* she do about it? She felt out of control again.

Oh, how she disliked those emotions. They were uncomfortable and unfamiliar.

She returned to the window and knelt down and prayed. She prayed a long while until, finally, the burden of fear lifted from her spirit. She broke out in a song of worship and enjoyed the beauty of her Lord's presence in her spirit.

She decided to seek help from Eunice to find a new copy of the Scriptures. Surely someone on this planet had another copy of the holy book.

She rose to her feet and made her way downstairs. Eunice was on the phone in a deep conversation with a friend. Cynthia pointed to the beach and waved goodbye. She would talk with Eunice later about helping her find her lost Bible, or perhaps how to acquire a new one.

The walk to the beach was pleasant and rewarding. The ocean breeze was a godsend. It had a certain feel of security to it, a tingling sense that everything would be okay. She was not alone. She was a child of destiny. She opened her arms wide and let her skin enjoy the salty air. She removed her shoes and placed her bare feet on the sand. It was still rough to the touch, though not as rough as the first time she stepped on it. Her feet were now calloused a bit, and the gritty shore was less annoying. Cynthia casually flung her sandals back and forth as she strolled the water's edge.

Spotting the perfect resting place, she plopped down on the warm sand and studied her painted toenails. They were a bright color depicting a sunrise. She liked it. She never had a pedicure before, but it was something she and Eunice had done together a few days back. She gazed once again at the horizon.

She got lost in the steady ripples of sea and meditated on her journey. She contemplated her newly formed relationships from her journey to find her parents.

She thought about Madeline and their developing relationship. Cynthia dismissed the thought of Madeline being her mom for two reasons: First, Madeline wasn't anything like the person who was described to her by her friends in Paradise. She wasn't the great lover of children who sacrificed her life to help those in need. Second, Cynthia didn't feel any connection with Madeline. She assumed that she would know her mother by trusting her feelings, naively using her untrained faith to guide her.

Cynthia's thoughts then turned to Eunice. Could it be possible that Eunice had unknowingly gotten pregnant sometime in her past and conceived her? There definitely was a connection between them, but her biggest question was why was the process taking so long? She wished Sebastian would just show up and point her in the direction of her parents. She missed him and Angela so much. She loved being goodwill ambassador for Ziggy's, but she was confused on what it had to do with her reason for being here on Earth.

"Cindy!" She turned to see it was Bobby. Her feelings became a jumbled ball of string. Uncertainty about how she should react to him caused her to pause a brief moment.

She rose and greeted him coolly. "Hello, stranger."

"Ouch! I was hoping to be more than that to you by now," he said, his tone playful.

"Me too." She smiled sadly and looked down. For some reason she sank her feet into the sand, not wanting to show him her painted toes.

He pulled out a box of Cracker Jacks that he had been toting in his back pocket. "Here, bought these for you."

"Cracker Jacks? Are you sure? These are your favorite."

"See what's inside."

She pulled back the cardboard top that had been opened and nearly half of the popcorn treat had been eaten. She smiled.

On top of the caramel corn laid a small prize packet. She pulled it out. "What's this?"

He moved closer to her and touched her hand that was holding the gag gift. "A prize worth keeping."

She opened it and pulled out a smiley-face sticker. "Oh, how cute."

"That day I dropped you off at your house, you kind of lost your smile. I figure I had something to do with that, so I thought I'd help you find it again."

"Thank you." She leaned in and kissed him gently on the cheek.

"Listen, I came down here to pick you up. Madeline has a gig she wants you to speak at. I guess she's being detained as a keynote at some big-shot breakfast this morning…"

"Oh?"

"And … I'm your escort."

"I'm glad to hear that." She smiled and moved her dark hair behind one ear. "What kind of gig am I speaking at?"

"Some kind of beach concert down the road a few miles to feed orphan kids in Africa. A bunch of high school kids will be there from all over the county, and you have been designated as the special celebrity guest of honor."

"I guess we should go, then."

"Actually, it's not until later. I showed up a little early hoping we could, you know, spend that day together that I kinda blew."

"I'm delighted you came early. What should we do?"

He grinned. "How about we start with a morning stroll?"

"Perfect." She offered him some Cracker Jacks as they headed west. "How did you know where to find me?"

"I have great instinct for the whereabouts of pretty ladies. Especially those who like Cracker Jacks."

"Eunice told you?"

"Yep." They shared a laugh and a friendly shoulder bounce. "Follow me, my lady," he said with the awkward smirk of a kid who just got a date with the prettiest girl in the class.

They walked side by side along the seashore. The morning turned out to be a whirlwind of fun. They did just about everything that came to mind. Bobby helped her catch sand crabs, find perfectly shaped seashells, build a somewhat dilapidated and deplorable sandcastle, and even made sand angels, in which Cynthia etched certain details that reminded her of the angels she had grown to love.

When they arrived at lifeguard tower number nine, Bobby froze, and the giggling abruptly stopped.

Sensing his sudden change in demeanor, Cynthia asked, "What's wrong?"

Looking pensively at the tower, Bobby replied, "A sad ending of happily ever after."

"I'm sorry," Cynthia sincerely apologized, not wanting to pry.

"All right." He took a deep breath and let it out with a sigh. "You want the Cracker Jack version of the worst day of my life?"

"If it would help you, sure."

"Met the girl of my dreams on a shoot. Last day of the job. One of my very first paid gigs as a photographer. It was for a kid's summer school event at a private school. She was nice. I was funny. We connected and dated for about sixteen months. I felt this was it, you know. This was the girl." He paused. "She was kind of like you."

"In what way, Bobby?"

"She kinda taught me about God and all that. A greater purpose, you know?" He waited for her to respond but she just prayed. Cynthia sensed that meeting Bobby was a divine appointment and there was something special that her King wanted for him and maybe even for her. She longed to draw close to him and get to know him in a deeper way; something more than friends. Her body surged with waves of unfamiliar feelings and desires but as much as all that felt good and enticing, the timing wasn't right, and she knew it.

Bobby abruptly continued his story. "Anyway, one day when we were supposed to spend the day together, she called me and…"

"What's her name?" Cynthia asked just above a whisper.

"Julia Caldwell. Strawberry blonde. Cute as can be. So, she called me and said something had come up and that we would have to put our 'friendship' on hold. I couldn't believe what I was hearing. Friendship? Really? A year and half of giving her everything and sharing what we shared, and she refers to me as her friend?" Bobby's anger subsided and his voice softened. "Anyway, this is where I first told her that I loved her. After she broke up with me, I came down here and threw a gift she gave me right into the ocean."

"What was it?" Cynthia inquired.

"Oh, just a key chain with a Bible verse about love on it. The last thing I wanted was a constant reminder of the pain she caused me."

Cynthia listened closely but felt there was more to Julia's side of the story.

"I'm sorry. That must've been so difficult."

He picked up right where he left off with the story, appearing to have not really heard her. "So I made the decision to just write it off as a fun time with a friend and move on."

"And you were able to do so? Just like that?"

"Sure!" He paused and gulped.

Cynthia could sense it. "And what about God? What did you decide about Him?"

"I decided to pour everything I am into my photography and forget about her and the whole God thing. If that's the way that those people act, then I don't want any part of it."

She just stared at him, giving him a moment to process it all.

He seemed uncomfortable with the silence. "That was it. Moved on with my life."

"I'm not sure you have moved on, Bobby." Cynthia paused. "Do you ever think about calling Julia to see how she's doing?"

"Not a chance. What makes you think I haven't moved on?"

"Aren't you the slightest bit curious as to why Julia called you that day? Surely, there was a valid reason she called you."

"Yeah, she found some other guy."

"Are you sure? Or, maybe there was something in her life she was afraid to share with you."

"Like what?"

"I think you need to find out for yourself. You deserve to know. You were in love with this girl." Cynthia cringed a little when she said those words.

"Four years is too long."

"Perhaps. Perhaps not." She paused then decided to bring up the issue of God again. "And your relationship with the King. Did it survive the breakup?"

"You'd have to ask Him. I felt He left me that day too."

She placed her hand across his shoulders. "I can assure you that's not the case."

"How can you be so sure?"

"I know Him. He never leaves His own. You can give Him a call too." Cynthia playfully smiled at him. "He'd love to hear from you."

A strong wave rolled up on them and splashed against their feet. Bobby realized time was flying by and they needed to get to their destination.

"Come on. Time to go," Bobby said, hoping they were finished with the conversation.

"On one condition."

Bobby shrugged, a little irritated.

Cynthia felt moved to press it a bit more. "Do yourself a favor. Find out why she called you that day."

He sighed.

"If nothing else it will give you the answer you need to hear. You'll be free to love someone else." She wanted to include herself in that statement but decided to stop there.

Bobby smiled and took her by the arm and escorted her up the beach. "We'll see."

Madeline was on stage speaking to over fifteen-hundred bored teenagers, doing her best to buy time when Bobby and Cynthia showed up at a makeshift stage. They were several minutes late. Madeline hated tardiness, especially when it reflected a bad image on her or Ziggy's.

Bobby took Cynthia by the hand and helped her up onto the platform. Madeline spied the two holding hands and made some quick assumptions. She finished her remarks on Ziggy's new mission of being a philanthropic theme park and introduced Cynthia. "You know her from social media with over a hundred million views! Now, as promised, here is our goodwill ambassador, Cindy Hope."

Madeline extended an inviting hand to Cynthia, but when Cynthia took her hand, Madeline pulled her close. Madeline pretended to kiss her on the cheek but instead growled in her ear. "Don't ever be late again."

Cynthia addressed the students and, when the polite applause died down, she passionately spoke to the boys and girls of eight local high schools about making a difference by putting others first. Students and various representatives from the local press took photographs as well as video and audio recordings.

Madeline stepped off the stage and quickly found Bobby, who was busy capturing stills of Cynthia speaking. She grabbed his arm and pulled him to the back of the stage.

"I thought you were a professional," she scolded. "I have been calling you for over thirty minutes. A professional shows up on time. I didn't hire you so you could find your next girlfriend. She works for me and so do you. You fail me again and I find a new…"

"Madeline, I…"

"Bobby! What's up, bro?" Bobby was interrupted by a stout man in his mid-thirties with wavy blonde hair that would fall down only to get flipped up time and again.

"Hayden. How are you, man?" They performed a routine embrace by gripping each other with their right hand and power embracing with their left arm, almost like a chest bump.

"Look, it's not the best time right now," Bobby said, watching Madeline out of one eye.

"That's okay," Madeline replied coldly. "We're done here. Bobby. I want to see you and Cindy in my office when this is over." She briskly walked away as she headed to her car.

Cynthia had the large group of teenagers listening intently but hesitated mid-sentence when Hayden pushed his way to the edge of the stage. He grinned a sideways smile and snapped up a bunch of close ups, leaving her with an unsettled feeling in her spirit. He winked but she quickly looked away.

Moments later, Cynthia finished her remarks and stepped back from the mic. The crowd cheered for several moments. They asked for a song. Cynthia was slow to respond but after a few chants of "Cindy! Cindy! Cindy!" she saw the band standing off stage, looking on. They offered her smiles of encouragement and a thumbs up.

She stepped up to the mic and began an acapella version of a song about one's journey through life, based on the beloved poem "Footprints in the Sand."

The crowd's chatter silenced. After the first verse they cheered her on to continue. She felt awkward but closed her eyes and moved into the second verse.

Though the depth of the lyrics were still a bit out of her experience, she felt the spirit within her provide the means for connection to the words. Her voice rang loud through the speakers and her emotion moved the audience to a stunning silence. The band stepped in and, with a soft interlude, picked up on the melody and carried her through the entire song.

When the song concluded, a large crowd rushed the stage and jockeyed for position up close. The pushing and shoving was nerve-wracking for Cynthia.

Hayden forced his way in and captured some unflattering shots of her grimacing and trying to hold herself up. Bobby stepped in and created space for her.

She tried to tend to the kids who were calling out her name, but it became far too difficult. It was something of a rock-star experience. For a woman who had never had her picture taken before she met Bobby, it was a baptism of fire. Cynthia felt compelled to try to meet those who called her name and begged for her time.

Untold numbers of girls and boys pushed their way just to get a picture with her. She resisted the demand of some of them to stand in questionable poses and had to turn her back on the groupies. This did not fare well with them. They suddenly threw vulgar names at her. She wanted to answer the accusations of the indignant fans, so she tried to speak to them, but they just held their phones up, filming her and the confusion around them. She realized they had no interest in hearing her out and felt panic surge through her body.

Bobby came to her side and worked hard to keep her safe. He finally got her off the stage and away from the screaming fans. He pointed to a city bus that was about to make a stop along the nearby highway and rushed her across the sandy beach. They arrived just in time to jump on board and leave the madness behind. Passengers on the bus stared at her. Some recognized her and shared whispers of gossip with each other. She felt at odds with the strangers who gawked at her. They gazed as though she were an idol of sorts, and she didn't like it.

The crowd she had just escaped stirred feelings of paranoia and isolation, and now she had to deal with being ogled like a desired commodity. She looked away, unsure of where to rest her eyes. In her heart she was both grateful and saddened that the passengers chose to leave her alone.

Bobby and Cynthia eventually made their way back to his truck and then drove straight to Ziggy's. They parked in the first spot they found and hurried across Ziggy's to Madeline's office. Cynthia paused and looked at Bobby. "Bobby, I don't want Madeline to know about what happened at the beach this afternoon."

Bobby seemed a bit uncertain but eventually shrugged in agreement. She smiled and squeezed his hand as they entered Madeline's doorway.

Down the hall in Radcliffe's gloomy office, an email from Hayden arrived in his inbox. After his encounter with Madeline and Cynthia in Danny's office, Radcliffe had hired people he felt could help him take the princess out once and for all. He opened the email and scoured the plethora of shots, looking for something specific.

Moments later he emitted a happy grunt. His chin nearly folded into itself as he beamed a nasty smirk.

"Those are my money shots." He looked intently at the close ups of Cynthia grimacing and the videos of angry fans calling her out for rejecting their demands. He fantasized about what could be done to the images with the help of Photoshop. He created an email with definitive instructions and attached the shots he wanted to be used. After he hit send, he slapped his stubby hands together and coughed out a laugh.

❧ 11 ❧

IT WAS LATE WHEN MADELINE, CYNTHIA, BOBBY, AND Danny finished their meeting that night. They shared a Chinese dinner in Danny's office and laid out plans for the next several months of public appearances. Invitations were pouring in from around the country. Social media was blowing up and Ziggy's was gaining enormous attention. Visits to the website were up more than 500 percent. Twitter, Instagram, and Facebook followers were through the roof. The numbers for the park were up nearly thirteen percent and showed no signs of slowing down. They were celebrating their success when Madeline got a text from an employee urging her to look at Ziggy's social media.

Madeline opened Instagram and was shocked to see one of many unattractive candid shots of Cynthia in the midst of the frenzied crowd. The pictures were disturbing.

"When were you planning on telling me about this?" She spun the laptop around so all could see the less-than-complimentary shot of Cynthia. Madeline eyed Bobby and Cynthia suspiciously and waited impatiently.

"Things got a little crazy today," Bobby said slowly.

Madeline scrolled through several more shots that were unnerving and frightening. She gasped.

Cynthia shot a glance towards Bobby and started to speak, but Madeline blurted out first. "Walter!"

Danny looked at her curiously.

Madeline walked the laptop over to his desk and flipped through the pictures she had just seen. She had recently begun having nightmares of something bad happening to Cynthia, something of considerable consequence that she couldn't stop or control. She couldn't make sense of it. She had no rational explanation for the fear but now paranoia began to lure her into its dreadful web, and she hated it. She had spent much of her time trying to figure out ways to not lose her.

Madeline referred to the photo of the chaos on her laptop and the lewd comments and death threats that were below it.

"I think we should hire security for her. Twenty-four seven," she said to Danny as though Cynthia wasn't in the room.

"How much will *that* cost me?" Danny interjected. Madeline ignored him.

"I'm quite happy with Bobby and Eunice as my companions, thank you," Cynthia said.

Madeline did not like the idea of Bobby and Eunice being the only protection for her, especially in light of what she suspected was going on between Cynthia and Bobby. "No, I'm not happy with that idea. Bobby, you said yourself that today got out of hand."

"It was a little crazy," he agreed.

"This looks like more than just a little," Madeline shot back.

"What exactly would this twenty-four-seven security be like?" Cynthia asked when she moved close to Madeline.

Bobby answered for her. "It's like a millstone around your neck."

Madeline shot a dagger at Bobby with her eyes.

Cynthia turned to Madeline and Danny. "I'm sorry, but I have absolutely no interest in having a bodyguard hover around me as though I were a prisoner."

"I'm sure there's another way," Cynthia stated emphatically, with the firmness that Madeline respected so much in her. "I'm afraid I'll have to insist on it."

Suddenly, Madeline no longer appreciated Cynthia's firm resolve, now that it was being used against her.

Silence filled the room. Madeline got the last word. "It's not negotiable, Cindy."

"I'll agree to it on one condition," Cynthia stated firmly. "He'll stand watch outside the house only. No following me in cars or shadowing me on my walks down the beach."

"Deal!" Madeline said, giving in.

Danny silently shook his head in surrender.

The following day, Cynthia asked Eunice to take her to the hospital to see the children. She had not visited the hospital since learning that Logan had left. As they exited the house, they were met by a tall man dressed in a dark shirt. The man introduced himself as the hired security guard and asked them where they were going.

Cynthia politely told them, "The hospital," and the man promised that he would remain at his post awaiting the women's returned.

"Thank you. We're grateful that you're here..." Cynthia said, unconvincingly.

Eunice and Cynthia climbed into the car. Eunice backed out and drove down the street. She peered over Cynthia.

"You look exhausted, Cindy,"

"I'm all right."

Eunice squeezed her hand in encouragement.

Cynthia gazed out the window. "How do you know when it's time to move in a different direction? I'm so busy working for

Ziggy's I have no time to find my family. I feel terrible saying that because of all the people I've met since I started working there."

"You have helped so many people, Cindy. You certainly have helped me and Portia. We've never had a relationship like we have today … and it's because of you."

"I'm only a vessel."

"I really want to help you, Cindy," Eunice said, touching Cynthia's arm. "Maybe I can help you find your parents." It came out of her mouth with less zeal than she intended.

"How?"

Eunice hesitated. "Well, I can do most of the searching online. Remember Palmer Labs has been sponsors of Ziggy's for some time now. They help people find their families every day."

Cynthia glanced out the window at the people in the cars next to them. She looked back at Eunice. "You don't have to do that."

"Please let me do that for you," Eunice said. "You've done so much for me. While you do your princess gig, I'll do the research, and then we'll go over it together and see what we find."

"You would help me with that?"

"I'm on it, girl. And after we've scoured the world, if nothing emerges, I just might adopt you myself." Eunice waited, tight-lipped, for Cynthia to respond.

A squeeze of her hand and a grateful smile told Eunice that Cynthia appreciated the spirit behind Eunice's good intentions.

The possibilities of how this could work streaked across Eunice's mind faster than she could process. But at the same time her heart was torn between wanting to find Cynthia's parents and the prospect of losing her. She had become such a blessing to her.

A worship song came on the radio and Cynthia sang along. Eunice started singing along with her. The more they sang, the better they felt.

The two sang in unison as they drove down the highway in the convertible VW.

When they arrived at the hospital, there was a huge commotion. Nurses were rushing about pushing two gurneys with two small infants. Cynthia and Eunice caught a glimpse of them. They were twins, of Asian descent, and looked sickly; one was turning blue.

Cynthia approached a nurse at the desk and asked about the babies. The nurse had been following Ziggy's social media and was a huge fan of Cynthia's, so she shed as much light on the situation as she legally could letting Cynthia know that the babies were abandoned in a nearby dumpster and left to die.

Cynthia watched in agony as the doctors tended to the babies. The sounds of heart monitors and breathing apparatus unnerved her soul. Her eyes peered through the ER's glass window, searching for any sign of hope that all would be well. Her heart was conflicted and confused.

Soon she became overwhelmed and quickly made her way to the small chapel on the third floor and found a place to pray at a front pew. She prayed, and then she prayed some more. Her strength was waning, and she could feel it. Eunice sat next to her, quiet.

"I hope it's ok with you. I texted Madeline and let her know where you were in case she needed you. She'll be here shortly."

Cynthia nodded with appreciation and resumed praying.

Moments later Madeline arrived, with Danny beside her. Madeline sat down next to Cynthia and hugged her. Feeling her embrace, Cynthia wept. The picture in her mind of those sweet girls not being able to breathe haunted her. Somehow in Madeline's arms she felt it was okay to be weak and that brought more tears. Madeline held her tight as Cynthia's body convulsed uncontrollably.

Cynthia recovered herself and was the first to let go from the hug. To her surprise, Madeline kept her grip tight and kissed her on the top of her head. Cynthia pulled away. "I'm sorry, Madeline. I really couldn't help myself."

"No, that's okay, Cindy. That had to be hard seeing those babies struggling to breathe." Madeline's voice quivered, and her glistening eyes were filled with compassion.

"I've… I've never really had to see this side of their pain before. I've always been on the other side when they arrived," Cynthia said without thinking as she wiped away her tears.

"Arrived? Where, Cindy?" Madeline asked. Danny and Eunice waited for the answer as well.

Cynthia realized she was speaking of the role she once had in Paradise at the Gate of Entry. *Was that role she loved so much forever gone?* she wondered. *Was she stuck down here with no way back?* And then a terrorizing thought rumbled inside her psyche, shaking her to the core: *Was she going to die?*

She jumped into the aisle and fled the chapel. Finding the stairwell exit, she dashed to the first floor and through the doors to outside. She sucked up as much fresh air as she could. Panic had stricken her, and she shook like a scared child. *Where are these thoughts coming from?* She repeatedly asked herself.

Eventually Madeline, Danny, and Eunice found her sitting on a bench outside the hospital. She had begun to recover from her panic and sat quietly whispering prayers of hope and thankfulness.

"Cindy? Are you all right?" Madeline asked with obvious concern.

"I think so. I can't explain what happened to me up there, but I'm better now."

"Would you like me to take you home?" Eunice asked.

"That's a good idea," Madeline said. "Why don't you come home with me, and you can relax. I'll cancel your meetings for the afternoon. I've got some comfortable clothes you can slip into."

Madeline smiled at Eunice, who looked a little taken back. Then Madeline turned to Danny. "Would you mind if Eunice drove you back to the office? I'm going to take Cindy home with me."

Danny was caught off guard and eyed the VW. "In that?"

"Yeah, great idea, don't you think?" Madeline quipped. "Do you mind, Eunice?"

"No … no, not at all."

"Good. Thank you. Come on, Cindy."

With that, they all parted ways.

On the way home, Madeline called Danny's cell. "I have an idea. Wanna see me shock Danny?" she asked Cynthia as she waited for Danny to pick up.

Cynthia was unsure of what to say. "Um, why not?"

Danny answered his phone. "Yes?!"

"Hey, why don't you join us for dinner tonight at my place?"

"Uh, at your house?" Danny stammered. "With you and Cindy?"

"Yes. Of course."

Her casual reply made it seem as though this was a common occurrence. They listened for Danny's response. It was slow to come.

"Um. Okay. Sure," Danny finally said. "What time?"

"Six sharp, please."

"Okay."

Madeline ended the call with a smile of accomplishment. "I have a sneaking suspicion my ex-husband is a bit befuddled."

Cynthia grinned with confusion.

Madeline drove her BMW SUV into a large circle driveway that was kept secure by oversized gates made of wrought iron and painted black and gold. The driveway was broad with a perfectly manicured green lawn supporting it. The exterior of the mansion boasted large gneisses stones. It was like a castle yet felt very inviting. *Madeline has excellent taste*, Cynthia thought as she climbed out of the car and surveyed the estate's beauty. The front door was tall and wide with large door knockers giving it a portrayal of royalty. "Everything is so beautiful, Madeline. It reminds me of home."

"Thank you." Madeline turned on the lights with a remote, and the living room with its high ceilings and white-carpeted floor lit up. The bright light of the chandeliers looked like crystal candles.

"Care for a cold drink? Lemonade? Tea?"

"I'll take whatever you're having. Thank you."

"You're easy," Madeline replied as she sauntered into the kitchen. It was spacious and bright with the finest marble a kitchen could display. Off to the side was a wooden table configured similar to those in ancient Middle East times. It allowed its occupants to sit in a semicircular fashion.

Cynthia stood near the table, thinking about home, when Madeline interrupted her thoughts. "Make yourself comfortable on the patio while I make you my favorite tea in the world."

"Do you cook?" Cynthia asked as she scouted the intricate detail of each kitchen appliance, all perfectly matched colors and styles.

Madeline laughed. "Uh, no! But I can do tea." She put the kettle on the stove. "I'll order in for dinner."

Cynthia casually found her way to the patio and opened the door. The view was breathtaking. The backyard had perfectly groomed trees and bushes, with a steep drop-off revealing a beautiful white sand beach. The deep, blue ocean extended out as far as you could see. Cynthia leaned against the wall of the patio and took a deep breath. She instantly liked where she was. In a small way it had the feel of where she had come from. Beauty and majesty stretched out before her, beckoning her soul to rest and enjoy it all.

She uttered words of prayer as emotions swelled up inside her. She shuddered in fear when she began to reflect on what had happened a few hours earlier and she didn't understand the wave of emotions that were hitting her.

She missed Sebastian, the citizens of Heaven, and the exquisite beauty and perfection of Paradise. Above all, she missed her King. For some odd reason, she felt disconnected from Him, as though she had done something wrong and He was angry at her. A chill ran up her spine just as Madeline approached her with a glass of tea.

"You okay?" she asked. "That was quite a chill you just had. Let me get you a sweater."

"Okay," she hesitantly replied. "I feel a little tired. Would you mind if I took a nap?"

"Not at all. *Mi casa es tu casa.*"

"*Gracias, señorita,*" Cynthia responded with a perfect accent.

"You speak other languages?"

"*Maxime in prompt,*" she answered in Latin as she followed Madeline into the house.

Madeline walked Cynthia upstairs and sauntered to a guest bedroom. She found some comfortable-looking sleeping clothes and handed them to her. "Here, try these. They should fit you well."

It was a lovely guest bedroom, highlighted by a large bed with a goose-down comforter. "I'll wake you in a little while and then we'll have an early dinner with Danny."

"Could I ask a favor?"

"Ask away," Madeline offered.

"Would you check and see how the twins are doing? I'm deeply concerned."

"Of course. I'll have an update when you wake up."

Cynthia offered her hand to Madeline. "Thank you, Madeline. You've been such a dear friend to me today. I'm grateful for your compassion."

Madeline accepted the shake and smiled. "Sweet dreams," she said as she closed the door

Cynthia fell asleep quickly and slept for a couple hours. Her spirit struggled as she dreamed of the people she had met since arriving here. Every time she saw the face of a woman she had met, the woman said she was Cynthia's mother. The different men in her life all said that they were her father. Even Bobby claimed to be her dad. The nightmare seemed to repeat in her subconscious.

Interestingly, the only ones who were missing from her dream were Danny and Madeline. She finally awoke with a gasp when Radcliffe stared up at her over his glasses and barked, "I'm your father."

She found the bathroom and refreshed herself. She chose to stay in her borrowed clothes and made her way downstairs.

Danny and Madeline were standing in the kitchen, discussing business, when Cynthia poked her face around the corner. "Hello."

"Hi, sunshine," Danny said as he offered her the option of a glass of wine or a glass of tea to drink.

"Just tea, thank you."

"You were out for quite a while. I chose not to wake you," Madeline said warmly. "Dinner was just delivered. Shall we?" she asked. "Oh, and I called the hospital, and the twins are still in NICU but doing a lot better."

"I'm so glad to hear that! I must go see them first thing in the morning. Thank you, Madeline, for checking"

"Please, call me Mattie." She waved them toward the patio door where the food, still in to-go containers, sat on the outdoor table.

As they took their seats and draped their napkins across their laps, Cynthia paused. Madeline and Danny both started to dig into the food, but she waited. "Something wrong?" Madeline asked, swallowing her first bite of lemon chicken.

"May I give thanks, please?" Cynthia asked graciously.

Danny and Madeline exchanged looks and then set down their utensils. Cynthia offered a hand to Danny and then Madeline. Both hesitated then took the hand being offered them. Cynthia smiled, squeezed their hands tightly, and prayed. "Lord, thank You for the kindness of Madeline and Danny. They are so gracious and loving. We invite You to bless this meal that You have provided. May we honor You in our conversation. In Your name we pray, amen." When she finished, there was a long pause.

"Thank you, Cindy. That was very sweet of you."

She said nothing as she took her first bite and enjoyed the savory taste. It was delicious, but still did not compare to the food she ate in Paradise, at least as far as she could remember. Memories of that sacred place seemed to be diminishing for her.

"Cindy, where did you learn to speak so many languages fluently?" Madeline asked.

"From Sebastian. He taught me all of them. I have so many more to learn, I can't wait."

"Is he your father?" Danny asked.

"He's like a father to me. I love him dearly. But no, he's not my father… he's my guardian angel." Cynthia felt a bolt of anxiety shoot through her brain after those words left her lips.

Madeline furled her brow and quietly chewed her salad.

"Excuse me?" Danny insisted.

"You mean, *like* a guardian angel?" Madeline said.

"Actually, he is indeed an angel of a higher rank. I was blessed enough to have him care for me along with so many others, who did such a marvelous work." Cynthia didn't know why this information was spewing out of her, but it was. For some reason, her walls were down.

Danny glared at Madeline, as if wanting her to fix the situation. She shook her head and shrugged to indicate that she wasn't sure what to say or do.

"And are these others angels too?" Danny asked with impatience.

"Oh, no. They're like my sisters and brothers of sorts. But Angela and I are really close and–"

"Oh. That's nice. So, how do you know Angela? Friend-of-the-family kind of thing?" Madeline asked.

"I was assigned to care for her after she arrived. She's learned to help so many children who don't make it down here."

"What do you mean down here?" Danny asked slowly and deliberately, looking very closely at Cynthia.

"Earth."

Danny snapped his napkin in the air and replaced it on his lap. "Earth. Okay." Danny gave Madeline a "she's crazy" look and took another bite of dinner.

"How about your family? Where do your folks live?" Madeline asked.

"I'm not sure, really. I've been told they reside around here, but I haven't found them yet."

"When's the last time you saw them?" Madeline swallowed a bite of chicken and waited for an answer.

"Actually, I've never met them before. We were separated before birth. I'm here to find them."

"So, you're an alien orphan?" Danny quipped. There was a loud thud.

"Ow!" Danny grimaced and sneered at Madeline. He reached down and rubbed his leg.

"I don't feel like an orphan," Cynthia said, trying to not stare at Danny.

"What do you know about them? Anything?" Madeline stopped eating and focused on what she was saying.

"Oh, I've been told that they are absolutely divine. My father is like a king. He is so incredibly warm and caring and gives of himself and what he owns sacrificially. I've been told he is a great leader to many. In fact, under his employ are hundreds of hard-working souls. He cares for children as though they were his own … That's what I've been told."

Danny grunted. "Yeah, right," he said, then went back to eating. "Ouch!" Again, he glared a sneer at Madeline. "Will you stop kicking me, Mattie?"

"Oh, I'm sorry. Was I being *rude*?" She turned to Cynthia. "Sounds like a wonderful man. Perhaps he's a monarch or king of sorts. What do you know about your mother?"

Cynthia was wise to their skepticism but maintained her belief in who she had heard her mom and dad to be. "My mother, I am told, is a most beautiful woman with a heart of absolute gold. She cares for the weak and encourages the despondent. Above all, she loves her children with a pure heart and sacrifices dearly for them. She is a mother of many."

Danny choked on his food and proceeded to cough for the next several seconds.

"They sound like a lovely couple, Cindy," said Madeline. "I'm sure they are everything you say but I would encourage you to leave a little room for error in your assumptions of them. I'm certain they would be extremely grateful if you did."

"Look, Cindy," Danny said as he cleared his throat and swallowed some wine. "There's no way on God's green earth that two people can be as perfect as you're describing."

"Danny, they're her parents. She's entitled to her opinions of them," Madeline chided firmly.

"I'm just saying. Angels and aliens … now we got kings and queens for parents and …"

Cynthia was being tested but remained calm. "I believe everything I was told about my father and mother. If that bothers you, or anyone else, for that matter, well then, I'm sorry, but it's what I've been taught is true, and I believe it is so."

"I don't care what you say, no such parent exists," Danny interjected while taking another bite.

"Perhaps if you had children you would think differently," Cynthia said with less patience than she cared to display.

"Well, you'd be surprised to hear that I am a father, or was, kind of. I had a stepson for three years during my second marriage, and I can tell you for certain that the people you're describing do not exist."

"Walter!" Madeline said with a chastising tone. "Where's this coming from?" She turned to Cynthia. "We really wanted kids and tried to get pregnant, Cindy, and it just didn't work for us."

Danny was agitated. "Whoa, wait a minute. You said you were glad that we never had kids!"

Madeline responded in anger. "Really, Danny? You're kidding, right? I said that I was glad we never had kids because of the *divorce*. Geez, Danny, you can be so clueless!"

Cynthia felt the heat build but did not pray. Instead, she got caught up in the tension and began to resent Danny.

"Well, my sperm count was fine," Danny replied smugly.

"I can't believe you just said that." Madeline stared at him with hurt in her eyes.

"I don't need this. I don't need any of this. And guess what! I don't have to take this anymore! Enjoy your dinner with Alien Girl." Danny jumped up and tossed the napkin down. He took several steps, stopped, and turned around. It seemed as though he was going to apologize, but he didn't.

"We are done talking about this, Ms. Brewer." He cocked his head toward Cynthia. "In my office first thing in the morning, we'll see if you're still qualified to represent Ziggy's." With that, Danny left.

Cynthia squeezed Madeline's hand.

Madeline looked away. "Cindy, I'm so sorry you had to see that. We have a long, painful history. I should take you home. Why don't you change, and I'll meet you out front."

Madeline rose and left Cynthia sitting alone on the patio. Cynthia had never felt so unsure of herself or her purpose on Earth. It haunted her.

On the drive home, Cynthia attempted to console Madeline about the dinner conversation, but Madeline wouldn't go there. Madeline couldn't help but think through all that was said and decided that Cynthia must have some sort of mental illness. Madeline was mad at herself for trusting Bobby to do a thorough background check. She was conflicted about what to do next. Ziggy's was deeply committed to using her to promote the park and she couldn't pull her out of her engagements now.

Since Cynthia's latest speech, invitations were coming in by the dozens. Several new hospitals called, as did girls' clubs, high schools, and corporations. Madeline was smart and knew that Cynthia's popularity would soon fade, and once it did, she would let her go quickly and quietly. Until then, she would use Cynthia's newfound fame to Ziggy's advantage and do her best to keep the truth hidden from the public. It wasn't long before Madeline's thoughts returned to promoting the park, and at this point, her ideas still included Cynthia.

"I keep thinking it's time for us to do something special at Ziggy's for the kids. We did such a great thing with the food and jackets, and I feel like we can do more, you know?" Madeline surprised herself at how keenly interested she was in helping people she didn't know and from whom she would never receive anything in return. There was something about helping others that had become addictive.

"What is an event you would love to see Ziggy's host? Something that could really make a difference for a lot of people who need our help?"

"A grand ball for every child who has ever wanted a parent but never had one," Cynthia said with a burst of enthusiasm.

Madeline had forgotten that Cynthia made this same request in her office weeks earlier, a request that irritated her for some unexplainable reason.

"An orphans' ball?"

"Absolutely!" Cynthia said, smiling as she gazed out the windshield. "Imagine Ziggy's hosting a ball that brought together children and parents who have never known each other. Young girls dancing for the first time with the father they've never had."

"How in the world would we pull off something like that?" Madeline teetered on regret over asking the question.

"It would take some work, but I would be willing to do it all. Eunice says there are websites that specialize in finding parents for children who are looking for them and finding children for parents who may be looking for their kids. We could contact every adoption office and work with the foster-care centers."

Madeline was abruptly struck with an idea and turned to look at Cynthia. "Cindy, we have a longtime sponsor at Ziggy's who does DNA testing that might be able to help you look for your parents. The woman who manages it is a friend of mine, and I can call her for you if..."

"Mattie! Look out!"

Madeline was so busy staring at Cynthia that she ran the red traffic light in front of her. An elderly woman stepped out into the crosswalk and started crossing without paying attention. Madeline slammed on her brakes and swerved the SUV to miss the woman, running over the curb and stopping just inches from a palm tree.

"Cindy! Are you all right?" Madeline screamed.

Cynthia didn't answer but hopped out of the car and ran to the fallen woman who lay helpless in the barren street. The moon was shining off the ocean and provided light in addition to the overhead streetlamp.

Cynthia reached down to help the lady but got her hand slapped away. The woman rose to her feet and started to yell at Cynthia and Madeline.

"Crazy stupid driver!"

"Violet!" Cynthia exclaimed.

"You know this lady? Is she okay?" Madeline asked frantically.

"Princess?" Violet asked.

"Are you okay? Where on Earth have you been? I haven't seen you for so long," Cynthia exclaimed while brushing Violet's hair back and straightening her dirty blouse. Violet appeared unharmed.

"Got my whiskey?" she grumbled.

"Cindy, what's going on? Who is this woman?"

"She's a friend. I'll explain later. We must help her find shelter for tonight." Cynthia attempted to find Violet a place to stay and some clean clothes, but Violet would have nothing to do with it. She asked for money for whiskey and when she didn't get it, she took off hobbling down the beach sidewalk.

Though it didn't turn out the way she wanted, Cynthia was happy she got to see Violet again, knowing the sweet old woman was still wandering around the area.

On the drive home, Cynthia told Madeline of her encounter with Violet at the coin shop and the clothing boutique. She didn't mention the name of the coin shop for some reason, nor did she mention the names of the girls who worked at the boutique.

Madeline pulled up to Eunice's house. Cynthia climbed out of the car and said goodnight but then turned back before closing the door. "Mattie?"

"Yes."

"I'm sorry you and Danny didn't get to have children. I think you would make an extraordinary mother. Thank you for the dinner and the hospitality." Cynthia closed the door.

Madeline paused and said goodnight. Cynthia watched her back out of the driveway and drive off.

She then turned and walked towards the well-lit house, nodding to the lone security guard sitting on the porch.

Eunice was waiting for her inside the house.

She had been doing research on various family locator websites and had purchased a DNA kit. She explained to Cynthia that there wasn't much detailed information on the last name of Hope in the area. Its roots were Scottish and English and did not carry much to the United States in recent decades. In fact, there were no younger families with that last name within a couple hundred miles. This confused Cynthia. How could she be so far off course? This was where Sebastian had left her to find her roots. This was the area she felt called to.

Cynthia told Eunice about her idea for a grand ball for uniting families but wasn't sure if Madeline and Danny would go along with it. Eunice encouraged her to not give up on the idea of the dance so quickly. Perhaps in her efforts to connect other families she might meet her own.

Eunice explained there were many ways for professional organizations to locate families, sometimes through blood but most often just a saliva test. With this type of technology, a ball would be an ideal place for birth parents and adopted kids to meet for the first time.

"Who knows?" Eunice remarked. "This just might be the idea that will lead you to your parents."

"Madeline mentioned something about a friend of hers who does DNA testing. Do you think it's the same thing?"

"I don't know. Probably. I'm using Palmer Labs, who I think is still a sponsor at Ziggy's." She held up the kit that showed the

Palmer Labs logo. "Would you like to take the test and see what information comes back?"

"Sure. What would I have to do?" Cynthia asked, a bit excited and nervous.

Eunice grabbed a cotton swab and offered it to Cynthia. "Wipe the inside of your cheek with this."

Cynthia did as instructed and handed it back. "That's it?"

"Now we send it off and wait for the results." Eunice stuck the cotton swab into the bag that came with the DNA kit and slid it into the accompanying envelope.

Cynthia let out a sigh. "That simple, huh?"

"I guess so," said Eunice.

A surge of excitement ran through Cynthia's body. *What if…*

It was about midnight when a weary Cynthia climbed the stairs and crawled into bed. Before falling asleep, she prayed for Madeline and Danny and their broken hearts. She prayed for the children at the hospital, especially for the health of the twin girls. She asked for guidance and clarity and, above all, she asked for help in being obedient to the plan that was unfolding before her.

The saliva test gave her a newfound hope, and she was feeling both nervous and excited about it at the same time. She giggled in anticipation as she thought about what the results may reveal. She then pulled the blankets up to her chin and drifted off to sleep.

Miles away, Radcliffe's computer screen lit up with several mock images of social-media postings as they appeared in his inbox. The stories were scandalous and harmful to his employer, but he knew that in any great war, there were always casualties.

He was willing to see his longtime boss and conniving ex-wife take the fall. His position would be secured in the eyes of the clueless board of directors, catapulting him to a higher income and greater authority.

The plan to take down the princess from nowhere was set to launch. Its success was certain and unquestionable.

He responded to the email with one line: "Open the floodgates."

❦ 12 ❦

THE NEXT MORNING DANNY SAT AT HIS DESK PERUSING over several social media sites on his phone. He was waiting for Madeline.

She entered his office and before she closed the door, Danny confronted her.

"After the dinner fiasco last night, I went home and Googled 'Cindy Hope.' The first site I clicked on I found a video of the high school event she did at the beach."

He held up his phone, forcing Madeline to lean in for a closer look. There was Cynthia, in the midst of a crowd, pushing a girl off the stage. The expression on Cynthia's face looked like one of rage, but the video was grainy and jerky. The comments next to the picture suggested a duel personality for Ziggy's good-will ambassador.

He scrolled down and clicked on another site. This post had a sweet picture of Cynthia hugging the disabled boy, Logan, next to a still shot of her pushing the high school student. Following that post were the angry comments of trolls with ugly accusations.

Madeline was shocked.

"What's going on, Mattie?" Danny demanded as he handed her his phone, which displayed Ziggy's Twitter account with

#fakeprincess trending. The tweets called Cynthia a fake and said that Logan was a set-up for publicity.

Of the more than three hundred tweets in response, most called her names, challenged Ziggy's choice of an ambassador, and some even boasted that they knew Logan personally and said he wasn't really disabled. They accused the boy of lying, saying he had faked the whole thing for money.

"I … I don't know." She read more comments.

"What do you mean you don't know? It's your job to know. First last night, and now this. She's unstable, Madeline, and a liability. Didn't you check this girl out before you gave her the keys to the kingdom?" Danny got up from his chair and began to walk around the room, running his fingers through his hair.

"Yes, we checked her out. I had Bobby do the background on her before we signed the contract."

"Bobby? The photographer? Mattie! The guy's dizzy over this chick. Of course he's going to tell you she's cleared."

Madeline stood up abruptly and stared him down. "This is all bull, Danny, and you know it." She waved his phone in front of his nose. "You were there just like I was and saw what happened with that boy. Somebody is trying to take us down."

"This isn't like you, Mattie. You hardly know anything about this girl and suddenly she's traipsing all over the city speaking on our behalf, sleeping at your house, wearing your clothes. What's with you?"

"She is innocent, I'm telling you. She may have a couple screws loose, but she's a nice girl! Someone wants to ruin us, and this is their attempt to do so."

"Then I suggest you find out 'who' and get us out of this mess. This was all *your* idea." He grabbed his phone from her hand.

She glared at him in a way he had not seen for some time and stormed out. Danny sighed and plopped down in his chair.

Madeline made a beeline for her office and called Bobby.

"Hello," Bobby answered.

"Bobby? Madeline. You have exactly five seconds to tell me what the heck is going on with the social-media nightmare we're in surrounding Cindy."

"I ... I don't know. I just saw some of the posts myself and I have no idea where this stuff is coming ..."

"I'm paying you to know. I left you in charge of her that day, and now I'm looking at the worst publicity nightmare this company has ever seen. What exactly happened on the stage at the beach?"

"There was some pushing and shoving and kids trying to get selfies. I got her off the stage and put her on a bus." Bobby gulped.

"Where is she now?" Madeline demanded.

"I don't know. I haven't seen her. Look, Madeline. I'm really sorry, but I assure you what you see in those photos didn't take place that day on the beach. Someone's trying to mess her image up pretty bad."

"Just stay close in case I need you." Madeline hung up the phone without saying goodbye and left her office.

As she drove to Eunice's house, she tried to reason with herself as to why in the world she cared so much about this strange girl who had turned her life upside down. She came up empty, with no answers.

Madeline made her way to the front porch. She nodded to the security guard she had hired to protect Cynthia as he stood his post. She knocked on the door harder than she intended. Portia answered.

"I'm Madeline Brewer from Ziggy's Island. Is Cindy here, by chance?"

"Yes, Madeline! Hi! I've heard so much about you. I'm Portia. Cindy and Eunice should be back soon. Please, come in."

"Thank you." Madeline entered the house. She had never been inside before. Scanning the modest dwelling, she sized it up as warm but not livable for her by any means. It looked like a property to rent to snowbirds.

"I don't know if it's my place to say, but Aunt Eunice says you've really cared for Cindy. She says you've really taken her under your wing lately."

"Well, thank you, I guess," Madeline said hesitantly. She contemplated whether she should engage in conversation with the young woman. "How well do you know Cindy?"

"Not very well, to be honest. I'm not really her kind of person, if you know what I mean."

"No, what do you mean?" Madeline scanned the room again, now curious.

"Well, she's, you know, a real lady, and I'm kinda clumsy and goofy. She's kind of special, almost like she's not from around here."

"Do you know where she's from?"

"No, not really. Aunt Eunice says she's an angel from Heaven. Sure has changed us. I mean, not Deidre, really, but me and Eunice, we're different people now from before we met Cindy,"

Portia eyes filled with emotion. "She's made me feel loved by my aunt, and no one's ever loved me before."

Madeline reached into her purse, pulled out a tissue, and handed it to Portia.

"Me and Aunt Eunice and Cindy all pray for Deidre and Dad ... I mean Radcliffe. He hates it when I call him Dad."

Madeline furled a brow. She had never connected the dots between Radcliffe and the two girls. She knew he had daughters, but he never talked about them. She also knew Eunice was his cousin but hadn't known she was caring for Radcliffe's daughters under the guise of being their "aunt."

"Would you care for some tea?" Portia asked.

"Would love some. Thank you."

Madeline didn't want tea, but she did want the freedom to look around and see if she could find evidence of anything that would give her a clue about what was going on with Cynthia. When Portia disappeared into the kitchen, Madeline made her way to a desk just off the dining room, where Eunice had been researching ancestry sites.

Madeline spotted a brochure for Palmer Labs placed next to Eunice's laptop. She opened it and saw a receipt for a saliva test, which she quickly stuffed in her pocket, making a mental note to call her contact at Palmer Labs the next day.

Moments later, Portia emerged from the kitchen with a gray plastic tray of tea and cookies. Madeline joined her at the table and sized her up. The tray looked like it was from the '70s. She wondered if she could get new ones for the '70s lot.

Portia made a loud slurping sound as she sipped her hot tea.

"Why don't I ever see you at the park? Your dad can get you in anytime," Madeline inquired.

"My father wants nothing to do with me or my sister."

Madeline wasn't all that surprised, when she thought about it. Radcliffe was a miserly and miserable man and Madeline never understood why Danny kept him on as CFO.

Just then, the door opened and Cynthia and Eunice walked in.

"Madeline!" Cynthia exclaimed. She walked up to hug her.

Madeline did not reciprocate the gesture. "Cindy, we need to talk."

Cynthia furled her brow as if bracing herself for what was to come.

That afternoon, Cynthia and Madeline met with Danny in his office. Danny was cold and distant and showed no signs of believing Cynthia's claims of innocence.

At first Cynthia was hurt, but then her feelings moved to anger when he addressed her as damaged goods and hurtful to the park. Madeline was not as cold, but it was obvious she wouldn't be inviting Cynthia back to her house anytime soon.

Bobby showed up and once again took heat, this time from Danny, for not having proof of a better background check on Cynthia.

Madeline decided to confront Cynthia. "Cindy, why won't you tell us where you're from? Are you trying to hide something?"

"I have nothing to hide, as you say. I told you, I'm from the other side of the ocean. I'm here visiting family."

"You mean *looking* for family?"

Cynthia stared at Madeline, afraid of how hard she was going to push. "Yes."

"That's what you told Danny and me at dinner, remember?"

"I do."

"So, please, for the love of God, tell me where you are from!"

The room grew thick and silent.

"I'm from a place a great distance from here."

"Ugh!" Danny exclaimed, "I'm afraid that's not good enough, Cindy."

"You will just have to trust me then. If leaving the park is in your best interest, I will leave now and you will never see me again."

Danny grunted out of frustration. Bobby rubbed the back of his head, his nervousness growing more obvious by the minute.

Madeline persisted. "Why can't I find anything on you? You have no Social Security number. No official ID. You're either an alien, angel, or my worst nightmare. Which one is it?"

"I'm none of those. My name is Cindy Hope, and I'm here to find my family."

Danny was exasperated. "That's it. This is ridiculous. She's just crazy, Mattie. Let's just cut our losses and move on."

"Cindy," Madeline stated very matter-of-factly, "I will give you until tomorrow morning to get me some form of identification. If not, your employment with Ziggy's Island will be terminated immediately."

In the other room, Radcliffe was still wearing his headset as he feverously took notes on what he just heard. As he was finishing up, he got an email that was just what he was waiting for.

Radcliffe opened up a file that contained edited footage of Cynthia and Violet in his coin store the very first day Cynthia had arrived. It had been doctored to look as though Cynthia was an accomplice to Violet reaching around the counter and stealing merchandise while Jacob was in the backroom.

He now had all he needed to take Cynthia, and possibly Madeline, down. He sent the video to Deidre along with a message for her to post it on all social-media sites and to use every means possible to make this girl look like a thief. He also warned her *not* to indicate in any way the name of the store.

He called Jacob. "Jacob. Close the store and go visit your brother. Do not return until you hear from me."

"How long should I expect to stay? He is sure to ask."

"A week. Maybe more. I will call you when it is time to come back. And Jacob, do not speak to anyone about anything regarding our business at the store. Understood?"

After hearing the groveling, "Of course, of course," Radcliffe hung up the phone.

That night, before the strike of midnight, the video had been posted with the headline "Ziggy's Princess Robs Store." Comments flew back and forth. Radcliffe closed out the apps on his phone and went to bed certain he was now in the driver's seat of his rise to power.

When Madeline got home from the office, she turned on the TV to relax. On the late-night news there was a full-blown story about the viral video. Over and over they showed the replay of Cynthia aiding Violet with the coin-store robbery.

The local news teams, broadcasting in front of Ziggy's with a large iconic Ziggy Rocket in the background, accused management of exploiting sick and disabled children for their own profit and hiring girls with questionable pasts to represent their own interests.

Madeline's heart sank; she shook with fear.

The next morning Danny phoned her just as she was finishing brushing her teeth. "Hello," was all she got out before he unloaded on her.

"Mattie," he said with the sound of gritting his pearl-white teeth. "I just got off a conference call with three of our key board members who had the audacity to blame *me* for this cockeyed mess you got us into. Not only did they blame me, but they demanded your immediate resignation." His volume increased on the word *immediate*. "Do you understand what I'm saying? The game is over. Either she goes or I fire you. Is that clear?"

"I will find out what's going on and who's behind this. If I don't, I'll be glad to leave you and your miserable board for good."

"Forty-eight hours," he snapped and hung up.

Madeline spent the next hour playing the video over and over on her computer. She gasped when she recognized Violet in the video and remembered her from the near hit a few nights before.

Familiar with the video-editing process from her years at Ziggy's as the one who approved all videos used by her company,

Madeline knew the secrets of making something look real. To her, the video looked fake.

But why was Cindy so vague about her relationship with Violet? Madeline had to learn the truth. She drove to Eunice's and stopped in front of the house. Members of the local press stood around the front lawn, waiting to see if they could get their inside scoop on what was going on with Ziggy's Princess.

She glared through her passenger window at Bobby and Cynthia, who were inside the house talking and smiling.

"How could they?" Madeline jumped out of her SUV and rushed past the security guard, who was busy trying to hold back the reporters. She banged on the front door, not caring what anyone thought.

Cynthia opened the door and cameras clicked and flashed.

Madeline cut to the chase as she pushed herself through the door, not waiting for an invitation. "You want to tell me the truth about your friend Violet?" She played the video for Cynthia on her phone.

Cynthia's eyes lit up with confusion. "She's my friend. We did not steal from that man."

Bobby ran over to the front door and closed it in an attempt to save the day. "Wait a minute. This girl has never stolen a thing in her life."

"How do you know?" Madeline demanded.

"Because she's a good soul and wouldn't do something like that. Besides, she doesn't need the money."

Madeline turned on her. "Why is that, Cindy? Why did you insist on working for free? Who works for free?"

"When I arrived in town a friend gave me a valuable coin, which I traded in. That's why I was in the coin store that day. It has provided me what I need for the time being."

"Really?" Madeline was skeptical. "One coin covers all of your living expenses, allowing you to work for free? And where did your friend get this rare coin?"

Cynthia didn't bat an eye and answered forthrightly. "From the mouth of a fish down at the beach."

"Ha!" Madeline faked a laugh. "Of course he did! And let me guess, your angel friend got it just for you."

Cynthia nodded.

"Angel?" Bobby nervously asked.

"His name is Sebastian and–" Cynthia stopped explaining when Madeline approached her.

"Tell me straight if you had anything to do with this robbery."

"There was no robbery. I would not do such a thing, and neither would Violet."

Madeline turned on her heels and started to walk away. She stopped and then spun back to look at Cynthia. "Do not talk to anyone about anything. Do you understand me? Anyone! It's time for me to put out some fires."

At the mirror beside the front door, Madeline fluffed her hair. She exhaled, touched up her lipstick, and gave herself a smile. It was time to do what she did best, pour on the charm and leave smelling like a rose.

She opened the front door and walked over to the press. Soon she was bombarded with microphones, cameras, and lights.

She assured everyone that Ziggy's would be doing a complete investigation into the matter and they would fully cooperate with the police. When questions arose regarding Cynthia, Madeline simply responded that, in her eyes, she was innocent until proven guilty. She smiled, winked and charmed her way into the heads of the unsuspecting reporters. It had been a long time since she used that side of her personality. It was exhausting.

When the interrogation finally finished, Madeline once again found solace in her car, just as she did decades earlier. As she drove home, she felt scared and out of control. A familiar ominous feeling of loss began to penetrate. Feelings she had not experienced since…

Abrupt thoughts from her unconscious spilled into her conscious mind. Memories flooded her spirit; memories of being alone and scared, pregnant and afraid to tell anyone, having a secret love that no other person knew about growing inside of her. Anxiety and panic over losing that someone surged through her body. She hated the emotions that she promised she would never feel again.

She pulled over and parked along the coastline.

She removed her shoes and made her way down to the water. The sand was grainy and uncomfortable, so she found a place to sit and plopped down. Letting out a huge sigh, she could no longer hold in her emotions and began to cry. The sound of the waves absorbed her sobs as she sat for a long while and wept. She had not felt pain like this since her miscarriage. The walls keeping it all back started to topple.

The next day Cynthia arose early, the bright sun presenting a gorgeous morning. She heard commotion downstairs but ignored it. After dressing, she made her way downstairs. Eunice was peering through her front window when Cynthia walked up behind her and glanced over her shoulder. She saw a crowd of people standing around. Eunice gasped and pushed her back, dead bolting the door. After locking it, she stared straight at Cynthia.

"We've got to get you out of here. Now!"

Cynthia glanced over at the kitchen table where Deidre was staring at her while eating. The moment Cynthia glanced toward her she hid her face behind the cereal box. Cynthia looked through the front window a second time. There were men and women of every shape, size, and nationality with recorders and phones and cameras in their hands mulling about the edge of the property while the security guard kept them off the front porch.

Cynthia drew near the door. "What is it they want from me?"

"They want to drill you about the video leak. Come on." Eunice stepped away to lead Cynthia out the back, but Cynthia turned the knob of the front door and opened it. There was a flurry of camera flashes as reporters began to yell questions at her.

"Who are you? What did you do with the money you stole? How did you get to be the goodwill ambassador? Who's the bag lady"

Wanting to clear her name, Cynthia started to answer them as best she could. "She's not a bag lady—I'm Cindy Hope, and I'm in town to find my family. No, I'm not a thief. I told you I'm from out of town and–"

Radcliffe emerged from the crowd, walking confidently up the front porch stairs. The security guard was quick to intercept him.

"Whoa, whoa, mister," the guard said, "this is private property. You can't come up here."

"It's my private property, you idiot!" Radcliffe replied smugly. "I own the place. Now remove yourself from my porch!"

The security guard looked at Eunice, who had just come out to retrieve Cynthia. She heard the whole exchange and nodded to the under paid guard to let him pass.

Radcliffe smugly snickered at him, tugged at his tie, and walked right up to Cynthia. She was overcome by fear and anger and leaned back a bit.

He glared at his cousin, dismissing Cynthia as though she weren't there. "I had a feeling she was bad news from the beginning. That's why I never hired her. I can usually tell when something's rotten, unlike my counterparts, who seem to get sucked into the web of every hireling that comes along."

"Radcliffe! You know she's not a hireling," Eunice blurted out.

"Do I?" he sneered.

Cynthia remained steady and quiet. She felt his wrath toward her, so she raised prayer after prayer to the heavens, expecting some type of intervention. None came.

"Is there no one besides my befuddled cousin that claims your innocence?" he taunted.

Eunice showed fear for Cynthia's well-being, which made Cynthia feel even more afraid.

Radcliffe stayed on the porch and yelled out for all to hear. He pulled out a coin and held it up high for all to see. "Do you remember this unusual coin, my dear?"

Cynthia said nothing.

"I believe you brought it into my store the day you robbed me. Do you recall that day?"

She remained silent.

"It held my curiosity for some time. I finally had it appraised by an expert archeologist. Do you know what he had to say about this particular item?"

The press was recording Radcliffe's every word. No one wanted to miss the punchline, and Radcliffe intentionally spoke loud enough for all to hear.

"It seems you came into possession of a coin that has historically belonged to royalty, those of Caesar Augustus's family. A mere commoner such as myself and the others around here would not have access to such a marvelous piece in mint condition."

In a patronizing voice, Radcliffe mocked Cynthia, "Are you a child of the King my dear?"

Cynthia was now aware that Radcliffe was not speaking of his own accord. Nor was he referring to the house of Caesar. He was referring to *her* king. Her spirit quaked as she sensed a stronger force standing in front of her. She jerked with fear as she remembered the encounter with the demons in her transition to this planet. *Who was this man? Where did he get his power from?*

Her eyes betrayed her, showing Radcliffe her weakness. He pushed harder.

"And how is it you would possess an item such as this?" He pulled her precious Scriptures from the inside pocket of his jacket.

Cynthia gasped when she saw her personal Bible in the claws of a man who loathed its very existence.

"This is not just any book, is it, my dear alien child? It's a one-of-a-kind copy of Scripture that was written on alum-tawed skin used nearly two thousand years ago for sacred documents."

He flashed it so the crowd could see its pages. "This too seems to be a byproduct of the first century!"

Cynthia shrunk back and prayed for intervention. None came. He pressed into her.

"Are you perhaps from another time? Another realm?"

"No, I'm not!" she blurted out. Her spirit sank as she lied. Guilt and shame crashed down on her.

"No?" He stepped in front of her and stood on his toes to stare her down. "You do not belong to a king?"

"No, I don't know what king you're talking about." Her spirit began to scream inside her. She had never betrayed her Creator before. What was she saying? And why? She was utterly confused.

"You don't know to whom you belong or from whence you come? Is that what you're telling us?"

"No. I mean, yes. I do. I mean, no, I'm not what you think…"

Eunice couldn't take it anymore. "Radcliffe! Stop this nonsense. Let's go inside."

Radcliffe persisted, not skipping a beat. "Who are your mother and father, anyway?" His breath smelled deplorable to Cynthia's nose. It caused a wave of nausea to surge though her body.

"I don't know. That's why I'm here … to find them."

"Radcliffe!" Eunice yelled again onto deaf ears.

"Perhaps your parents don't want to be found. They obviously didn't want you … or maybe they're dead. Perhaps this king you supposedly love has set up a cruel joke. I think he lied to you."

"He would never do that," she shouted back. "He loves me!"

A gasp swept through the press on her admission of belonging to an unknown king.

Eunice walked toward Cynthia to save her, but Radcliffe quickly intervened.

"One more step, Eunice, and I will evict you tomorrow," Radcliffe threatened. She stopped in her tracks. "Besides, I'm almost finished."

Radcliffe sneered, stepped behind Cynthia, and growled in her left ear. "Tell me, child. You're somewhat of a mystery. I think we all want to know." He motioned to the gathered press. "When were you *born*? What is your date of birth?"

She shook with anxiety. Panic filled her veins and set her mind on fire. It felt like her brain would explode. "I … I … I don't know."

"You don't know because you're a freak. You don't have a birthday. You're not from here, are you?"

"Yes, I am. I–"

He moved right up into her face and yelled, "You're lying, aren't you?"

"No! I mean … yes!" The confession came gushing out of her mouth before she could stop it. Everything she knew about who she was came crashing down inside her. She remembered Sebastian's warning to never lie about her identity. She burst into tears and buried her face in her hands.

"Radcliffe, stop it now!" Eunice shouted.

He growled victoriously at his cousin. "I'm done here." He threw her Bible down at her feet. "I have no more use for this rubbish."

Cynthia bent down and swept up the sacred Scriptures, holding them close to her chest.

Eunice had enough. She grabbed Cynthia and held her tightly, trying to move towards the front door. Radcliffe blocked their way into the house.

"Don't try to stop us," she warned Radcliffe, who smiled in victory as he moved aside. Eunice took Cynthia into the house and closed the door.

Once the door was shut Radcliffe turned to leave and then spotted Deidre to the side of the front porch. He hesitated and then meandered his way to her. He sensed she was waiting for a pat on the back. Normally he would not accommodate such a notion, but he felt so giddy he decided to be generous. "Well done, child."

She gave him an awkward smile as he patted her hand resting on the porch rail. She attempted to give him a hug, but he turned and wobbled down the stairs, leaving her behind.

Terry Harris

⚬ 13 ⚬

AFTER PACKING A BAG, EUNICE AND CYNTHIA TOOK A
drive along the coast and stopped at a bed and breakfast two
hours from home. Cynthia, riveted with the thought of failure,
was a shell of herself. She had not said a word the entire drive.

Feelings of failure beget fear and fear beget distance. She
felt alone and removed from who she once was. A dark chasm
she had never known before filled her soul. All her moments
in Heaven had been filled with an awareness of the King and
His acceptance and approval for her. Never before had she felt
abandonment and shame as she felt now.

She could only mumble, "*Why? Why have you left me?
Why have you forsaken me?*" She began to entertain thoughts
of running away. She felt anger at her King; inside, she blamed
Him for her failure to tell the truth.

A voice in her head answered: "*Because you failed.*" She knew
the accusing voice was correct. She had failed miserably. She
lied. She didn't stand for truth but cowered instead. She denied
the very One who gave her this opportunity. She reminded
herself that no other human ever had this incredible gift to cross
the span of Heaven and experience a taste of the life on Earth
that had been denied to her in the beginning. She felt unworthy

and wondered if she would be allowed back home. The feelings were unbearable.

They arrived at their room. Eunice closed the shades and Cynthia dove face-down in the bed and wept. *What would happen to her now? How would she get back to her place in the King's court? Would she ever be welcomed back again? Would she die here? How could anyone ever want her back now?* She was stained. She was broken. She was … a transgressor and she had no recompense for her failures.

Eunice watched over Cynthia as she fell asleep in her clothes, curled up in the fetal position. The night was long and silent.

In the morning, Eunice texted Portia and asked for an update on the home situation. Was it safe for them to return? Portia texted back and asked what was wrong. She had been working at the store, and Deidre refused to give her the details. Eunice gave her the abbreviated version and asked to be informed when it was safe to return.

Like most residents of Paradise Bay, Madeline saw several social media videos of Radcliffe confronting Cynthia on the porch steps. Her blood began to boil as she watched Radcliffe relish his "gotcha" moment with Cynthia.

Morning couldn't come quickly enough for Madeline as Radcliffe's smug smile of satisfaction replayed over and over in her head. Once at work, she went straight to his office to confront him.

Terry Harris

Without knocking, she charged through his door. Radcliffe was on his computer and calmly looked up, almost as though he was expecting her.

"Okay, Radcliffe," she attacked as she stared him down, "I've known some underhanded dirtbags in my life, but you really take the cake. What in the world were you thinking? How could you treat Cindy like that? And do you have any idea what this will do to Ziggy's? No! You just think about yourself! That was the most pitiful display of narcissism I have ever seen! You are pathetic! Give me one good reason I shouldn't fire your stubby butt right now!"

Madeline cringed as Radcliffe gave her the same smile that had been haunting her all morning.

In a calm, matter-of-fact tone, he replied, "Well, Madeline, first of all you don't have the authority to fire me and second… the way I see it, Ziggy's, and you, should be thanking me."

"What!?" Madeline exclaimed.

Radcliffe responded more forcefully. "Look, I knew that girl was trouble from the beginning and you and Danny were just too stupid or starry eyed over her to see it. I saw right through her, and you should be thanking me that I exposed her for who she really is, a fraud, before this went on further."

"Your butt is mine. You posted that video without permission," Madeline threatened.

"Do your homework, Madeline, I didn't post that video…"

"I know you're behind it, Radcliffe. How else could your precious daughter get a hold of that footage? I don't know what you're scheming, but I'm going to find out." Madeline turned to leave the room.

Radcliffe coldly replied, "Be careful, Madeline. I know you don't want me to press charges against the bag lady and your precious Cindy."

Madeline paused in the doorway but decided to hastily exit his office. She could no longer tolerate Radcliffe Finklemeyer. She turned left to the big office down the hall.

She knocked on Danny's door but didn't wait for him to invite her in. She marched straight to his desk and hung up his office phone, ending Danny's conversation with a friend.

"I found the problem."

Offended by her rudeness, Danny glared at her and slowly set his phone down in its cradle. Madeline was too angry to care. "It's not Cindy. It's Rat Fink!"

Danny was not amused. He sat back in his chair and looked at her, saying sarcastically, "Are you saying that Radcliffe set Cindy up to rob him? I think you might be accusing the wrong person here, Mattie."

"The video, Walter! It's a fake, and I know he's behind the posting of it."

"Fine, show me your evidence and I'll call him into the office right now."

"I don't have any evidence, but I know he did it."

"And you know this because…"

"My instincts."

Danny sighed and rolled his eyes.

"Danny, who else had access of that footage besides Radcliffe? I confronted him. I know his daughter got the video footage from him, and he didn't deny it."

"He didn't deny posting the video?"

"No, he denied posting it but then pretty much admitted his daughter posted it and that we should be grateful because it exposes Cindy as a fraud now, as opposed to later. He was completely insubordinate and offensive. I want him fired, Danny. Today! Now!"

"That's not going to happen Mattie. Without iron-clad evidence, we're inviting a lawsuit and quite frankly, we can't handle that right now."

"Fine, then I'll quit. I'll resign, you've given me the forty-eight hours I asked for."

Danny groaned. He sighed, ran his fingers through his hair, and looked her in the eyes. "Mattie, I don't want you to quit. I'll take the heat from the board." He paused. "Why are you protecting this girl?"

Madeline welled up with emotion, and unwanted tears leaked from her eyes. "Because I have to."

"Why?" he asked with persistence.

"I don't know why. There's just something about this girl. She's so naïve and vulnerable. I've got to protect her," Madeline quietly replied, surprised by the words she just spoke.

"Remember, Mattie, we're running a business here. Sometimes hard decisions have to be made."

Madeline shook her head and left the office, once again feeling misunderstood.

A day later, Eunice informed Cynthia it was safe for them to return home. She had received a text from Portia that all was quiet and no one was around except for a new security guard.

Cynthia offered small talk on the drive home and then returned to her dismal state of mind. She had not eaten for a couple of days and was, in fact, fasting and praying, though she had not told Eunice what she was doing. It had occurred to Cynthia in the wee hours of the night that her King was known for His compassion, and perhaps He would forgive her of her shortcomings and find a place for her back in His dwelling.

In the Psalms, she found hope from the writings of David. While in Heaven, she had shared in a few conversations with him but had never seen his laments from the perspective she now held. Like David, she struggled to believe God would totally forgive her, but her time in meditation that night was a start to the process of healing. She was so grateful that her Bible had been returned to her, albeit in such a slanderous manner.

Cynthia desperately missed her friends Angela, Sebastian, Peter, and all the others. They seemed so distant now. She believed she had lost her honorable place of service but hoped that perhaps she could serve her King once again.

Eunice pulled into the driveway and parked. They climbed out of the car and made their way into the house. Walking on the front porch, Cynthia shuddered as she recalled the horrible experience with Radcliffe and the paparazzi just days before. Anxiety lunged through her body and caused her to pause near the doorway. Somehow, she knew Deidre had a hand in the ordeal, but she was uncertain as to what Portia's contributions were, if any.

She lumbered up the stairs and closed the attic door behind her. She sat on the edge of her windowsill and gazed out across the landscape. The beach was gray and fogged in, just like her mind. Then, something caught her eye. She leaned out to see what was on the eave that extended just below her window. She didn't know what it was at first. It looked like a chunk of dirt until she noticed the orange and yellow stripes. Cynthia gasped.

Holding onto the windowsill with one arm, she extended her body just far enough to grab hold of her feathered friend. She brought the bird close to her bosom as she retreated back into the attic. Sitting on her bed, she opened her hands to reveal the lifeless bird. Gone was the beautiful song the bird had blessed her with so long ago. Gone was the joy it once gave her. Tears poured down Cynthia's cheeks as she looked upon the bird.

In her sorrow, she pondered how those around her could live an entire lifetime in a place that inflicts so much pain. She imagined the pain of losing a loved one: a friend, parent, or a child. Then she remembered the wounds on the hands of her King and shuddered. Cynthia decided that death was the worst part of this world. She took a shoe box out of the closet and placed the bird gently on top of the tissue paper inside. Tiredness swept over her like a powerful wave, and she gave into its call by slipping into bed and under the covers fully dressed.

The citizens of Heaven were watching and were moved with deep compassion for Cynthia. They also stood in awe of God's plan as it carefully unfolded. Their dear friend looked to be on the brink of ruin, yet they fully understood from their eternal perspective that she was on the verge of a great revelation.

The King at that very moment bent down and began to sing a melodious song of comfort and strength over His beloved child as she slept. He was by no means surprised, disappointed, or angry with her. On the contrary, He was orchestrating her development and maturity as his precious daughter, carefully overseeing every wrinkle in the process with His wise and all-seeing eyes.

All of Heaven became silent as His song over her rang through the portals of glory, shaking its very foundation. At that moment, the King was in his most cherished role: a servant to his children.

Cynthia awoke the next morning to find herself surprisingly refreshed. She felt a tug on her heart to visit her two favorite places on Earth; the beach and the small chapel in town, which had become her home away from home for worship. She surrendered to the call and immersed herself in both.

When she entered the chapel, she smiled as she noticed the crucifix that once hung at the front was now gone, and in its place was a plain brown cross with a green wreath attached to its center.

Perhaps she had been instrumental in helping Pastor Timothy find freedom from serving a "dead" King. She found a quiet, candle-lit corner and escaped into an extended time of prayer. She concluded her quiet time with a song of thanksgiving and inconspicuously slipped out the door before anyone noticed she was there. She left feeling hopeful.

The next day, Madeline knocked on Eunice's door. Eunice invited her in. Cynthia sat at the table, looking pale and thin. A plate of cold food sat untouched in front of her. Depressing thoughts of the accusations whaled hard against Cynthia that morning. She found herself once again wondering where her King was and why she felt so alone and unworthy. She longed to be back to her real home.

"Cindy, I just came by to see how you're doing."

Cynthia shrugged and offered her a small smile. Madeline drew near. As a flawed and sinful human being, Madeline didn't fully understand the emotional roller coaster that Cynthia was on. "So many thoughts and feelings that I've never known before. I'm just not sure who I am anymore," Cynthia stated somberly.

"I'm sorry for some of the things I said to you recently. I know that a lot of this is not your fault. I wish you had a better explanation for many of the questions about your identity. Heaven knows that would alleviate a lot of the anxiety Danny and I have about you. We have to let you go as Ziggy's ambassador. I'm sorry. I'm sure you understand."

Cynthia sighed. "I've never been fired before either. It feels awful." She looked Madeline in the eyes, her gaze sympathetic. She could tell Madeline was very uncomfortable with the decision but was trying to cover up her feelings.

"Come on. I took the afternoon off," Madeline said. "Let's take a trip to the orphanage. The twins are there, and I've made arrangements for us to visit them."

Cynthia perked up a bit. She stood and smiled, but then cowered. "Are they okay?"

"Yes. They are doing well health-wise. They could use some company, I'm told. Care to join me?"

"I'd love to, if you're sure you want me to go with you."

"I'm sure," Madeline stated with a smile.

Cynthia took a bite of food, hugged Eunice, and then left the house with Madeline.

As Madeline was set to start the car, Cynthia said, "I'm sorry for the trouble I have caused you. I don't deserve your kindness, though I must confess I am utterly confused as to what I have done wrong."

"I'm sorry for the behavior of our CFO. Whatever happened that day in the coin store does not warrant the kind of slander and character damage he has brought against you."

"Why does he hate me so much? What would cause him to lie about me?"

"Sometimes good people, like yourself, get in the way of the plans of those who aren't so decent. And that's when you become a target. It happens in politics and it happens in business. Knowing Radcliffe as I do, my guess is that it's a power play. He wants to be king in a kingdom he did not build, and you're the pawn he's using to accomplish his goal." She backed out of the driveway and drove away.

Cynthia stared out the car window and pondered Madeline's words for several minutes. "I've never met such a man as Radcliffe before. That day in the house he looked at me as though he was the lion and I was his prey."

"I remember when I was a little girl in Sunday school they taught us that our enemy looked to devour us as a roaring lion. I didn't really believe that there was evil in the world, but now I'm beginning to wonder."

Cynthia had not given any thought to the idea of Madeline in Sunday school, where children learn the truth of who they are and the call on their lives. She sensed there was hope that Madeline would be open to hearing about the King and how much He cared for her.

"What else did you learn in Sunday school?" Cynthia asked bravely.

"Jesus loves me this I know..." Madeline laughed.

Normally, Cynthia would have laughed along and then pursued a deeper conversation with Madeline. But now she felt she had lost that privilege and was no longer worthy to tell anyone about His lovingkindness. She remained silent.

They pulled in front of the run-down orphanage. The faded sign in the front yard was painted in gray with black letters: Hope House. Cynthia was excited to see not only the twins, but some of the other children she had met at the hospital weeks before.

Cynthia recognized the little boy sitting alone on the front steps as the one who had played the harmonica at the hospital. He was wearing a bright-yellow shirt that had blood stains on it. He told her he had been whacked a few times by some of the other kids who didn't care for his music. Cynthia's confidence strained as she attempted to console him with a smile and a handful of jokes. He wasn't the same boy she had met before. He slowly warmed up to her and she sat down on the wooden bench near the porch and held him. He seemed to respond as she rocked back and forth and sang softly in his ears, which aided in calming his anxious heart.

Madeline sat quietly on the steps next to them, saying nothing.

After a short while, the boy grabbed Cynthia by the hand and led her into the orphanage. They made their way to the upper floor where the halls were lined with rooms that all looked the same. There was no life to them. No color or sense of hope. The walls were painted an off-white color that highlighted dirty handprints and black scuffs.

The beds in each room were single cots with thin, faded blue sheets. Mismatched pillowcases partially covered the stained pillows. Four children shared one dresser per room. The drawers were open, showing the kids had few possessions. The twins were kept in separate cribs in a room void of life. The rickety beds of faded blonde wood looked old and unkept.

Cynthia gasped as she moved toward one of the girls. The baby's big brown eyes showed no signs of alertness or engagement. She looked sad and aloof. Cynthia gazed at Madeline, who winced, and then at the caseworker who was filling out a form. The caseworker, an overweight middle-aged woman, looked at the girls in their cribs with what appeared to be little pity or compassion.

"May I hold her, please?" Cynthia asked, trying to hold back tears.

"Sure," the woman said with a shrug.

Cynthia gently lifted one of the infants and held her close. The baby pushed away at first but after several moments accepted the love Cynthia was offering. "What's her name?"

"We call her Ann."

"Orphan Annie?" Madeline asked, sounding annoyed.

The caseworker hacked a laugh.

Cynthia missed the humor but cuddled Ann and whispered her name a few times in her ear. She walked around as she held and kissed the infant gently on the forehead. After several moments of loving the child, she moved toward Madeline. "Would you hold Ann for me, please, while I hold her sister?"

She waited for Madeline to take the baby in her arms. Madeline appeared awkward, glancing at the door. Cynthia didn't back off her request. Madeline dropped her purse and moved her arms around as if she didn't know what to do. Cynthia gently laid Ann in her arms and waited until Madeline was in control before she let go of the child.

She turned to the caseworker. "And what is her sister's name?"

"We haven't decided yet. We're voting between Lucy and Kylie. Sometimes we just don't name the orphans at all and let the adoptive parents do it. We'll call them orphan one or two…"

Cynthia was unable to hide her feelings of agitation in response to the caseworker's indifference. "Can you please not refer to her as an orphan? She's an innocent child who needs love and care, just as much as you or I."

Cynthia bent down, picked up the baby, and held her close. The infant put her little arm around Cynthia's neck, which caused Cynthia to smile and nearly cry at the same time "It's okay, baby. It's okay." Cynthia began to sing a lullaby, which filled the room with a spirit of peace. It also filled her soul with a steady flow of familiar joy and purpose. "I think her name should be Emily," Cynthia said softly. The nurse nodded in agreement.

Madeline bonded with baby Ann and even kissed the child's face a few times. Cynthia could see that things were beginning to feel natural to her and that intuitions on how to care for a child emerged that were perhaps never before given the chance to awaken.

"Is your family looking to adopt the girls?" the caseworker asked Madeline out of the blue.

Madeline threw a quick glance at Cynthia and then back at the caseworker. "Uh, we're not related. And, no, we're just visiting."

"Oh, sorry. I thought she was your daughter, since you look so much alike." The caseworker looked at Cynthia and

Madeline closely and seemed surprised when Madeline said they weren't related.

Cynthia didn't mind the mistake. She was focused entirely on the baby in her arms. She hummed for a few seconds than began to sing another soft song of comfort.

Madeline was obviously uncomfortable. "So, what's going to happen to them … uh, the twins?" she inquired quickly.

"It's looking more and more like they will be split up and put in different foster homes." The caseworker seemed a little bothered by the idea, but then quickly added, "Probably best for them. At least they'll have a home."

Madeline's face sunk at hearing of the twins being separated. Cynthia felt the suffering of the girls and stopped her singing. The peace and joy that had entered the room from Cynthia's melody faded, and the deep sense of hopelessness returned. When the ladies placed the girls in their cribs, they glanced at each other, concerned. A part of Cynthia's soul now belonged to the infants, and it tore her up that there was seemingly nothing she could do to solve the problem the girls faced: a life of separation and loneliness. Cynthia left the room in silence and descended the stairs, wondering if Madeline felt the same.

Madeline followed behind her, not saying anything.

When they arrived at the bottom step, several kids, in the range of eight to twelve years old, stood around chatting. They were talking about Logan, the boy in the wheelchair.

"Excuse me," Cynthia interrupted. "Can you tell me how Logan is doing?"

The kids shrugged.

"Is he here? May I see him please?" Cynthia continued.

"Got moved to another orphanage. He was causing trouble and got put somewhere else again," a shorter blonde boy blurted out.

"*Again* is the keyword there," a red-haired girl chimed in.

"What do you mean, trouble? What did he do?" Cynthia touched the boy's shoulder.

"He was getting mad. He bit Tommy," the blonde boy pointed to another boy, "really hard and made him bleed."

"Why would he bite Tommy?" Cynthia was getting concerned about someone she cared for very much.

"Tommy said he was a liar 'cause of that stuff that's on Snapchat and Instagram about you. You know… saying he faked everything."

Cynthia's head began to swim. "But it wasn't fake. The nurses said he couldn't walk and then when I held him he–"

"That's a lie! You're a liar!" Tommy shouted.

"She's not a liar. She's a princess. Leave her alone," someone yelled.

"Liar!" another accused.

Arguments for both sides of the story erupted within the group and grew loud very quickly. Caseworkers rushed into the room. Madeline stepped in to help Cynthia and walked her out of the orphanage, but Cynthia resisted.

"Come on, Cindy. It's not your fight," Madeline insisted. "Let's get you out of here." With her arm firmly around Cynthia's waist, Madeline moved her out the door and into the car.

Once inside the SUV, Cynthia sat tight against the door and said nothing. As Madeline drove, tears streamed down Cynthia's face.

"I'm sorry, Cindy. Those kids were wrong. They had no right to treat you like that."

Cynthia sighed. "It's not their fault, you know. Those kids are hurting inside, so they try to hurt others. I wish I could do something to help. If only we could find someone who would love each one of them for who they are."

"You still didn't deserve that."

"I'm just so confused," Cynthia confessed unintentionally.

"About?"

"Who I am. Why I'm here. I thought it would all be so different…" She trailed off and stared out the window.

"Cindy, may I ask you a direct question?"

Cynthia nodded.

"Are you in trouble with the law?"

"In trouble?"

"Are you running from something you don't want us to know about? Why is there no background information on you? Is Cindy Hope your real name?"

"Yes. Partially."

"So what is the rest?"

"Cynthia is my proper first name."

"Cynthia Hope?"

Madeline's face wrinkled as though in pain. Cynthia Hope was the same name she had chosen for her baby girl so many years ago.

"I like that name. If I had a daughter, I think that's the name I would give her," she muttered almost to herself.

Cynthia smiled. "You would make a great mom."

Madeline began to look uneasy.

"Maybe you can adopt me if I can't find my parents," Cynthia offered her as a joke.

"I just might consider that," Madeline assured her with a smidgen of seriousness. She put her hand on Cynthia's arm to comfort her. "Cindy, we're going to make a quick stop at the park. I need to phone Danny about something."

Cynthia felt awkward at the idea of revisiting Ziggy's. "Are you sure it's okay since I'm no longer working there?"

"If I say it's okay, it's okay. Besides, I might not be working there that much longer either." Madeline chuckled nervously.

Cynthia chose to go along with whatever was unfolding, trusting that the King still had her best interest in mind.

It was getting dark when they pulled into Ziggy's back lot. Madeline and Cynthia heard the familiar sounds of Ziggy's guests cheering as the nighttime lights whimsically brightened the park. Cynthia breathed deeply as she scurried to keep up with Madeline's fierce pace toward the main office. Madeline walked with determination and focus as she mumbled aloud a one-sided conversation with herself.

"What's with you?" Cynthia playfully asked, slightly out of breath.

"You'll see," Madeline assured her.

Once they arrived at the office suite, Madeline asked Cynthia to wait in the lobby while she made a phone call. She stepped into her office and searched her phone for a number and tapped the number. It read Palmer Labs.

The phone rang until it went to a voicemail. "Ruby, hi, it's Madeline. Hey, I got a favor to ask…"

A moment later Madeline finished her voicemail and hung up. When she was done, she left her office and found Cynthia waiting in the lobby. "Now, let's go talk to Danny."

They took three steps, turned the corner to Danny's office and ran smack into Radcliffe. "What the–" he growled as he spilled open his manila file folder. Radcliffe bent down to pick up his papers. Madeline tried to move around him, but Radcliffe blocked her way as he slowly straightened up, glaring at Cynthia. Madeline recognized the stare. Cynthia had been correct in her assessment of him—he did look as though he wanted to devour her.

Cynthia stepped back to retreat so Madeline stepped between them, forcing Radcliffe to abort his attack.

"Move it, Rat Fink," Madeline demanded.

Radcliffe pushed his glasses up off the bridge of his nose. He didn't acknowledge Madeline but peered around her, staying fixated on Cynthia. He slowly stepped aside, and the women resumed their way toward Danny's office. Cynthia couldn't resist looking back at Radcliffe. When she did, she shuddered. Madeline put her arm around her and glanced back at Radcliffe. He grinned and gave her a mocking wave.

Danny was on the phone when Madeline and Cynthia entered. He furled a brow at the sight of Cynthia and threw Madeline a curious glance. He abruptly ended his call and closed the emails he had been reading.

"Mattie, why is she here? We fired her! Haven't you had enough?"

Cynthia took a seat at the far corner couch, as far away as she could get from the center of attention.

Madeline jumped right in. "I have an idea. Actually, it was Cindy's idea… but now it's our idea and I want to share it with you."

"No. I don't care what it is, the answer is no. Why are you even listening to her? Look at where she's gotten us. Our image is shot!"

"Really, Danny? Yes, look at what she's got us. Double-digit sales increases and social-media traction like we've never seen before. Now just hear me out."

Danny glared at her.

She eased her tone. "Danny, you've been in this business long enough to know the one thing worse than bad press is no press. I know Cindy is innocent in all this, and when it clears, I want to be standing by her side. As far as I'm concerned, she's our good-will ambassador, at least in spirit, until all of this blows over."

"Mattie, I have no idea why you are being stubborn about this girl. She can potentially ruin everything you've worked so hard for. It's not like you."

Madeline paused and didn't address what he was saying. "Care to hear our idea?" she asked.

"I'm all ears." Danny stood and met Madeline at the front of his desk, meeting her eye to eye and toe to toe.

"I think we have a chance to right the ship on this. I know for a fact, and I believe you do too, that this whole thing is a bunch of horse hockey splattered around by someone who wants to see us take a fall." When she said "someone," she pointed toward Radcliffe's office.

"Madeline, what you're accusing Radcliffe of makes no sense."

"I don't want to get into that right now," she said dismissively. "I think we can turn this around and not only get back what we lost but come out on top bigger than ever. And your face will be all over the campaign. It's what you've always wanted: a reputation for being the greatest guy in the land, with a heart the size of Texas."

"I'm listening," he said quietly.

"Ziggy's should host a grand ball for orphans."

Danny's eyes darted from Madeline to Cynthia, and back to Madeline. "An orphans' ball?"

"Danny, what is our mission statement?"

Danny rolled his eyes but played along. "Connecting families with their past, one decade at a time."

"Exactly," Madeline said forcefully. "*Connect*. Let's connect families! Foster kids who are looking for a home can come and meet parents and families who are hoping for a child or an adolescent adoption. We invite birth moms and their potential adopting family to come and enjoy an evening under the stars. We bring in Palmer Labs to reach out to clients in their database who want to connect with birth parents or children that were adopted.

"We give our guests a place to meet, connect, and possibly begin the process of becoming a family. We'll have interactive games, music, and great food, plus support booths set up to guide families. And at the very least, we'll give these 'orphans' a chance to feel wanted, loved, and cherished for one special night."

Danny seemed to be impressed by Madeline's passion.

"And no, Danny. No sponsorships. This one is on us."

Danny's face fell. He challenged her. "What's the admission price?"

"That's on us too," she said, smiling.

Danny shook his head, but Madeline continued. "Ziggy's needs this, Walter. We need to repair our reputation now!" Madeline looked out of the office window to Ziggy's Island below. She had always loved the park at night. "Just imagine a huge event, under the stars, kids and adults dressed to the nines, laughing, dancing." She looked back at Danny. "And the press! We'll have a ton of good press."

Madeline gave Danny a flirtatious smile and locked into his eyes as she walked over to his desk. "You can wear your tux that you look so handsome in, and I'll get a deep-red dress."

Danny didn't respond and appeared to look right through her. Madeline felt a sinking feeling of failure in her gut. It was the first time she could remember where her charm and beauty didn't "close the deal" with Danny. His silence was deafening to her.

Madeline gathered her thoughts. Danny showed no signs of continuing the conversation, so she spun around and gazed out the large window overlooking the park. The colorful lights called to her spirit. Something special was about to happen, and she really wanted Danny to be on board.

Not wanting to give up, she turned back to Danny. "Can we take a walk?"

Danny shrugged. "Why not? I was about to close out the day anyhow." Danny logged off his computer, and Cynthia sat back on the couch as though she would wait for their return.

"Cindy, would you join us, please?" Madeline asked.

Cynthia looked confused for a moment, but then sprung off the couch with a smile like that of a child who was asked by her parents if she wanted to go out for ice cream.

Madeline led Danny and Cynthia to the center of the park. Ziggy's rocket was about to launch for the night, and the crowds had gathered to watch the show. Two men dressed in overalls covered with black soot stopped and said hello to Danny and Madeline.

Danny patted the men on the shoulder and asked how they were doing. They made a joke about "life in the pit" and left him laughing as they opened the door behind the enormous rocket ship. The workers descended a set of cement stairs into a basement that contained the fire pit for the rocket launch.

The door slammed shut behind them and Danny, Madeline, and Cynthia walked around the rocket ship to the entrance of the 1970s lot. Throughout the streets, men and women laughed and shared stories of favorite childhood memories.

Madeline and Danny stood and watched the people. Madeline locked her left arm in Danny's and leaned her chin on his shoulder. This surprised him. He smiled at her. "What?" he asked, suspicious with a hint of flirting.

"Do you remember why you started this park?"

"Because I thought it was a killer idea?" he asked.

"You told me that you wanted to create a place where people could go to remember a time when life was, perhaps, happier."

"Yeah. I believed there was a market to own in nostalgia. And, I was trying to impress you."

She sighed.

"What is it you want from me, Madeline?"

"Danny, I want you to have what I believe you really want. The feeling, the knowledge that you have indeed made a difference. Can you tell me the name of one person you feel you've truly had an impact on?"

"Look, I've given over seven figures to help build hospitals and banks and daycare centers, and if that isn't enough for you, I'm not sure what to say. My money has helped thousands of people. Just because I don't know a name doesn't mean that I didn't help."

Madeline slowed down and paused a moment. "Oh God, help me with this," she quietly said to herself. "I want something more, and deep down, I think you do too. I need... we need, to do this ball for these families. I can't explain why I feel this way, but I feel that it's what we're supposed to do."

He paused and sighed. Madeline understood he was comfortable in his world. He had grown accustomed to surface relationships and not having to get messy with people's problems. Her request challenged his lifestyle and shook him up a bit. He rubbed his neck with agitation. "I don't know, Madeline. Do we really have to invite all those people? Can't we just... you know, invite a few orphans and some foster parents for a free night at the park?"

"What are you afraid of Danny?"

Danny walked over to a kiosk selling beverages and asked for a bottled water. Her question hit a nerve and irritated him for a second. There was something about the idea of family that scared him. He flashed back to his dad rejecting him and his younger brother when they were kids. And, of course, his failed marriages didn't help his cynicism. He took a few gulps and walked back to her but said nothing.

He scanned the park and observed the people. Hearing their laughter nudged his spirit. He took a deep breath and let it out. "It's funny you should ask me to do this. I just spent the last couple hours poring over dozens of emails telling me how much people have appreciated our donations to help the homeless, including a call from a writer at the *Paradise Times* who wants to do a feature about it. Who would have guessed that after all we've done to put Ziggy's on the map, helping the unfortunate would be our greatest marketing success? Maybe we can do the same for orphans."

Danny stopped walking and turned to Madeline. He grabbed her shoulders and looked her straight in the eyes. "Okay, Mattie. I'm trusting you on this. Go for it."

"I want us to do it together." As soon as she said that, Madeline's eyes teared up and she looked away, embarrassment creeping across her face.

Danny squirmed; he was not used to this side of Madeline and wasn't sure how to respond. It had been many years since he'd seen emotion like this in her. He needed to break the tension. "All right. We'll do this together," he replied softly. After an awkward pause, he quickly changed gears, took his hands off Madeline's shoulders, and began walking. "So, what's it going to cost us?"

Madeline laughed and wiped her eyes as the three of them walked. "More than you can imagine."

Danny groaned. "Can't we have at least one title sponsor?"

"No sponsors," she emphasized. "We have to cover the costs on this one; otherwise, we can be accused of doing it for the wrong reasons. If we're going to see this through, we have to do it with our own money."

"Madeline…" Danny stopped in his tracks. He hated the idea of no sponsors. Sponsorships were a financial safety net.

Cynthia chimed in. "If this turns out the way Madeline envisions, you'll have the greatest success you've ever seen. I believe you'll see a miraculous response."

Danny raised an eyebrow. Madeline nodded, agreeing. "That's not why I want to do this, but yes, it will be the best investment the company ever made."

He liked hearing that. "Anything else?"

"Yes. You're the face of this event."

He was about to blurt out, "What about Cindy?" but he reminded himself she no longer officially worked for them. He looked at Cynthia but said nothing.

"Every royal ball needs its king," Cynthia added with an undertone of respect.

Madeline waited on Danny for a commitment.

He rubbed his chin for a moment as he mulled it over. Finally, he cracked a smile. "Rat Fink ain't gonna be too happy about this."

They all burst into laughter. Madeline put her arm in Danny's as they continued to walk.

"Great! Maybe after this he'll quit, and we won't have to fire him," Madeline quipped.

Danny threw her a glance of caution. "So, when's the big day?" he asked.

Madeline and Cynthia exchanged looks. The question surprised them.

Madeline stared into Cynthia's eyes. "September first," she announced.

"That's only a few weeks away. This kind of thing takes months to pull together, Madeline. You know that."

She let go of his arm. "We can do this. It feels right."

Cynthia squealed in excitement and wrapped her arms around Madeline's neck. "Thank you. Thank you. The children are going to love it."

Madeline didn't acknowledge the burst of excitement, as her eyes were locked in on Danny's.

Cynthia stepped back. "If you'll allow me to, I'd be honored to help however I can."

"Are you kidding me?" Madeline asked. "You bet you're gonna help. This whole thing is for people like you, my dear."

Cynthia's face glowed. "Do you think there's a chance that *my* parents will be there?"

"They just might be," Madeline said kindly.

Cynthia looked at Madeline. "I took a saliva test that apparently can help locate them. If that happens, I can send them an invitation. Wouldn't they be surprised?" She couldn't help laughing.

"I imagine they would be," Madeline said. There was a moment of silence.

"Am I missing something?" Danny prodded.

"Nope." Madeline locked arms with Danny on one side and Cynthia on the other. "Let's go get some ice cream to celebrate our grand ball."

Danny led the three of them into the crowded street, headed toward his favorite malt shop. Soon he and the ladies blended in with the hundreds of other happy families in the park that night. The screams of roller-coaster riders and the loud roar of Ziggy's rocket ship filled the nighttime air, giving Danny an unusual sense of peace.

⤚ 14 ⤙

DURING THE NEXT FEW WEEKS, CYNTHIA, MADELINE, AND Danny worked tirelessly on getting the park ready for its big night.

Cynthia connected with Bobby so she could thank him for bringing her to the park. They spent a few afternoons together planning the promotion of the event, including pictures of Danny. Cynthia felt her heart beat faster each time she saw Bobby, but she always kept it to herself, uncertain if he was destined to be with someone else.

"Have you had any success in getting in touch with Julia?" she asked one day.

Bobby was slow to respond. "Actually, I did locate her through Instagram. We're following each other. I guess that's a good sign, huh?"

"That's wonderful, Bobby. My guess is she would love a box of Cracker Jacks."

Cynthia laughed, prompting him to break a smile as well.

Madeline loved the choice of pictures Bobby gave her of Danny and the orphans' ball ad campaign. He had delivered his best work yet and provided fuel for a fantastic social-media campaign.

Her favorite was a shot of Danny holding a baby boy, looking as though he had just won the lottery. It took some work to get the pose, but not quite as much as they first thought. Danny had seemed to take to the little guy more so than Bobby, Madeline, or Cynthia would have imagined. *Perhaps he does have a "daddy gene" in him*, Madeline mused to herself.

Besides the marketing, Madeline's focus was on connecting with every reputable ancestry and adoption organization she could find. She spent hours sharing her vision with each of these companies about how they could provide their clients, who had already identified their families, an opportunity to meet each other for the first time at the ball.

On the day they officially announced the ball, they used every available media source possible. Madeline and Danny conducted press tours defending his desire to do something good for the orphans. The announcement was covered on social media, radio and TV, and in newspapers. Ads and public service announcements broadcasted the news that Ziggy's Park would be closed to the public on September first to host the inaugural orphans' ball. The park invited orphans, potential adoptive parents, birth mothers, birth fathers, and adopted adults seeking to find their birth parents to attend the dance for free.

Madeline, Cynthia, and Eunice carved out time to visit the twin girls. The babies required a great deal of human contact, more than what the workers at the orphanage could provide. Madeline began to give her heart to the girls. They became part of her daily conversations and part of her life. She talked in great depth about them with Danny, though oftentimes he was distracted with work, leaving Madeline to feel as though he was just playing along with the conversation, indulging her in her "midlife crisis." One day, she finally convinced him to go with her to see the girls, as a favor to her.

Danny was surprised when he saw the girls again. He commented that the last time he had seen them was at the emergency room, when they looked like they wouldn't make it another day. Now they looked healthy and happy and like children who had everything they needed.

Madeline took Annie and laid her in his arms. She had mastered the art of holding the babies, so now it was her turn to show Danny. His discomfort was obvious at first, but eventually Annie's big brown eyes and bright smile seemed to both calm his fears and melt his heart as her little hands clung to his strong fingers. Madeline held Emily. Together they swayed and played with the babies.

Just then, a nurse at the orphanage walked in with a man and a woman. "Oh, I'm sorry. I didn't know Annie had another family looking at her," the nurse said.

"No, we're not here looking to adopt. We're just…" Madeline stopped herself. The words felt like gravel in her mouth. She looked to Danny for help. Then she looked at the man and woman standing in the doorway. She didn't like them. They looked poor and unkempt. They didn't look right. Annie and Emily deserved better than these people.

Danny put Annie in a crib and then took Emily from Madeline and laid her in a crib. He smiled at the couple. "We're done here. They're beautiful babies. Enjoy your time."

Madeline had difficulty leaving the room, but Danny lovingly escorted her by the arm. Once in the hall, he put his arms around her and held her for a moment. They heard the nurse ask the visiting couple, "Are you looking to adopt both children?"

The woman quickly replied, "No, we wouldn't be able to handle both kids, I'm afraid."

Madeline stared into Danny's eyes and whispered her fear: "They're going to separate the twins." Madeline was horrified, and tears welled up in her eyes as he walked her down the stairs and out the front door. She looked at him with red eyes and then climbed into the car.

He paused for a second, then said, "Madeline, ever since Cindy arrived, you're not the same."

Nothing more was said on the drive back to the office.

Madeline and Cynthia spent the last couple days before the big event overseeing the transformation of Ziggy's. Madeline wanted a classy look and decided on only black and white in all the décor. She installed huge, round paper lanterns that appeared to float in thin air as they hung over the park's entrance and down Main Street, giving plenty of light below. The lights would guide their guests along a red carpet to the sunken amphitheater at the center of the park, where each of the decade lots converged. The venue had been enlarged since the first ball so many years before. It could now hold up to nearly a thousand people or more.

Music would fill the air as guests would descend the marble steps to discover thousands of small crystal bulbs strung together lighting up a beautiful, varnished hardwood dance floor below. One of the finest local 1940s-style orchestras would assemble at the northern corner. Candle-lit tables covered in white linen would be set up around the perimeter of the dance floor, giving potential moms, dads, and children a chance to converse for the first time or to deepen an already established relationship.

Madeline and Cynthia worked diligently with each foster-care agency, adoption center, and ancestry organization involved to ensure that the seat assignments would connect the children with the appropriate potential family. Their planning was strategic and judicious, while at the same time rewarding for their relationship. They grew to care for each other deeply.

When she was not working alongside Cynthia, Madeline worked with Danny doing guest appearances, public service announcements, and tracking the marketing campaign. It was obvious to Madeline that while he was on board with the goodwill of the event, he still wanted to know that it somehow would bring in a profit to the company in the end.

The day before the ball, Madeline sat at her desk combing over the insurmountable list of things to do when the phone rang. It was a friendly voice.

"Hi, Madeline! It's Ruby from Palmer Labs calling you back."

Surprised, Madeline replied, "Ruby! I heard your voicemail message. Are you okay?"

"I'm healing. I had back surgery two weeks ago and I'm laid up. The surgery went well, but it's driving me nuts just being in bed."

"Oh, Ruby, I'm so sorry."

"Don't be! My back's been bothering me for years. I finally took care of it. The doctor said that I should be good as new in a couple of months. But I'm calling about that saliva test you were inquiring about. I was able to do some research from home and I got some results for you. Is it a good time to talk?"

Madeline's heart stopped. "Yes, of course!"

"Well, I'm happy to report that Palmer Labs passed the test and got you a 99.2 percent match!"

"What do you mean?"

"That's what this was, right? A test to prove the accuracy of our DNA tests? Why else would you have your daughter submit a saliva test? I can't believe after all this time of working together, I never knew that you even had a daughter!"

"A daughter?" Madeline exclaimed. "I don't have a daughter!"

Ruby paused. "Sure you do, Cindy Hope."

"No … I never had kids."

"Madeline, our results conclude that you and Cindy Hope are not only related, but that you are her mother."

Madeline laughed. "Ruby, I think I'd know if I had a child! Did Radcliffe put you up to this?"

"Radcliffe? No! Look, I don't know what to tell you, but DNA tests don't lie. Especially with over ninety-nine-percent accuracy. What's going on, Madeline?"

"You're talking crazy, Ruby! Email me the results," Madeline demanded.

"Madeline, I …"

"Email me!" Madeline heard Ruby's fingers typing on her keyboard.

Ruby continued, "Do you remember years ago when we offered free ancestry kits to your employees as part of our promotion at Ziggy's? You and Danny were among those that submitted your DNA, and we've had it on file ever since. There is a definitive match. The two of you are Cindy's parents."

Madeline's heart began to race as she hovered her hand over the button to open the attachment. Something inside her knew that Ruby was telling the truth, but *how* this could all be true was mind-boggling to Madeline.

"Madeline, did you receive the email? Are you okay?"

Madeline couldn't respond. She felt a surge of emotion burst through her insides while scanning the twelve-page document. Her head began to spin. It was all there right in front of her, her entire family tree, including many people she knew to be part of her lineage. Cynthia's name was at the top of the list as the most recent member of her family line.

Madeline was stunned but refused to let her emotions get the best of her. "This must be a mistake."

"No, Madeline. I don't see how. We always run the numbers twice."

"Years ago, I was pregnant, but I lost baby Cynthia..." Madeline's voice drifted off. "I... I need to go now."

"Madeline, I don't want to hang up and leave you alone right now. Is there anyone you can call?"

"I'm fine," Madeline softly replied. "I'm going to see a friend."

"Okay, good." Ruby breathed a sigh of relief. "I'm sorry, Madeline, if this causes you pain. I hope you can work it out."

"Bye, Ruby." Madeline hung up the phone, eyes fixed on her computer screen. It was too much to process. How could this be? *There must be a mistake*, she thought. *There must be a mistake.*

Madeline cleared her mind and printed the documents. She shoved them in her purse and left the office in a rush. When she climbed into her SUV, her mind began to organize her priorities. One of them was to make sure she didn't run into Cynthia. She knew she couldn't handle that conversation at the moment. She called Bobby and instructed him to find Cynthia, pick her up, and keep her busy—away from the park and away from Eunice's house.

Bobby asked why, but Madeline gave him no direct answer. He surrendered and agreed to do it. Within thirty minutes, Bobby texted Madeline and said they were on their way to an early dinner. Madeline thanked him and drove to Eunice's.

Eunice was reading when a pounding on the front door startled her. Her heart jumped for a second, but she was relieved when she spied Madeline through the drapes. Surprised to see Madeline at her doorstep, Eunice noticed her anxious rocking back and forth. She opened the door and Madeline pushed by her, something she'd never done before.

"Madeline, are you okay?" Eunice asked with concern.

"I was wondering if you could help me with some information I just received that's very important to me."

"Of course. I'd be glad to help anyway I can. Would you like to sit down?"

Madeline nodded, but stayed on her feet. "What do you know about Cynthia's past?"

"You mean Cindy?"

"Yes, Cindy. Do you know where she came from?"

Eunice giggled. "Huh! I wish I did!" After she said that, her face wrinkled with fear. "Why do you ask? Is she okay?"

"Did you ever hear back from that ancestry company on her saliva test?" Madeline asked, ignoring the question.

"No, I lost the paper with the identification code and wasn't able to retrieve the results. But Cindy said you were helping her find her parents, so I just let it go."

Madeline bit her bottom lip, then asked, "How well do you know this girl? You've lived with her for some time now."

"Yes, I have. Over a year now. It seems like just yesterday she stood on my porch and sang to me."

"Sang to you?"

"Yeah. A song that my dad used to sing to me years ago. The thing about it is, I never told anyone about our special song. It was something my dad and I kept to ourselves. It's like she knows things that no one knows, you know?" Eunice snickered.

Madeline, seeming a bit distracted, asked, "Has she ever said anything about where she comes from? Who she is, how she got here… anything at all?"

"I'm sorry, Madeline, she hasn't. But I've wondered about that ever since I met her. If you ask me, I'd say she's an angel."

"An angel?" Madeline perked up. "What do you mean by that?"

"You know her as well as I do, if not better. Have you ever met anyone like her? She's no ordinary person. She's ... I don't know ... different. She's an angel."

Madeline drew close to Eunice. "Do you really believe in angels?"

"I didn't before I met her. But now ... Well, remember she told us about that guy Sebastian and how he was her angel?"

"That's right. I forgot about that." Madeline's brow furled. She expressed a great deal of mental anxiety.

"Madeline, what's this about?"

"Is there someone I could talk to that might know about angels and stuff?" Madeline whispered loudly.

"You can talk to Pastor Timothy at our local chapel down the street. If anyone knows about angels, it would be him."

"Is that where you go to church?"

"Me, Cindy, Portia ... We go every week."

"So, he knows Cynthia?"

"I'd say so. She sings in the choir sometimes."

"Where is this chapel?"

"Right off Center Street on Marshall Drive."

"Thank you. You've been a big help." Madeline hugged her and left the house.

Eunice prayed for Madeline while she watched her peel out of the driveway, headed for the chapel.

Madeline reached the chapel in less than five minutes. She opened the double doors to the pristine house of worship and made her way towards the front of the chapel, locating the back office off to the right. She knocked on the door and Pastor

Timothy greeted her with a friendly handshake. He invited her to sit down and talk, but she didn't like the claustrophobic feel of his tiny old space. She asked if they could take a walk. They found a place to chat on the top step of the platform in the empty sanctuary.

Madeline asked about angels and how to identify them. She also interrogated him about angels taking the body of humans who had died. He carefully walked her through the difference between angels and humans and did his best to clear up any confusion she might have.

"Angels can appear as humans, yes. But they do not indwell the body of a human who has passed. Nor do they take on the DNA of a baby who did not live."

This left Madeline perplexed and even scared. How could this girl, whom she'd known and worked with for over a year, have the same DNA as that of her baby, who died over two decades ago?

She didn't realize it, but she had voiced her question out loud.

Pastor Timothy stared at her with compassion. "Who are we talking about?"

"Cynthia. I mean Cindy. You know her as Cindy."

"Cindy Hope?"

"Yes, I understand you know her quite well."

He smiled. "I guess you might say we are what you would call friends. She's quite an extraordinary woman. Uh, please excuse me." He adjusted his glasses. "Are you saying she's your daughter?"

Tears filled her swollen eyes. "How can that be? I lost my baby over twenty-five years ago. I was in that room when they told me the baby had passed. I lost my baby, yet I'm told by the experts in ancestry research that there's almost a one hundred percent chance that it's Cynthia. How can this be, Pastor?"

He spoke softly. "Madeline, have you talked about this with anyone else?" His German accent was more apparent in a whisper and made him harder to understand.

She pondered his words. "No, I haven't. I wouldn't know who to talk to."

"Does your husband know?"

"We're divorced." Her voice broke. "After losing the baby, we found we couldn't get pregnant again and our marriage fell apart."

"I'm sorry to hear that. It must have been a very difficult time for you. Does he know yet about the test results?"

"Danny? Oh, he has no clue. He never even knew I was pregnant to begin with. I kept it a secret that he was a father ... is a father ..." She trailed off, confused.

"Maybe it's time he found out." He placed his hand on her shoulder, offering comfort.

Madeline shook to her core. *How in heaven's name did my life get to this point? What did I ever do to deserve the hell I'm going through?*

She rose and extended her hand to the perplexed reverend. "I wish I could say that you've been of help to me, Pastor, but I think I'd be lying. And the one thing I'm not is a liar."

They shook hands.

"I understand, Madeline."

She turned and walked down the aisle toward the front door, then stopped and turned around. "Tim?"

"Yes?"

"Have you ever heard of anything like this before? I mean ... you're in the miracle business, right?"

"I can honestly say no." He scratched his head, perplexed, and then pointed to the plain wooden cross hanging behind him. "But this girl you're referring to, I hardly know her, yet she has turned my life upside down. She talked of this King as though she knew Him. I mean really knew Him. So, I changed the cross that hung up there for more than fifty years and now my board says change it back or they will terminate me. I wonder. What should I do?" He looked up towards the cross.

Madeline followed his gazed, not understanding everything but felt the man's pain and dilemma.

"If it's of benefit to you," he said, "I believe if anyone could be such a miracle baby … she's the one."

Madeline felt a glimmer of hope and cracked a smile. "If she is a miracle baby, as you suggest, what in the world do I do with such news?"

"Tell the world," he said. "Tell the whole wide world that even in death there is life. In loss, there is gain."

"I'll let you know." She left the chapel and walked very slowly to her SUV, mulling over all that she'd just heard. Danny flashed through her mind. She had no idea how to break the news to him but strongly felt that it was the right thing to do.

Bobby was chatting with Cynthia at a local café when Madeline texted him. She wanted assurance that Cynthia was nowhere near the office. He secretly texted back that she was not; they were about to finish eating and make their way back to the house. Cynthia was getting tired and wanted to go home.

Madeline thanked him for his help and insisted he not tell Cynthia of their conversation. He sent her a smiling emoji with the comment "you owe me." There was no reply.

Madeline arrived at the park and made her way to the administrative building where she hesitated nervously at the door to

Danny's office. Her hands were sweaty. She had not felt like this since the night she stood on the grassy hill waiting to tell him they had a baby girl. How ironic that, nearly three decades later, she was nervous about telling him the same thing. The old fear that she would be rejected once again sent panic through her veins. She overcame them with anger and barged into his office ready for a fight.

As usual, Danny was on the phone. She motioned for him to end the call. The look he gave her conveyed an annoyance at her gall to give him such a demand. She paced back and forth in front of his desk with her shoulders back and her face grim.

"George, let me get back to you. Something has come up." He hung up the phone. "What now, Madeline?"

She sat down and took a deep breath. She silently prayed. *Oh God! Help me and help me now!*

"Come on, Mattie. What's so important that I had to cut short my conversation with our local senator?"

"Have you noticed any similarities between me and Cynthia … I mean Cindy?"

"Where's this going, Mattie?"

"Just answer the question."

"Yeah. I've noticed a few things here and there."

"Like?" She was getting more anxious, which made her more irritated.

"Like, how much you look alike. Or how you seem to have identical expressions and mannerisms at certain times."

"Like?"

"Like when you sit down, you both cross your legs one way, and then a moment later cross them the opposite way. Or when you scratch your nose, you both use your pinky."

"So? What's wrong with the way I scratch my nose?"

"Nothing's wrong with it. You asked me about similarities and that's something that sticks out to me. That's all. And you both laugh the same."

Madeline was surprised by his list and how observant he was. She looked down at her fingers. She felt paranoid all of a sudden, like she had a shadow or a clone of herself mimicking her every move. She shook it off and stood up.

"I need to tell you something, Danny, and I have no idea how I'm going to say it, or how you're going to understand it."

"Try me. Nothing's gonna surprise me anymore."

She removed the papers from her purse and sifted through them. Once she found the report she was looking for, she handed it to Danny. Her hand shook. "These are the findings of a saliva sampling conducted from several thousand tests. You are holding the results of those tests."

"I don't understand what I'm looking at."

"Read the names at the top left corner."

"Madeline and Walter Richards."

"Now read the name at the far right corner."

Danny eyed her for a moment and then glanced at the name. "Cynthia Hope Richards. Madeline, what is this?"

Madeline was frightened to look at him for fear of rejection but forced herself to make eye contact. "It's a scientific document stating that you and I have a daughter."

"That's impossible. We were never able to get pregnant!"

"That's not true."

Danny stopped and slowly asked, "What do you mean, Mattie?"

Madeline's voice shook. "Do you recall that night we had our first ball? I asked you to meet me on the grassy hill because I had something to tell you?"

"Vaguely. I remember something made you so mad you swore we would never have another one."

"That night I tried to tell… I tried to tell you that I was pregnant."

Danny rose to his feet and met her in front of his desk. "What?"

Talking nervously and quickly now, Madeline defended herself. "I was afraid I would lose you. You made it very clear before our wedding that you were *not* interested in having kids. I tried telling you the night of our grand ball, but you were not in a place to talk about it."

"That's not fair," Danny said, his tone defensive. "If you knew the lousy childhood I had, you would understand my reasons for not wanting kids. I know what I am and what I am not, and I am *not* dad material." He stopped and looked in her eyes. Danny softened in his response. "I'm so sorry, Madeline. I had no idea. What happened?"

Madeline struggled to get out the words, her body shaking. "I lost her in my eleventh week. I was hiding the pregnancy from you until I could find the right time to tell you. Then, one night I woke up feeling scared. I lost her sometime that morning, September the first." Madeline started to cry as the memories came crashing in, "The doctor couldn't find a heartbeat! I'm so sorry, Danny. I'm so sorry for hiding it from you and not telling you. I'm so sorry I lost our daughter."

Danny rushed over and put his arms around her. He held her convulsing body tightly as decades of repressed tears streamed down her face.

"No, Mattie. No. It's not your fault. I'm so sorry that you had to go through all of that alone. Thank you for telling me." He let her cry and continued whispering to her over and over, "I'm so sorry."

Madeline couldn't think. All she could do was surrender to the tidal wave of emotion that covered her. The wounds of loss had never left her, they were just stuffed away, slowly tormenting her. Now, her walls crumbled, and her secret was no more. She sobbed uncontrollably, finding comfort in the arms of the man she had once loved—and perhaps still loved.

Madeline eventually composed herself and stepped away from Danny. "So here we are, more than twenty-five years later, and they're telling me she's alive."

"What? So you didn't miscarry?"

"I did lose her, Danny, but this report shows that she's baby Cynthia. Cynthia Hope."

"Wait, wait. Cindy Hope? Are you saying that Cindy Hope is our daughter?"

"I don't know what to say or think. But that's what the saliva test confirms."

"That can't be!" Danny grabbed the papers again and started rifling through them.

"That paper in your hands says that it's over ninety-nine percent true."

Danny plopped down in a chair with a thud. "Mattie, do you know how crazy this sounds? I mean... How is this even possible?"

"I have no clue, but evidently it's real. And it's happening to us."

In the dark, cluttered room down the hall, Radcliffe's portly face twisted with anger and disbelief. Stunned, he grumbled to himself over and over, "I knew there was something wrong with that girl. She's not human!" He also knew that if Cynthia was indeed their daughter, she would be poised to inherit the bulk of the company, shattering his delusions of grandeur at owning Ziggy's Island.

Radcliffe turned up the volume on the speaker that provided his unauthorized eavesdropping and started to chew his fingernails.

Terry Harris

Madeline watched Danny's reactions carefully. His phone buzzed. Without flinching, he hit the do-not-disturb button on the phone, causing it to go silent.

Madeline breathed a sigh of relief. He cared; she felt it. There was a sudden jolt of connection between the two. Her fear of being rejected diminished noticeably.

Danny took a deep breath and rose to his feet. He drew close to her and grabbed her hands.

"Mattie. I am so sorry that I was unapproachable that night when you tried to tell me. I'm also sorry you had to go through the loss of our baby alone. That had to be the worst time of your life. With all we've been through, no wonder we couldn't work things out. I promise you now, no matter how crazy this gets, I will be here for you. We'll see this madness through together, okay? You and me."

She teared up again but kept control. "Thank you, Walter. You have no idea how much I needed to hear that."

She fell into his arms, and they held each other until they couldn't hold each other any longer. A deep flood of healing surged through both their souls. It was almost as if the years of separation were being swallowed up and they had their entire future before them. This hug was one of unity, not of condolence. They shared tears of joy and felt as though they were one soul.

Danny was the first to speak. "Oh Mattie, you're the only woman I ever really loved."

Madeline was very selective with her words and tried to be as honest as possible. "I love you too, Danny, and I need you, now more than ever." She stopped. She didn't know what to say next and suddenly felt extremely vulnerable. She jumped out of his arms.

Danny looked at her, concerned. "We need to find Cindy."

Madeline corrected him. "Cynthia. Her name is Cynthia Hope Richards."

He smiled. "That's a beautiful name. Do you know where she is?"

Madeline nodded. "She's with Bobby. I had him keep her away from the office 'til we talked." She grabbed her purse and Danny opened the door for her. She smiled, kissed him gently on the lips, and stepped into the hall to leave.

Radcliffe sat in his office, frantically dialing his cell.

"Deidre? This is your father. I have a job for you that is of critical importance. I want you to find that girl Cindy, and I want you to take her somewhere, anywhere, I don't care where. Then call me once you have her. Do you understand?" He listened impatiently as she spoke, then cut her off. "We don't have time to wait. Do it now. Leave the shop and get over to the house and see if you can find her. If you find her, do as I told you. You've got very little time. Now do it!" He tossed his phone on the desk and stewed.

Radcliffe's darkened mind formulated a plan to rid himself of Cynthia once and for all. He had to if he wanted to see his plans to own the company fulfilled. Nothing was going to get in his way. He scanned his computer files and located the security service that Madeline had hired. He then placed a call to them and let them know they would no longer need their services of guarding Cynthia; effective immediately.

15

AFTER LEAVING THE OFFICE, MADELINE CALLED BOBBY and asked about Cynthia. Bobby had dropped her off back at the house less than thirty minutes earlier. Madeline thanked him for his help and confirmed he was ready for the ball the next day. He assured her he was. Madeline ended her call with Bobby and then turned to look out the window.

Her nerves were getting the best of her, so she asked Danny to hurry. He said nothing but obliged her request and sped up.

Deidre entered the house and found Cynthia home alone. She acted scared and made up a story about something being wrong with Portia, and then begged for Cynthia's help. Cynthia grew concerned and promised to do everything she could to help.

Deidre pulled her out of the house by the hand, leaving Cynthia's purse, keys, and all other personal items behind. They hurried into Deidre's car and roared down the street away from the house.

Deidre had no clue where to go next, so once she reached a stop light, she quickly texted her father. He texted back a moment later and instructed her to bring Cynthia to the park. They were to meet him near Ziggy's rocket ship at the center of the grounds.

As they drove, Deidre concocted more of the lie about Portia and got Cynthia to agree to meet her at Ziggy's.

Deidre pulled into the employees' parking lot of Ziggy's, where Radcliffe had arranged clearance. Once they were cleared to enter, she rushed Cynthia through the gate and into the park.

A new text told Deidre to take Cynthia down into the fire pit, and he would meet them there. Deidre became stressed. How would she get Cynthia to go there? As they walked through the park, Deidre pretended to get a text from Portia. "What? How weird is that?"

"What's the matter?" Cynthia asked.

"It's Portia. She's telling me she got herself stuck in the fire pit behind Ziggy's rocket. Oh, brother. How can you be so dumb? Maybe we should just leave her there."

"No, we can't do that to Portia. If she needs our help, we've got to be there for her."

"I don't wanna go down into that stinking pit and get my new dress all dirty." Deidre bit her lip, hoping Cynthia would take the bait.

"I'll go. I'm not worried about this old dress." Cynthia showed genuine concern.

Gotcha! Deidre thought. She gave Cynthia's sky-blue dress a once over as a sign of playing along. "All right. Suit yourself. They're your clothes."

She smiled to herself devilishly as they maneuvered through the crowd. She imagined Radcliffe telling her how proud he was of her. She couldn't wait to see his face when she delivered the princess to her dungeon. She hoped that Portia would be jealous of their new relationship and fight hard to get in her good graces.

At the rocket ship, Deidre had a sudden surge of panic that the plan might not work. But Cynthia eagerly placed her hand on the steel door handle to the pit. "Is this the way down?"

"Uhhh, yeah. That's it, I think," Deidre declared, trying to conceal her nervousness.

Once inside, Deidre closed the door behind them as the steamy air enveloped them. They stood at the top of the narrow cement steps to the fire hole until their eyes adjusted to the darkness.

"She's down there," Deidre said coldly as she nudged Cynthia down.

"Portia?" Cynthia called out. The room was loud with the rumbling of the furnace that lit the thirty-foot rocket. Sweat dripped down Deidre's back as she stepped onto the dirt floor, following Cynthia.

"Over here." Deidre led her to the small room that held fuel and black coal for the rocket. The room had iron bars around it, with a small entry point that could be blocked by closing an iron gate.

Just then, the door at the top of the stairs opened up, letting in light. A loud clomping echoed within the small space as someone clumsily descended the steps.

Deidre pushed Cynthia into the coal room and slammed the gate closed, barricading it with her body until she could get some help.

"Deidre. What are you doing?" Cynthia called out, her voice full of fear and tension.

Radcliffe stepped into the space in front of the gate. "She's doing exactly what she was told to do."

"I don't understand. Where's Portia?"

"You fool. Portia's not here. But you are, and you'll stay here until I move you elsewhere." His voice gurgled eerily, like a death rattle.

With that, he shoved a thick board between the handles to lock the gate shut.

"But why? What have I done to you?" Cynthia pleaded.

"You were born!" He growled like an angry dog. "Actually, let me correct that. You were not born. You were aborted and now you've come back to haunt those who got rid of you in the first place. Your parents never wanted you, not then and not now. I'm going to do them and everyone else a favor. I'm going to sell you to the highest bidder and ship you off to a faraway land on the other side of the ocean." He laughed hard and loud. "Isn't that where you told everyone you were from? Well, I'm sending you back."

He laughed even harder. Deidre laughed with him and secretly waited to hear *Well done, my child*, but she never did.

Cynthia reached through the bars, grasping for help.

He swiped at her neck and ripped her necklace off.

"No! Give that back to me."

He held the necklace up, reading it. "Cynthia Hope! Well, well, well... ain't that a pretty name." He laughed and threw the necklace into the fire.

Cynthia wept, begging to be released.

"Come on, Deidre. Let's leave this scoundrel to the rats. But first I want you to load the fire pit up so no one will need to refill it before I transport her to the ends of the earth."

Deidre just stared at him, not understanding.

"Go on. Grab that shovel and fill the pit."

She glanced over by the bowels of the rocket ship and stared at a stack of coal piled against the concrete wall.

He waved her on.

She begrudgingly picked up the shovel and began to heap the coal into the fire pit. When she finished, she wiped her hands on her dress without thinking.

He sneered at his daughter. "Good god, girl, you're as dirty and ugly as she is."

She looked down at the dark soot that covered her expensive dress. Radcliffe's humiliating laughter bounced off the walls.

Deidre slowly lifted her head, and with tear-filled eyes, cast a look of pity toward Cynthia. Seeing her caged didn't feel as good as she thought it would. Her hatred of Cynthia took a back seat to feelings of compassion. Deidre darted up the steps, bawling, leaving her ungrateful father behind.

Unfazed by his daughter's outburst, Radcliffe slowly approached the cage holding Cynthia. "Oh, by the way. I just want you to know that I know who your parents are. But I'm not going to tell you." He grinned, letting the pain of his words pierce her soul. "You'll be shipped off never knowing who you belong to. Good riddance, Princess!" Radcliffe hacked a hard cough, then clumsily hobbled up the concrete steps.

Cynthia cried out, "No, Radcliffe. Please tell me. You can't leave me here. Help! Somebody, help!"

Radcliffe exited the fire pit and slammed the door shut with a hard thud. He then padlocked the door handle, securing her fate. He chuckled to himself and then waddled away, slipping the key to the padlock into his suit pocket.

Meanwhile, Madeline and Danny pulled into Eunice's driveway. They knocked on the door, but there was no answer. They looked through the windows but saw an empty house. Danny knocked again and then tried to open the front door. It was unlocked.

When they entered, they saw Cynthia's purse on the couch, her Bible, and a warm, half-empty cup of tea. Madeline called out as she walked around the small house. There was no answer, and Madeline grew concerned. She ran up the stairs and opened the door to the attic. Cynthia's bed was made. All looked normal. She went to the backyard and searched the garage. No signs of anyone.

Danny suggested they wait for her to come back, as she was probably on a walk and would return shortly. Madeline agreed and sat down on a chair on the porch. Danny sat next to her and held her hand.

An hour later, worried and tired of waiting, Danny and Madeline left Eunice's house to look for Cynthia and then returned a few hours later. They had searched everywhere they could think of, to no avail. They called Bobby and put him on alert, with orders to call them the moment he heard from Cynthia.

They returned to Eunice's house and knocked on the door again, surprising Eunice.

"Is Cynthia here?" Madeline asked anxiously as they entered the house.

A look of worry on her face, Portia stepped away from the dinner table to stand beside Eunice.

"No, she's not. I'm not sure where she is, but she left her purse here so she can't be far," Eunice tried to assure them.

"Yeah, I know. It's been here all afternoon."

Eunice gave Madeline a look as if to ask how she knew that.

Danny stepped into the conversation. "We were here earlier and found the front door unlocked, so we came in uninvited, thinking we would find her upstairs or something. I'm sorry about that, but this matter is quite urgent."

"Sure, I understand," Eunice said. "What's wrong?"

"I don't know," Madeline mumbled. "Cynthia's nowhere to be found. We've searched this entire area thinking she took a long walk or something, but she should have come back by now. Something's not right."

Eunice panicked. "What do you mean something's not right? How long has she been missing?" Eunice went to the phone and picked it up. As she was dialing, Madeline continued to talk.

"We've looked everywhere. No one knows where she is."

"Hello, yes, my name is Eunice Finklemeyer. I would like to make a missing person's report. No, she's an adult." Eunice looked to Madeline. "How long has she been missing?"

"Only about five hours, but I know something's wrong. My mom alarms are going off!" Madeline hesitated, surprised by her words of such intimacy.

"Yes... no, I understand," Eunice said into the receiver. "It's just that it's so not like her and nobody knows where she is. Okay. Well, hopefully we won't have to call you again. Thank you." Eunice hung up the phone. "The police won't even consider a report until an adult has been missing for twenty-four hours."

Madeline groaned. "So what do we do now?"

Eunice began to cry. "If anything were to happen to her, I don't know what I'd do." Portia went over to her aunt and put her arms around her.

Madeline realized that they were just wasting time by staying in the house. She had to get out and look for her daughter now. "We're gonna go back out and drive around and see if we can find her."

Danny jumped up to immediately oblige.

"Please, of course, let us know if you hear anything. Here's my cell." Danny handed Eunice his business card. "Stay here so that if..." He instantly felt Madeline's anxious eyes stare him down, so he corrected himself. "*When* she returns, you can ask her to give us a call right away. Regardless of the hour. Okay?"

They shook hands and Danny escorted Madeline toward the door. Madeline stopped and turned and hugged Eunice. "Thank you for taking care of Cynthia for me." It was an awkward but completely honest emotion. The tears in Eunice's eyes indicated her love for Cynthia and her appreciation of Madeline's gesture.

As soon as they left, Madeline grew more anxious and pressed her mind to figure out their next move. "The orphanage!" she blurted out. "We forgot to check the orphanage."

"I'm on it." Danny sped down the street. Madeline pulled out her cell phone and called the orphanage. It rang four times and then went to a generic voice message. Madeline waited forever for the beep and then left a message trying to cover up her anxiety: "Hi, this is Madeline Brewer. I'm calling to see if Cynthia Hope is there visiting the girls. If she is, can you please let her know I need to speak to her? It's rather important. She has my number. Thank you."

When they finally arrived, Danny hadn't even stopped the car before Madeline opened the door and jumped out. She left him behind as she shot up the steps and barged through the entryway of the old brick building. Inside, there was no sign of Cynthia. She scanned the halls and then ran upstairs to the room where the twins were kept. Madeline froze at the sight of an empty room. The twins were not there, and the bedding was being changed. *No*, she thought. *Are they gone?* She couldn't take another loss.

"Mattie?"

She heard Danny calling her name from downstairs. "Up here," she called out.

Danny entered the room and found Madeline staring at the empty cribs, then she turned and stared at him. "She's not here."

"Cindy?" he asked to confirm.

"Cynthia," she snapped, correcting him. "And it looks like the twins are gone too."

Madeline's mind raced with two frightening thoughts that converged into one heartbreaking possibility: *Something's happened to Cynthia, and someone has taken the twins away.* If both were true, she would never be able to see them again, and that was too unbearable to accept.

Danny spoke up. "Let's go talk to the director and see what's going on. Maybe they've seen Cynthia. Better yet," he said perking up, "maybe Cynthia's with the twins."

Madeline breathed for a moment, considering that as a possibility.

"Come on." On their way down the hall, Danny asked a worker where he might find the director. They were told to go to the office building behind the orphanage.

They found the director in her office, poring over some adoption papers. Their bubble of hope popped when she told them that Cynthia hadn't been there for a couple of days and that the twins were undergoing medical exams for their imminent departure. The girls would be separated and live with two different families. Madeline lifted her eyes to see Danny looking back at her, sympathetic. Madeline turned on her heels and left the tiny room, holding back the tears at hearing that news.

Back in the car, Madeline was on her cell phone, calling everyone she knew and asking if they had seen Cynthia. Danny said nothing as he drove back to the office.

By the time they arrived at Ziggy's, it was after eight p.m. Most of the office staff had left for the day, except Radcliffe, who was trying to plot his exit strategy for the princess held captive in the fire pit.

He listened with glee as Madeline divulged her fear that Cynthia was gone and wasn't coming back. She feared just as Cynthia seemed to magically appear, she could disappear as quickly. "My heart aches at that thought. There is so much I want to say and do with her. You know, I've even considered canceling the ball but can't break the hearts of so many people anticipating the life-changing event."

Radcliffe enjoyed the sound of Madeline's pain, until he heard her whispered confession to Danny: "I was thinking we could hand the reins of this place over to Cynthia in a few years, if indeed she is our daughter. You and I could retire and live the life I dreamed about when we were first married."

After hearing that, Radcliffe grew more desperate than ever to make sure Cynthia wouldn't be seen or heard from again. His dark, narrow mind searched for ways to sneak Cynthia out of the park and sell her to the highest bidder. He made some calls to some seedy acquaintances and threw out the bait. It wasn't long until he got a call back from an interested party.

At first, he was furious with the man on the other end of the phone, as the trafficker stated he could not pick her up for another twenty-four hours. He was being watched by the FBI and had to lay low for at least one more day.

Radcliffe was about to hang up on him when he nearly begged to be the purchaser of such an incredible find. "Wait," he said. I'll give you more money for her than you'll get anywhere else."

Radcliffe's beady eyes widened. "I'm listening."

"If she's the princess I'm looking at right now on your website, she'll bring one of the highest prices ever paid for a human being. There are kings, tycoons, and even sheiks who will pay any price I ask."

Radcliffe's mouth watered. "Just how much are you offering me for her?"

"We're talking a lot of money. Half when I pick her up and half when I get her out of the country."

"A lot to you may not be a lot to me. How much are we talking?" Radcliffe snarled with greed.

Sweat broke out on Radcliffe's lip when the man named the price. He gulped.

"You keep her hidden until my people pick her up tomorrow night, and you'll be set for a lifetime."

Radcliffe snickered and snorted at the thought of that kind of pay day. He prided himself on figuring a way to not only get rid of Cynthia for good but also to make himself filthy rich.

"I'll give you the twenty-hours, but I better see a bag full of money or you can kiss her and your sheiks goodbye."

"You'll have your money. Tomorrow night. This time. Text me the place."

The phone went dead. He looked at the receiver, then set it down in its cradle. His mind raced as he daydreamed about what he could do with all that money. All at once, he let out a gut-splitting laugh that could be heard up and down the empty halls of Ziggy's executive offices. He couldn't wait for the orphans' ball. It would be the perfect thing to distract Madeline and Danny while he snuck their precious princess out the back gate, never to be heard from again.

As dawn broke the next morning, the day of the grand orphans' ball, Madeline pulled herself out of bed and checked her phone. No messages. She had spent a sleepless night crying. Despair and loss eerily reminded her of that dreadful morning years ago when she lost her baby. The feelings had overtaken her, leaving her empty and despondent. She had no idea how she was going to pretend that she was having a good time at the ball when so much pain besieged her soul.

How was it possible that she could be facing the loss of the same child twice? Who would even *think* of playing such a cruel joke on her? What had she done to deserve such punishment? Those dead-end questions had plagued her all night, draining her of any sanity she had left.

After a long-needed hot shower, she checked her phone again to see if any emails or texts had come in with news of

Cynthia's safety. Danny had texted her, letting her know he had called in every favor owed to him by anyone with whom he had ever rubbed shoulders in law enforcement. They promised an investigation first thing that morning.

Bobby had spent sleepless hours trying to track Cynthia down, without any clues whatsoever. Somehow, though, he believed that she was all right. He knew that if she could be at the dance, she would be. He told himself that he wouldn't worry unless she didn't show up to the ball. He would know then, and only then, that something was truly wrong. His heart told him he would see her again, and he chose to trust it.

Despite his conflicted feelings, that afternoon Bobby kept his promise to Cynthia and called Julia. On the third ring, she picked up.

"Hello?" Bobby's heart leapt as he heard her familiar voice. He froze.

"Hellooo?" Julia asked again.

Bobby spoke up. "Uh, Julia. Hi, it's ... a ..."

"Bobby?" Julia broke the ice. "How are you? Are you okay?"

"Yeah. How are you?" Bobby was still nervous.

"I'm good. A little surprised to hear from you."

"Well, I promised a friend that I would call you."

"That sounds like an odd promise. Did you lose a bet or something?" Julia joked.

"Oh, no, no, no. It's not like that. Look, Julia, I'm sorry to bother you. I just ... I just need to know ... I ... I need to know something about what happened with you and me." Bobby gulped. "I really wanted to hear from you why you broke up with me." He breathed out a heavy sigh.

Julia changed her tone and spoke softly. "Bobby, I was going through a tough time." She gave an awkward chuckle. "After all this time, really?"

"Please, Julia."

"Okay." She paused. "I stopped seeing you because I honestly thought you could do better."

"What?" Bobby was completely surprised.

Julia's voice was faint as she went on to explain how she had not been entirely honest with him about her past and it haunted her. She said she had felt guilty and ashamed, so she ended their relationship.

"I really wish you had trusted me a little more with what you were feeling. Do I suddenly sound like a woman?" They both laughed. Then there was a long pause. Julia sighed.

"I can't believe that you're asking me this now."

Feeling the awkwardness, Bobby quickly chimed in. "Look, if it's too much, or not a good time..."

Julia cut him off. "No, no. It's perfect timing. I'm just surprised. I've been thinking a lot about you lately and was actually thinking of calling you myself." Bobby was relieved and stayed quiet.

"I've been spending this last year reflecting, healing, crying. I think this conversation is another step that I have to take." Julia's voice broke as she continued. "You see, Bobby, I had something in my past that I had to deal with, and I couldn't do it with you. And I definitely couldn't tell you."

Bobby couldn't stay quiet any longer. "What?"

Julia sighed. "When I was a teenager, I got pregnant. And I got an abortion." Her tears were heard over the phone and words began to flow out of her. "I just never dealt with it, you know? I knew it was wrong. I didn't want to, but I didn't know what else to do. I did it. It was horrible and I regret it every day. I think about my baby and her due date and how old she would be, or he would be.

"I wonder what would've happened if I didn't do it. Would we have made it? Would everything have been ok? Why was I so afraid? What would my daughter be doing now? What would she look like? What would she be like?

"I never dealt with it. I hid it from everyone. And I never grieved. For the sake of my child, I needed to grieve. I thought that my baby at least deserved that.

"When we were at the beach that day, Bobby, I just knew that I had to deal with it, without you. And I couldn't tell you. I felt so much guilt. There was no way I could tell you. I'm so sorry."

Julia abruptly hung up.

Shocked and confused, Bobby stared at his phone. The conversation was a complete surprise to him. He got up and paced his room, his phone still in hand. *Now what?* he thought. Not feeling satisfied, he dialed Julia again. The phone rang four times before it was answered.

"Hello?"

"Okay, Julia, just hear me out," Bobby started. "First of all, thank you for sharing that with me. I know that was really hard on you. And, Julia, it's okay. I don't think you're a horrible person. You don't need to apologize to me, I get it. I'm, uh, sorry for what happened. You're an incredible lady and that had to be pretty tough for you to come to grips with, let alone talk about it with someone like me."

Bobby continued to encourage her to forgive herself and let go of the past. "I want you to do yourself a favor. Talk to someone who knows about this stuff. Get some help. Don't keep beating yourself up. Maybe even talk to God about it. You always told me He knows and understands everything."

Julia laughed nervously.

Before hanging up, he felt moved to rebuild the bridge of friendship with her. "You're a pretty incredible person, Julia, and when we were together, I felt like the luckiest man on Earth." After a pause, he asked, "Are you okay?"

"I am better now, yes. Thank you, Bobby, for being so awesome. If it ever works out on your end, I'd love to see you sometime. Maybe we can have coffee at that little French café on Coast Highway."

"I'd like that," he said, letting her hear the smile in his voice. "I'll be in touch."

"Okay, Thanks for calling, Bobby. It means a lot to me."

As Bobby hung up the phone, a familiar peace flooded his soul. He remembered why he had enjoyed being with her so much. They had a special connection.

He paused for a moment, thinking about what just happened and how wrong he had been about the reasons for their breakup. If it hadn't been for Cynthia's encouragement, he probably would have never known the truth.

Glancing at his camera, his attention was suddenly drawn back to the evening's event. It was going to be a busy night.

As she got dressed, Portia had her own mixed feelings about the ball. The night had held so much promise for them as a "new family," but Cynthia's strange disappearance cast a dark shadow over the whole event. She was the reason there was a ball. Without her there, nothing seemed right.

Deidre, on the other hand, seemed curiously giddy and pranced around the house, flaunting her new dress. Recognizing the designer, Portia wondered where Deidre had gotten the money for it.

As Portia was trying to put the finishing touches on her makeup, she reached into Deidre's purse to grab a lipstick. She noticed a new text from Radcliffe on her sister's phone. Portia was shocked to see his name; he never made contact with them in such a personal fashion.

As she reached for the phone to read it, Deidre shrieked and grabbed the device away from Portia's grasp.

"What are you doing snooping around my stuff?" Deidre snarled, sounding much like their father.

"Why is Radcliffe texting you?"

"He may be Radcliffe to you, but he's Dad to me."

"What's that supposed to mean?" Portia demanded.

"Enough, girls," Eunice chastised. "It'll be midnight by the time we get there, the way you two are carrying on. Now, can we go to the ball please?" She opened the door and waited on them to exit.

Deidre stared her sister down, then stuck her tongue out at her. "Jealous!" she snarled as she sauntered past Portia and Eunice and out toward the garage as if she were going to her personal chariot.

Portia walked up and slapped Deidre's backside with her shiny blue purse, which matched her evening gown. "Unbelievable. She's up to something, I can smell it," she grumbled.

Rushed and distracted, Eunice didn't hear Portia's comment. She opened the garage and backed the VW out. "Get in, please!"

Deidre angered Portia again when she claimed the front seat and forced Portia to cram her plump figure into the back of the Volkswagen. Portia stewed until an idea popped into her head. "Aunt Eunice, since it is such a special night, wouldn't it be fun to put the top down and ride to the ball in the open air?"

Eunice smiled big in the rear-view mirror and lowered the convertible top as she slowly drove down their street. Once they hit the highway, the wind blew Deidre's hair all over the place, ruining the style for which Portia knew Deidre had just paid nearly a week's wages.

Deidre squealed and panicked, trying to hold her hair in place. Portia relished in the revenge on her devious sister. Eunice ignored Deidre's pleas to put the top back.

At Ziggy's, the ball was in full swing. Danny entered the event looking dashing in his role as host of the affair. He gazed at the hundreds of well-dressed men, women, and children that stood around chatting. He could feel the anxiety and elation in the air. Tears were being shed as long-lost family members met for the first time. Ancestry, adoption, and foster-care representatives were acting as matchmakers for people who came as strangers but would leave as family. He felt a little uncomfortable in his role as host even though it was probably Ziggy's best event ever.

Never before had he seen a sight like this on the grounds of his park. Dozens of birth moms sat around decorated tables sharing stories with potential adopting couples. The evening offered each of the birth moms a unique and fun environment in which they could connect in a deeper way with the couple who wanted to adopt their baby. It was intended to be a safe, neutral place for the girls to see their baby's potential parents in a whole new light.

Among the many visitors that Danny hosted were parents looking to adopt a foster child. Some of his biggest checks had been written to foster care and orphan agencies in the past, and now they were his guests at an event he never would have imagined himself throwing, let alone paying for. How life had changed for him in the last year. Hearing the laughter of the prospective families enjoying themselves, he tightened his bow tie and grabbed himself a refreshment from a server walking past him.

He smiled to the visitors as he made his way downstage next to the orchestra. A tall man with a distinguishing aura walked up and greeted Danny. While the band played behind them, Danny struggled to hear what the man was saying but did his best to make sense of the conversation—something about

Danny being ready to be a dad and the need to reprioritize his life for his family.

Danny figured the man didn't know who he was and probably thought he was there looking to adopt or something along those lines. But then he could have sworn he heard a reference to the twins. Danny found the conversation peculiar, but he was too distracted to make sense of it.

Madeline had arranged for some time alone so she could watch the ball from the grassy green hill she had once considered her favorite place at Ziggy's. She surveyed the quiet cove and the view she had of the entire park. It sparkled. The lighting was breathtaking, and the park had never looked better.

As the band played a moving rendition of "You Are So Beautiful," Madeline teared up. Her thoughts went back to Cynthia and filled her with dread and fear, the same feeling she'd had when she stood there afraid to tell Danny she was pregnant. Now she was in the same spot with the same horrible feelings.

She wiped the tears, grumbling, "How could I be so stupid, to come back to the place I've avoided for so many years?" She started to leave but then felt impressed to pray for Cynthia. Her little girl needed her. She didn't know how to pray, but she spoke softly and honestly to a Person she hadn't thought about since the days of her youth. Her heart was soon raptured by the music in the background and the words that welled up inside her soul. She prayed harder. Soon it felt as though something was being birthed in her. She couldn't explain it, but it was real, coming from within her, but it was not of her.

She paced back and forth as she prayed. Forceful words flowed from her spirit, powerful words of truth that were foreign to her. She felt connected, as though Cynthia was standing right next to her. Anger and a desperate longing for hope welled up inside her. Her heart raced. Finally, she called out in a loud voice, "CYNTHIA!"

The music stopped. Madeline heard nothing other than her own hard, fast breathing. Her thoughts came to a screeching halt. "Danny!" She had to talk with him now. She ran down the hill and found him in the crowd. He was chatting with a man. She interrupted them. "Excuse me."

The man turned to face Madeline and smiled at her. "By all means."

She acknowledged him, then quickly turned to Danny as the stranger stood attentive to their conversation.

Madeline grabbed Danny by the arms. "She's here."

"Who?"

Irritated he wasn't on her wavelength, Madeline said, "Cynthia! She's here in the park. I can feel it."

"Where?"

"I don't know where, but she's here. We have to find her."

"Your daughter is safe," the man stated emphatically. "You will see her shortly. I would recommend you not stray too far."

Both Madeline and Danny turned to him with angst.

"You've seen her?" Madeline pleaded. "You saw Cynthia?"

He smiled and stepped away from them into the crowd.

"Hey, come back here. Who are you?" Danny demanded. He reached out and grabbed him by the arm, then immediately released it.

He looked up at Danny with grace and understanding, then turned to Madeline. "My name is Sebastian." He bowed his head, took three steps into the crowd, and by the fourth step, he was gone.

Danny ran through the crowd, moving people to the side as he searched for him. The man had vanished. Danny glanced back to Madeline, who looked a bit dumbfounded. She mouthed the name "Sebastian" as though she was asking who he was. Danny shrugged and made his way back to her.

"What should we do, Danny?" Madeline asked as she fell into his arms and clung tight.

"Wait. As hard as that sounds, I believe we are to wait," Danny said, as though he believed it was their only option.

He put his memory to the test and tried to remember Cynthia's conversation about Sebastian. It was that night they had dinner at Madeline's. He had left hurt and angry. It all seemed so long ago. Now here he was, holding Madeline in his arms in a way he had never held her.

They were together. Everything he deemed as important before now seemed senseless and irrelevant to who he was and what he wanted. He tightly held Madeline's hand. She needed him, and that felt good. He needed her, and where that had caused him anxiety before, now it brought peace to his soul. Together they would see this whole thing through, for better or for worse.

Terry Harris

16

CYNTHIA LAY ON THE DIRT FLOOR OF HER CELL. THE light from inside the furnace lit the muddy tear streaks that stained her face. Her mouth was dry from dehydration and she was painfully hungry and scared. The twice-daily roar of Ziggy's rocket igniting and seemingly taking off was frightening and robbed her of the rest she needed. The entire fire pit shook every time it was lit and left thick, heavy smoke hanging in the air. It had felt as though she were in the bowels of hell itself.

Distant sounds of crowds and music filtered in from outside. Cynthia wondered if the ball she had dreamed of and helped create was in full swing.

The soft flapping of bird's wings startled her. She pulled herself up off the ground and looked around. Then, she heard it again. She craned her neck and got up on her tiptoes, trying to find its source.

A moment later, a white dove flew past the cage and landed on the ledge of the small window up and to her right. The glass was disguised behind black paint to keep light from shining through.

Startled, Cynthia fell backward, but the bird remained unfazed and stayed perched on the ledge. The dove was a pleasant sight, giving her hope that she wasn't alone. Smiling, she got back up on her feet and spoke to the bird as though it were a friend, extending her hand to it.

Faint memories of when she served in the King's court reminded her communication between humans and animals should be a normal part of life. Down here, it was not so. She had to work at it.

She hummed a few notes of a song, hoping the bird would look her way, but it showed no signs of response. She called to it again and again, desperate for interaction in the dark, dismal abyss. As she turned her back on the bird to stretch her legs, the bird flapped its wings and flew into the darkness of the pit. She spun around and screamed, "No! Don't leave me. Please come back."

She called after it several more times, hoping, praying, and even begging God to bring the bird back. There was no reply. Heaven seemed a million miles away, where no one could hear her cries, or worse, no one wanted to. She fell to the floor and wept loudly.

Deidre and Portia stood at the far end of the dance floor, feeling like outsiders looking in. Deidre decided she would keep an eye out for a potential dance partner/husband while she awaited instructions from Radcliffe. He had texted her earlier telling her to be available in case he needed her.

Deidre felt her sister's eyes drill holes in the back of her head. So, after several minutes, she turned on her heels and confronted Portia. A shouting match ensued, followed by hair-pulling and shoving. Eunice, who was returning with her hands full of beverages, dropped the drinks and ran to break up the fight. Her face intercepted a punch thrown by Deidre, knocking Eunice back and causing Deidre's purse to spill, including her phone.

Deidre shrieked as she watched Portia plunge to the ground and sweep up the device. Deidre fought to keep her sister away from the phone, but Portia entered the password and scanned the texts. When she stopped at the conversation between Deidre and Radcliffe, her shock left Deidre an opportunity to overpower Portia. Deidre shoved Portia to the ground, but not before snatching the phone away.

Deidre took off running through the crowd, knocking innocent bystanders off their balance and causing a ruckus. The band kept on playing as she escaped into the night to meet Radcliffe.

Back in the pit, the distant music soothed Cynthia's nerves, allowing her to lift herself off the dirt floor and sit up. Her eyes had played tricks on her in the dark cellar. At times, she saw people moving about in flames, as though a man was standing in the middle of the burning fire talking with someone. Other times, it appeared there were several of them, laughing and conversing like they were at a dinner party. It seemed so odd to her. Yet, she knew her reality was a nightmare.

She was caught up to the sound of her own breathing when a bright light flashed from the core of the fire. She covered her eyes with her hand and screamed. Fear that the rocket ship might suddenly explode caused her to jump to her feet. She threw her body back into the corner of the cage and tucked her face into her body. Suddenly, the light from the flames began to permeate the room, overtaking every inch of darkness.

Cynthia lowered her hands to see where the light was coming from. Her eyes bore the intensity of the light without flinching, though it was as bright as the midday sun. A man appeared out of the brightness and stepped toward the metal frame that kept her a prisoner. He looked strong, but she knew him to be more angelic than human.

"Cynthia." His voice was as calming as the soft gurgle of a stream.

Cynthia recognized him immediately. "My King!" She ran to the metal bars, tears streaming down her face.

"Why do your tears sound so final?" He moved closer to the cage.

"I have failed! Forgive me, Lord. I have failed in every way." She resumed crying.

"Open your hands, child." Suddenly, He stood before her inside the cage, with the gate still locked.

She looked down at her fingers, which were clenched shut. She slowly opened them.

"What do you see?"

"Nothing. They're bare and dirty," she replied.

"Look again, with eyes of faith."

She searched again, but her hands were still empty. She raised her eyes to His face. "I don't understand."

As she said that, He placed an item onto her palms. She was slow to lower her eyes from His face, as He was so pleasant to look at. She felt the object as it laid across her nimble fingers. It felt familiar. She glanced down. The necklace that bore her name stared back at her, bringing a gasp from deep within. It was her necklace, the symbol of her identity, the very stone given to her in the portals of glory, the one that Radcliffe had hurled into the fire.

"I don't deserve this," she groaned. Just as she voiced that belief, accusing and conflicting thoughts swirled about her mind, reminding her of her failure. "I have sinned and denied my King." In her soul, Cynthia believed she had lost her place in the King's family. She felt condemned and cast out.

Terry Harris

When He took the necklace from her hands, she felt more guilty than ever before. She dropped her head and closed her hands once again.

"Open your hands, child." His voice was uplifting and compassionate.

She looked up, and her King was right next to her, looking at her with compassion and love.

She reluctantly acquiesced. She felt warmth on her palms. She lowered her eyes and there before her were the nail-pierced hands of her Lord.

"Now, what do you see?" He asked.

"You... I see you, my King."

"Then nothing is lost. You have everything."

Her mind flashed back to the times she watched Him enter the Great Hall in the King's court. So many who had lived on Earth and then entered Heaven wept tears of joy and celebration when they touched His hands. But she had never had that kind of response; she had not understood the meaning of His wounds, until now. For the first time, she understood the need for His sacrifice, forgiveness, and grace.

She waited in a solemn moment of weakness and vulnerability. Silence filled her soul. "I'm so sorry, my King, for denying you. I... I understand if I cannot be part of your kingdom, perhaps I could–"

From nowhere, He presented a loaf of warm bread and a gold cup. He broke the bread and handed it to her. She took it, slowly lifted it to her lips, then placed it in her mouth. It was sweet to her parched tongue. Her taste buds tingled and danced with each chew.

He handed her the cup. She sipped it. At first it was bitter, but as her body absorbed it, it refreshed her spirit. She felt cleansed.

"Remember," He said.

Remember she did. A flood of thoughts, images, and memories of the meal she had shared with Him before leaving the shores of the Celestial City flashed across her mind. Her skin came alive as she recalled her true identity as His child and what her life was like in His presence. A new beginning erupted inside her.

Her eyes widened with a smile. Her soul was born anew. A deep appreciation of her Master and Creator emerged within her mind and heart. Her conscience was clean. She felt whole. The cellar she stood in released its hold on her soul. The pit that threatened her life and held her captive became her own personal sanctuary of salvation.

She dropped to her knees and cried great tears of joy. She thanked Him for His forgiveness.

He touched her head with His hand and more tears fell from her eyes, landing on His feet. One by one, she wiped them with her hair. He knelt and placed the necklace around her neck. "You are my beloved daughter, and I will never leave you."

She exalted Him in ways she had never worshiped before. Her heart beat faster with each word she sang.

He raised her up. She felt nourished and strong.

"Come, my child. Your time is here. You have a ball to attend."

The metal door behind them swung open with ease. He stepped back and allowed her to exit first. With deep humility, she stepped past Him into the open space.

She watched His every step. He moved in the same manner in the small cave as He did in the Courts of Glory. He was majestic, humble, and inviting. She felt free to ask the one question of Him that had burdened her since she arrived.

"My Lord, my family ... Will I meet them soon?"

"You already have." As His words penetrated her mind, a clear image of Madeline and Danny flashed through her consciousness. Tears of joy filled her eyes when she reached down and pulled her necklace up to examine it. "Cynthia Hope Richards."

She gasped with delight.

From the top of the steps, another man appeared out of nowhere. It was Sebastian, standing inside the locked cellar.

"Sebastian," she spoke softly. Under normal circumstances she would have ran up the stairs to greet him, but her desire was to remain close to the King. She smiled, content to be exactly where she was.

"If you will allow me, I'd like to accompany you to the dance," Sebastian announced as he descended the steps. He approached her and offered his hand as though she were a princess, because, indeed, she was.

She looked to her King for direction. He smiled and kissed her forehead, much like a father would who was sending his daughter off to her prom. "Your time is short. There is much to do. Sebastian will guide you."

She bowed her head in obedience and when she lifted it again, the King was gone. Her heart jumped a sad beat.

"He abides within you now," Sebastian said. "You will never be alone." Cynthia's heart was filled with love and gratefulness for her King and her friend. She missed them both so much. Cynthia squealed and gave Sebastian the biggest hug she could muster. She laughed and cried at the same time as she held her long lost friend. He felt like home.

"It's time for the ball," Sebastian gently spoke as their arms released.

Cynthia wiped her eyes as Sebastian extended his hand as her guardian and escort to the dance. She accepted his invitation and laid her hand in his. Together, they ascended the narrow stairwell. The door opened before them. Cynthia breathed a deep breath of freedom as she stepped out into the night air.

The sights, smells, and sounds of Ziggy's Island enveloped Cynthia. She turned and looked back at the chains hanging from the door handle. Her body shuddered at the thought of where she had been. Sebastian touched her shoulder. "That which held you captive has been broken."

She took another deep breath, this time to inhale the wonderful truth just spoken to her soul. Cynthia smiled as she locked arms with her guardian and strolled through the park.

Being fully alive as never before, Cynthia noticed even the smallest detail. She marveled at the sights, sounds, and smells that invaded her senses. Bright lights, laughter, perfume, and the aroma of cotton candy filled the air. She gave thanks for every vibrant color, every aromatic tickle that permeated her nostrils, and every sound that rang harmoniously in her ears. The distant music of the orchestra led her and Sebastian to the heart of why she had journeyed to Earth.

Together, they approached the edge of the staircase that led down to the dance floor and looked below at all the attendees. It was a beautiful sight. So many people laughing, chatting, and even dancing. Children of all ages played and giggled among their new friends under the watchful eyes of their guardians. The celebratory spirit of the night washed over her and renewed a deep-seated joy that had been previously squelched.

Cynthia couldn't help but scan the large open space looking for her parents. Sebastian motioned for Cynthia to go down. She blushed a humble smile and then slowly descended the staircase in the same manner she had entered the Great Hall: with elegance and the assurance of who she was and to Whom she belonged. In the distance, some dancers left the dance floor, and she spotted her parents. Her heart jumped.

"Mom," Cynthia whispered as she darted down the stairway.

Madeline and Danny stood on the far right side of the dance floor as they held each other and gently swayed to Louis Armstrong's "What a Wonderful World." And it *was* wonderful to be back in Danny's arms, but everything would not be as it should until she knew what had become of their daughter. Though it was difficult, Madeline chose to hope and believe what they had been told earlier: that Cynthia was safe and they would see her soon.

Madeline buried her face in Danny's shoulder, but Danny began to turn her awkwardly. Madeline lifted her head to say something, looking perturbed. Before she had a chance to speak, her body was turned in such a way that she could see what he seemed to be transfixed on.

Cynthia, all alone, descending the stairs. She was gazing at them, smiling.

Madeline gasped at the sight of her daughter.

Her simple blue dress was soiled. Her face was stained with soot and streaks from her tears. Her hair was unkempt and dirty, but she was absolutely … radiant. Her natural beauty rivaled the finest-dressed woman in the crowd.

Madeline's eyes locked with Cynthia's, then she cried aloud, "My baby!"

Madeline flew out of Danny's arms and ran toward her daughter, pushing dancers out of her way. Cynthia wove around dancing couples, making her way towards her mom. Mother and daughter met and embraced in the center of the dance floor. As they hugged each other and wept, dancers backed away to give them space.

Danny stepped in and embraced them both. They all wept tears of joy mixed with laughter. The crowd applauded, and applauded, and applauded even more. Soon the entire company of guests were standing and cheering the reunion of all reunions. Madeline's mind reeled with questions but one thing she knew; they were all witnessing a miracle that could not be explained. In that moment she felt as though Heaven itself were watching, and those on Earth could not help but be pulled into the wonder of this divine appointment.

Eunice watched with tears in her eyes. Standing with Portia, Eunice had seen the whole interchange with Cynthia and Madeline. She was divided in her soul, wanting the moment to include her. Cynthia must have sensed her feelings, as just then she looked up and locked eyes with Eunice. Smiles were exchanged and then Cynthia slowly stepped away from her parents and hugged Eunice.

"I thought I lost you," Eunice replied.

"No. I'm okay. Better than ever. I'll explain everything later." Cynthia broke their embrace as Madeline and Danny walked up behind her. Eunice held onto Cynthia's hand, not wanting to let go. "Eunice, Portia, I want to introduce to you my parents." Eunice gasped, but knew it to be true. She stretched her arms wide to invite them all into a group hug.

Portia stood alone, watching. Eunice gazed at Portia with a motherly love that she had never felt before. Letting go of Cynthia, Eunice reached over to Portia and pulled her close. Portia wrapped her arms around Eunice.

Back at the fiery pit, Deidre waited, just as Radcliffe had asked. She shook uncontrollably in her high heels at the sight of the open door and broken chains. Peeking her head into the dark abyss, she saw and heard nothing. Cynthia was gone.

Deidre contemplated what Radcliffe might say or do when he discovered their prisoner had escaped. A chill ran down her spine and she turned to leave. On her second step, she smacked into Radcliffe's short, portly body. She panicked.

Terry Harris

On either side of him were two angry-looking Asian men. They stared her down, unimpressed with her stature and looks.

"Is this the merchandise?" the one with a partial right eyebrow asked.

"No, you fool. This is my daughter." This time Deidre did not care for the reference to being Radcliffe's relative. The sound of the words made her stomach turn.

Radcliffe pushed Deidre into the other man and peeked into the dark cellar. The man grabbed her arm and held on tight. Deidre tried to squirm lose but was unable to break the grip.

"I didn't do it!" Deidre exclaimed. "She was gone when I got here."

Radcliffe was furious. "Where is she, Deidre?" he growled.

"I don't know."

"No one else knew she was here, Deidre. Now where is she?" He glared at her and moved closer.

Fearful, Deidre started to cry and blurted out, "You have to believe me. I didn't do it. Somebody must've let her out. You locked the door. I didn't do it."

The two thugs exchanged looks. "We came to buy a girl, and that's what we're going to do. No girl in the pit, then we take this one," the shorter one barked with a thick accent.

"What the hell? No!" Deidre cursed and called the men names as she tried to free herself.

When Radcliffe flinched and showed concern, they seized the opportunity. "Seems like she's worth something to you, so we keep her and call it even for wasting our time."

Radcliffe opened his mouth, then paused. After a long moment, he said, "What about fifty thousand for her? Surely, she's worth that and more..."

"WHAT? DAD!"

The taller man holding Deidre tightened his grip. She cried out in pain.

The shorter one with the scarred eyebrow poked him in the chest. "You promised a princess. She's no princess. The girl is worth nothing! We take the girl and let you live. Got a problem with that?" He stepped into Radcliffe's face.

Deidre watched Radcliffe swallow hard, but he showed no sign of fear.

"All right this time, but next time I get my asking price plus a finder's fee."

Deidre started to shriek, but they bent her arm behind her back, sending intense pain to her shoulder as a warning to quiet down.

The men sneered at Radcliffe. "Get us out of here," one of them demanded. The three of them marched Deidre back into the shadows and toward the back-lot entrance, Radcliffe leading the way.

Deidre was about to be pushed through the exit gate that led to the employee parking lot when they suddenly stopped in their tracks. A tall man stood directly in front of them, looking like a Samurai warrior, and staring them down. The goons holding Deidre yelled a few threatening words at the man, but he didn't seem to be intimidated.

"Let the child go," he commanded. "She doesn't belong to you."

The shorter man spouted back in broken English, "Who she belong to?"

"The Lord Almighty."

"The lord. Who is he? We never heard of no lord mighty."

They scoffed at the stranger and then shoved Deidre forward toward their car. She screamed. The man flexed his back and muscle-like wings appeared, ready for battle. Deidre shrieked. With one lightning-fast move, the creature knocked both men backwards, causing them to land hard on their skulls, knocking them unconscious.

Deidre turned to her dad.

Radcliffe froze as the mysterious man turned his fierce gaze on him. Radcliffe howled for mercy and fell to his knees, trembling with fear. Deidre couldn't speak as she watched him step into Radcliffe's space, looking down on him.

"Radcliffe. Your ways have led you down a path you do not want to see to the end. It's time for you to stop."

"Yes, yes. Whatever you say... I'll do," he pleaded with his head bowed. "Who... who are you?"

"My name is Sebastian."

Radcliffe cowered, whimpering loudly. "Please don't hurt me. Please."

"Go!" Sebastian commanded.

As Radcliffe slowly lifted his head, Sebastian pointed in the direction of Radcliffe's Mercedes. Radcliffe rose to his feet, glanced at his daughter whom he had just betrayed, and ran into the night, showing no sign of shame or remorse for his failure as a father.

Deidre flinched. She was petrified and had no idea who this stranger was or what he might do to her. She stared at her captors, now lying unconscious on the ground.

"Please don't hurt me," she begged Sebastian.

He lowered his wings and extended his hand in compassion. "Child, I'm here to help you, not harm you."

She breathed a sigh of anxious relief.

"Go to your family. They await your return."

"I don't have a family," she replied, looking toward the darkness into which Radcliffe had disappeared.

"Yes, you have been rejected, but by one only, not by all. Those with whom you share a house are more than roommates. They desire to be your family."

Deidre's hands were shaking so violently she could barely grab her purse. She could sense Sebastian's watchful eye as she ran from the dark parking lot into the lights of the park. She trusted him, though they had never met before. After what felt like a safe distance, she turned and yelled back, "Thank you, whoever you are."

Sebastian bowed his head in humility.

She watched him disappear in a flash of light. Deidre let out a great sigh of relief as she ran back towards the center of the park.

This flash caught the eye of a security guard patrolling the parking lot. A minute or so later, he pulled up in his car and spotted the two unconscious men on the ground. He placed a call on his radio and waited for backup.

Once the police arrived, the traffickers were put in handcuffs and escorted to the back of the patrol car. Not only were the men carrying illegal firearms, but the background checks had shown both were on an international most-wanted list.

"You're going away for a long time," announced the young security guard. They men growled under their breath and hung their heads.

Bobby had been away from the center of all that was taking place, capturing pictures of families who were introduced to each other for the first time. He had grown weary of pretending that he was having a good time. Without Cynthia, it felt too much like work. He missed her and wanted to be with her.

He meandered his way toward the dance floor and saw her. Their eyes locked.

As Cynthia and Bobby gazed at each other, time stood still. He saw her dirty clothes and unkempt appearance, but he still felt she was the most beautiful creature he had ever seen. He forced himself with all his might to play it cool, even though his insides erupted like a volcano. He loved this woman. They took steps toward each other and met near the edge of the dance floor. Their eyes did most of the speaking for several moments.

Finally, he had to speak. "Are you okay?"

"I'm better than ever," she spoke softly.

Her voice was so sweet to his ears. His soul battled within him. He looked deep into her eyes for signs that he was free to love her, but he did not find what he was looking for. He saw love reflected in her face but did not see a future with her, which tormented him.

He drew her near. "I prayed for you."

"You did?"

He shrugged in an attempt to play it cool. "Well, yeah, of course." As she studied him, he felt exposed. His voice broke. "I was so scared I would never see you again. I thought I did something to push you away, like…"

He stopped.

"No. Not at all. I was simply… detained for a little while," Cynthia replied.

"I felt different after I prayed for you. Like I was being heard or something, you know? It was cool the way He, I mean God, showed up. It was so real at times that I knew you were gonna be okay. I was just hoping that you weren't hiding from me."

"Of course not. I wouldn't leave you like that. I care for you and feel that–"

"You have feelings for me?" he asked with a nervous crack in his smile.

Bobby knew that a relationship with her could not be serious until he had made his own commitment to the King. She had told him on several occasions how she prayed that he would find his place in God's kingdom and together they could serve Him.

"I do."

Just then, Danny tapped Bobby on the shoulder. "Heh, um…"

"You interrupted our family reunion."

Bobby furled his brow in confusion.

Cynthia smiled with delight. "Bobby, I'd like to introduce you to my mother and father."

Bobby cracked a grin. He always saw striking similarities between Madeline and Cynthia, but now it seemed ridiculously obvious.

Madeline moved her family into position for a picture. "Bobby, would you mind taking our first family photo?"

Bobby lifted the camera to take some shots, but Cynthia seemed distracted. She stared at Madeline and then at Danny, as if drinking in the sight of the two of them together.

Bobby waited as she held them both for a long moment. All three laughed and cried with their arms wrapped around each other, wiping each other's tears.

Danny drew Madeline close and exhaled a huge sigh. Bobby caught the pose on his camera, then positioned them for more shots. The spontaneous candids captured the love between them. Bobby quickly reviewed them and gave himself a congratulatory smile.

When the music faded and the dancers returned to their tables, Bobby saw it as an opportunity and turned to Cynthia. "May I have this dance, Your Highness?" To Bobby, she looked like a princess, though one who had just climbed out of the cinder bin of the palace.

Cynthia looked to her father for permission. Bobby tilted his head as if to ask Danny if he could interrupt their family moment.

Hesitant, Danny looked at Madeline, who nodded with a smile.

Bobby and Cynthia walked toward the dance floor arm in arm.

"No, wait!" Madeline interjected.

Bobby and Cynthia turned toward Madeline as she grabbed a napkin, wet it in a water glass, and ran to Cynthia. They all laughed as Madeline wiped her daughter's face like she was a toddler.

"There. Much better." Madeline gleamed. Bobby winked at Cynthia as they started to dance.

The interlude in the music was perfectly timed for Cynthia and Bobby. With many of the dancers off the floor, they had their space to move about. Having photographed many a formal event, Bobby recognized the waltz that commenced and worked to lead them through the first awkward steps. Cynthia seemed to catch on quick with how he was leading, though he sensed neither of them were intimately familiar with this type of dance.

They looked intensely at each other. He felt he was at his best in his perfectly fitted black tuxedo, while she was as elegant and lovely as he had remembered, albeit with a smudged dress and dirty hair. The connection between him and Cynthia rivaled any fairy tale romance he had ever been told. The more he relaxed in his role as lead, their dance steps flowed and were in concert with the smiles they gifted to one another.

For several brief moments, he felt they were the only ones on the dance floor. Their eyes never left the other. Not even the slightest glimpse went to another soul around them. They waltzed, then he spun her around, then they waltzed some more. The attractive lighting above them became a blur. With each step came a glimmer of hope that they would be together like this forever.

The song ended and forever came to a halt. They stood in the middle of the floor, gazing at each other.

Applause for the young couple erupted. The end of the orchestra's beautiful rendition of the "Vienna Waltz" snapped them back to reality. They laughed, then joined in with the clapping for the conductor and his band. The maestro bowed, then threw the spotlight back on Cynthia and Bobby. The crowd obliged and roared with approval.

The young couple blushed with embarrassment. Finally, Cynthia bowed in honor of their kind cheers and applause. She rushed over to her mother and nuzzled close to her. Beaming with pride, Madeline kissed her daughter on the cheek. The music changed beats and drew a large crowd back onto the floor, filling it instantly.

Danny stepped in front of Cynthia and smiled. He held out his hand. "Care to join your father on the dance floor?"

Cynthia gasped. Her dream to dance with her dad was about to be realized. Her heart beat fast. She blinked twice to assure herself this was really happening. He smiled. She placed her hand in his.

They were just three steps from the dance floor when Cynthia's arm was yanked by Juanita, the chairperson of the board at the orphanage. Cynthia had personally invited her to the ball, hoping she might find families for many of the children in the orphanage.

"We have an emergency," Juanita said urgently. She dragged Cynthia by the arm to an area away from the crowd. Danny, Madeline, and Bobby followed close behind, anxious to hear the news.

"The twins are going to be separated." It sounded almost fatal.

Madeline drew close to her daughter's side. "When?"

"About midnight tonight. At twelve a.m. they become the property of two different families who have no intention or desire to keep them together." Juanita's words were void of hope.

Cynthia turned to Madeline and said, "Mother, we've got to do something to stop this." She continued, "Those girls need each other." Everyone agreed. Splitting them up could prove to be harmful to either one.

Cynthia turned to Danny, looking for help.

Danny drew a deep breath and sighed. He motioned to Juanita. "What can we do to stop this from happening?"

Juanita shook her head. "Nothing, unless you want to adopt them yourself and prove to the court that their well-being is at stake."

Madeline asked abruptly, "What do we need to do to get a postponement of the adoptions?"

"A judge's order. But at this late hour, I'd say you're going to need a miracle."

"Tonight's all about miracles," Madeline stated firmly as she squeezed Cynthia's hand.

"Judge Martinez just happens to be sitting at table number five," Danny informed Juanita. "Come on. You can explain the whole thing to him."

Cynthia led the four of them over to the judge's table with Bobby in tow. She tapped him on the shoulder, interrupting the judge's conversation with another couple. Cynthia started to speak but Madeline jumped in and quickly explained what they needed and the urgency of the situation.

The judge questioned Juanita briefly, then made a phone call. When the call was finished, he told the group that they better hurry and get to the orphanage to ensure that the babies did not leave the premises. He promised that the paperwork would be sent over to the orphanage just as soon as it was ready. In the meantime, he would have an official email drafted in minutes and sent to Madeline's phone.

GONG! The clock that stood high at the front of Ziggy's entrance chimed loudly. Cynthia and Madeline spun to gaze at the large timepiece, which showed that it was midnight.

Cynthia gasped. "Oh my goodness, we gotta go, now!" She turned to Bobby and gave him a kiss on the cheek. "Thank you. I'll never forget tonight. You're an incredible dancer." With that, she turned on her heels to run.

Bobby called after her. "Cynthia, wait..."

Madeline grabbed Cynthia's hand. Together they pushed themselves to run hard.

GONG! The bell gave Cynthia a surge of adrenaline. The Richards family made a mad dash up the large staircase and across the park as the clock continued to sound. Danny called his valet to have a car brought to the front of the park; he explained to Cynthia and Madeline it would be quicker than going to the employees' lot.

The clock continued to reverberate mercilessly.

Heads turned at the sight of Madeline running in her ball gown and high heels, with Cynthia in tow, looking like a younger version of Madeline dressed in rags.

Moments later, Danny was the first to arrive at the front exit. His jaw dropped at the sight of the car that was waiting for them. It was an old, beat-up, burnt-orange Volkswagen Beetle.

Danny let out a gasp. "An oversized pumpkin?"

"A VW?" he yelled at the valet.

The valet tossed the keys to Danny. "You said it was urgent. It's my car."

"GONG!" The final toll of the midnight bell rang loudly and then stopped.

Madeline and Cynthia ran up to the car. "Just get in, Danny!" Madeline barked.

Cynthia took the back seat. Wanting to be close to her daughter, Madeline sat next to her. With precious minutes slipping away, they sped down the road toward the orphanage.

Madeline spoke louder than normal in an attempt to be heard over the clanking metal frame they were squeezed into. "Cynthia? I have to ask you a question, and I'm praying I don't offend you or anyone who may have helped you get here." She waved her hand in the air as if to refer to an invisible being.

Cynthia waited with an understanding smile. She and Madeline reached for the other's hand at the same time.

"Where did you come from? I mean, exactly how did you get here? You died in my bell–" She choked on the words, so she looked away and took a deep breath trying to figure it all out. A nauseating pain pierced her gut.

Cynthia waited for her mom to process her feelings. While she waited, she prayed a brief prayer as though to ask permission from her King to share the story with her sweet and confused mother. She felt peace with the idea.

"So much has happened since I arrived here," Cynthia said. "I can honestly tell you that I have forgotten many things. But what I can remember I would love to share with you."

"Please!" Madeline begged.

"I second that," Danny said from the front seat.

Cynthia giggled, then began to reflect on her other life, which seemed so distant in time and memory.

"It seems like a lifetime ago," Cynthia quietly replied. After a pensive pause, she continued, "I was happy, perfectly happy. It's beautiful there. I was surrounded by love. I would play with Angela and Sebastian and sing. We would always be singing magnificent praises, and even though I was completely content, for as long as I could remember, I wanted to meet you."

Madeline hung on her every word.

"I wanted to meet you, and my King knew that," Cynthia said. "He knew my heart's desire and even though it has never been done before, He let me come to you. Out of love for me, He gave me that gift. Sebastian led me here. I took my first steps on the beach. It was cold and the sand was rough. He gave me the coin from the fish's mouth on that beach. Then I met Violet. It was the coin from Sebastian that Violet and I brought into the coin shop … Radcliffe's coin shop."

Madeline shuddered when she mentioned Radcliffe's name. Cynthia squeezed her hand and continued.

"Then I found Eunice, then Ziggy's, then you! It's been a wonderful, scary, lonely, and fascinating journey, and I know now that He has been with me all along. He's been with *us* all along." Cynthia smiled. "He loves us that much."

Madeline put an arm around her daughter and pulled her close. Cynthia inhaled her lovely perfume and closed her eyes.

Cynthia was just about to mention her relationship with Bobby and how God used him to bring the three of them together but stopped abruptly when the car came to a screeching halt in front of the orphanage.

"I'll tell you more after we know what's going on with the twins," Cynthia said.

Madeline squeezed her daughter's hand and kissed her on the cheek before exiting the car. Cynthia teared up and followed her out of the car. Madeline left her side and trotted up the stairs toward the front door.

Danny stopped Cynthia as she was about to follow Madeline. "Sweetheart, when this is all over and the time is right, I'd like to hear more about this King you were talking about. Sounds like He's someone I should get to know."

"I'd be so honored to, Daddy." She kissed him on the cheek.

She grabbed his hand and together they ran up the lawn to catch up with Madeline.

∞ 17 ∞

THE DARKENED BUILDING SHOWED NO SIGNS OF LIFE. Madeline was peering through the windows, hoping to see someone, when Danny came up behind her and abruptly knocked hard on the door. It sent a booming noise through the house, and in no time the head nurse on duty appeared.

Seeing Madeline and Cynthia through the glass, she opened the door with a friendly smile. The nurse was dressed in a flowered robe that was pulled tight around the waist and emphasized her portly figure. Her name tag said *Clara*. "Wow! Aren't you fancy to–"

Madeline cut her compliment short. She shoved her phone displaying the email with the judge's order to delay the adoption in Clara's face.

"We have a judge's order. Where are they? Are we too late?" she asked.

Madeline scanned the house, looking for signs of couples ready to steal away the twins.

"Too late for what?" Clara asked, Madeline's phone in hand.

Frustrated, Madeline asked, "The twins. Are they gone?"

"Oh! Is that what this is about? Well, I'm sorry, but I don't need this." She handed Madeline's cell back to her, which caused Cynthia to gasp and Madeline to flush red with anxiety.

"You mean, they're gone?" Danny demanded as he stepped into the conversation.

"Who?" Clara asked quizzically.

"The twins!" Madeline and Danny shouted simultaneously.

"The twins? Oh, heavens, no. They're both upstairs sleeping like a rock. Checked on them myself not twenty minutes ago. They're not going anywhere soon."

A collision of confusion and relief splattered across the faces of Madeline, Danny, and Cynthia. They just stared at each other, then at the nurse. Madeline shook her head, trying to drum up some understanding.

"So are the girls being adopted by two different families or not?"

"No." She smiled and folded her arms as she answered.

"But we were told they were being separated at mid–" Cynthia said.

"Okay, yes," Clara interrupted, "We had the girls cleared to go to their new homes, separate homes. All the tests were done, the paperwork in place, and then earlier tonight the phone rang, and I was told that Annie's adoptive family had a sudden change of heart. Just like that." She snapped her fingers, then continued.

"They wouldn't be coming by to pick her up. I hung up the phone and wouldn't you know, not more than a minute or two later, a second call came in with the news that a baby boy would be brought to the house tomorrow."

Madeline waited, but the nurse stopped telling the story as though it all made sense. "And?"

The nurse nodded and then resumed. "The family that was considering Emily had really been wanting a boy. So, once they were told about this boy, who just came out of nowhere, they went to see him tonight at the hospital, loved him at first sight, and signed up to adopt him, just like that." She snapped her fingers again then smiled.

"This new baby boy just appeared out of nowhere?" Cynthia quickly queried.

"Like a ram in the bush," Clara assured her with a wink.

Madeline, Danny, and Cynthia all let out a sigh of relief and then displayed nervous grins. "This is all so crazy," Madeline murmured.

Danny nodded in agreement. "I feel like I'm in some B-movie mystery where we're suddenly the main characters in a thriller that could rearrange our lives forever."

Madeline furled her brow. Danny shrugged. "What?"

"I know it's terribly late, but do you suppose we could just peek in on the girls for a moment?" Cynthia asked.

"By all means, I'd be sad if you didn't," said the jubilant Clara as she motioned for them to go up the stairs. "There was a phone call yesterday from a family out of state who is interested in meeting Annie. But they won't be able to come out until next week."

With Danny just a step behind, Madeline and Cynthia climbed the narrow staircase. The hall light fanned its warm hues across the faces of the twin girls as they quietly laid awake in one crib. Their smiling eyes stared back at the ladies. Madeline and Cynthia gasped when they spotted their tiny little fingers outstretched and touching.

Madeline turned and looked at the empty crib a few feet away.

As though reading Madeline's mind, the nurse spoke in an audible whisper. "Sleep comes much easier for me when they're together. Separate the two, and you're in for a long night of crying."

"They're so beautiful," Madeline said out loud. Danny rubbed her shoulders with his strong hands. Madeline leaned back into his grip. Emily let out a cute baby sound.

"So, are you ready to be parents?" the portly woman interjected in her faint Irish brogue. The nurse kept on. "It would be an answer to prayer to have these two girls together in a loving two-parent home."

Madeline spoke up. "Oh, we're not married."

"Oh, forgive me. I just assumed." Clara paused. "So, you're considering adopting yourself?"

Madeline thought about the question and hesitantly leaned over and picked up Emily, carefully separating the girl's fingers. She looked at Emily and felt her vulnerability. Madeline's face wrinkled with fear and yet her heart bonded with the bundle of life she held.

Cynthia stepped close to her mom and embraced her. She whispered in Madeline's ear, "You're a wonderful mother. Don't be afraid."

"Now, I have to be honest," Clara replied matter-of-factly. "A two-parent family gets priority over a single parent. If this family coming in next week is willing to adopt one, or both, of the girls, they will more than likely go to them."

Madeline looked intently at Danny while she swayed back and forth, holding Emily.

Danny smiled back at Madeline while talking to Clara. "What if it wasn't a single-parent adoption? What if they were adopted by a couple who were very much in love and would give them the home they deserve?"

Danny walked over to Madeline and put his hand on Emily's head. "A family that gets a second chance?"

Madeline spoke softly. "Danny, what are you saying?"

At that question, Danny leaned in close to Madeline. "Make us a family, Mattie. This is our chance to have the family we always wanted. Marry me ... again."

Madeline's eyes filled with tears. "Are you sure?"

He gulped. "I'm sure."

Madeline nodded, and Danny hugged his fiancée and prospective new daughter. Cynthia squealed in delight.

Clara spoke up. "You're willing to take both of them home and keep them together?"

"Absolutely!" Danny exclaimed. Madeline laughed as tears fell down her cheeks.

"I'm gonna be your big sister," Cynthia shouted as she looked at Annie. She reached down and picked her up and placed her in Danny's arms. There was a peaceful moment of silence as Danny gazed upon his other soon-to-be daughter.

"She's so beautiful," he said, tears now welling up in his eyes. Madeline brought Emily over to hold the babies side by side.

"*They* are so beautiful," she added.

Cynthia gave a shout of praise and thanks to her King for all that He had done that night. She celebrated her family, including her new sisters, and their future together.

Clara smiled, then wiped a tear away with her robe. "Hallelujah!" She whispered her praise in a strong Irish accent.

Madeline pondered it all deeply, wondering what was happening in her life.

That next morning, Madeline and Cynthia were still in their pajamas when they took a seat at the table on the patio. The view of the ocean was spectacular. The sky looked as though its blue horizon stretched on infinitely. Madeline grinned as she poured her daughter a cup of hot green tea. Breakfast sat invitingly on silver-trimmed plates. The sun glistened off the fine silverware next to their portions atop linen napkins. It was all so perfect. Madeline was in a daze over the beauty of the moment.

She reached over and pinched Cynthia. "You are real, aren't you?"

"Ouch!" Cynthia winced. "Very much," she said as she pinched her mom back.

"Ow!" They both laughed.

Madeline's light tone suddenly became serious. "Cynthia, I'm very grateful that you shared some of your story with us last night. Things were crazy with the ball and rushing to the orphanage." She drew a deep breath and exhaled.

"Please forgive me if this is too soon, but there's so much I need to tell you."

"Please," was Cynthia's simple response, her compassionate eyes captivated with the mother beside her.

"Oh, this is so hard," Madeline murmured, fighting back the tears. "I can't believe how much I've cried lately," she joked. She looked into Cynthia's eyes and grabbed her hand. "I need you to forgive me, Cynthia."

"Why?"

"For failing you as a mom." She swallowed hard as she spoke. "I was supposed to take care of you, and I failed. I failed miserably. I was supposed to protect you, keep you safe. I couldn't even do that when you were inside of me. Imagine what a disaster of a mom I would've been if you had survived."

"No!" exclaimed Cynthia. "That's a lie."

"Cynthia, please forgive me for failing you and not giving you a chance. Somehow, I failed you. What did I do wrong? What didn't I do? Why? *Why didn't you live?*" Madeline was sobbing, releasing decades of guilt and shame.

Cynthia was visibly shocked at her mom's words.

"And now I'm thinking of being a mother of twins. *Twins!*"

There was a pregnant pause. Madeline exhaled her anxiety.

Cynthia leaned in close. "You are a remarkable mother and what happened, happened, not because of something you did or didn't do, not because you did something wrong.

"It just happened. For whatever reason, it was allowed to take place. Please understand. You *are* my mother and I *am* your daughter! I always have been and always will be. The veil of life that has separated us is only for a moment. We have eternity to spend with each other."

"Do you really believe that?" Madeline posed the question almost as though she was the child asking her mom for reassurance.

"I know it to be true. I've been on both sides. Before I came here, the love I felt for you and Dad grew stronger each moment. I learned so much about the two of you and was taught great and mighty things. You are royalty in the eyes of those on the other side."

Madeline furled her brow and squirmed in her chair.

"No, Cynthia. I'm not *royalty*."

"Why not?" Cynthia prodded.

"I guess because I know who I am. What I've been. What I've done. How I've failed."

"In the King's presence, each soul is viewed from the complete picture of their life and not just a snapshot of it. Who you are is not based on what you have or haven't done … but to *Whom* you belong."

There was another long pause. The battle within Madeline's soul was raging. She glanced at her daughter, looking for help.

"I do like the idea of spending eternity with you." She smiled as she gazed at her teacup.

"I can help you with that." Cynthia held her mother's hands and started to speak on her behalf. "Yeshua, my King. Thank You for choosing Madeline to be my mother and Danny to be my father. I am so grateful for both of them. We celebrate our reunion under Your watchful eye and rejoice in the truth that we are loved; loved by You and by one another. How great is Your perfect plan that has brought us together!

"Now, my Lord, would You help my mother to see Your outstretched arms inviting her to accept You and believe in You as her eternal Savior? Do Your work in her now, Lord, so she may receive the blessings You have in store for her. It's in Your mighty name I pray this. Amen."

When the prayer was concluded, Madeline stared at her daughter, waiting for direction.

Cynthia opened her eyes and smiled at her mother. "Would you like to say anything?"

"I'm not sure what to do."

"Just tell Him how you feel and that you love Him."

Madeline was relieved at what she heard. "I can do that." She swallowed and squeezed Cynthia's hand. She began to stutter and fidget, not realizing she was squeezing Cynthia's hand so hard. "Lord, I, uh, want to say thank You for, um… helping us find each other."

She shrugged off the distraction, took a breath and then continued, squeezing her daughter's hand even harder. "I guess I just need to trust that all this is real and that…" Madeline paused and looked up at Cynthia.

"I'm sorry, sweetheart. This is all new to me. I haven't prayed since I was a little girl in grade school and…"

"What is it, Mom?"

Madeline's heart melted when Cynthia called her "Mom." She remembered her passionate prayer for her daughter the night before at the orphan's ball. It had come deep from within her soul and now they were together, and her daughter was praying for her.

"Never mind. I think I can do this," Madeline said, and then finished her prayer. "Thank You for sending my daughter to me to prove Your love for me. I am so sorry for rejecting You and avoiding You all these years. Please come into my heart and fill my soul with Your life. I need Your forgiveness and ask that You would wash me clean and make me new. I love You."

"And, Lord," Cynthia, said concluding their prayer time, "please help my dad to see his need for You and move his heart to seek You first and foremost in everything. We love him so very much. Amen."

When she finished, she smiled at her mom. "You ought to see the banquet of celebration going on for you in the King's court at this very moment."

Madeline grinned curiously.

Danny awoke with a start. He had slept in for the first time in years. His phone repeatedly buzzed with texts and voicemails congratulating him on the success of the evening from the night before. But he didn't seem to care. The morning sun brought him a sobering dose of reality. Fear and anxiety began to fill his spirit about what had transpired the previous evening.

What did I do? After two failed marriages and some bad dating experiences, he swore to himself that he was done with walking down the aisle. *How can I be so impulsive and stupid?* He paced around his room as questions swirled in his mind. What would happen to him and Madeline? Where would they go from here? What about Cynthia and the twins? How in the world could he learn to be a father? *I gotta call this whole thing off,* he thought. *I can't do this.*

Then he thought about Madeline. It was true that he loved her, and he knew the risk of losing her forever. *She will never forgive me if I back out now. What if she quits the company? I can't run Ziggy's without her. But I'm not ready to be a father,* he argued with himself. *I'm in my fifties and they're twins. Twins! What was I thinking?*

Danny became desperate. He was at a pivotal crossroads in his life and neither option had a good outcome. The only thing that was certain was that Danny was overwhelmed and scared.

As he stared into an abyss of anxiety, for the first time in his life he had no answers.

Danny drove into Madeline's driveway. He had never been so nervous in all his life. His internal struggle made him anxious and jittery. He was scared to death of facing Madeline with the news that he had made a mistake the night before, but he was even more frightened of the commitment into which he had jumped.

The old Madeline would curse him out and possibly throw something at him. The Madeline he'd seen lately would probably just break down and cry. Either way, he was convinced he would lose her forever. He took a breath before ringing the doorbell.

Madeline was still in her pajamas but looked more beautiful than ever. When she opened the door, she didn't say a word, but instead shrieked with delight and gave Danny a big hug. "Good morning!" she exclaimed as she held her fiancé. Danny stiffly put his arms around her, and she let go.

"What's wrong?" she asked, looking intensely at him.

"Mattie. Can I come in?" he asked.

"Of course." The joyous mood was instantly extinguished.

"Where's Cynthia?" Danny asked as he walked in.

"She's in the shower." Danny knew this was his moment. They both sat down, and Danny took her hands. His heart was racing. He had no idea what the fallout would be.

"Mattie, I… I can't…" He stopped.

"You can't what?"

"I can't… Look, a lot happened last night. Some very wonderful, even miraculous, things. But I've had some time to think some of this through, and I think you'd agree with me that we were very impulsive last night… and… I'm just not ready."

"So what are you saying? That you regret proposing to me?" She pulled her hand away from his.

"No, no. I'm not saying that I don't want to marry you; I do. But with you comes the part of being a dad, and I don't think it's right for either one of us to rush into that part of it. Especially not an instant family. It's all too fast, Mattie. You gotta agree with me on that." Danny was desperate to find common ground.

"But what about the twins? You held them. I thought that you loved them too."

"I do love them, but I can't be their dad! I know me, and I know I'm not dad material. I'm sure they'll find a great home. Maybe that couple coming in will be a perfect fit. I just can't do this. At the risk of losing you, I can't do it."

There it was. The truth was out, and Danny braced himself for the repercussions.

Madeline became quiet. She just looked out into the distance as if deep in thought. The house was silent.

After what seemed like an eternity, Madeline spoke. "You're telling me you can't do this?"

"I'm sorry, Mattie, I just can't."

She gave him a warm, understanding smile. "You're right. You can't."

Danny's mind came to a screeching halt. A surge of confusion coursed through his body. Madeline was handling this in a much different way than he expected.

"I'm glad you agree, but I'm not sure what you're saying. What are you saying?"

"You're right. You can't do this on your own... and neither can I." She paused. "But I just met someone who can."

She stood up and made her way to the kitchen and poured herself some tea.

Confused, Danny watched her from the couch. His mind was racing with intrigue and curiosity. Who was this strange man she was referring to? Danny braced himself to hear about an affair that Madeline was going to confess to. *Who is this mystery man?* He rose to his feet and made his way to the kitchen.

With a cup of hot tea in hand, Madeline glided her way to the patio, and Danny followed.

For the first time in her life, Madeline poured out her heart to him with unbridled transparency. Her spirit was humble, caring, and sensitive. She told him about her shame and guilt for so many things in the past and her need to keep the world at bay lest someone remind her of her failure as a woman, which appeared to surprise him.

Then she stunned him with news of her newfound relationship with the King and the prayer that Cynthia prayed over her. He stared at her, revealing his consternation.

"And Danny ... there's more."

Danny braced himself.

"I'm sorry but ... I can't marry you," Madeline said.

He let out a painful sigh of confusion. "I ... I thought that's what you wanted."

"Danny, everything's changed," she continued carefully.

"I don't understand. What happened to you in the last eight hours?"

"That's what I'm trying to tell you. I'm not the woman you proposed to last night. I know it sounds crazy, but I need to pursue this new love that I've found. I'm alive! For the first time in my life I am truly alive. And I don't ever want to go back to the way I was. I love you, Danny, I really do. But I need a husband and father who is united with me in this new life."

"Okay. I'm with you in your new life."

"It doesn't work that way, Danny."

"Well, how does it work?" he asked with impatience.

Madeline looked up and saw Cynthia in the kitchen. "I don't know exactly, but I think it starts with a prayer."

Danny glanced up and saw Cynthia watching them from the kitchen.

As Cynthia slid the patio door open and stepped outside, Madeline caught a glimpse of Danny gazing at her. "I've never seen you look so, so … at peace."

She smiled back at him and then kissed Cynthia on the cheek. "Sweetheart, why don't you tell your dad about this wonderful King who sent you down to us."

Madeline stepped into the kitchen, closing the sliding door behind her.

Danny felt the tug in his heart to turn and hide, like he had always done. He learned to build walls around his heart and pretend all was well with him and the world, but today something stopped him from doing that.

He motioned for Cynthia to join him as he sauntered toward the rim of the property that provided them a spectacular view of the ocean and beyond.

They stopped at the edge of the lawn and stared out at the blue water. Danny let out a sigh. "Before you arrived, I thought I had life figured out. Make money. Be famous. And take love where I could find it."

"And now?" Cynthia asked.

"I feel like I'm about to get wiped out by the biggest tidal wave of my life. It's scary out here."

"Yes, it can be scary when you feel alone."

"I gotta ask you. That day out here on the patio when you talked about your parents being so perfect, like they were royalty or something. Who were you talking about? Because it sure isn't us."

"Why can't it be you?"

"Sweetheart, you're obviously an intelligent woman. You can see the disaster that our family life is in right now. That's not who you described to us. But that was before you knew we were your parents. So how would you describe us now, if we were having that same conversation?"

"I wouldn't change a thing."

Danny laughed nervously, almost as though he was on the verge of being angry. "Why is that, Cynthia?"

"Because what I heard from the citizens of Heaven about you and Mom is true. It's spoken from a perspective not of this moment but from beginning to end. It's not just a single snapshot, but the whole picture."

"Are you saying that what you heard about us is in the future?"

"Past, present, and future," she said, putting her hand on his shoulder. Then she laughed to herself.

"What's so funny?"

"It's happening even now."

"What's happening now?" he asked with a strong slant of childlike curiosity and nervousness.

"You, becoming a great man."

Danny liked being considered a great man. Tears welled up in his eyes. He looked at his daughter and was flooded with immense love and gratefulness for her. She saw him not as he saw himself but as the man he had always wanted to be.

"I want to be that man, Cynthia. Not for myself but for you and for your mother. For something greater than myself..." He stopped. "*Someone* greater than myself." He looked her in the eyes. "Will you help me?"

"Yes, Daddy. Of course. I'll do anything I can to help you and Mom be who I know you really are."

He embraced her and kissed her head a couple times, absorbing all the love his child had to give. "Let's start with you telling me about this King who sent you to us."

Danny listened intently as Cynthia shared the good news of the King and His forgiveness with her father.

"Is He the man your mother said she met this morning?"

"He is, and more," she said confidently.

It was the faith of Cynthia in this King that opened Danny's heart to a relationship he had never considered in his entire life. "So, how do I meet Him?"

She smiled with conviction. "You can meet Him right here, right now. But you're not the boss anymore."

Danny was more than curious by her statement. "Care to explain that one?"

"A relationship with the King means, as I learned, once you invite Him in, you don't run the show anymore. He's in charge. But I promise you, Dad, you'll be so grateful He is. He has plans and ideas for you and Mom that you've never imagined. But you have to trust Him and follow His lead."

Danny sighed in relief. "Sounds refreshing. I have to tell you, sweetheart, I haven't been happy. Not really. Except when I'm with you and your mom."

Cynthia took her father's hand and looked him in the eyes. "Why don't you tell Him that and invite Him into your life? He's right here now, waiting to be invited."

Danny looked around as though he might see someone. "Do I just close my eyes and talk to Him? How do I do this?"

"However you want. Eyes open or closed, doesn't matter. It only matters that your heart is open."

He smiled nervously and then shared his heart with the King. He then asked God to come into his life and make him a better man, the man he had heard from Cynthia that he could be; someone who was generous and loving, a man who wouldn't be run by fear anymore. He paused, allowing himself to be in the moment and aware of what was transpiring in his life.

When Danny and Cynthia finished their prayer, Danny grabbed his daughter and held her tight. "Thank you."

Taking her hand, he pulled Cynthia into the house and went straight to Madeline.

"Honey, let's go get the rest of our family."

⌖ 18 ⌖

AFTER THEIR EVENTFUL MORNING, MADELINE, DANNY, and Cynthia went to Danny's attorney's office to discuss the adoption. Madeline and Danny had not finished their conversation about getting married, so when the attorney told them he had spoken to the orphanage and there was a hiccup, it got Madeline's attention.

"By state law," he stated, "the orphanage can't 'hold' a baby for anyone, and the out-of-state couple is still interested in meeting the girls. Since the other couple is married and have great references, they will most likely take priority over you two, despite my recommendation otherwise."

"So what do we need to do?" Madeline asked. She didn't want to give up.

"Well... if I may... If you two are really serious about this, you need to get married fast."

Danny looked to Madeline. He shrugged to let her know it was her call. He looked a bit unsure.

Cynthia sensed it and squeezed his hand.

All eyes were on Madeline as she pondered what to do.

"When's the other family coming in?" Madeline inquired.

"Four days."

Madeline stood up and made her way to the large office window. She stared out at the busy street for quite some time. She wasn't contemplating. She was praying.

Danny joined her. "Mattie, I've messed up in the past, I know."

She gently put her fingers on his lips. "If my fiancé will agree, we'll be married in three days!"

Madeline, Cynthia, and the attorney all looked at Danny, waiting.

He moved close to Madeline, and with his eyes locked on hers, said, "Cynthia, we're going to need help. Call the troops. We can do this."

Madeline leaned into Danny. "You bet we can," she said, then kissed him firmly.

"Yes!" Cynthia shouted.

Danny and Madeline laughed, breaking their embrace, and opened their arms, inviting their daughter into the celebration.

"You may now kiss the bride," Pastor Timothy announced with pride as he closed the ceremonial book that held the church's traditional wedding vows.

Cheers broke out as Danny kissed Madeline as passionately as she could ever remember him kissing her. After a long moment she stepped back, catching her breath. The radiant couple stood at the front of a small, elegant altar that was centered in the backyard of her estate, which would now be their family home. The panoramic view was her idea for the perfect setting for their last-minute wedding.

Madeline took a deep breath and grinned big. Never had she been so efficient and organized and laser-focused in her life with her to-do list, delegating tasks wisely. She had contacted all the vendors they used for the orphans' ball to streamline the process.

Terry Harris

Pastor Timothy had accepted her request to officiate the ceremony. Bobby agreed to post the event on Instagram and Facebook. Eunice's job had been to find a dress, and of course, the perfect shoes.

Madeline and Cynthia had worked tirelessly around the clock to pull off the single largest wedding the coastal town of Paradise Bay had ever hosted. They had agreed that the guest list would not be complete without those who had attended the orphans' ball. Scores of emails flooded her office, describing the enormous blessing the dance had brought into their lives and confirming their attendance at the wedding. Social-media sites following the grand night told the world how much the event had meant to them and their new families. Never before had one single evening done so much good for adopting families, children in foster care, and those looking to unite with their relatives.

With such a large response to the wedding invite, Madeline and Cynthia determined that the reception would have to be held someplace big enough to handle so many guests. To simplify, Madeline decided to hold a small ceremony with close friends and family on her patio overlooking the ocean, and the reception would take place down below on the beach. She arranged for a large, opulent tent with a solid wood floor to be erected along the seashore.

After the ceremony concluded, Cynthia found her father standing outside one of the bedrooms that had been used as a dressing room for the bride and the bridesmaids.

Cynthia could not help but gaze at her father. He stood tall and handsome in his tuxedo. He wore his tailored clothes like a great leader.

She recalled many of the stories she heard of her father's greatness by those in the King's court, and now they were coming to pass. The selfish man she had known in the past was not the man standing in front of her. He reflected compassion and humility. She was so proud to call him Dad.

"Dad?"

"Hi, sweetheart. Waitin' for your mom."

She put her hands on his firm shoulders. "I'm so proud of you, Daddy. You are an amazing man."

He choked up. "I want to thank you, Cynthia."

"Thank me for what?" she asked as she stepped aside for some of the wedding party to pass by.

"Lately, I've been thinking a lot about how my life has changed since you arrived. I'm not one to share the credit, at least I wasn't before, but now … you've changed everything, and I've never known happiness like I do now. Your mother and I are more in love today than we had ever been, and it's because you came along. If it wasn't for you …" His voice cracked.

"Daddy, I'm so happy for you both, but I can't take the credit for it." She paused, seeing his clear blue eyes tear up. "Everything that has come to pass is because of the generous heart of the King. He sent me here, and it was He who brought us together as a family."

Danny touched her cheek. "Last night I had a dream that you were suddenly gone. I couldn't find you. Everywhere I looked I saw the faces of children I've never met before. But when I looked at them, it was as though I knew them, like they were my own kids."

She shuddered and choked back her words.

He continued. "Look, I don't know if tomorrow I'm going to wake up and all this will have been a dream, but regardless of what happens, I want you to know that I love you, and I will never go back to being the man I was before you came into my life."

She threw her arms around him. "I love you, Daddy, so very much."

"I love you too, Cynthia."

Several voices called Cynthia back outside for group photos. "I have to go. Will you promise to save me a dance at the party?"

"Our dance is already reserved."

She looked at him in confusion.

"Don't you know every wedding has a father-daughter dance?" He kissed her on the forehead and smiled.

As Cynthia left her father's side, she suddenly realized that her dream to dance with her father was a small part of a much larger plan the King had in mind for her family. It was the seed from which He harvested an entire crop of fruit that would last for generations. She couldn't wait to see their future. She also couldn't wait for the dance.

Bobby was finishing the groomsmen group shots when Cynthia approached the altar. He snapped several final shots then caught a second glimpse of her as she took the last few steps onto the runner. She was waiting, along with the bridesmaids, for their instructions from him. The exquisite flowers and plants from around the world that were placed all throughout the patio could not compete with her majestic beauty.

For a brief moment, Bobby pictured himself as the groom, waiting for her to join him in the exchange of their vows. The thought of such an emotional plunge triggered both joy and terror inside his soul and caused him to shudder. He nearly dropped his camera but caught it before it crashed to the ground.

"Are you all right?" Cynthia asked.

"I think so," he said and then instructed the bridesmaids on where and how he wanted them to pose.

When the final photo was taken, the women asked if they were free to go to the front of the house to help send off the bride and groom with showers of flowers and confetti. Bobby agreed, hoping to have a moment alone with Cynthia.

Deidre, who had been quietly sitting behind Eunice and Portia, stepped into the aisle to speak with Cynthia. "Cindy, I was thinking a lot about what you said the other day when I apologized, and I was just wonderin' how, err, why, you would just forgive me like that and not want your 'pound of flesh,' if you know what I mean? It makes no sense to me. Who does that?"

"I'm only giving to you what was given to me by Someone far greater than myself," Cynthia said. "Please accept my forgiveness. I give it freely. No strings attached."

"No strings?"

"Not a one."

Deidre awkwardly reached over and hugged Cynthia tightly as Eunice and Cynthia exchanged smiles.

Inside the house, on a cue from the bridesmaids, Danny led Madeline down the stairs and out to the front of the house. Their guests and the wedding party greeted them outside with confetti and flower petals. As the newlyweds stepped out onto the cobblestone driveway, they were showered with the blessings and good wishes of people who had known and loved them much of their lives. Danny and Madeline's story was an extraordinary one of second chances and renewed hope.

Once he cleared the shreds of paper from his eyes, Danny looked up, expecting a long limousine to be waiting for them. Instead, he was greeted by the same orange VW he drove the night of the ball. The car's owner, one of his loyal employees, was leaning up against it and smiling at Danny.

"You're kidding, right?" Danny asked.

"Gotcha! Here's your real ride," Cynthia shouted as she ran up behind them, laughing.

From around the corner came a beautiful white carriage with red-and-gold trim, pulled by a pair of Windsor Greys and a pair of Cleveland Bay horses. "These breeds have been used by royalty since the fourteenth century, and they are a present to you and mom," Cynthia announced as she hugged them tightly.

The carriage took Madeline's breath away. Danny helped his bride into the coach and then turned to Judge Martinez, who stood nearby. Danny pulled a set of folded white papers from his jacket pocket. "Judge, you'll find our adoption papers signed and completed with a copy of our marriage certificate. Please see to it they get processed immediately so we can officially take our little girls home."

"I will see to it personally," assured Judge Martinez.

Danny leaned in and kissed Cynthia on the cheek. "We have a great future as a family, sweetheart, and we owe it all to you."

Danny stepped up and took his seat next to Madeline. He held her close. As they rode off into the sunset in their two-seated carriage, Danny kissed his wife like they were a couple of young lovers.

The reception was a short hike down the hillside for Cynthia and Bobby. Rocks framed the beach ahead, making it somewhat of a cove. It was much like the spot where Cynthia had arrived on that early gray morning not too long ago. In the distance, she could hear music from the celebration that had already began.

Words were few between her and Bobby as they strolled arm in arm toward the beach. She found herself pondering the strange feeling swirling inside her. Watching her parents ride away into the sunset without her seemed surreal, almost prophetic. Oddly, she wasn't bothered by her thoughts and feelings but viewed them as matter of fact rather than frightening.

Her mind drifted to all her friends in the King's court. She had so much she wanted to share with all of them. Everything she had ever dreamed of, and considerably more, had happened, and now she recalled how each of them had been part of that dream and its fulfillment. She knew from her own experiences that they had a certain degree of awareness of all that had transpired over her time on Earth.

Her cloud of witnesses was cheering her on, and she believed that the fulfilled dreams she and her family had realized to this point were being celebrated this very hour by the hosts of Heaven. She suddenly missed Angela and Sebastian and all her family in Heaven so much that she forgot she was with Bobby.

"So, what do you think?" he asked.

Cynthia stopped and looked at him, not having heard a word he said. "Please forgive me, I'm a little distracted. What were you saying?"

"Dancing? Tonight? You and me?"

"I would like that very much." She kissed him on the cheek, and then laid her head on his shoulder as they took the remaining steps to the reception.

When the bride and groom arrived at the reception, the carriage came to a soft stop at the entrance to a gargantuan tent that supplied seating and dining for the crowd. Cynthia greeted them with a wide smile and helped Madeline step off the carriage. She then proudly ushered her parents inside to a spectacular sight of crystal lighting and soft-seated chairs placed around fine- linen-covered tables. Gold and white were the colors of choice, with splashes of royal blue. Madeline complimented her daughter on the color scheme, knowing it was her choice. "So beautiful, my dear."

Madeline and Danny made their way through the crowd, greeting friends as they went, and finally found their proper seats at the head table. The wedding party soon joined them in their assigned seats. Cynthia sat next to her mom and listened closely to the inspiring words of blessing and promise that were spoken over the couple by their family and friends. As their story was shared in bits and pieces through various toasts, it became clear how incredibly unique and profound their reunion and marriage was.

Cynthia knew that only the King was capable of weaving such an unimaginable set of circumstances into a masterpiece such as theirs. She prayed a silent prayer of thanks, and when she opened her eyes, she saw Sebastian standing at the far entrance to the tent. She was elated. "I'll be right back, Mom," Cynthia whispered to Madeline as she kissed her on the cheek and jumped to her feet.

Cynthia made her way across the tent and found her friend standing outside the entranceway.

"Sebastian!" she exclaimed, hugging him. "I've been missing you so much today."

He greeted her with an embrace and a warm smile. In his hands, he was holding her clear glass shoes, the same pair she had surrendered to him the morning of her arrival.

"I'm so delighted to see you," Cynthia bubbled. "Oh, how I do miss everyone."

"And they miss you, my child."

Her eyes fell on the shoes he was holding.

"It's time," he said as he held them out for her to take.

"Cynthia?" Madeline's voice interrupted the moment, giving Cynthia time to process what she knew Sebastian was saying.

"Mother, this is Sebastian."

"Yes, we've met. The night of the ball. It's nice to see you again. I never had the chance to thank you for giving my husband and me hope that night." She extended her hand to thank him.

He shook her hand and bowed his head in humility. "I was merely a messenger of the King. May I say it was indeed a most grand event that evening, as is tonight's."

"Neither would have been possible without this one. She is remarkably gifted in so many things," Madeline said as she pulled her daughter close to her.

Madeline craned her neck and looked closely at the crystal footwear in Sebastian's hand. "What beautiful shoes. But they look terribly uncomfortable."

"Oh, not at all," Cynthia perked up.

"Are they yours, Cynthia?" she asked.

Sebastian held them out for Cynthia to claim them.

"They are," she replied slowly as she took hold of them.

Madeline admired them and stroked the glass throat of the shoe with her finger. "They're soft. Certainly not from around here. Where did you get them, if I may ask?"

Cynthia smiled with a moment of intimate recall. "They were given to me by the King."

Tears filled Cynthia's eyes and she looked to Sebastian for guidance.

Madeline noticed the tears sliding down her daughter's cheeks. "I see." She reached over and gently pulled the shoes out of Cynthia's hands and held them.

Cynthia could feel her mom's struggle to understand what was happening, so she spoke up, hoping to alleviate some of the pain. "There's not another pair like them in all of Heaven. Every daughter of the King wears her own uniquely created slip shoe."

"So, one day I'll get my own pair?" Madeline asked as she choked back the tears.

"One day, yes …" Cynthia's words fell off, realizing her mom understood more than she had imagined.

"Madeline? Cynthia?" Danny walked towards them, with Eunice two steps behind him. Madeline glanced up at them and then back to Cynthia.

"But not today," Cynthia whispered aloud as she retrieved the shoes from Madeline.

There was an awkward silence when Danny and Eunice approached. Danny smiled when he recognized Sebastian. "Hey, how are you, umm . . .?"

"Sebastian," said the angelic being with extraordinary humility.

"Yes, of course," Danny obliged apologetically. "From the orphans' ball. I can't believe that was just a few nights ago. I never had the chance to show my gratitude for the assurance you gave me that night. I needed it." Danny looked toward Madeline. "We needed it."

Cynthia stepped close to Madeline and gently wiped the tears away that rolled down her cheek.

"Mattie, is everything okay?" Danny asked, confused.

Madeline didn't look at Danny right away but turned her eyes to Sebastian.

Cynthia looked at her dad with a smile that revealed pain.

"Cynthia?" he asked.

Cynthia stepped out of the wedding heels she had been wearing all day and slipped into her glass shoes. They still fit perfectly.

She gazed at her dad and grabbed his hand. "Dad, I'm so proud of you. You're everything I dreamed you would be and more. I'm eternally grateful I got to know you and Mother."

She leaned in and kissed him on the cheek. "Thank you, Dad, for everything."

"You sound like you're saying goodbye."

"Yes, I am, but only for now. Soon we'll be together, all of us, never to say goodbye again."

"Wait! Where are you going?"

Madeline stepped up next to Danny and touched his sleeve. Danny scanned the eyes of his wife, then Sebastian, then finally Cynthia, who could not look at him. Fear rose up inside him, followed by a flush of anger. He was about to interrogate Sebastian.

Then a calm voice inside his soul whispered a thought to him: *Her work here is done.*

Danny's heart skipped a beat when he processed what that meant. He realized in some strange way that there had been a plan for all of this, a great, unimaginable plan, and he, his wife, and their daughters, were all a part of that plan. It felt so surreal to him.

He looked at Cynthia with a new selfless love that gushed up from his soul. She was a walking, breathing miracle. She was, under any other circumstance, not supposed to be here, yet there she stood reflecting back to him the love he felt for her. His mind flashed back to the moment in his office when Madeline had told him she had been pregnant with a daughter, Cynthia, whom she miscarried. The word sent chills up his spine.

"Cynthia, I ..." His tongue was suddenly tied. His heart broke over the thought of losing her, then and now.

She reached over and hugged him tight. Madeline turned away for a moment, pain etched across her face.

Is this what it felt like for Madeline those many years ago when she had to face the news of having lost our daughter? Danny

Terry Harris

wanted to say he was sorry to Madeline, and so much more, but he knew now wasn't the time or place. He vowed in his heart to speak with her before the night was over.

Cynthia was grateful when others from the wedding party made their way to the wedding couple, bringing laughter and celebration with them. It refreshed the somber mood that had disrupted the Richards family's wedding-day celebration.

Cynthia stepped up and kissed Eunice on the cheek.

"Thank you for everything you did to make me feel like I had a home."

Eunice held her by both arms. "I have never been the same since you arrived on my doorstep singing my favorite song. For the first time in my life, I have a family. Thank you for that. God bless you, my dear." They hugged. Then Cynthia embraced Portia, who was too choked up to speak.

Cynthia spied Deidre hanging back, obviously unsure of what to say or do. She let go of Portia, touched her cheek with a kind gesture, and then walked over to Deidre and embraced her. Deidre cried. Cynthia stepped back and encouraged her with a smile. Deidre made eye contact with Sebastian and gasped. She held onto Cynthia's arm for safety until Sebastian gave her a smile and bowed as if to say, "At your service."

"He's as gentle as a butterfly," Cynthia assured her.

"I never saw a butterfly with wings like his," Deidre confessed.

Cynthia didn't quite know what that meant but hugged Deidre one last time and then looked around for Bobby. She didn't see him. Just then, he split the crowd and made his way to Cynthia. "Hey, there you are. What's going on?"

She smiled a broad smile then held him close. He smelled good. She always enjoyed his cologne. It made him stand out.

He carried himself so well, and she knew that if she had the chance, she would have seen him grow into the man the King created him to be. A man she might have been able to spend the rest of her life with. She released him, then opened her purse and pulled out her brown leather Bible. She handed it to him.

"What's this?" he asked.

"A prize worth keeping. I was going to get you a new one, but now it seems right that I give you mine. That book has meant everything to me since coming here."

He gazed at the Bible, then held it tightly. "I'll read it, I promise."

She touched his face with her hand. "Never lose your smile." She opened the Bible to reveal the smiley face sticker that Bobby had given her nearly a year before.

He chuckled and looked up. Their eyes locked. There was so much to tell Bobby, but she couldn't. She just gazed deep into his eyes and felt the heartbreak of losing him.

"Take me with you. I don't know where you're going, but I have a pretty good idea. I want to be with you, no matter the cost. I love you, Cynthia, and I have to be with you."

"Oh, Bobby, I wish I could. It's not within my control. You'll have a happy life. I'll be watching over you."

She kissed him passionately on the lips and whispered in his ear, "Thank you. You were the one chosen for me, for my time here. Our memories together will be stored in my heart forever."

Bobby tried one last time, quietly objecting, "No."

He let her go. She knew from his expression that his heart was breaking as he watched her move away from him and toward her parents, who were holding each other tightly.

Cynthia fell into their arms and the three of them hugged and cried, not saying a word. She conveyed every ounce of love she had for them in her embrace.

"I can't do this again," Madeline pleaded with Cynthia. "I can't lose you again."

"Mom, it's not goodbye. We'll be together soon." Cynthia pulled away from her mom, looking into her eyes. "Very soon."

Danny pulled Madeline away from Cynthia. "Let her go. We'll be okay. We'll be okay," he whispered in her ear.

The crowd gathered watched in silence as Cynthia turned and stared toward the shore. She glanced back at her friends and family.

Sebastian bowed in honor to Danny and Madeline, then motioned to Cynthia. Madeline and Danny watched helplessly as their daughter slowly backed away. Hearing murmurs from the crowd about where she was going, Cynthia decided it was time.

She walked to the shoreline and hesitated, then slowly turned to catch one final glimpse of her family. A single tear, rested on the corner of her eye, glistened in the night light of the moon. She blinked and it rolled down to her lip. As she stood there, she reflected on all that had happened to her. Her mind took her back to the day she had stepped on the cold shoreline of this world, not knowing how her desire to meet her parents would be lived out.

Her eyes scanned the beach as she looked for someone. The woman Violet she had met on that early morning was not there. She missed her and pondered what might have happened to her had she not run away. Cynthia knew she had to leave that in the hands of the King. She resumed her walk further toward the water that now nipped at her feet.

"Cynthia!" her dad called after her. She spun around, hoping that somehow they could all stay together.

He called out again. "Cynthia!"

Cynthia watched her dad run toward her. She looked to Sebastian, but he offered no answer.

Danny yelled to her from the shoreline. "What about our dance? Doesn't your dear old dad get his father-daughter dance?"

Cynthia's heart fluttered and she gasped. She had been so close to walking into eternity without fulfilling the one true dream she had since she could remember. She looked to Sebastian for permission. Sebastian smiled and gave her a slow, single nod.

Danny trekked through the water and filled the space between them. She held out open arms, inviting him to come closer. To his astonishment, Cynthia was standing atop the water.

She gazed down at her ability to float atop the sea, remembering how she used to do it with such ease before arriving on this shore some time ago. Her transformation had already begun to take place. Her bridesmaid dress had transformed into a dazzling white-pearl gown, the kind she wore in eternity.

He stared dumbfounded at his daughter standing on water. Glistening white and pure.

Her voice snapped him out of his shock. "It's okay, Father." She held out her hand and invited him to dance. His hesitation caused her to step toward him and meet him where he stood. With a touch of her hand, he rose to meet her on top of the waves. They took each other's arms and slowly stepped in time to the distant music that wafted in the salty air.

Though they had never danced before, Danny and Cynthia were a perfect pair and danced eloquently. Madeline could tell Danny was fully captivated by his daughter as they waltzed atop the water as sure-footed as if on a hardwood floor. The moon smiled its splendid light across the ocean waves, providing the perfect spotlight for such a dance. Madeline stared at the waves that appeared to be held in check, making the ocean calm like a glassy sea.

Unable to stop the tears from flowing, she watched her daughter dance with her father on top of the ocean. She whispered words of gratitude and praise to her King and lifted her eyes to the sky.

Why was she so fortunate to have a miracle such as this happen to her? Her mind raced with a thousand questions for which there was only one answer: tell the whole world that even in death, there is life.

She now understood that what she had lost would one day be fully returned to her. What had been taken from her in turmoil and pain would be restored to her in jubilee and celebration without end. Madeline gasped at the majesty of the moment and was filled with unspeakable and incomprehensible joy. Her pain had finally given birth to life and purpose.

As the father-daughter dance continued, music filled the sky. A song of another stratum replaced the earthly sounds and swept the wedding guests off their feet. A myriad of colorful bright lights appeared around Cynthia and Danny, and from the midst of those beautiful shades of magenta, royal blue, emerald green, and deep purple emerged images of people: the saints.

They were the witnesses who had been observing and cheering the events of Cynthia's visit from the grandstands of the King's court. The heavenly onlookers were those who had raised Cynthia from a baby to a young woman. All her friends who had shared in her well-being and had encouraged her dream looked on with wonder at the unveiling of answered prayer, the prayer of a child who had arrived in Glory as a miscarriage.

Angela was accompanied by the citizens of Heaven as she sang songs of praise to the King while their dear friend danced atop the sea with her handsome father. Beautiful music and breathtaking colors surrounded them as their figures glowed on the water.

Madeline, Eunice, Portia, Deidre, Bobby, and all the guests privileged to be present were profoundly moved and reflected awe and wonderment at Cynthia's dance, a miracle story conceived and birthed by the King of Kings long before a single child of His had ever been born.

∽ EPILOGUE ∽

THIS WAS THE END OF CYNTHIA'S TIME ON EARTH BUT only the beginning of her impact on the lives of those she touched. Danny and Madeline became the proud adoptive parents of several children and raised each of them to carry on the mission of caring for orphans. Eunice became the mother she always wanted to be to Portia, and, after a while, even Deidre. Radcliffe's many sins were revealed and he fled the country, never to be heard from again.

Ziggy's Island established the Annual Orphans' Ball, igniting a fire of enthusiasm for family reunions and adoptions of orphans and foster-care children. They sponsored outreaches to various shelters and care centers for young moms who faced single-parent pregnancies and even started the best-run orphanage in all the land.

To Bobby's surprise, his heartbreak over Cynthia was short lived. If he were to be completely honest with himself, he always knew that her love was not his to keep. He also had suspected all along that his heart was meant for another. Months later, he made good on his promise to Cynthia and met with Julia. Through their time apart, they both had been able to find healing and lose the shackles of their past. Their romance reignited with a foundation of truth and trust. After they were married, they were blessed with a daughter and a son of their own whom they raised in a loving home focused on serving the King.

But the miracles didn't stop there, for once Cynthia resumed her place in the King's court, it was made known to her that Angela Marie, the very same girl Cynthia had mentored in Paradise, and considered her closest friend, was after all, the baby girl Julia had lost to abortion years before.

Never again would there be a young woman as unique as Cynthia and never again would there be a father-daughter dance quite like this one. In the end, because of a princess named Cynthia, scores of families would unite and live their lives together in love, happily ever after.

Join our community at Cynthiasdance.com

TERRY HARRIS AND HIS WIFE LOST THREE BABIES DUE TO miscarriage between 2007 and 2009. Through their grief and loss, Terry had the idea to write a simple story about a girl who never had the chance to be born, but who gets a glimpse at life and brings healing into the lives of her parents and those around her.

In 2006, Terry was awarded Honorable Mention by Writer's Digest for his short story "Always," in the Inspirational Category. There were almost 19,000 entries that year.

Terry lives in Huntington Beach, California, with his wife and three precious children. He currently is writing his second novel.

Printed in Canada